HARLEY MERLIN AND THE FIRST RITUAL

Harley Merlin 4

BELLA FORREST

ONE

Harley

Getting myself sucked into an interdimensional pocket wasn't how I thought I'd be spending my night.

I dove to the ground and slammed into the marble with a hefty thud. A bright light flooded the space above me, cutting off my air supply as the golden bubble started shrinking around me. My lungs clawed for oxygen, and I scrabbled against the floor in a vain attempt to break free of the rapidly narrowing pocket. A *pop* sounded and the bubble exploded outwards in a spray of sparkling shards.

Jacob came running toward me. "Are you okay? I didn't mean to do that!"

I lay on my back, panting like a dog at the beach. "No worries. Everyone makes mistakes," I replied, raising my hands. "Your mistakes are just a little bit more powerful than other people's." I sat up and dusted myself off, taking his hand as he pulled me to my feet.

He looked bashful. "You sure you aren't hurt?"

"No harm done. What was that, anyway?"

"The last thing Isadora taught me before Katherine took her was how to make interdimensional pockets by opening up four portals at once—they kind of work like corners on a soccer field, though way smaller," he explained shyly. "I just don't have her skill. This is all useless without her guiding me."

"Gee, thanks for the vote of confidence," I said.

"No, I didn't mean it like that!"

I flashed him a grin. "I'm only teasing, Jake. I obviously don't have any experience in this stuff." I was thankful I hadn't broken any ribs. An ache shot through my chest, but it would soon subside. I'd probably just bruised my side or something—nothing I couldn't handle. "I've been thinking... there must be a way to *feel* this stuff out. I mean, how did magicals do this back in the day, when they first started shooting out of the womb? They must've done some guesswork and worked on instinct, right?"

He nodded uncertainly. "Not sure they came shooting out, but I catch your drift."

"That's what you need to do."

"I thought that's what I *was* doing?"

"Could you feel the bubble getting unstable?" I prompted.

"Yeah... kind of."

"And what did you do about it?"

He frowned. "I pushed it outward."

"And what happened?"

"It came loose from its... I don't know what you'd call them—anchors, maybe?"

"Right, so maybe you need to draw them inward instead; keep the bubble steady."

His eyes brightened. "That's not a bad idea. Isadora kept telling me I needed to show restraint and be more precise in my actions. I kept destroying stuff around the hideouts we were staying at, which she said was a control problem."

I tried not to show my panic at his words. "Then let's start again and try something different."

"But I thought we wanted to develop an escape route for the coven, if all of this goes to sh—"

"Language, Jacob," I chided playfully.

He smiled, his eyes turning sad. "You sound like Mrs. Smith."

"I guess she rubbed off on me after all."

Jacob had been masquerading as Tarver for just over a week now, and we'd started training in secret each night. With him here at the coven, there was no time to waste in trying to get his abilities up to snuff—not that I had any idea what I was doing. Nevertheless, Alton had given us the key to the preceptors' private training room and instructed them to use the public ones instead. I wasn't sure how much he'd told them about Tarver-aka-Jacob, but they'd kept away from our sessions. I'd even asked Alton if he thought I was the woman for the job, to which he'd helpfully replied, "It's not as if we have a bunch of Portal Openers at our disposal to help him hone his skills. Follow the list of instructions I've given you, and you'll do just fine."

My ribs did *not* think I was doing just fine, nor did the cut on my cheek or the scrape on my forearm. Training Jacob was a risky business. Then again, I couldn't let him go through this alone. He and I shared the same sadness over Isadora, not to mention a mutual helplessness. I hadn't been able to save her from Katherine, back in the warehouse, any more than he'd been able to when Katherine's cronies had come for her. Besides, I could sense his contentment at having me in the room with him, helping him with this. He evidently thought I was doing a decent job. *Fake it till you make it, right?* Plus, I was going step-by-step through the processes Alton wanted Jacob to work on, which took a small bit of the strain off.

"The end goal is to create an escape route, but even if that's just you making a big-ass portal that everyone can run through, that'll be better than what we currently have," I assured him. "Yes, a comfy little pocket of interdimensional space would be ideal, but if you're not ready for it, that's okay. There's no pressure on you, Jake. Don't let anyone tell you otherwise."

"Like Alton, you mean?"

I narrowed my eyes in curiosity. "Has he been pressuring you?"

"Not in so many words, but he keeps letting me know how important this escape route is."

"You need me to have a word with him?" I grinned impishly.

"I'll let you know if I do." He smiled. I liked seeing him smile. He wasn't the type of kid who did that much, despite his young age. I knew this was a trait in most foster kids, but that didn't mean I thought it was okay and normal. It wasn't. It was heartbreaking.

I understood his pain a little too much. He and I were in very similar boats. There were big old skeletons in both of our closets, and we were the ones left to deal with the aftermath of our parents' choices. Putting my efforts into him stopped me from wallowing in my own history, since that was a downward spiral I *really* didn't want to start slipping down.

One thing was for sure: our moms were heroines. I kept wanting to tell him that, but it didn't seem appropriate to bring it up. *Zara and Hester... your legacies live on. We're still here.* My dad had done some pretty great things too, to save me from Katherine. Although I didn't know enough about Elan Sowanoke—Jacob's dad—to make any judgments.

Jacob sighed. "I just keep thinking about all these kids, and what we're going to do when we get them back... *if* we get them back. They won't be safe here. If I could create that pocket of space and get it to hold, just for a while..."

"I know, Jake, but there's no point in beating yourself up over something that's momentarily beyond your control. You do what you can, and we'll be grateful, okay?" I patted him on the shoulder, sending a jolt of pain up my torso.

"Are you okay? I knew I'd hurt you." He dropped his gaze.

"No, I slept funny on my side, that's all. Seriously, it's all downhill when you hit nineteen."

He laughed. "You sure?"

"Positive. Now, let's get some portals opened and see what else happens," I urged. "Why don't we start with short-range portals? A controlled opening from here to somewhere else in the coven? Let's say the Banquet Hall so we don't disturb anyone."

He nodded. "Sounds good."

As I watched him walk to the far side of the training room, with its beautiful arched ceiling painted with ancient images of magical warriors on the backs of dragons, I thought about what he'd said. The missing kids had been playing on my mind a lot. We had Micah and Marjorie, but that wasn't enough, not when other lives were still at risk.

Alton had put Micah and Marjorie in two of the secret rooms that seemed to be dotted all over this coven—little hidden spaces, which were frankly quite depressing with their black marble and windowless walls. Marjorie had asked for things to decorate hers with, and we'd happily obliged. However, even with a sack-load of Christmas lights and pretty lamps and posters of her favorite K-pop band, it still seemed gloomy.

Micah, on the other hand, was a little easier to placate. He was happy just to play with Fluffers and a couple of toys we'd stolen from Kid City. Although he was the one who worried me the most. Since returning to the coven, he'd Purged a small goblin-like creature that he'd let run amok in his room until Alton caught it. Micah called them his "pets," which had made us all wonder how many of these "pets" he'd created in the past. Dr. Krieger's Reading confirmed that the boy did, indeed, have Necromancy powers, alongside the beginnings of a fierce Telekinetic ability. Pretty scary stuff in a five-year-old boy who had no control over his emotions. We'd already had to strap things down after he'd heard about his family. Alton had put it as kindly as possible, giving it the usual "fell asleep and didn't wake up" clichés, but the little boy was smarter than that and had been completely devastated by the revelation.

Speaking of which, I should probably tell Marjorie about the Hamms having their memories wiped. I was dreading that particular duty, which was presumably why I continued to put it off. Alton had given the task to me, for some reason; maybe he thought it might be character-building. I couldn't avoid it forever, though. She already knew something was up—I could sense it coming off her in subtle currents of suspicion.

"Did Krieger say anything else about your Reading?" I asked Jacob. "Like, your strength or anything? Light and Dark—that sort of stuff?"

He shrugged. "According to him, being a Portal Opener tends to mean you're pretty strong, and I'm well within the Light side of the spectrum."

"Yeah, I can vouch for the strength."

Part of me felt relieved that he was a Light magical, though I knew that had nothing to do with how a person ended up.

"How's Dr. Krieger, anyway?" Jacob asked, as he stretched out his muscles in readiness for the next portal. "He seemed pretty wiped out when he did my Reading the other day. Or is he always like that?"

"He wasn't well for a while, but he's doing better now. To be honest, I think he needs to sleep for an entire week, but he keeps telling everyone he's fine to keep working," I replied.

Alton and Preceptor Bellmore had performed a dangerous hex on Krieger shortly after Jacob's arrival that had seemingly removed all trace of the curse, at great cost to both Krieger and Bellmore. Alton seemed to have come out of it okay, but then he normally had Necromancy to deal with. Krieger and Bellmore had both been walking around the place like zombies ever since, neither of them accepting the fact that they needed more downtime to recover. Still, at least we had our physician back. After Adley de la Barthe, we didn't want the San Diego Coven to be known for its inability to retain its physicians. Our rep was tattered enough as it was. Before the removal hex, Alton had been going out of his mind, trying to figure out whom he could get in as a replacement, since nobody could be trusted anymore. Paranoia was rife in this place now, more so than it had ever been, and it left a sour taste in everyone's mouth.

"That's good. He seems like a cool guy," Jacob said.

He closed his eyes, and I imagined he was digging deep to draw upon the power of Chaos. His hands glowed green. Time and space tore open behind him, the gap much more restrained than it had been during his previous attempts, the edges smooth where they'd formerly crackled and spat.

Hey, maybe I'm getting better at this teaching malarkey.

"Shall I throw a sandbag through?" I asked.

He nodded, a trickle of sweat meandering down the side of his face. "Sure, let's start small. If this works, it'll end up in the Banquet Hall."

I picked up one of the small, colored sandbags that we'd been using to test the end points of his portals and tossed it through. He closed the portal a moment later, breathing hard with the exertion of having kept it open.

"How did that feel?"

"Better," he replied.

"Let's see if it ended up in the Banquet Hall." I went to the side of the room and turned on the small monitor that Alton had given me, so I could use cameras to mark Jacob's progress, and the whereabouts of these sandbags. It only granted me access to three—the Banquet Hall, the Assembly Hall, and the Aquarium—but we were starting small, which suited me just fine. I peered at the camera showing the Banquet Hall. Sure enough, there on the floor lay a red sandbag.

"Did it?" he asked.

I nodded. "Yep—bang in the center of the room. Okay, do it again when you're ready, and I'll go through," I said confidently, though my heart was hammering in my chest. The sandbag had gone through, but Lord only knew where I'd end up. *Banquet Hall, Banquet Hall, Banquet Hall... You can do this.*

"I just need to catch my breath."

"No problemo."

I grabbed one of the water bottles that sat at the side of the room and chucked it to him. He caught it deftly and tore off the cap, chugging the liquid down as though he hadn't seen water in weeks.

"The Rag Team doesn't suspect anything about me, do they?" he asked, mopping his brow with the back of his forearm. "I thought I might have given myself away the other day, in the Banquet Hall. Wade kept calling my name and I just ignored him. I totally forgot I'm supposed to be Tarver."

"I don't think anyone noticed anything. Wade hasn't mentioned anything to me, anyway. They probably think you're a bit dense, that's all." I cracked a smile, which seemed to amuse him.

"Speaking of the Rag Team, you're friends with Tatyana, right?" he asked tentatively, wiping his mouth on the back of his hand.

I arched an eyebrow. "I am. Why do you ask?"

"She's super hot."

I laughed. "Please don't tell me you have a crush on her."

"Why not?"

"She's not called the Ice Queen for nothing," I retorted, with an affectionate smile.

He shrugged. "That makes her so much more interesting. Women like her are so mysterious, don't you think?"

"Note the word 'woman.'"

"You don't think she'd be interested in me?" He looked crestfallen. *Bless him.*

"She's too old for you, Jake. Besides, she's seeing Dylan."

"The puffed-up jock?"

"Hey, he's more than that… but yes, him. And let me add that he's also a Herculean, so don't go trying to challenge him to a duel or anything stupid like that, okay? They think you're Tarver. They don't know you're Jacob, so I need you to behave. No flirting, understood?" I chuckled at the weirdness of it. Still, I couldn't help feeling a little bit sorry for him. Teenage crushes were hard enough without being unrequited. I mean, he'd gone all gooey-eyed just talking about her, when the harsh truth was Jacob was still a kid while Tatyana was a full-blown woman. He was barking up the wrong tree.

A smile tugged at the corners of his lips. "Maybe I'll play the long game. Charm her first, compliment her all the time, and see where that gets me. I reckon I can get a kiss on the cheek before Christmas."

Ah, grasshopper, you have so much to learn about women. And how inappropriate this is.

"Or a swift kick to your crown jewels."

He laughed. "You talk like her sometimes, you know? Isadora, I mean."

"Do I?" His words took me by surprise.

"Yeah, you both have this bluntness about you, but I think you're both just hiding a soft, squishy center," he teased.

"I definitely do *not* have one of those, thank you very much!"

He grinned. "You know, Isadora never used to let her guard down very often, but she'd do it now and again, in the evenings, when the two of us were up late. She'd always talk about you, and how much you meant to her. I admit, I got a little jealous from time to time," he added, with a mischievous smile. "Sometimes, she'd tell me about those three years you were on the run—her, Hiram, and you. The places you hid and the lengths your dad went to, to keep you safe. You might not have known it when you were stuck in the foster system, but you've always been loved, Harley."

Tears pricked my eyes, prompting me to turn away for a moment. "I wish we could save her," I murmured. "There's so much I still want to know. Nothing important; just the simple stuff, you know? Those kinds of stories, about the years we had together. I don't remember any of it."

Isadora's letter had given me a whole torrent of information, which I was still struggling to process. So much so that I'd been trying to shove it back into the darkest recesses of my mind, with very little success. That thing was like a magnet, drawing me in. Nevertheless, I only wanted the easy stuff right now: the cute tales, the adventures, the love that my dad and my aunt had shown me, without me even knowing it.

"We *will* save her, Harley."

I turned back around. "Yeah… yeah, we will. Now, come on, we're not going to get her back without a decent portal, so get one opened pronto!"

He smiled and set to work, tearing a hole in the fabric of the universe. "Banquet Hall, madam?" he joked.

"Much obliged." I stepped toward the portal and teetered on the brink for a moment, before jumping through. These things never got any easier to deal with.

A split second later, I tumbled out of the portal exit and landed with a bump on something firm and uneven. Darkness surrounded me as the portal snapped shut behind me. Wherever I was, it definitely wasn't the

Banquet Hall. A shout went up, causing me to panic and scramble backwards, getting tangled in a throng of vine-like things that grabbed hold of my limbs and drew me under. I fought back, thrashing violently, trying to break free. Up ahead, the weird mass that I'd landed on was moving and groaning, a shadow growing taller in the pitch-black room as my eyes slowly adjusted to the gloom.

Oh, crap... I'm going to die here. Wherever here is.

A light flickered on. My eyes flitted up toward the figure, fearing the worst. Wade Crowley stared back at me with deeply unamused eyes, his bare chest looking like chiseled freaking marble in the soft glow of the bedside lamp. I couldn't take my eyes off him. Only when his legs wriggled beneath me, and I realized I'd tangled his lower half in the sheets during my battle with the bed linen, did I look down and gulp. My cheeks burned furiously. I'd pretty much had my head nestled in his crotch this whole time, while I'd thought I was fighting a vicious monster. *Yeah, actually, if you could go ahead and kill me now, that'd be swell.*

"Harley, what the hell?" he growled.

I jumped back as though I'd been zapped by an electric shock, doing my best not to stare at either his muscular chest or the defined dip of his abs as they slinked below his boxers. "I—I can explain everything!" I babbled. "I was training Jacob and he sent me through to here. Well, not here—it was supposed to be the Banquet Hall, but I guess he misjudged."

Surely he wouldn't have purposely sent me here? That'd just be cruel. Then again, I had teased him about Tatyana. *Is this payback? It'd better not be.* If it was, Jacob was on borrowed time.

"Wait... what?" He rubbed his eyes and sat up straighter. "Jacob?"

Ah, crap... His name had spilled out without me realizing it. Now, I had two options: try and wriggle my way through a convoluted lie, or come clean to Wade. Although the first choice was tempting, I knew it would be easier to tell the truth. Given my slip-up, he probably wouldn't have believed a lie anyway. *Right, then, time to face the music.*

"Tarver. Tarver is Jacob. He's wearing a creepy-ass mask to stay hidden. Alton knows—I mean, of course Alton knows, duh. Anyway, long story, nothing to worry about. A simple accident," I rambled. "I've been helping him, and I guess he needs a lot more work because here I am… in your room… landing on your bed and getting all tangled in your sheets. I, uh, thought they were creatures trying to grab me. Sorry about that." I smoothed down the covers like a class-A idiot, my hand rubbing along his thigh. I snatched it away, my face burning.

Slow it down, Merlin. He's going to think you've downed a gallon of coffee and a case of Red Bull.

"Let me get this straight," he said calmly, his face half-shrouded by shadow. "Jacob is Tarver. Alton disguised him in order to protect him— after everything that happened with Isadora, I'm guessing? And you've been helping him with his portal work, but he sent you here by mistake?"

"Bingo! We were working on short-range openings." I clung to the technical side of things, using it to ease my rapid heartbeat. It jumped up a notch as my gaze lingered on his half-naked body once more. *Stop looking at his beautiful damned abs!* Sure, they looked like they'd been carved by the gods themselves, but I needed to focus and quit making a fool of myself.

"And you didn't tell me any of this because…?"

I shrugged in apology. "Alton told me not to."

He sighed and threw back the covers, revealing himself in all his Calvin Klein glory. I sat down on the edge of the bed and stared like a starving woman as he padded over to his closet and grabbed some clothes. He threw on sweats and a T-shirt—two items I'd never seen Wade wear in all the time we'd been here—and turned back to me. A flurry of something like anxiety washed over me, coming from him. It was mixed with stifled desire that he was trying desperately to hide from me. After all, I was here, in his bedroom. It was just the two of us.

"I'm coming back to the training room with you," he said, his voice catching in his throat. "It's late and since I'm not getting more sleep anytime soon, I might as well make myself useful—see what you two have been hiding from me. It might be worth knowing who else's bedroom you've accidentally tumbled into, in the middle of the night."

There was no anger in his voice, only that same undercurrent of unspoken desire.

"Nobody's!" I protested. "Just… uh, yours."

"Good to know."

With that, he pulled on sleek sneakers and headed for the door, leaving me to follow after him, wishing the ground would open up and swallow me whole. Of all the rooms in all the coven, why did it have to be his? On second thought, I pictured myself landing unceremoniously in Alton's bed, and figured there were worse ways this could've turned out.

TWO

Harley

We hurried back through the empty hallways of the coven, passing a few guards in the magnolia courtyard who looked about ready to stop us in our tracks. Wade put his arm around my shoulders and flashed them a wink, most of the male contingent giving him a sly nod and letting us pass through. *Wow... Alton really needs to get better security.* Still, it felt nice to be pulled close to him, even if it was just for the sake of a ruse. He smelled good, of sleepiness and the faded aroma of a spicy cologne, the scent intoxicating at such close proximity.

As we moved down past the Banquet Hall and on to the training rooms, his arm dropped from my shoulders but stayed stiffly at his side, his fist clenching and unclenching in a tense rhythm. He was fighting to keep his emotions away from me, but I was too close and too attuned for that. Something like longing made its way toward me, twisting my own insides into knots. I missed the weight of his arm draped around my neck and the closeness of being pressed to his side. But how the heck was I supposed to tell him that? Every time I tried to speak around him, I ended up tongue-tied and looking like a complete dingbat.

He cleared his throat awkwardly. "Sorry about that. Didn't want anyone getting suspicious. I know you've got Alton's permission and everything, but it's best not to draw too much unwanted attention, especially with the coven on edge," he said quietly, as we pressed on.

"No, no, it's totally cool. After landing in your lap, what boundaries are left, right?" I choked on my forced laughter.

He cast me an odd glance that set my heart racing. It held a thousand unspoken things, some of which I could feel flooding out of his body and into my veins, making them brim with a sudden urge to push him up against the nearest wall and kiss him hard on the lips.

Get your head back in the game, Merlin! No more doe eyes at Crowley. I kept my gaze fixed ahead as we made our way to the preceptors' training room without any further frissons. Still, by the time we walked through the black double doors and into the baroque-style room, I was exhausted from the effort of keeping my thoughts to myself.

Jacob looked up in surprise, lunging for his mask.

"It's okay, he knows," I said.

He paused. "Oh... well, I guess that's a relief. It's claustrophobic in that thing."

"I bet it is," I replied.

"Did you end up in the Banquet Hall?" he asked hopefully, his tone genuine. So, it hadn't been some underhanded ploy to get me back for teasing him earlier. It had been a genuine mistake. I tried not to let my disappointment show, but part of me wished it had been a trick. Then it might've been clearer that we were making some progress with these portal shenanigans.

"Not quite," I replied, trying hard not to look at Wade.

Jacob frowned. "Where did you end up?"

"In Wade's room."

He looked shocked. "What? How?"

"I was hoping you could answer that." I gave a wry laugh and patted him on the back. He was trying his hardest to get to where we needed him to be. I could only imagine the pressure he was under. There was a constant current of unease coming off him, but I knew that only scraped the surface of the strain he was feeling. Even if I told him not to listen to Alton's comments about coming up with the goods, that wouldn't stop *Monsieur Director* from breathing down his neck.

"I must have been thinking about—uh, it was after I told you about that thing that I mentioned." He gave me a pointed look that I understood all too well. He meant the Tatyana thing. "As soon as I thought about that, I started thinking about similar *things*. My mind must have focused on something else when I was conjuring the portal, and it led you to… well, Wade's bedroom."

I was grateful to him for not outing me there and then. Although he'd been suitably vague, I got the gist of what he was trying to say. He'd picked up on my crush a while back, after watching me fumble through a conversation with Wade, and he could've exposed me if he'd wanted to. Fortunately, Wade himself didn't seem to have a clue what was going on, as he'd taken to inspecting the colored sandbags that lined the edge of the room.

"Have you been sending these through?" he asked.

Jacob nodded. "We figured it was easier to start with small objects before either Harley or I stepped through one of my portals. My precision comes and goes, and Harley insists on safety first."

Wade shot me a surprised look. "Really?"

"Hey, I can be Captain Health and Safety too, when I want to be," I retorted. "Anyway, sorry we took so long getting back to you, Jake. Do you want to try again?"

"Ready when you are," Jacob said with a shy smile. "Shall I do short-range again? I promise I won't let my mind wander this time. I'll focus on the Banquet Hall and nothing but the Banquet Hall."

I smiled. "Then take us there."

Wade and I stepped back as Jacob prepared to open another portal. I'd lost count of the number he'd managed to create that evening, but desperation seemed to be giving him a burst of stamina. He was determined to get it right. Who was I to stop him? In his position, I would've been, and still was, just as stubborn.

He lifted his palms, gathering the power of Chaos to him. His sleeve slipped back to show a leather bracelet, with a black stone fixed in the center. He'd returned from his last visit with Isadora with it on his wrist—a gift, which had found its way back to him. Apparently, his mother had given it to Isadora who, in turn, had given it to him. One thing was for certain; it wasn't an ordinary bracelet anymore. Jacob had found his Esprit, which was extremely lucky for a guy with that much power. He'd already improved by leaps and bounds, the sandbags reaching their destination more often than not. I might not have reached the correct destinations quite as often, but nobody was perfect.

The black stone glowed as the light of his Chaos shone emerald at his fingertips. He closed his eyes to slow everything down, just the way Isadora had taught him. He'd told me all about it when we'd started these evening training sessions and the idea fascinated me, making me wonder if I could use it with my own powers. However, that wasn't important now. Jacob's abilities took center stage here, not mine.

He clapped his hands together with measured force, the energy pouring out behind him, feeding into the tiny cracks in the fabric of the universe, the imperfections that allowed him to dig in and bust open a huge tear. With an almighty roar, a portal opened behind him, revealing the gaping void of the wormhole beyond. As soon as it appeared, I knew something was wrong. The gap was far bigger than it had been before, the edges crackling and spluttering. Gold and green sparks flew every-where like a glittering rainstorm. The entire fissure seemed to shudder with innate violence.

I looked to Jacob, whose eyes flew open in panic. His body was trembling all over, his face drained of color, his lips opening and closing as though he were trying to say something to us. The glow that shone from his hands was building in intensity, and the light grew so bright that it was hard to see him properly.

I squinted against the glare, trying to get a better look at him. It was clear he was struggling to control his powers, even with the Esprit to help him, but there was something else as well—through the blinding light, it looked as though Jacob was starting to disintegrate. Parts of him were ablaze, while tiny flecks of gold and green peeled away from him like dust motes. Only, they weren't dust motes; they were part of him. His atoms, being dragged into the portal, one by one.

"*Help!*" he cried out, his voice weirdly muffled.

"Oh, my God," I muttered in complete shock. "It's killing him."

Wade glanced down at me. "What?"

"It's killing him!" I yelled.

Without another word, I lashed out with my Telekinesis lasso and hurled it toward Jacob. I felt the edges slip around him, my hands and mind working together to gather the invisible tension around him before I tugged him back. He jolted forward, flying toward us as I yanked him as far from the wormhole as possible. I hoped that, by taking him out of the equation, it would sever the connection to the portal.

The trouble was, the moment Jacob landed on our side of the room, I felt a tug of my own. It sent me sprawling to the ground, an unseen power dragging me along the floor. The portal had somehow managed to grab hold of my mental lasso and was now pulling me toward the gaping tear. I felt the particles of my magical energy get eaten up by the vortex of the wormhole, the enormous power sucking in the very essence of my Telekinesis' Chaos.

"Break the link!" Wade yelled, as he sprinted over to grab me. His arms encircled my waist as he played a tug of war with the portal, with me at the center. "Let go of the lasso!"

I realized that I still had Chaos rising from my palms, the light glowing from my partially broken Esprit. Those two empty sockets still grated on me. In the panic that had ensued, I'd kept hold of it, somehow thinking it would keep Jacob safe if I just held fast. Immediately, I severed the link between myself and the lasso, the last of the energy surging into the vortex. As soon as the final wave barreled into the mouth of the portal, it snapped shut, having sapped all it could like a hungry beast who'd finally been sated.

However, a second later, a faint rumble emerged from the thin line of light that remained, where the portal had just been.

Wade grabbed me and dove to the floor with me in his arms as a silent wave of power rushed through the entire coven, pushing out of the training-room doors. It pulsed over our heads in a visible torrent of electric gold, shot through with veins of piercing white, the hairs on the back of my neck standing up on end as it passed us by.

As the initial burst ebbed, I lifted my head higher to check on Jacob, only to realize that something terrible was happening to the walls of the room. And, possibly, the rest of the building. The entire section of the interdimensional pocket that formed the training room shuddered and blinked for a second, as though it wasn't quite sure if it was going to hold out. A few bronze particles peeled away in a flurry of eerie light, cascading down like the last of fall's leaves.

"Something's wrong. The pocket's failing," I murmured, my heart hammering in my chest.

"What do you mean?" Wade asked.

"Look!" I grabbed his head and turned it toward the coven walls.

His eyes went wide in horror. "No… It can't fail. It can't."

As if sensing his words, a swell of bronzed light flooded back in the opposite direction to the blast, restoring the integrity of the walls. Like a defibrillator starting a heart back up again, it looked as though the explosion had only jolted the Bestiary generator for a moment, before it dutifully came back online. With it being so late at night, I hoped that nobody from the outside world had noticed the little glitch. Citywide panic was the last thing we needed. Moreover, I hoped that the rest of the coven were asleep and hadn't noticed the momentary lapse in protection in this section. Alton in particular.

I glanced over my shoulder to look at Jacob, who was in a heap on the floor against the far wall. Scrambling to my feet, and ignoring the fact that Wade's hand lingered on my waist for a moment as I stood, I rushed toward Jacob. He groaned as I neared, his eyes blinking rapidly as if he couldn't stand the light.

"Jacob? Jacob, can you hear me?" I asked, kneeling beside him. I took his hand and held it tight. *Please don't die, please don't die, please don't die.*

He stirred. "Harley?"

"I'm here."

"What happened?" he murmured. "I felt like… I don't know. It was weird. It was like I was fading away, like the portal was dragging me into a place I wouldn't be able to get out of."

"You overworked yourself, that's all. We shouldn't have tried to do so much in one evening. That last portal was one too many. You're not injured or anything, are you? Is anything broken? I pulled you away pretty hard."

He smiled weakly. "Doesn't feel like anything's broken, except my pride, maybe. Did anything bad happen?"

I shot a look at Wade, who walked up at that moment. "There was a bit of an explosion when the portal closed, but everything's okay. Harley had to pull you out, which meant the connection got snapped instead of it being magically disconnected. That must have caused an imbalance in the portal, which led to the blast. Anyway, there's no harm done, as far as we know. You did good—you just need some rest," he said, to my surprise. I'd expected the usual tough-love attitude.

"I messed up, didn't I?" Jacob dropped his gaze.

"No, Jake; you're just exhausted. You want to help, so you pushed yourself too hard. We've all been there." I squeezed his hand gently, wanting to encourage him. If he lost his confidence, we'd never get him to try this again.

"I'll do better next time," he said, a yawn stretching open his mouth.

"I know you will. You've got the talent; you just need a bit more training."

Regardless, it was becoming clearer and clearer that Jacob's powers were massively temperamental. They relied on a lot of precise factors and focus, which Jacob didn't always have handy. He couldn't help his mind wandering, or his stamina slipping, especially considering he was still a novice at all of this stuff. Isadora had done what she could, but their time had been cut short.

We'd need to call in some outside help, but I had no idea where to start. Who the heck could I ask when the only two people with these portal powers, whom we knew of, were Jacob and Isadora? I resolved to think about it and speak with Alton. He'd put me in charge of Jacob's training, so it was my duty to tell him when things weren't working. If Alton didn't want any more accidents like this happening, he'd have to come up with a solution himself. Although he'd likely just tell me to carry on doing what I was doing. He had a lot on his mind with this traitor still amongst us and the continued threat of Katherine.

"Come on, we should probably get you to bed," I said, reaching out for Jacob's hand. With Wade's help, we pulled him to his feet and held him between us as we made our way toward the exit.

"I can walk, honestly," he insisted, pulling away.

I was about to argue when a figure in the doorway made me freeze. A shadow stood across the threshold, lurking in the darkness. I stared at them in abject fear, worried we were about to be found out. The preceptors knew the situation, and knew we were using this facility, but this person didn't look like a preceptor. If they were, they would have walked in by now.

"Show yourself!" I shouted, stepping in front of Jacob to protect him. Meanwhile, Wade kept his arm around the boy's shoulders.

The figure stepped forward, the dim light of the training room casting its glow on the face of Dr. Krieger. "I apologize for the intrusion," he said calmly. "I was with Tobe in the Bestiary when something strange happened. I came to investigate on his behalf, as he was busy recalibrating the energy source. He told me the glitch had occurred here. I trust everything is well in here?"

I nodded. "A training accident with Jacob, but everyone's fine. I know it looks bad, but it's okay now. I'll give a full report to Alton about it." Krieger already knew that Jacob was Tarver. The only reason that Alton had let the good doctor in on the secret, after the whole curse debacle, was because it was up to Krieger to do the Reading. Alton's eagerness to discover the strength of Jacob's powers couldn't wait.

"Glad to hear it. Are you sure it was just an accident? The glitch was fairly sizeable." He looked much better than he had a week ago, the dark circles less prominent around his eyes, and a bit of color having come back into his pale complexion. Clearly, the guy had finally got a bit of rest after the trials of the removal hex.

"Yep, absolutely positive. Sorry for dragging you down here. Actually, I was wondering if I could have a word with you, doctor?"

"About the Dempsey Suppressor?"

"Got it in one."

He smiled. "Well, actually, I have some news regarding that," he replied, glancing around as if he didn't quite believe me about the room being fine. "And I was hoping to talk with you some more, at some point, about the magical-detection technology I've been working on. I believe I may have made a breakthrough, though I should very much like your opinion. Perhaps this meeting is more serendipitous than I initially suspected."

"My opinion?"

He nodded. "Yes, you seemed rather interested the last time we discussed it. I thought we could kill two birds with one stone, as the saying goes. Do you have time now? I realize it's rather late, but Alton told me you might be up and about."

"Did you say magical-detection technology?" Jacob perked up behind me, his tone eager.

"I did." Krieger tapped the side of his head. "Ah, yes, the Sensate. That's right. I did your Reading, didn't I? Wait... did I? I can't quite remember what is real and what is not. To be honest, I was almost certain I'd dreamt we had a Sensate among us." He sighed heavily. "You must forgive me for my mental sluggishness; this hasn't been the most straightforward of weeks for me, and I'm still regaining some of my former faculties. A severe hex will do that to a person. Indeed, you may be extraordinarily useful in this, if you wouldn't mind accompanying us."

I frowned. "You should really get some sleep, Jacob."

"You sound like Mrs. Smith again," he said, with a smile. "Come on, let me stay for a while. An hour, max, and then I'll go straight to bed."

I rolled my eyes. He wasn't my kid—what right did I have to stand in his way? "Fine, but just for an hour."

"Thank you!" He grinned with glee, practically shoving Wade away in his eagerness to follow Dr. Krieger. He snatched up his mask on the way out and tugged it down over his face.

As Wade and I headed out of the training room behind Jacob and Dr. Krieger, I paused for a moment to lock up the double doors. Wade hovered beside me, almost like he was awaiting an invite to the infirmary too. Still, I couldn't help noticing the weary expression on his face. Evidently, the night's events had taken a lot out of him.

"You don't have to hang around. Jake and I will be fine with the doc," I said sheepishly. "I want to hear Dr. Krieger out, and then I'll get myself to bed. No portals, no shortcuts—just plain old walking. You should head back. I'll fill you in on everything I hear tomorrow."

He arched an eyebrow. "No secrets?"

"No secrets." *Well, aside from the gigantic elephant in every room we step into together.*

"You sure you don't want me to come with you? I know Krieger didn't technically invite me, but I don't mind coming along."

"Nah, we'll be fine. Honestly, you get some shuteye. I feel bad enough about waking you up as it is, though I'm kind of glad you were there when things got out of hand. That could've all gone south so fast." I couldn't bring myself to look him in the eye, in case I gave myself away. "Anyway, you'd still be in dreamland if I hadn't landed on you in the middle of the night. Go on, we'll be okay. And I promise, no more secrets."

"Okay... Well, goodnight." He didn't look like he wanted to leave. "You did a good job back there, Harley. Jacob wouldn't be alive right now if you hadn't stepped in the way you did. What you did back there was... well, like I said, you did a good job."

"You sure you didn't crack your head when you knocked me down?" I teased, wishing I could take the words back as soon as they slipped out. He looked a little disappointed.

"Goodnight, Harley," was all he said, as he turned to go.

"Goodnight, Wade."

With that, he left, taking the right-hand hallway while I took the left, hurrying after the fading figures of Jacob and Krieger. The thing was, there was more to my reluctance about having Wade there than met the eye: unless it was good news about the Dempsey Suppressor, I didn't want him to know about it. In fact, if it wasn't good news, I didn't want to tell anyone about it.

Besides, after all my promises about not keeping secrets, there was one big one that I'd been hiding from most people: Isadora's letter. I'd already had enough bad news from that to last me a lifetime. Right now, the only news I wanted to share was good news. Something that would tell me, without doubt, that I could get this stupid Suppressor out of my body, once and for all.

THREE

Harley

Catching up with Jacob and Krieger, I walked with them the rest of the way to the infirmary. They were chattering away like hyperactive birds, barely acknowledging my presence. Jacob wasn't usually so talkative, but he tended to get excitable about things that intrigued him. Krieger had clearly pushed the right buttons. I didn't mind; it gave me a spare moment to think about what had just happened… and what might have happened if I hadn't stopped Jacob. The thought of him literally disintegrating sent a shiver down my spine. It filled me with dread. Now that Isadora wasn't here to protect him, that role fell to me. I'd pushed him too hard, insisting we carry on. *I'm no better than Alton.* But my heart was in the right place. I wanted him to progress for his sake; anything else was just a perk. A useful perk that could save our asses one of these days.

"Are you sure you're okay to do this, Jake?" I asked, as we stepped through the empty ward, with its eerie strip lighting and clinical white walls, and into Krieger's private office. "It's pretty late and we've got an early start in the morning. Plus, you've had one hell of an evening. Maybe I could fill you in on everything tomorrow, instead?"

He shook his head. "I'll be fine."

"Really? That last portal must've taken a lot out of you."

"Honestly, I'm all good. You don't need to worry so much." He offered a smile, but there was a warning in his tone. *Stop henpecking me.*

I shrugged. "Fair enough. Don't blame me if you need tape to hold your eyes open tomorrow, that's all I'm saying."

"Noted," he replied with a laugh. He didn't seem too affected by the portal mishap. Either that, or he was good at hiding the fact that he was on the brink of exhaustion. Beneath the stoic façade, I could feel the weariness emanating off him in sluggish rolls, like a marsh at low tide.

"If the young man says he's fit and well, then let him stay awhile," Krieger agreed. "If he starts to feel unwell or overtired, he's in the right place. I might have been somewhat compromised these past few weeks, but I am still a doctor. And a good one, at that."

I chuckled despite myself. "Point taken."

Jacob and I sat on the nearside of Krieger's almost ostentatiously large mahogany desk, while he walked around and sat on the other side. He had several files stacked up beside him, one of which he took from the pile and opened wide. He drew his finger across the page in a flourish, before settling on a cluster of notes at the bottom.

"Ah, yes, here it is," he said, his soft Germanic accent creeping through. "As you know, thanks to my former affliction, I've had a great deal of time to give to personal study. The removal of the Dempsey Suppressor has been at the top of my list for some time and, you will be pleased to know, I have made some headway with it."

"And you're feeling better now? The curse has definitely been lifted?" I pushed away the note of concern in my voice. If Alton had given him the all clear, there was no reason for me to doubt his state of mind. Still, Alton likely hadn't seen what I'd seen.

"Indeed it has, Harley. You need not trouble yourself," he assured. "Preceptor Bellmore and Director Waterhouse did a splendid job of removing it, with few side effects. I have become somewhat hard of hearing in my left ear, and there is a permanent exhaustion deep within my bones, but it's nothing I can't treat with a colorful array of medicinal potions."

"Good to know."

"Now, shall we proceed, or would you like to talk about my health for a while longer?"

Chastened, I gestured for him to carry on.

"Excellent," he said, glancing down at the page. "So, the good news is, I have discovered a way to remove the Suppressor successfully, but the bad news is, it will involve some rather intensive surgery. The Suppressor is designed to attach to nerve endings, so it can send constant pulses to block the flow of Chaos through your body. Which, in simple terms, means it is really stuck in there. That's the intention, as these things aren't usually meant to be removed once they've been implanted."

"And this is good news how?"

He smiled. "Well, I'm glad you asked. I've been thinking about utilizing Tatyana's skill set in order to lessen the collateral damage to your nervous system. With her healing powers, it may simplify the procedure a fraction. It will still be an enormously difficult task, for both you and me, but if she can maintain a current of healing energy through you as I work, then we might be able to make the removal a success. Limited side effects, which is precisely what we want."

A flutter of excitement made my heart rate quicken. "Limited side effects? Like what?"

"There's a wide range of things that can go wrong in all surgeries. I couldn't say for sure what might happen. Surgery is always unpredictable, and it will be difficult, as I've said."

"I can handle difficult, believe me. If I can take on Katherine Shipton in a tiny, dark hellhole in the earth, I can deal with a bit of surgery."

"Correction, a *lot* of surgery. We're talking hours and hours under the knife, with a very real chance that you might end up with paralysis, loss of motor function, as well as the risks to your magical abilities."

"I'm willing to do whatever it takes," I insisted. "I'll spend a week under the knife, if that's what I need to do. Yeah, it won't be pleasant, but if it's worth it then I'll do it. I just want to know if you can get this thing out of me for good?"

He nodded slowly. "I can, but I must be assured that you understand the gravity of the endeavor."

"I understand. Just tell me what I have to do."

His fluffy eyebrows pinched together in a frown. "Well, the surgery preparation itself will take a few months to organize, as work like this requires very specific tools that one cannot simply pick up at the nearest hospital. I have already taken the liberty of ordering these surgical instruments, but they have to be cleared for use by the magical authorities. That process is lengthy at best, interminable at worst. Once that's out of the way, there will have to be a period of two weeks, before the surgery, in which you will be required to enter a state of Euphoria."

I looked at him anxiously. "Surely you've got something in your pharmaceutical stash for that? Can't I just take something to put me in this Euphoria thing?"

"You misunderstand me, Harley," he said sternly. "Euphoria is not something you can ingest or imbibe, but a trancelike state, which cleanses the magical body of all power. You must train yourself to perform this act and maintain the restraint that comes with it so that a sudden surge of Chaos does not interrupt the surgery. It's a time-consuming and exhausting process, whereby the magic within you is pooled into a localized region in your body, where it will remain in stasis until you release it again. Bearing that in mind, the energy will have to be released back into your system slowly, to prevent a catastrophe from occurring." He paused, casting me a concerned look. "It is an extremely hard method to master and will require a great deal of effort on your part. Even then, there may be risks that we will all have to face: myself, you, and Tatyana, if she obliges."

"I told you, I'm not scared of a challenge. I'll jump through every hoop you've got if I can have the full force of my powers at the end of it. Tatyana isn't one to back down from a tricky situation, either."

He clicked his tongue in response. "Once again, I must ensure that you understand the gravity of this. Euphoria is a dangerous act that can leave a magical vulnerable for a prolonged period of time," he said gravely. "Magicals of old used to plunge themselves into intense states of Euphoria, as a means of strengthening their powers and improving their clarity. The sensation is said to be overwhelming. However, I would not normally advise or suggest it. Your case is the exception, as I can see no other way of performing the surgery without it."

My heart sank as realization dawned. I might have been willing to go through the entire rigmarole of this surgery and all its prep, but even then, it was going to take a long time to get done—longer than we likely had, before Katherine struck us again. I'd been so excited about the prospect of getting this thing out of me that I'd neglected to process the length of time it would take. *Reality bites.* I didn't want to seem ungrateful for all the research he'd done, but I needed something to get this Suppressor out of me faster.

"Is there any other way? A quicker way, maybe? Like, if I were to break it myself, would there be a safer way of doing that?" My mind turned toward Isadora's letter—I needed to reread it, if this was the only solution that Krieger could offer me.

He shot me a stern look. "Not if you want to survive the Suppressor's destruction, no."

"Then I guess we're playing the waiting game," I said with forced cheer. "You make all the preparations, and I'll do whatever it is I need to do to see it through." I was by no means ready to give up on a quicker solution; I just needed some time to do some digging of my own. There had to be something between the lines that I hadn't picked up on, or a lead I could follow. This couldn't be it—months of waiting, a lengthy surgery, and a bevy of risks to go with it.

Krieger smiled. "I know these months of persistence won't be easy for you, but you have the strength to make it through, and see excellent results on the other side. You will not find a surgeon in all of America who is better equipped to perform this than I am, and it will be my honor to do it, when the time is right."

"Thank you, Dr. Krieger. That means a lot." I hated lying to him, even if it was just a slight bending of the truth.

"I don't want to seem pushy or anything, and I'm really glad that you've figured stuff out with the Suppressor thingy," Jacob chimed in, taking me by surprise. I'd almost forgotten he was there. "But it's getting late, and you mentioned something about magical-detector technology?"

Krieger chuckled to himself. "Nice to see a young mind with such focus!"

"I didn't even know something like that existed, aside from what I can do. Did you come up with it?" Jacob's eyes were as wide as saucers, his backside perched on the very edge of his seat.

"Well, as a matter of fact," Krieger paused, tapping his chin thought-fully. "Actually, let me start from the beginning, so you get all the facts. You see, the previous physician here, a young woman named Adley de la Barthe, had begun some research into how this kind of technology might be possible, and how that would translate to a broader spectrum. She was trying to amplify certain subtle vibrations that magicals have been known to exude, but her calibrations weren't that accurate. Those vibrations are faint to pick up across a wide expanse, which is the end goal for this technology, so we may discover hidden magicals far and wide." He took a breath before continuing. "Anyway, I used her findings, and some of my own, to come up with several prototypes that could detect the faintest of these energy waves."

Jacob nodded along thoughtfully. "I get why there might be magicals out there who are reluctant to reveal themselves to covens, but in times like these, they're better off with a coven than without one. You're going to use this tech to help, right? Not to force anyone into anything?"

Krieger seemed delighted. "I would never allow this technology to be used for nefarious ends."

"Then can I help you develop this technology? I'm pretty handy with putting things together, and I've got my Sensate abilities to add to the mix," Jacob said.

"Why, of course!" Krieger replied. "I could use your Sensate exper-tise. You may even quicken the entire process."

"You've also got a lot of other things going on, Jake," I said softly. "Not to mention the fact you're supposed to be undercover. People might start to suspect something if you, as Tarver, suddenly start spending a bunch of time in Krieger's lab. There's enough suspicion going around this place as it is, right now. I don't know if it'd be safe for you."

"I'll be subtle about it," he replied animatedly.

"I'm really not sure this is a good idea."

"Nonsense." Krieger waved me away. "If anyone asks what he's doing here, I'll tell them he's my new intern. People tend to get tired of asking questions when you give them a dull answer. Anyway, I will be able to keep a close eye on him while he's here, to make sure he doesn't come to any harm."

"Even so, I—"

Krieger cut me off, the conversation about Jacob helping apparently over. "There may be a way to channel your Sensate abilities into one of my prototypes, Jacob, thus improving its ability to locate and identify magicals. Vibrations are all well and good, but they are nothing compared to actual Sensate capabilities." His voice was practically bouncing with excitement. "You see, one of my prototypes is a device able to hold certain powers within it. The gathered fragment of power can then be used by the technology to seek out whatever I program it to."

I frowned. "Wait, that sounds familiar. Do you mean an Ephemera?" Jacob's mom had used one of those to open a portal and escape with Jacob. His father had poured some of his Portal-Opener abilities into it, to give her a one-shot use of that particular skill.

Krieger shook his head. "No, this device is similar to an Ephemera, but it is not the same. The device can amplify the essence of a power, but it's not a one-time-only situation. If I'm being entirely honest, it is a modified version of an Ephemera, though much less potent. Here, the device, rather than the ability itself, does most of the work."

"How can I help?" Jacob asked eagerly.

"I will use the Ephemera-like device to extract a fragment of your unique Chaos signature, which I'll then connect to the magical detector and calibrate it, so it can pick up on those faint magical vibrations," he explained. "It is a minor procedure and will not affect any of your power. It's the same as making a small cut in the skin—the Chaos will heal it over and restore the missing piece."

"I think it sounds dangerous, but that's just my two cents," I said. "Your keeping a little bit of his ability doesn't sit right with me." I realized I was being slightly hypocritical, considering my own determination to break the Suppressor by myself. However, it was one thing to take the responsibility of endangering yourself, but it was a whole other ball game for someone else to endanger a person.

Krieger smiled. "I assure you it is perfectly safe. He won't miss it, and it will be of enormous benefit to all of us."

"Maybe some magicals don't want to be found, like Jacob said."

"Nevertheless, my job is to abide by the rules of the coven, and that encompasses the protection of magicals all over this nation. I have been instructed to develop this technology for the greater good, so we can serve more of those out there who have no coven to go to, or do not even know of their existence. If you're concerned about other people using a device like this, then you needn't fear. Alton has assured me that the most intricate security checks will be implemented when this technology passes the testing stage. Only coven physicians will be allowed to use it, and they will have to undergo rigorous background checks. He made a mistake with Adley, and he won't make it again. I wouldn't ask Jacob to assist me if I thought he might come to harm."

"I'll do it," Jacob said firmly. "Whatever you need to give this thing juice, I'll do it."

I stared at him in disbelief. "Why are you so eager to do this?" I was a firm advocate of taking time to think about stuff. I'd had Isadora's letter in my possession for a while now, and I was still mulling over a lot of what she'd said. No point rushing headfirst into potential danger.

"I have my reasons."

"Care to elaborate?"

He sighed. "I want to help. I didn't have a coven, and didn't even know what one was. That put me in danger with the Ryders. I want to stop that from happening to other people."

"Well, maybe you should sleep on it. I get why you want to do this, but if there's one thing I've learned that still serves me well, it's that you should never jump into a decision about something this complicated. If you wake up tomorrow, and it still feels right, then go ahead."

Jacob frowned, the cogs whirring in his head.

Krieger nodded. "How about you both return to your rooms and, as Harley says, sleep on what I have suggested. Jacob, you can come back to me in the morning with your answer. I am in no rush to extract the tiny fragment, and if you decide against it, I will find another way to fine-tune the detector so that it can pick up on these frequencies."

"I think that sounds like a good idea," I said, wishing Jacob hadn't just blurted out his agreement like that.

Jacob shrugged. "No problem; I'll sleep on it. Can't say it'll change anything though."

With a cursory farewell to Dr. Krieger, Jacob and I left the infirmary. Krieger watched us go, a half-amused look on his face. Even so, in the low light of his office, he looked exhausted. His shoulders sagged, his body collapsing into the comfy armchair as though it were the only thing still holding him up. *Poor guy.* He'd been through a lot. I could only imagine what a removal hex could do to a person.

"What did you do that for?" I whispered as we made our way back through the dark hallways, heading for the living quarters.

Jacob turned to me. "What do you mean?"

"Why did you have to go and agree like that? You don't know what could happen."

"Krieger said it was safe. I trust him."

"That doesn't mean it is." I sighed. "You said it yourself—people who know about you are going to try and pressure you into using your abilities for their own ends. Isadora must've taught you that much."

He shrugged. "She did, but this seemed like a risk worth taking. If this works, this'll benefit a whole lot of people like us, Harley—people who don't have anyone else, and are living with these weird abilities that nobody around them has. If some magicals don't want to join a coven, they'll still have the right to say no. But, this way, like Krieger said, it gives the covens a chance to find and help more magicals, one way or the other."

"At what cost to you, huh?"

"A fragment of my ability. Krieger said he'd only take a small piece." He came to a halt, looking me dead in the eye. "I didn't think you'd be the one to have a problem with this. Can't you see why I'm offering to help?"

I frowned. "I don't know. I suppose it's very noble of you."

"I want the freedom to make my own choices, even if they turn out to be mistakes. Otherwise, I might as well have stayed where I was," he said quietly. "Plus, if Krieger manages to develop this machine, then I won't be under the thumb of the coven for the rest of my life. They need my powers—right?"

"Right."

"And they want to use them for their own ends, like you said—yes?"

"Yes." I could see where he was going with this.

"If this thing works, then they can have the machine instead of me. I'll be free to leave without feeling a load of guilt about not using my abilities to help out, for the so-called 'greater good' that everyone keeps harping on about. I don't want to be selfish, but, like you mentioned, Isadora also taught me not to get trapped in places like this."

"I guess I hadn't thought of it like that," I said, feeling bad about laying into him.

"If I'm not distracted with using my Sensate abilities, then I can focus on portal-opening, and use *that* to help the coven instead," he added. "I mean, after tonight, we both know I need to put all my energy into getting the portal stuff right. I'm not stupid, Harley; I know what you did for me, and what could've happened if you hadn't."

I dropped my gaze. "You did your best, Jake."

"And it wasn't good enough. I nearly destroyed this place. Don't pretend like I didn't, because I know you're only trying to protect me."

I gave him a wry smile. "All I can think about is keeping you out of harm's way—I guess I keep forgetting the fact that you're a bright spark.

You've stayed one step ahead by yourself for this long. I suppose part of me is trying to fill Isadora's shoes."

"I know, and I appreciate it. I just need you to ease off on the gas a bit." He chuckled. "Right now, I'm thinking about the coven. But, when all of this is over, I need to know that there's going to be a life out there for me. I need to put those plans in place now, if I can. Does that make sense?"

"Perfect sense. You're putting me to shame."

"Nah, you're handling yourself like a pro. Honestly."

"I just keep wishing Isadora was here too, so she could give me a bit of guidance."

He nodded. "Me, too. Did the letter not help at all? She wouldn't tell me what was in it, but I'm here if you want to talk about it."

I pulled a face. "I can't even talk to myself about it."

"That bad, huh?"

"Parts of it, yeah. The truth is, what she wrote, it just... it hurts like a bitch. A lot more than I thought it was going to." After hearing the news from Krieger, I was even more downhearted about the letter's contents. It had offered so much and taken so much, all at the same time.

"I'm sorry. Should I have hidden it?"

I flashed him a sad smile. "Who knows—maybe. At the end of the day, I was the one who forced her to tell me all that stuff. I could've stayed in blissful ignorance, but I didn't want to. I just *had* to know more. She was just doing what I'd asked. It's not her fault, or yours."

"It's not yours, either."

"Thanks, Jake."

"Anyway, when we get her back, you can ask her for more of the good stuff, to take the edge off the bad," he said brightly. "Her stories are great."

"That's the thing—where do we even start with getting her back?" I murmured, running a hand through my hair. "How do we rescue her when we can't track Katherine? And you said you hadn't sensed anyone with that kind of power in the coven."

He grinned. "Well, that's another reason I agreed to help Krieger.

You really need to keep up." He winked and nudged me in the arm. "If I do some Sensating, or whatever it's called, then maybe we can discover Katherine that way."

"Do you know something, Jake? You might be the smartest one out of all of us."

"I've got youth on my side."

I shoved him playfully. "Yeah, and you're not too old for a smack."

"So, you think it's a good idea?"

"Now that you've put it like that, I think it's the best plan we've got. If that machine could somehow track Katherine, then we might have a way of sneaking up on her. An advantage, at last."

I glanced at him for a moment. He might have been wearing Tarver's mask, but his eyes were those of a kid. A kid with a lot resting on his shoulders. I wished I could reach out and take some of the strain for him, but that was an ability I hadn't been granted. He was going to have to do this on his own. But I vowed, right then and there, that we'd be behind him, every step of the way.

FOUR

Harley

After sleeping like the dead, I rolled out of bed to find that it was only half past five. The sun had just come up outside my bedroom window, the sky looking all the more mesmerizing through the gauzy filter of the interdimensional pocket. I stood there for a moment and watched the bolts of hazy orange and dusky pink trail across the dawn. It was rare that I simply stopped and took a moment to myself. Gazing out, I could pretend that my life was stress-free.

Tearing my eyes away from the beautiful view, I padded over to my desk and opened the top drawer. A single letter lay inside, beside the note that my dad had left for me. The crinkles from where I'd crumpled his note ran like veins through the paper. My dad and my aunt, side by side in words. I took the letter and sat cross-legged on the floor. I'd read Isadora's letter every day since I'd received it, but the words didn't get any easier to swallow. My heart ached with every reread, while tears threatened to fall down my cheeks.

My dearest niece,

I'm sorry I'm not there to tell you this in person, but I hope this letter finds its way into your hands. There is much to tell, and not a lot of time to tell it, but I can't write to you and not say this—I love you, sweet girl. I have loved you since the moment you were born and I held you in my arms for the first time. I cannot replace Hester, and I would never attempt it, but I have felt like part of your life for so long, though you didn't know I existed. I was a vision in your dreams, no more, but you have always been a very real thought in my every waking moment. Your survival is all I care about. It is all your father and I cared about. And when I see your face, I see his pride and his love. His eyes are your eyes, and he would have been so overcome with joy at the woman you've become. It was our all-consuming love for you that drove us to save you, and to keep you hidden. It was that love that forced us to put the Suppressor in you, though I know it's a source of great frustration and pain for you. I'm sorry for that.

And so, that's where I'll begin—with the Suppressor. I know you've been searching for a way to rid yourself of its boundaries, but I have to warn you before you try anything. It's my duty as your aunt, and as the last person who can keep you safe. Not only from Katherine, and the threats surrounding you, but from yourself, as well.

A knock at the door made me jump. *Who the heck is knocking for me this early?*

"Come in," I said, rattled. I hurried to hide the letter in my pajama pocket as I hastily wiped my tears away.

Santana poked her head around the door. "Hey, I was on my way to the gym and I saw your light on. I thought you might want to—" She stopped, her expression morphing into a mask of worry. "*Dios mio,* are you okay? Did something happen?" She rushed to my side and wrapped me up in her arms. I guessed a teary-eyed me was a rare enough sight to cause some alarm.

I buried my face in her shoulder. "I… I got a letter."

"A letter? From who?"

"Isadora."

She pulled away and held my arms. "Before Katherine took her?"

"Yeah." I might've been ready to talk to someone about the letter, but I wasn't about to blow Jacob's cover at the same time. I'd already done it once with Wade; I didn't want to make that same mistake again.

"Do you want to talk about it?"

I nodded.

"Is it bad news?"

I nodded again. "There was a lot to take in."

"Well, start at the beginning and I'll sit here for as long as you want me to," she said, in her usual Santana way. Sitting back, she folded her legs under her and waited for me to speak.

"You sure about that? We might be here all day."

"No problem. Now, shoot."

I took a shaky breath. "There were a couple of things she wanted to tell me, but the first thing she mentioned was the Dempsey Suppressor. She told me that, if I try and break it by force, there's no way of knowing if I'll come out the other side with any power at all. Apparently, it can go either way—leaving me with too much or nothing at all. No in-between, as far as I can tell, though she didn't go into much detail about that aspect of it. By all accounts, my unused Chaos energy has been building up inside the Suppressor since I was two, which means the eventual release will be massive."

I paused to wipe the rest of my tears away. "It might even emerge in the form of a dangerously powerful Purge beast, or something called a Purge plague. She said a plague like that hasn't happened in thousands of years, but it's a possibility, considering how much of this energy has been collecting in me all this time. The truth is, she doesn't know what'll happen, which freaks me out more than if I had actual details."

"I'm sorry, Harley," Santana murmured.

"There's nothing I can do about it," I said, with a wheezing sigh. "All I know is that, if I try to break it myself, I might end up risking my life, and the lives of everyone around me. The risks need to be lessened somehow, but that's the hard part—figuring out how. Even if I succeeded, and nobody got hurt while I was doing it, Isadora said that the return of my full powers would tip the scales of Light and Dark. Given my family's track record, sinking into the Dark side probably won't do me any favors. Anyway, she told me that I'd likely plummet into Darkness, and end up in a lifelong battle of trying to control all my abilities. They'll be too much for me at once, and there's a risk they might consume me." I looked at my friend. "Bet you wish you hadn't knocked, right?"

She shook her head. "Not at all. If you're going through something, then I damn well want to know about it. You're *mi hermana,* remember?"

I smiled. "Thanks, Santana."

"Don't mention it." She flashed me a grin. "So, we've got problems with the Dempsey Suppressor and what might happen when it breaks. That's all doom and gloom, granted, but there's got to be a solution, right? Any thoughts on getting around it? I mean, you're tough as old balls—there's got to be some way you can pull through the breaking and the aftermath of it."

I sighed wearily. "There probably is, but I've got no idea what. Like, there must be some way to balance me out—a spell, or an object, or some crazy magic voodoo. There *has* to be a way; I just don't want to do anything reckless. I learned that lesson with our half-summoned, smoky friend in New York. I don't want to kill everyone while I'm breaking this thing, you know? *If* I can even break this thing."

"It's *when,* not *if.* Seriously, it'll happen. We just need to figure out some angles that'll keep you safe, and everyone else safe."

"I really hope so. I know it's a big risk, but it seems worth it. It might be the one thing that gives us an edge over Katherine, if it comes to a one-on-one face-off again. I barely scraped out of that last fight alive. I don't want to be in that situation again, not if there's a way I can face her with a great big barrage of power."

"Too right, *mi amiga.*" She glanced over her shoulder, checking the door, probably to make sure nobody was listening in. "Plus, I know you've got some crazy mojo going on in there that makes you tougher than all these *ifs* and *maybes.* I spoke to my mom about your affinity with Grimoires. Don't worry, I didn't mention you specifically. I just asked her if it was possible to read from an unfinished one. She said that the most ancient of magicals had the ability, but it got watered down over the centuries. Nobody has that talent anymore, or so she seemed to think. Still, she mentioned that it had something to do with bloodlines and their connections to the raw center of Chaos itself."

My shoulders sagged. "Which leads me right on to Isadora's next point of business."

Santana seemed surprised. "It does?"

"Yeah. She said that, throughout history, the Merlins and the Shiptons have been getting themselves into a whole heap of trouble. Anyone with a leaning toward the Darker side of things, in both families, has ended up on some watch list or another, for unspeakable crimes against humans and magicals. Naturally, all this juicy stuff gets covered up, but you'd think they'd have given my mom and dad a warning before they made me, you know?" I forced a laugh, gaining a look of sympathy from Santana. "Apparently, we're descended from the Primus Anglicus—the first magicals who came into being. I guess all magicals are, in a way, but our connections are stronger. We're rooted deeper into the fabric of Chaos than others. Our name comes from the old man in the pointy hat from Arthurian legend for a reason. Mother Shipton, too. They're not famous for being understated."

She nodded. "My mom said that a deeper connection to the very core of Chaos could allow someone to read an unfinished Grimoire. It's why the ancient magicals could do it—these Premium people your aunt talked about. I guess, with you having all these abilities, and being the product of two ancient lines, you're rooted firmly in the heart of Chaos, in a way that hasn't been seen for a long time."

"Lucky me, right?"

"Yeah, one-hundred-percent lucky you. This is a gift, Harley, not a curse."

"I know. It's just a lot to take in."

She nudged my knee. "You've got this. Think of it as a good thing—this connection might be the very thing that keeps you from going under when the Suppressor breaks. It might be this strength that helps you control your full-whack abilities when they all come tumbling out."

I laughed. "See, this is why I'm glad it was you who knocked on my door."

"So am I. It sure beats pretending to run on the treadmill." She sat back, a funny look passing across her face. "By the way, I meant to tell you yesterday—I spoke to Marjorie about the Hamms having their memories of her wiped. It didn't go too well, but at least that's one thing off your mind. I know you were dreading it, so I got it out the way for you. And anyway, Alton should never have asked you to do it."

My heart sank. "How is she?"

"Devastated."

"I can imagine."

"She wouldn't leave her room. I tried to get her to come out for something to eat, but she just put on this terrible music and drowned me out. I thought I should leave her to herself for a bit and let her deal with it in her own time. Poor *chinguita* has been through the wringer. Part of me wanted to ask Wade to do some of his forgetting witchery on her, but that seemed crueler. At least, this way, she's got memories of being loved."

I nodded. "It'll hurt for the rest of her life, but it's better that she gets to think about them. They thought the world of her, and I know she loved them. It just sucks that it had to end the way it did."

Another kid whose pain I want to take away.

"Anyway, we can think about how to get Marjorie out of her room later," Santana continued. "What else did the letter say?"

"Well, Isadora told me why she hates the covens so much," I went on, my mind still dwelling on Marjorie. "She explained how they treated her, back in the day. I guess she doesn't want me to get stuck in the same cycle that she got stuck in, feeling like she was beholden to them because they looked out for so many people."

Santana frowned. "How do you mean?"

"She said they used her for her powers and forced her to help them do certain questionable things. If she ever refused, they threatened and manipulated her to make her do their bidding."

"What kind of stuff?" Santana's eyes shone in the light that glanced in through the window.

I sat back against the wall. "They had her break into high-security facilities, like armories and repositories, and into other covens, to spy on them and steal information. She was their pawn, just like she said to me back at the safe house. They locked her in the New York Coven's prison cells a couple of times, to give her a taste of what she could expect in Purgatory if she didn't do what they asked." I paused, feeling tears rise again. "I keep wondering if that's what they'll do to me if I don't comply, especially if I manage to break the Suppressor. It's the same fear I had when I read from my parents' Grimoire, given that I wasn't supposed to be able to do that. I can't help but think that, if they can't control me, they'll throw me in a cell somewhere, for the good of everyone."

"They wouldn't do that."

I arched an eyebrow. "Wouldn't they? I mean, I know I don't have any particularly rare abilities, unfinished-Grimoire reading excluded, but I do have six skills to my name." I glanced down at my broken Esprit, the two missing gems standing out like a sore thumb. "Well, four that I can control, right now."

I was still trying to wrap my head around how I'd managed to use my two most temperamental abilities in the fight against Katherine, but I guessed it had something to do with the desperation and adrenaline-fueled necessity triggered by the scenario. The need to save my friends, and to get Micah the hell out of there, had been a powerful motivator in getting my abilities right. Although, without that chemical help in my veins, I knew I was at risk of causing more destruction than I'd done at my pledge, if I tried to use those abilities in a more ordinary setting. Plus, a giant sinkhole wasn't exactly useful in most scenarios. Somehow, I'd gotten lucky. I didn't know if I'd get that lucky again, without my Esprit to help the flow of my powers.

"Harley, if anyone ever tried to throw you in a cell, they'd have to go through me and my Orishas first. They might be small, but they're mighty. Not to mention the rest of the Rag Team—they'd form a human shield around you if it meant protecting you from something like that."

"You think Wade would go against the authorities?"

She smiled. "For you, absolutely."

My cheeks flushed. "I haven't told him about the letter."

"And you don't have to unless you want to. He's a delicious specimen of a man, make no mistake, but he doesn't own you. He doesn't get to dictate what you tell him and what you don't. Besides, these guys love a bit of mystery in a woman."

"Yeah, I'm not sure this is the kind of mysterious he's after."

"Harley Merlin, you are *exactly* the kind of mysterious he's after. Half the time he looks at you, I want to snap his tongue back into his head. I keep thinking he's going to turn into a cartoon wolf and howl at you with his eyes popping out like balloons." She imitated the mental image for me, stamping my foot on the ground as she wailed. I couldn't help but laugh, clutching my stomach as she finished up.

"I'm glad you're here," I said, stifling a giggle.

"Me, too—someone needs to talk some sense into you. Anyway, I digress. Was there anything else in the letter?"

I wanted to tell her, I really did, but I couldn't get the words to come out of my mouth. "No, that was pretty much the gist of it."

The truth was, there was one other thing that Isadora had written. She'd saved it until last. Even in that moment, as I thought about it, I couldn't get it to process in my head. *"Alton Waterhouse was the man who sentenced your father to death. I don't know what he might have told you, but I was at the hearing. I created a portal into the jurors' deliberation room and I hid in the corner to hear their conclusion. The jury of ten was split down the middle—five for a life sentence, and five for the death penalty. Alton was the deciding vote. After hearing all the evidence, he decided to give your father the death penalty. He could have spared him, but he didn't."*

That was a hard pill to swallow. My dad was dead because of Alton— not just because he'd been on the jury, but because he'd been the deciding vote. Not only that, but Alton had lied to my face about it. He'd told me that the jury was split eight to three, and that he was bound by law to keep his vote a secret. He'd made me believe there was a chance that he'd been one of the three, when all that was a load of crap. He hadn't mentioned anything about being the deciding vote. In fact, when I'd asked him whether or not he thought it was possible that my father was innocent, he'd said he'd never excluded the possibility. Back then, I hadn't thought to look into the public records myself, believing every word he'd told me. To do that now would have taken another request to the New York Coven, and I didn't feel like dealing with a bunch of red tape. Besides, Isadora had no reason to lie.

Since discovering the truth, it had been difficult for me to even look Alton in the eye. No matter how hard I tried to rationalize everything, wondering if he'd lied to spare my feelings, my anger remained. Yes, he'd been doing his job, but that job had been a lot more specific than he'd let on. With the odds at eight to three, I hadn't thought there was any way my dad could have been spared. At five to five, with one vote left to go, that had raised the stakes much higher. He could've lived if Alton had voted differently. In the end, I wondered if he'd lied to get me on his side, knowing I'd have left the coven for good if he'd told me the truth. I'd thought about confronting him so many times, but something always held me back.

What does it matter now? It was the question I kept asking myself. I couldn't change the past any more than he could.

FIVE

Harley

An hour after Santana left, my phone beeped. Wade's name popped up on the screen, with a typical Wade message underneath: *Need to talk. Meet me in Luis Paoletti in ten. W.*

At least he'd dropped the "C" after a lot of teasing from me. I remembered promising to tell him everything about my meeting with Krieger, but all I wanted to do was curl up under the covers and go back to sleep. Dragging on jeans and a sweater, I texted him back: *Will do. H.*

After I stole a glance at myself in the mirror, realizing there was nothing I could do with my unruly mane of copper locks, I reread the text. Although it had appeared to be one of his usual, blunt messages, he never normally put something like "need to talk." My mind started to work overtime, delving into every little scrap of subtext I could conjure up. What did he need to talk to me about so urgently? Was there something else he wanted to get off his chest? *His sexy, honed, Adonis-like chest.* My mind drifted back to the previous night, a small smile playing upon my lips.

Yeah... not gonna happen. I thanked the rational part of my brain for bringing me back down to reality. Still, my heart was undeterred, remaining convinced that there was something more to this little rendezvous than met the eye. I mean, why did he want me to meet him in the Luis Paoletti Room to talk, when we could talk in the Banquet Hall or any other public place? No, for this particular meeting, he wanted privacy. My heart jumped at the prospect of being alone with him again.

Swiping some cherry ChapStick over my lips to give them a bit of kissable juiciness, as per one of Santana's many useful how-to-land-a-guy tips, I ducked out of the room and headed for the meeting point.

"I said ten minutes. Long night?" Wade said as soon as I entered the room, his tone clipped.

"I've been up since dawn, actually," I replied stiffly. My romantic hopes were soundly dashed. This was pure business. "Anyway, if you text a girl at seven in the morning, you've got to give her a little leeway."

He shrugged. "It couldn't wait."

"What couldn't?"

He smiled like he had a secret he was excited to tell. "I received some good news this morning. The application I filed for you to access your parents' Grimoire was approved by the New York Coven. Now, all you have to do is get through the interview."

"You're kidding?" My voice sounded flat; I could hear it as the words came out.

I couldn't bring myself to feign excitement. I mean, I wanted to see the Grimoire again, for sure, but it wasn't that Christmas morning buzz of euphoria. Instead, I felt a deep sense of dread. If the same thing happened again, with the trance and the black fog and the mysterious presence, he would be there to see it. Would he tell Alton? Would he be scared of me? I didn't want either of those things.

As I glanced at Wade, a twinge of guilt and fear tied my stomach into knots. I really wanted to tell him about my last visit to the Merlin Grimoire, to come clean there and then, but that fear of being locked up crushed me in a powerful vise that kept me silent.

"I thought you'd be happier than that," he said, with a flicker of disappointment.

"I am," I replied with forced brightness. "It was a long night, like you said—I'm still waking up. Plus, you didn't even give me a chance to get coffee."

This seemed to satisfy him. "We can get one on the way back. Anyway, with regards to the Grimoire—I'm coming with you this time. No arguments."

"Aye, aye, captain." I mock-saluted, bringing the smile back to his face. He seemed happy for me, despite my own lack of enthusiasm. He really did want me to get some answers.

"Well, that was easy," he teased. "I thought you'd at least try and dissuade me."

"Nobody can diss-Wade you." My cheeks reddened. "Get it?"

He snorted. "You're not *that* sleepy if you're swinging dad jokes at this hour."

"Believe me, I'd come up with something snazzier if I had a latte in me."

"So, what did you and Krieger talk about?"

I sat down on a stool and recounted the details of what we'd discussed the previous night. Or, rather, in the wee hours of this morning. I told him about Jacob and the magical-detection technology, and the news about the Suppressor. As I mentioned the latter, I watched Wade's face change from happy to concerned, just as I'd known it would. He worried too much. *But he's worried about you, Harley.* My heart skipped a beat.

"And you agreed to wait?" he asked.

I nodded slowly. "Yeah." It wasn't a lie, as I didn't have another option in the pipeline. Plus, I wasn't ready to tell him about the letter yet. One word about it to him, and I'd end up in a puddle of tears on the floor. I'd already done my crying for the year, and I wasn't about to do more in front of Wade.

"That's surprisingly careful of you."

"What can I say; I've got enough excitement going on with Katherine and her cronies, without thinking about doing something dangerous to myself." A slight bending of the truth, but I really *didn't* want to do anything dangerous. I wanted to break this Suppressor as safely as possible, just quicker.

"And you're okay with the surgery aspect?"

I shrugged nervously. "I know it's really risky, which is probably putting it mildly, but if it works, then it'll be worth it. At least, that's what I keep telling myself. I trust Krieger to do a good job. He seems confident about it, which is slightly comforting. Not much, but hey."

"And you think it'll work? Did Krieger mention any side effects?"

Isadora's warning flashed back into my mind. I could be left with too much or nothing at all. Would it be the same if I waited for the surgery? I had no idea. Although I doubted that seventeen years of pent-up energy just went away because it got plucked out slowly.

"I have to believe him when he says it will," I said. "As for side effects, I don't want to worry you, or myself, for that matter. There are some, but I don't want to think about that too much. It's not like this kind of thing has been done a lot."

He looked me dead in the eyes, a wave of affection rolling off him. "Well, we're all here for you, when the time comes. I'm sure Tatyana won't mind using some of her abilities to get you through, as long as Krieger is sure of the measured risks," he said evenly. "Although, for you, the surgery will probably be the easy part. It's the Euphoria that'll wear you out. Sinking into a state like that is notoriously difficult, and it'll require a lot of focus. I'd be happy to help you, once Krieger sets a surgery date."

"Thank you; that'd be great." I smiled at him, feeling a bit sad. If I had my way, that surgery would never happen, meaning I wouldn't get to spend a whole bunch of alone time with Wade.

"And, if you need someone to hold your hand while Krieger operates," he murmured, setting my pulse racing, "I'm sure Santana or Astrid would oblige. They'll want to be in the room if they're allowed."

Ah, Wade Crowley, how he does giveth and then taketh away.

"And you?" I said boldly.

"I'm not one for blood and guts and scalpels."

"Hey, there'll be no guts, thank you very much. If any of my insides start spilling out, Krieger's cut in the wrong place."

He pulled a face. "You have such a way with words, Harley."

"Yes, Wordsworth would be proud." I flashed him a grin, trying to shove away my disappointment. "Anyway, has there been any progress on the Katherine case? I know you said something about looking through a stack full of folders the other day—any luck so far?"

He shook his head and sat down beside me. "Not really. There's no reference to these five rituals in any of them, and nobody seems to know anything about this Librarian or where to find her. It's like she's completely off-grid, whoever she is. I'm guessing that's the point."

"Yeah, with knowledge like hers, it's probably best to keep a low profile."

"Precisely. Only that's incredibly frustrating when you're trying to find said person."

I chuckled. "Like a needle in a larger stack of needles?"

"Right." He sighed and leaned back on the workbench. "Alton's been putting his feelers out, and he's asked Marjorie to try her Clairvoyance using only the name, but so far all that's thrown up were visions of old ladies in fusty libraries across the country, stacking and stamping books. Not exactly the kind of Librarian we're looking for."

"Did Alton think they might be able to form a link, given that they're both Clairvoyants?"

"I think he had something like that in mind, but Marjorie just hasn't had the time to develop her skills. They're all over the place, to be honest. I don't want to sound like an asshole, because I know she's trying, but it's like having a huge, super-useful weapon and no ammunition. Even when she's highly focused, she needs more than a name to get a clear image. Look at Micah—it took touching a Shapeshifter to get that location out of Marjorie."

"I hope you haven't given off any of these vibes to her, Wade," I said sternly. "She's been through a lot, remember. Her mind is probably a total mess. Even if she wanted to think more clearly, there are a million other things going on in there, especially now."

He frowned. "What do you mean?"

"Santana told her about the Hamms having their memories of her wiped."

"Ah."

"So, she's got a lot on her plate," I said. "Can't go wrong with a little compassion."

"You think we've got time for compassion?"

I stared at him. "There's always time for that; otherwise, we're no better than Katherine."

After a pause, he crossed his arms. "I guess you're right."

"You do?"

He chuckled. "Do you really think I'm that cold?"

"No, but I'm still trying to find your soft and fuzzy center. I know you've got one, somewhere in there." I reached over and pressed my palm to his chest. In one swift movement, he covered my hand with his and held it there for a moment longer, his heartbeat thudding against my skin. I looked up at him in surprise, and my tongue twisted itself into knots as I struggled for something to say.

"Have you found it?" he murmured.

A lump gathered in my throat. "Not yet."

"Then you'll have to look harder."

We were so close that I could've leaned over and kissed him. His eyes were fixed on mine, as though challenging me to make the move that he couldn't. Desire bristled off him like static electricity as he looked at me, his Adam's apple moving in a breathless gulp while his teeth grazed his bottom lip. *Oh, God... Could you be any sexier?*

"Still, what Marjorie is going through doesn't make our current overall predicament any less frustrating," he said, breaking the tender moment.

Yeah, and you looking at me with those bedroom eyes doesn't help, either.

"Just when I thought I'd found Mr. Soft and Fuzzy, you go and say something like that," I chided, removing my hand and sitting back on my stool. Even then, I wanted to lean back over and kiss that coldness out of him. My feelings for Wade were going haywire, amplified by a sudden need for human contact, brought on by my sadness over the letter and Marjorie discovering that her foster parents no longer remembered who she was. It was a fate almost worse than death, being forgotten like that by those we loved. It reminded us that life was short, and we should grab the proverbial bull by the horns. Or, as Santana would say, by the *cojones*.

"You seemed upset," he said, taking me aback. "I thought that, if I said something like that, it might make you feel better. I've seen most of the Rag Team sad before, and I know how to comfort them, but with you... I don't know what to do. I'm not cold, you know. I'm just good at hiding my emotions from people. Not you—well, most of the time—but everyone else."

I gaped at him in utter confusion. I hadn't seen this soft, vulnerable side of him before, and I couldn't decide if I adored it or I wanted to run from it. It was easier to deal with my feelings when he was in business mode, all stern looks and steely eyes. Honestly, this squishiness made me like him even more, if such a thing was possible. *My little onion has himself some hidden layers.* And they were about to make me tear up.

"There... you're doing it again," he said, a worried expression on his face. "Is something wrong?"

I wish I could tell you...

"It's just dealing with Marjorie and Isadora and my parents and trying to stop Jacob from beating himself up about his mistakes," I half-lied.

"Stay where you are. Don't move a muscle," he replied. Frozen to the spot, I didn't move as he scooted his stool closer to mine and pulled me toward him. His arms smoothed around my shoulders, folding me up in his embrace, his chin resting lightly on the top of my head. Slowly, I let my arms wrap around his waist and buried my face in his neck, inhaling the spicy-sweet scent of him as I let him hold me. Time seemed to slow down, the rest of the world falling away, leaving only the two of us.

After a few minutes, I lifted my head up. Our faces were practically touching as he looked down into my eyes. A couple of inches forward and his lips would be on mine. He swallowed as I held his gaze, his hands lifting up to cup my face as we sat there. With my palms now pressed firmly to his chest, I could feel his heartbeat again—it was thudding hard against his ribcage, as though trying to beat out a secret message in Morse code. *Kiss me?*

"We should go and get that coffee," he said, his voice thick with emotion. "You look tired, Merlin."

My heart sank as he moved his hands away and released me from his comforting arms. He had been so close to kissing me, I was almost sure of it. But now... well, now, I was back at square one, left to wonder about the "and then what?" of our relationship. *Relationship—don't make me laugh.* It was more like a constant exercise in mental aerobics, trying to figure him out. Just when I thought I was starting to break through the ice that surrounded him, he pushed me away. Then again, maybe that was for the best. If I shared my feelings and then he rejected me, or he confessed that he felt the same way—what would happen then?

I had no idea what it meant to be in a relationship, having never actually experienced one. My track record with all relationships, romantic or otherwise, wasn't exactly exemplary. All my life, I'd been handed off to one person or another, never staying longer than a couple of years. If Wade and I became an item, would the same thing happen? It scared me as much as it thrilled me. More than anything, I wanted to find out.

SIX

Astrid

"Keep your eyes closed," Garrett said, close to my ear. I walked awkwardly forward, feeling stiff and uncomfortable as his hands guided me. Romance of any kind, not just with handsome renegades, was an entirely new concept to me, especially when said renegade had his hands on my shoulders. Touching bare skin, no less! I didn't know whether to pepper-spray him or hug him.

He'd texted me late last night, asking if he could take me out on a sunrise date. Naturally, the word "date" terrified the bejesus out of me, since it entailed a social or romantic appointment or engagement. Dates were not my forte. I wasn't even sure I liked meetings. Rendezvous were even less palatable. Besides, appointments usually made me think of dentists and doctors; and engagements... well, that didn't seem like an appropriate thing to think about. Although it would certainly send Garrett running for the hills. The thought amused me as I let him push me forward.

Regardless, I liked to wake up early, so the time suited me, but I'd never had to get ready for a breakfast date before. Would there even be breakfast? I had no clue. I hoped so, because I usually kept to a tight schedule with my meals. Smartie was already beeping in my pocket, reminding me to take my vitamins. After you've been dead a couple of times, you learn that internal health is vitally important. However, I realized I hadn't brought them with me. *I hope my immune system doesn't take too much of a knock.* A few hours without wouldn't hurt, right?

I'd been desperate to request Santana's or Tatyana's advice on this sort of thing, but by the time he'd messaged me, it had been much too late for me to go and ask for their help. Then again, most of what they usually talked about, when it came to romance, went over my head. I was still trying to figure out what Santana had meant about the "ghoulies" when talking about Tatyana's date with Dylan. No doubt it was a sexual innuendo of some sort.

"Are we there yet?" I asked uncertainly.

He removed the blindfold that he'd helpfully placed over my eyes. I'd told him I was a known peeper, which had prompted him to bring the prop. I hoped it didn't give him any ideas… There was no such thing as Fifty Shades of Astrid. I doubted I even had one shade.

"Now you can open your eyes," he instructed.

I blinked to accommodate the change of light, letting my retinas do their miraculous thing. Beyond the interdimensional bubble of the coven, the sky was still dark, though an inkling of daylight was starting to emerge on the horizon. I thought of all the countries that had already had their sunrise and wondered if anyone else was doing what Garrett and I were.

Taking in the rest of my surroundings, I realized we were out in the dragon garden. The fountain trickled crystalline water onto the fanned-out shells below, its marble wings half-outstretched as though it intended to fly off as soon as it was finished spewing. On the floor beside it, a tartan picnic blanket had been spread out, with candles flickering in Mason jars all around it. *I hope you didn't take those jars from the Bestiary, Garrett.*

"I thought we could have breakfast as the sun came up," Garrett said, gesturing for me to sit. A cardboard box full of pilfered goods from the Banquet Hall sat in the center, though it all looked delicious: chocolate pastries, fresh fruit that had been cut to look like flowers, a cup of

Greek yogurt, crusty white bread and berry jam, all to be washed down with the pitcher of orange juice beside the box.

"This is lovely," I replied shyly.

"To be honest, I stole the idea from Dylan. I just replaced sunset with sunrise, and decided not to drag you out to some weird cemetery." He shrugged. "I guess it's down to personal taste. Tatyana likes ghosts. I didn't think you would."

I smiled. "Not particularly."

"I wasn't even sure you'd agree, what with it being so friggin' early. I had to sneak into the kitchens to nab all this stuff."

"I like to get up early, and I like breakfast. Consider me sold."

"Cool. It's all good then? Even with the stolen ideas and food?"

I nodded. "I think it's cute. Plus, this is one of my favorite places in the coven, so you picked well."

"Ah, that's a relief. I was going to take you to the pool balcony, but I figured this was a little more... private."

For what? I swallowed the thought and focused on him instead. In all my life, I'd never pictured myself with someone like him—someone handsome and roguish and a little edgy—but here I was, about to partake in a romantic breakfast. We'd had a few outings together, as a fledgling pair, and I'd come to like him a lot in that time. Where others tiptoed around things, he was blunt and honest. Even with the stolen ideas, he'd told me the truth instead of passing them off as his own. It was refreshing, to say the least.

"You know I like you, don't you?" he asked suddenly, just as I was about to reach for a pastry.

I paused, mid-grab. "Well, I didn't want to assume."

"Because it makes an ass out of you and me?" He flashed me a grin.

"I would've looked silly if I'd thought you liked me and you didn't, wouldn't I?"

"See, this is why you're so cool. You get me. You hear me say stupid crap and you don't roll your eyes; you just... I don't know. I guess you make sense of it."

I took the pastry and tore off a small piece. "For the record, I like you, too."

He grinned from ear to ear and leaned down to kiss me on the forehead. "You've got no idea how glad I am to hear you say that."

"You didn't know?" I flushed, my skin tingling where he'd kissed me.

"You're a tough one to read, sometimes."

I chuckled, looking up into his eyes. "Well, now you know."

"You're one of a kind, Astrid Hepler." He held my shy gaze. "Seriously, you are. The way you do things, and the way you think about other people—it's cool. Really cool. I wanted to thank you again for trying to stand up for me, by the way, about the body cams. I know I've told you before, but it meant a lot for you to defend me and the other Shapeshifters against Alton. We get a bad rap, and we don't deserve it. Not all of us, anyway," he went on, taking a strawberry and popping it into his mouth. I'd never seen anyone eat a strawberry in such a seductive manner. Nor had I ever wanted to be a strawberry so much.

"I know," I said, watching him chew. "It wasn't fair, what he did. And now you all have to go around with those things strapped to your chests, having to explain every time you turn it off temporarily to go to the bathroom. It seemed so hypocritical of him, when he'd vowed to protect you all from the coven's judgment. Why go through the rigmarole of doing that for so long if he was just going to expose you in the end, anyway? That's what I can't understand. There had to have been another way."

Garrett smiled bitterly. "I guess this was the easiest option. Surveillance."

"Still, it doesn't make it right."

He turned to me. "No, it doesn't."

"I wonder what would happen if you took it off?"

"Is that a challenge?"

I stared at him. "No... I just meant... uh, I don't actually know what Alton would do if you took it off. Would he come running? Would he send in the cavalry? I've been thinking about it a lot."

"Because of me?"

"I suppose. For example, this date would be far more romantic if you weren't wearing a piece of equipment on your chest, recording all of this."

"Some people like that, you know?" he teased.

"Yeah, well, I'm not one of them."

He laughed and reached down to the straps that held the camera in place. "Why don't we hide it for a while—see what happens?"

"I'm not sure if that's such a good idea." I looked down at the fine detail of the blanket's tartan weaving, temporarily distracted by the navy, red, and thin white bands crossing one another. "I wouldn't want anyone coming and cutting our date short."

He stopped fidgeting with the camera straps and moved his hands away. "You're right. Neither would I."

"I'm sorry you have to wear it, though."

"I know you are. See, that's another thing I like about you—you're one of the most genuine people I think I've ever met." He leaned over and tucked an escaped strand of curly hair back under the red-and-white spotted headband I was wearing. "I can tell you've got a good soul. It's probably why you keep telling death to go screw itself—your soul is too good to leave this world."

"Actually, it's Alton who keeps doing that." I giggled into my pastry.

"I'm not just doing this to impress you, by the way," he said. "I mean everything I say to you. It's like you draw it out of me. At first, I thought it was weird, and that someone had slipped some kind of truth serum into my coffee, but then I realized that it's just you. Your vibes make me want to talk to you about everything. It sounds crazy, at least to me, but I've never liked any girl as much as I like you. And it's unbelievably cool that you like me, too. Honestly, I was under the impression you thought I was some kind of dumbass wannabe bad boy."

"First impressions don't always stay the same," I replied. "You got in with the wrong people and you made some mistakes, that's all. If I were to shun everyone who's done something stupid at some point in their lives, then I'd probably end up talking solely to Smartie."

"You love that thing, don't you?" He nudged me in the arm, almost making me spill the orange juice.

"Smartie never lies, and he gives me all the information I could possibly want. What's not to love?"

He laughed. "As long as he's not muscling in on my turf…"

"Sadly, he's no substitute for actual human contact. I have these realizations sometimes, that I've just spent an hour talking to a machine."

"It's probably no worse than all of us being glued to our phones all the time, though."

"No, maybe not." I cast him a side glance, admiring the chiseled features of his sharp, handsome face. He always had a way of rationalizing my thoughts and making me feel less weird. Being the only human in a coven full of magicals made me feel pretty lonely sometimes, as though everyone was in on something that I couldn't be a part of. Garrett never made me feel that way. Instead, he made me feel included, in both the coven and his life. The Rag Team did, too, on some levels, but there were moments when they seemed to realize that I didn't possess the abilities that they did. I sometimes wondered if they thought less of me for that.

"I'm sorry about the way I acted when Finch was still around," Garrett said, as he took a huge bite out of a croissant. "I like to think it was all because of him, but I'd be lying. Being on the bad side of things is oddly liberating, and once you're in it, it's impossible to break free without a big event tearing you away. It's addictive."

"He was your friend, regardless of how things turned out," I replied. "That kind of betrayal must have stung something terrible."

"It did, Astrid. Man, it really freakin' did."

"Do you miss him?"

He shrugged. "Sometimes. I know it seemed like we were just these guys who went around making people's lives miserable, but we were tight. Tight enough for him to tell me about Adley, and how they got away with sneaking around. He seemed crazy about her. I'd see him get funny about it every now and then. I guess that was his guilt talking—if he even feels any guilt. I don't know anymore. But he and I talked about stuff I'd never told anyone before. Our dreams, our fears, even some of the things we'd done before the San Diego Coven. We had a solid friendship. The real deal. At least, I thought we did. Like, even now, I don't know if someone can pretend that convincingly, you know?"

"I think there's more to Finch than any of us know," I replied. "I don't like to play devil's advocate, but it can't have been easy for him, growing up the way that he did. And we all know what a master manipulator Katherine is. She probably had her claws so deep in him, he didn't even know life without her influence, or thoughts without her poison."

"I agree. It's still scary, though," he said. "The Finch I knew and the Finch he turned out to be are completely different people. I still can't wrap my head around it."

"I get why it's so difficult a concept to grasp," I murmured.

He sighed and bit violently into his pastry. "I guess I'm just glad that, after everything, the Rag Team have accepted me... more or less." He flashed me a wry grin. "As long as I've got your vote, I don't care about the others too much."

He'd changed the subject quickly, the topic of Finch evidently too hard for him to talk about. I might not have been blessed with magical abilities, but I knew a man in pain when I saw one. There was some residual heartbreak over the lost friendship, and the deceit that had marred it for life. To have been fooled like that couldn't have been easy to deal with, and to correlate one Finch with the other would've been just as harrowing. Finch clearly had two sides to him. As I'd said, I still believed there was more to him than any of us knew, though much of that particular truth lay between Finch and his mother. Our parents had a lasting effect on us, no matter who they were.

"What do you think of this whole Katherine-becoming-a-Child-of-Chaos thing, anyway? I keep meaning to talk to you about it, but it's hard to get you to myself with everyone else around," he said.

"I think it's terrifying."

He frowned. "Really?"

"Nobody should have that much power. It's different for the actual Children of Chaos—they're magnificent, omnipotent, omnipresent beings as old as time. They've been crafted from Chaos itself, born of the first particles of magic. But no one should be able to become or replace a Child of Chaos. I'd hate to know what someone like Katherine would do with that level of power."

He lay back on the picnic blanket and looked up at the brightening sky. My animal instinct drove my gaze toward the flat muscle of his stomach, where a strip of bare skin poked through the bottom edge of his T-shirt. Engaging my logical, non-lizard brain, I forced myself to look elsewhere.

"I know you won't judge me for saying this, but I kind of like the idea of it," he said, undeterred by my silence. "I mean, can you imagine the enormous power it would bring?"

"I can imagine that, yes, and I repeat—I don't think anyone should have that much."

"Yeah, but think about what you could do. You could do *anything*. You want world peace, go for it. You want to take revenge on someone, you do that. You want to be rich, by all means. You want to help your friends and family out, you just clap your hands and *bingo!* You can give them everything they've ever wanted, in the blink of an eye."

"I thought it was the clap of your hands?"

He smirked. "All I'm saying is, it'd be pretty cool. Not that I'd ever do it," he added hastily. "Still, I can't deny it sounds interesting. Like, how did she even come up with that? Did she wake up one day and think, 'Hey, I don't like how things are, so I'm going to become a Child of Chaos and do what I want'? I'd love to know what her mindset was. She's scary and all, but she's sort of intriguing too. Does that make sense?"

"In a way," I replied tentatively. I could see where he was coming from—I just didn't like the inference much.

"It's got to be a huge sacrifice though, if you think about it. I've been thinking about it a lot, to be honest. To become a Child of Chaos, do you reckon she has to give up her mortal shell, so to speak, and become raw energy, like the rest of them?"

"I honestly have no idea." I wondered why he was so fixated on the subject.

"Then again, if that's the case, as a consolation, I guess you get to go anywhere and do anything. Nothing would be off limits," he continued. "I don't believe there's a single person in this coven who doesn't find that level of power appealing."

I got the feeling he was almost in awe of Katherine's breadth of ambition, which worried me somewhat. He'd been led astray before by bad eggs—I didn't want Katherine snatching him away from me with all her manipulative witchery. In that moment, I was very glad that the cameras weren't recording audio; otherwise, Garrett would have found himself with a one-way ticket to Alton's office. This sort of talk was tantamount to treason.

However, I couldn't deny that his plain honesty, even peppered with his darker thoughts, made him extraordinarily appealing. He didn't try to hide or pretend; he simply said it how it was—whatever *it* happened to be. I admired him for that. Plus, every moment I sat at his side, I kept wanting to let my gaze linger on that small piece of skin. My fingertips were itching to know what it felt like. I imagined it would be smooth and warm, as most bodies were, but there was something about his that lit a fire in me. *This is very unlike you, Astrid. Switch off your amygdala before it gets you into trouble.*

"I wouldn't know what to do with power like that," I admitted.

"Really? No idea whatsoever? Not even in a distant, crazy-wild dream, somewhere on the bottom of your consciousness?" he asked, a smile tugging at the corners of his mouth.

I frowned. "I haven't really thought about it. I know some people here pity me for not being a magical, but I honestly think I prefer it. Having Chaos abilities seems like a lot of pressure and responsibility, especially when things go wrong. Which, by the way, they often do."

"It's funny, I can't even imagine a life without these powers, yet you're more of a magical than me, in a way. It's hard to explain." He propped himself up on his elbows and looked at me. "Your intelligence is your ability. Not a lot of people have what you have. And I'm in awe of you. I wish I had your brains."

"That's kind of you to say," I murmured, feeling my cheeks burn.

"I mean it. It's rarer than most magical abilities." He sat up straight, taking my hands in his. "You know what; there's another reason I hate all this constant surveillance. If there weren't eyes on us, I might even kiss you right now. Honestly, it kills a guy's game, having one of these strapped to him."

My heart leapt into my throat. I couldn't tell if he was joking or not. Reading people was more Harley's thing. I wished I could tell what people felt, the way she did. It would've made all my social interactions much easier. I would've loved to be able to feel Garrett's emotions right now… though of course even Harley's abilities wouldn't work on a Shapeshifter.

"Seriously, I hate these things," he muttered, his tone tinged with anger.

I couldn't blame him. Ever since the implementation of the cameras, the Shapeshifters in the coven had been avoided like the plague, their identities revealed. It was a sorry state of affairs, and it was one that I had so desired to stop from happening. Alton usually took my opinion on board and, more often than not, we were on the same page. With this, however, we seemed to be at opposite ends of the proverbial library.

"I've tried to talk Alton into removing the cameras," I confessed. "I know the damage has already been done, but I've attempted to make him see sense. As of now, he still refuses to budge."

"What's the deal between you two, anyway?" he asked, arching an eyebrow. "I've always wondered how you got here. There are a thousand stories going around, but I don't believe any of them. So, come on, truth time. How did Alton find you?"

I lowered my gaze, turning my face away. He might have been upfront and honest with me, but there were a few secrets that I wasn't ready to tell anyone, not even Garrett. And yet, the words started creeping onto my tongue before I could stop them. Deep down, I wanted to be vulnerable with him. I wanted him to see that side of me.

"If I tell you, you must promise not to—" I didn't get to finish my sentence, as a figure appeared on the threshold to the dragon garden. He loomed larger than life, his eyes narrowed.

"Apologies for the intrusion. Astrid, might I speak with you?" Alton said coolly. "There's some urgent business that requires your attention."

Garrett scowled. "We're a little busy right now."

"Nevertheless, I need Astrid's assistance."

Torn between the two of them, I cast Garrett an apologetic glance. I might not have liked the way Alton went about certain things, but I couldn't just sit here and continue with my date if he needed my attention. Although, I could smell the ruse from a mile off. I wouldn't have been surprised if there was no business at all. Either way, Alton obviously had eyes on certain cameras and had spotted me out here with Garrett. *What right does he have to do this?* I was never going to hear the end of it if I didn't go with him now.

"Rain check?" I asked hopefully.

"You're going?" Garrett's voice was ice-cold.

I sighed hopelessly. "I have to."

"Can I see you later?"

"I'll text you when I'm done," I promised, flashing him what I hoped was a roguish smile. He had a point about bad behavior feeling a little addictive. *Does this mean I'm becoming a renegade?* A secret part of me hoped so.

With that, I followed Alton out of the dragon garden and through the near-empty hallways of the coven. A couple of magicals passing us by dipped their heads or offered a sleepy "hello," but he barely acknowledged them. Nor did he extend any chattiness toward me. In fact, he didn't say a word until we were safely inside his office, as I'd expected. Alton was nothing if not a creature of habit, and he didn't like to air his dirty laundry for all to hear.

"Astrid, I have turned a blind eye for long enough," he said, the moment the door was closed. He began to pace, which was never a good sign.

"A blind eye to what?"

"To your romance with Garrett. I don't like you being in the company of someone like him. It can only spell trouble, and I won't see you mixed up in anything like that. You're too precious to this coven to be led astray."

"What do you mean, 'someone like him'? What do you think he is?" I snapped back.

"I didn't mean it like that. Don't turn this into something it's not."

I balled my hands into fists. "No, actually, I don't know what you mean. As far as I'm concerned, I'm doing what any normal young woman would do. I like a guy, so I date said guy. That's all there is to it. This has nothing to do with you, and, frankly, I'd be amused to see how you think you can stop me. After all, you've already gone so far as to strap a camera to his chest. How was the footage of our date, by the way? Did you enjoy it over your morning ristretto?"

He whirled around, glaring at me. "You don't get to speak to me like that, Astrid. I am your father, whether you like it or not, and you'll do as you're damn well told."

SEVEN

Astrid

"You were the one who suggested I keep our relationship a secret, and now you want to play the dad part, bringing down the hand of discipline? You can't have it both ways, Alton." I held his gaze, remaining steadfast in my resolve. I wasn't prone to tears, and it had been many years since I'd cried in front of my father. I wasn't about to break that excellent streak of stoicism now.

He flinched at his name. "I've asked you not to call me that when it's just you and me."

"You can't be my father only when it suits you."

"I'll always be your father, Astrid."

"I mean, you can't just decide to get parental with me when I'm doing something perfectly normal that *you* don't like. If this had happened a few years ago, I might've understood, but I am perfectly capable of handling a romantic relationship." My cheeks burned with anger. "Would you have me be an outcast for the rest of my life, or do I have to leave this coven to get some sense of ordinariness?"

He looked startled. "You wouldn't leave."

"Why not, since you seem determined to ruin any normalcy I might have here?"

"I'm worried about you, that's all," he said. "Garrett has trouble stamped all over him."

"No, he has a camera strapped to him. And that was *your* doing, remember?"

Alton sighed. "I mean it, Astrid. He's not good for you. He's not good for anyone in this coven."

"What are you talking about?" Curiosity was in my blood. My anger wasn't about to put an end to that. No, if he had something to say about Garrett, then I wanted to hear it come straight from the horse's mouth.

"I can't say anything about it."

My eyes rolled so hard I thought I was about to detach my ocular nerves. "Then why mention it? Evidently, you believe he's up to something; otherwise you wouldn't have alluded to it. So, tell me, what is it you suspect him of this time?"

"It's… it's just an inkling I have."

I gaped at my father in disbelief. "An *inkling*? You would judge him without any grounds or evidence?"

"I have grounds."

"Like what?"

He at least had the decency to look sheepish. "His friendship with Finch."

"His *former* friendship with Finch, before he realized Finch was a traitor. You can't be serious," I muttered. "This is because he's a Shapeshifter, and nothing more. Admit it—I dare you."

"I have nothing against Shapeshifters, and you know it."

"What, so it's only Shapeshifters who happen to be shaped like Garrett Kyteler? You just said 'someone like him' as though he was somehow less than the rest of us. I know what you *actually* meant, and it's got nothing to do with fatherly concern. You couldn't be more prejudiced if you tried!" I shook my head furiously. "How many hoops does he have to jump through for you to see that he's honest, that he's loyal? Does he have to be on fire? Must he perform the twelve labors of Hercules before you'll see that he's deserving of your respect?" I was on a roll now. "He almost died in that fight with Katherine. You must've seen it on the cameras. He fought with us, side by side. He didn't run off at the first sign of danger, or switch sides when it looked like we were losing. If he was in cahoots with her, he wouldn't still be here."

"I did find that quite surprising," he admitted, as a sudden realization dawned in my mind.

"Tell me you didn't."

He frowned. "Didn't what?"

"I'm not stupid. You have to give me more credit than that, *Father*." I almost hissed the word, but he and I were much too passive-aggressive for spitting and name-calling. "You set him up, didn't you? You implemented the cameras so you could see how he would behave with Katherine's cronies. You wanted him to switch sides. You wanted him to be the traitor. Go on, admit it—you wanted him to prove you right, didn't you?"

"Perhaps I did."

My shoulders sagged. "Why? Did you do it for me?"

"I do everything for you, Astrid. I may not always be the best at showing it, but you are my first priority in all things," he said, his tone desperate. "Every day, I wake up and I thank my lucky stars that you're still with us."

"That doesn't mean you can dictate what I do with my life. You can't save me from experience, and I wouldn't want you to." I knew he meant well, but this overprotective malarkey was not a pleasant attribute in him. To set someone up, all in the name of getting him away from your daughter—that was borderline despicable, and I didn't like the sour taste it left in my mouth. My father was better than that, and yet he had stooped to the lowest of the low.

"I'm looking out for you," he insisted.

"No, you're doing what you always do. You're hiding me away from something that might cause me pain or suffering. If that happens, and he breaks my heart, then so be it, but I don't think Garrett deserves to be made a pariah because he likes me." My heart felt heavy. "Do you want me to be alone for the rest of my life?"

He perched on the edge of his desk. "I'm protective because you're constantly in danger, Astrid. You're vulnerable, whether you want to believe that or not." His gaze turned sad, his face aging about ten years in front of my very eyes. "It's not the romance that worries me—it's the trouble that flocks to Garrett. If Katherine got to Finch, then who knows if she got to his friends, too. Garrett included. And I don't want to put you in any kind of situation where I might have to bring you back from the dead again."

I sighed. "I know."

"Please, I beg of you, understand what that's like, from my perspective: to hold your lifeless daughter in your arms and will her dead body back into existence. Once would be bad enough, but I've done it more than once. On the last one, I almost didn't get to you in time... I don't want to have to go through that again."

Me dying while helping the coven wasn't the only reason he'd resurrected me. As his daughter, he couldn't have let me die. I knew that, and I knew he'd suffered because of it, but that still didn't make this right.

"Garrett isn't going to get me killed. He's loyal to us," I said.

"And until I know that for sure, until I know that he isn't working for Katherine, I need you to understand why you have to keep your distance. All I'm asking is a temporary hiatus, until we can be one-hundred-percent certain about his loyalties."

"I already am."

Alton's head dipped to his chest. "Well, I'm not."

"Why can't you just be happy for me? I wouldn't mind a little fatherly bluster, but this is ridiculous," I said, unable to rein in my temper a moment longer. "Mom likes him, so why can't you?"

Alton's head snapped back up. "Wait... what? Your mother has met him?"

"Garrett doesn't know he's met her, but yes, they've been introduced," I replied. "I took him to the shop the other day, and the two of them got on just fine. Afterwards, she told me she liked him—that she felt good energy coming off him. You know she's honest to a fault. She tells people how it is, even when magicals come into Cabot's to try and convince her that their Esprit is the freaking Cullinan diamond when it's actually a raggedy old watch. Some want the fancy things, and she tells them they can't have it, even though it costs her a bunch in revenue." Esprits simply didn't work like that, of course. You received the one you were destined for, not necessarily the one you wanted.

My mother was Henrietta Cabot, of Waterfront Park's famed Esprit shop. A non-magical like me, she had an exceptional affinity for all things ancient and powerful, whether it be spells or Esprits. I admired her immensely for that, as people often mistook her for having magical abilities when, in fact, it was merely excellent instinct. Before she met Alton, she had traded in rare artifacts and one-of-a-kind jewelry, often traveling the world to uncover new pieces for the private collections she purchased items for. I was pretty sure she might have been a tomb raider, once upon a time, but she'd never disclosed anything like that to me. *See, women like us need a bit of mystique.*

"Your mom probably knew I'd dislike him," Alton said after a brief pause. "She'd do anything to make me look bad."

"No, she wouldn't. She'd never try to muddy *your* name, and you know it."

Alton and my mom had me after a brief fling. They hadn't lasted longer than a few months, but Alton had stayed by her side during the pregnancy and had insisted on being involved in my life. Even though they weren't together, they both loved me, and I didn't hold any resentment against either of them for not being able to make it work. That was life. It was messy and wonderful, and I still got to have two loving parents, even if one was terrible at showing it in ordinary ways.

He looked wounded. "Maybe not, but I always end up as the bad cop."

"It's not Mom's fault that you hate Garrett because of what he is. She hasn't turned you into the bad cop—you've done that yourself. I bet even Isabel wouldn't be so hard on him. Why don't we ask her what she thinks about him, see if she sides with Mom or you?"

"She'd tell you not to get involved with boys at your age."

"Really? You think an intelligent woman like her would just blindly side with you because you're her husband? Come on, we both know that's not true." Isabel Monroe was a fearsome woman in the field of molecular science, with a sharp mind and a sharper sense of humor. Whenever our strange, mixed little family gathered at Christmas or other holidays, she was always the one to rib Alton mercilessly, to the point of making us laugh until we cried. She and my mom got on like a house on fire, which I knew worried Alton sometimes. He felt like they were ganging up on him, which was both sweet and hilarious in equal measure. The great Alton Waterhouse, reduced to a blushing wreck by his wife and the mother of his child.

"It doesn't change my perspective on this 'relationship' you're embarking on, Astrid," he said pointedly.

"Why do you think you have the right to dictate what I do and don't do? I know you're my father, but it's not like you act very fatherly most of the time. I feel like your employee most days, rather than your daughter." I tried to stuff my bitter words back down my throat, but I'd opened the floodgates now. "The point is, you don't get to have a say in whom I choose to date, because—and I mean very little offense by this—you are the last person that anyone should take romantic advice from." I paused for breath. "Before Isabel, your track record of relationships wasn't exactly great. You can't stop people from living their lives or making their own mistakes. Life happens. I want mine to."

He sighed wearily. "I know I made some mistakes and didn't exactly have much longevity in the romance department, but I was never an actual danger to anyone. Garrett may well be."

"He isn't!" I barked, almost clapping my hands over my mouth to stop the words coming out so harshly.

"Astrid, I—"

"All I'm asking is that you see things from my side," I interrupted. "Garrett has done nothing to deserve this kind of suspicion. He's honest and loyal, and he's proven it in the field. Your setup should be the one thing that shows you he's innocent. You have it on film, for goodness' sake."

Alton shrugged. "Maybe he was told to pretend."

"Now you're being entirely stupid." I laughed tightly. "You didn't get the results you wanted, so now you're trying to find faults that don't exist. Please, please, please, remove the Shapeshifters' body cams. Not for my benefit, but for the benefit of everyone whose trust you've broken. You promised them you wouldn't reveal their identities and yet you went and slapped cameras on them. You put targets on them, Father. They put their faith in you and you let them down."

"I've lost count of the number of times I've said this to you, Astrid, but if Garrett has nothing to hide, then he shouldn't be so opposed to the cameras," he retorted. "Don't you think that's the slightest bit suspicious?"

"No. I see a group of hurt people who've lost their trust in you. You've singled them out—of course they're going to resist it."

"See, this is why this relationship troubles me so much. It has blinded you. The other Shapeshifters haven't uttered a word of complaint about the cams. They understand the necessity. Yet Garrett keeps griping on about it. Why is he the only one with a problem?"

I shrugged. "I don't know. Perhaps it's because they're scared to stand up to you and Garrett isn't?" I narrowed my eyes at my father. "Maybe you're the one who's hiding something, since you seem so eager to spread the blame and suspicion elsewhere. What secrets are you keeping, Father?"

"Now you're the one being ridiculous."

"Am I?" In a sudden burst of uncharacteristic impulse, I strode behind his desk and rummaged around, making a show of lifting all his documents and sifting through his files. I pulled open every drawer and dumped folders on the desk, flipping through in a dramatic fashion. He hurried around to my side and put himself between me and the desk, blocking my path.

"Enough!" he said, his tone cold. "You're above childish behavior like this."

"Apparently I'm not, seeing as I need to be babysat through a camera. You hate that you've lost control of me—that's all this is."

He huffed out a breath and turned his back to me, blocking my view. Straining to get a better look, I caught sight of something glinting under his hand as he swiped it off the desk and into the top drawer. A folded letter went with it. I frowned at the sight. Why would he do that? Why would he slip two objects into the drawer, and not the rest? I'd said it in vengeful jest, but now I had the unsettling feeling that he *was* hiding something from me.

"The cameras are staying, Astrid. They're there for the good of everyone. If a small group have to endure temporary discomfort, then we've got to accept that as collateral. If Garrett continues to have a problem, he can come and speak to me himself, instead of using you as a go-between."

"I won't stop seeing him."

He whirled around to face me. "We'll see."

"What's that supposed to mean?"

"It means… it means I won't stop watching out for you. If you go against my wishes, then that's your prerogative, but don't think I'll stop trying to protect you from anything that I see as a danger. Until I know for sure that Garrett isn't working for Katherine, he fits into that category. I'm sorry, but that's the way it has to be."

"And I'll continue to fight for my right to live my life, on my own terms."

"As you wish, Astrid." He leaned back against the desk, using his body to cover the top drawer. "You should go. I've got a lot to do today."

Without another word, I walked out from behind the desk and crossed the room. At the door, I turned and flashed a disappointed look at him over my shoulder, before heading out into the hallway.

As I walked back to my room, a thought came into my head. It wasn't one I wanted to dwell on, but it popped up anyway, as thoughts are wont to do: I wondered if there might ever come a time when I was forced to pick sides.

And if that happens… whose side will I choose?

EIGHT

Harley

W hen I was halfway through the Banquet Hall to meet up with Jacob for lunch, my phone vibrated. Pulling it out from my back pocket, a flicker of surprise ran through me at the name on the screen. *Ryann?* I hadn't spoken to the Smiths' daughter—my soul sister —in so long. A twinge of guilt churned in my stomach. Mrs. Smith had asked me to give Ryann a call sometime, when I'd last been to their house, but things had gotten so out of hand that it'd slipped my mind completely. Part of me wanted to let it ring, given how busy we were, but I knew I had to answer. I tapped the answer-call button and lifted the phone to my ear.

"Hello?" I said.

"Hello, stranger!" Ryann's cheerful voice echoed through. It brought an instant smile to my face. Man, it was good to hear from her. "I thought I'd give you a call to make sure you're still alive." Her tone carried a hint of a laugh.

"Yep, still breathing," I replied. *Just barely.*

"Glad to hear it! So, how's the fancy new job? They treating you well? Any perks?"

"It's a lot of work. Long hours, no breaks, busy, busy, busy all the time."

"Sounds awful." She chuckled. "You sure you don't want to go back to the casino life?"

I smiled. "Nah, it's not too bad, aside from all that. The people are nice, and I feel like I'm actually doing something worthwhile, you know? Handing in dirty players for cheating at the tables wasn't exactly a calling."

"At least tell me the money's good?"

"It's... uh, decent." Even without taking my shifts in the Fleet Science Center's archives, I'd been getting paid the same salary. I guessed running around, risking my life, was worth the same amount of dough.

"It better be," she replied.

"How's school? UCLA still treating you good?"

She groaned. "Speaking of too much hard work and not enough fun. It's fine, but I think I'm taking too many classes. Seriously, who knew college would be so exhausting? If I don't have twelve coffees a day, I end up in Anthropology 101 instead of Advanced Environmental Law, and that's when I'm not grabbing dinner in the library so I can read about tort law and human rights violations."

I laughed. "You need to get out more."

"Says you," she teased.

"Fair point. Anyway, a little birdie tells me there's a guy on the horizon? You can't be that busy with tort law if there's some delicious specimen taking up your time."

She giggled. "Let me guess. Mom asked you to do some spy work?"

"I told her I couldn't break sisterhood confidentiality."

"See, this is why I love you!" she said.

"So, spill the beans—who is he, what does he do, what does he look like?"

"His name is Adam Sirieux. He's French-Canadian, six-one, dark hair, blue eyes, swims for the college team. He's in pre-med and wants to be a pediatrician."

"Nah, no way—he doesn't sound real. You've got to give me the *real* goods. You can't just go making guys up," I joked. He sounded perfect.

She chuckled. "I promise you, he's one-hundred-percent real. He's romantic, too. He took me out the other night to this fancy restaurant, and showed up in this three-piece suit with a bouquet of roses in his hand. He asked me if I thought he'd gone overboard and had me laughing all the way through three courses."

"Ugh, where can I get me one of those?"

"Canada, apparently."

I grinned. "Ah, the Great White North, home of the last gentlemen."

"So, no luck where you are? No saucy security agents?"

My cheeks burned. "Well… there is one guy."

"I knew it!"

"Hey, it's nothing to get all excited over. He's nice, and I like him, but he's… well, he's not exactly showy with his feelings. He blows hot and cold all the time. It's pretty confusing, to be honest."

"I wouldn't bother if I were you," she said. "If a guy doesn't tell you he likes you or make you feel special, he's usually not worth your time."

I frowned. "He's a good guy. He's just more of the broody, silent type. I guess we can't all have romantic, fairy-tale guys sweeping us off our feet."

"You deserve one, though."

"Honestly, I think you'd like him if you met him," I said defensively.

"What does he look like?"

I smiled. "Tall, green eyes, dark curly hair. A bit Irish. The accent comes out when he's angry or passionate about something."

"Ooh, okay, you're persuading me," she replied. "Irish is good."

"He's smart, loyal, funny when he wants to be. And he's *really* freaking sexy. Like, I can't even begin to explain how sexy he is." I gulped, thinking of him shirtless in bed, staring at me in surprise. *Oh, and his lips… dammit, they were so close!* I almost wished I'd kissed him, back in the Luis Paoletti Room.

"Why don't you tell him how you feel?" she suggested. "What's the worst that can happen?"

"I lose a friendship."

"No way. If he likes you, even if it's just in a friendly way, you admitting you like him isn't going to change that. You're too cool to cast aside, believe me. It might be awkward for a bit, but then you'll both get over it. And, if he *does* like you, then everything will be peaches and cream, and you can find out just how sexy he really is," she said, a wink in her voice.

Honestly, it felt so good to have a normal conversation for a little while. A girly, gossipy talk about boys and school. No monsters, no terrifying Katherine, no heartbreak, no sadness, just a good old-fashioned chat with my foster sister. A girl who knew me better than a lot of people, even in this place.

"Maybe," I said.

"No maybe about it—you *have* to! If he isn't going to make the move, then you've got to be the one to have the balls," she replied sternly.

"But I want him to be the one with the balls."

She howled with laughter. "Let's hope he is, huh? Anyway, you can update me on it all when I see you in Hawaii for family vacay time. You're still coming, right? Mom didn't mention it when I spoke to her. Did you manage to get the time off?"

My heart sank. "Ah… Ryann, I'm so sorry. I put in the request but, because I'm the rookie, they wouldn't give me the days. I totally forgot to tell Mrs. Smith."

The family vacation had been the last thing on my mind, but now that I'd been reminded of it, I felt bad that I couldn't go. I really did want to join them. I'd missed having them around and being part of their family unit. Worst of all was the realization that I was going to have to break the news to Mr. and Mrs. Smith themselves. I knew I could've just texted them or called them, but that wouldn't have been fair. No, if I was going to tell them I couldn't go, I had to do it face-to-face, to soften the blow a bit.

"You're kidding! You have to come! Pull a sickie or something. It won't be the same without you." She sounded genuinely upset.

"I know. I really wanted to come," I replied. "Why don't you give your sexy Canadian my ticket instead, so the fam can get to know him a bit better?"

"Forget him—I want *you* to come."

I smiled sadly. "I'm so sorry, Ryann. There's been so much going on, and there's a ton of work still to do. If I could pull a sickie or get those days off, I would. I promise I'll make it up to you at Christmas, okay? Please don't hate me."

"As if I could ever hate you. You're one of my favorite people on the planet," she said with a sigh. "You just work too hard, that's all. It really won't be the same without you. I'd already pictured the Instagram photos—you, me, palm trees, fruity drinks with umbrellas, lying out in the sun."

"Ugh, that sounds like just what I need. Don't tempt me."

"That's exactly what I'm trying to do!"

I laughed. "I'm sorry, I really am. Next year, I'll be there with bells on." *Yeah, if I live to see next year.* That wasn't the positive attitude I needed, but it was a very real possibility.

"You better be!"

"I will, I will—I swear."

"You better take some pastries when you break the news to Mom."

I pulled a face. "I'll get an extra big basket of them. Hell, I'll buy the whole shop."

"Well, I've got to head into class now, but I thought I'd call you and see how you were," she said apologetically. "It's been good to hear your voice."

"Yeah, yours too."

"Don't be a stranger, okay? There's always an open invitation for you to visit me, whenever you want. I miss you, Harley. I know you're all busy and stuff, but it'd be cool to see you soon."

"I'll try and visit one weekend," I said, though I had no idea if that'd be possible.

"Promise?"

"Promise."

"Okay... Well, take care of yourself, do you hear me? Don't burn yourself out. And if this guy doesn't see what's right in front of him, and how bleepin' glorious you are, then forget about him. You deserve a nice one, Harley. A good guy, who'll treat you well. Sexy is good, don't get me wrong, but it's not everything."

I grinned. "Says you with the six-one Canadian fox."

"Yeah—I'm just hoping he's not too good to be true, you know?"

"He won't be. And if he is, let him know your sister works for Homeland Security."

She chuckled. "Right, well, I've got to go. I mean it, though—take care of yourself."

"You, too."

"Good luck with Mom and Dad."

"Thanks."

"Talk to you later, Harley."

I nodded, even though she couldn't see me. "Talk soon."

She hung up the phone, leaving me with a bittersweet sense of sadness. I really did miss Ryann and the Smiths. After the childhood I'd had, they'd been the light at the end of the tunnel, guiding me into adulthood with a kind hand. Plus, Hawaii would have been so good—a welcome break from the madness here. It made me stop and wonder where my life would be now, if I hadn't met Wade in the parking lot of the casino that night. Would I be happier? It was a tough one to call.

I was already picturing Mrs. Smith's disappointed face, and Mr. Smith's diplomatic words of understanding. This was going to sting, for sure.

I hurried toward the Banquet Hall, knowing I'd have to cancel my lunch with Jacob so I could pay a visit to the Smiths. There was no time like the present. I was rounding the corner onto the main hallway, when a figure stepped out of the shadows behind one of the bronzed dragons. Jacob wore a hood low over his head, an amused smile on his lips. I'd gotten so used to seeing him as Tarver that his actual face was pretty odd.

"Geez, you scared me!" I laughed, clutching my chest. "What are you doing out here? We're supposed to be having lunch in five minutes."

"My face needed to breathe."

"Careful someone doesn't call the cops on you, loitering around with your hood up."

He grinned. "Nah, I'm a master of blending in. Why the heavy breathing?"

"I was just running to tell you that I have to cancel on lunch. I just got a call from Ryann and I need to tell the Smiths that I can't come on the family vacation. So, I'm darting off to their place. I figured I'd get it out of the way, since Mrs. Smith is going to be majorly disappointed."

His face lit up. "Can I come with you?"

"I'm not sure if that's such a good idea," I replied.

"Please?"

"It might be painful, Jake. They won't remember you."

He shrugged. "I don't care; I just want to see them again. They did so much for me. Please let me come with you."

"You can't say anything about having been there before," I warned.

"I won't—I swear."

"Fine, but if it becomes too much, just let me know and we'll go, okay? And put your mask back on."

"Will do."

With an uneasy feeling in my chest, we headed out of the coven. With his Tarver mask on and the protective charms that Alton had put on him, he'd be able to fly under the radar. Still, I couldn't push away all my nerves about taking him out of the coven. Veering around toward the parking lot, we made our way to my Daisy and hopped in. He didn't say much on the drive over, his gaze fixed on the outside world, his fingertips tapping anxiously on the dashboard. I understood his desire to see them again, but he had no idea just how painful it would be, not to be remembered.

"So, how did things go with Krieger? Did you give him your decision?" I asked, breaking the silence.

He shrugged. "Yeah. I told you I wouldn't change my mind."

"Did he take that piece out of you?" I hated even saying it. It felt so very wrong.

"He did it this morning," he replied, showing me his arm. A tiny, red cut was visible across the center of his palm. "Didn't hurt at all."

"Do you feel okay?"

"Absolutely fine. He told us there was nothing to worry about, and he meant it. Stop panicking."

I smiled. "You don't feel weird or anything?"

"Not at all. Like I said, I didn't even notice him taking a piece of my Chaos. Was easier than getting a jab."

"Sure?"

"Sure—now stop asking." He grinned at me, covering his hands with his hoodie sleeves.

Half an hour later, after stopping by St. Clair's for a basket of pastries, we pulled up outside their house. Nerves pulsated off him in shaky waves, his eyes wide as he looked up at the house. It had been a while since he'd been here, and the last time hadn't exactly been great. The clean-up team had done an incredible job of fixing everything up, but that didn't wipe away the memories that Jacob and I had. I figured it might have been easier if they'd altered Jacob's memories too, but I wouldn't have taken them from him, not for the world. He deserved to have some happy thoughts, even if they were peppered with bad ones.

Together, we walked up to the door. Mrs. Smith answered a minute later.

"Harley, what a wonderful surprise!" she said, beaming. Her eyes drifted over to Jacob, an expression of confusion drifting across her features. There was no way she could remember Jacob, but there was a hint of something like recognition when she looked into his unchanged eyes, as if there was a memory on the tip of her tongue. Just out of reach.

"Hi, Mrs. Smith. I was just in the area and thought I'd swing by," I replied. "This is... uh, Tarver—he's an intern, so I brought him along."

"Well, the more the merrier. Will you stay for lunch?"

I shook my head. "We can't stay long. A cup of coffee would be great, though. Might be good to wash these down." I showed her the basket of pastries before handing them over.

"Of course! I love croissants, though my waistline doesn't." She flashed me a smile, taking the basket and leading us into the kitchen. We sat at the breakfast island, perched on the stools as she made coffee. Jacob couldn't stop staring, his eyes practically popping out of his head.

"Actually, there was another reason I wanted to come and see you," I admitted.

She glanced over her shoulder. "Oh?"

"Yeah, it's about the family vacation. I tried to get the days off, but they denied them. I haven't been there long, so I don't have all the perks and stuff yet," I explained, feeling bad for lying. "I spoke to Ryann earlier, and thought I'd come and break the news over coffee and pastries. Call it a peace offering."

Mrs. Smith's face fell. "Oh, no. Are you sure? Can't you even come for a few days?"

"Afraid not. I'm so sorry—I was really looking forward to it."

"Well, these things can't be helped," she replied, after a pause. "Mr. Smith will be disappointed, but we both understand how busy you are. Still, it won't be the same without the whole family there. You'll be sorely missed."

Jacob stiffened beside me, dropping his gaze. Not so long ago, he'd been part of the family, too. The Ryders and Katherine had taken that away from him. It didn't help that every time Mrs. Smith looked into his eyes, she had that same glimmer of recognition, as though she was trying to place him. I could tell he was desperate to say something, but he was fighting against it.

"I'm really sorry," I murmured.

"Never mind. We'll just have to do something extra fun at Christmas. You'll be able to get some time off then, won't you?"

I nodded. "For sure."

"Right, then, that's settled. I'm going to cook the biggest feast our kitchen can hold and feed you until you have to be rolled upstairs," she said, a little too brightly. I felt very lucky to have them in my life, but it made Jacob's loss all the more poignant. I might've arranged for their house to be warded by powerful charms, so Katherine couldn't get her revenge on me by attacking them again, but I couldn't bring their memories of Jacob back. It was for the best, but it still sucked.

An hour later, after copious cups of coffee and one too many pastries, we left the house and got back into the car. Jacob hadn't said much throughout the entire visit, but I couldn't blame him for that. It had been harder on him than he'd anticipated; I could sense the residual pain brimming inside him. He wanted what I had. He deserved to have that.

"Are you okay?" I asked, as I fired up the engine.

He nodded slowly. "I didn't realize it would hurt that much. She kept staring into my eyes like she knew who I was but couldn't quite figure it out."

"I knew I shouldn't have let you come," I said, not unkindly.

"No, no, I'm glad I did. I wanted to see them again," he insisted. "It just made me realize how much I miss having a family. It was easier when there was this hope that my real family might be out there, but now that I know I'll never see them, it's... I don't know. It's more painful, I guess. I'll never get that lucky again, finding folks like the Smiths. It feels like it's just me now, especially with Isadora gone."

"Hey, you've got us," I replied. "We're not going anywhere, and nobody's going to make me forget about you."

He smiled. "Yeah, I'm grateful for that."

"I know it's not the same."

"No..."

"But we'll be here for you, no matter what."

"I guess that's why I wanted to help Krieger," he said. "Doing this detection stuff makes me feel like I have a purpose, you know? Like, beyond the portal stuff. This is something I can help with, without damaging anything around me. It makes me feel useful."

"You *are* useful. And I'm proud of you for taking the initiative, even if I don't like Krieger rummaging around in your Chaos." He was pretty mature for his age, making decisions like that, based on more than himself. It made me wonder what kind of man he'd turn out to be. A good one, I guessed.

He turned toward the passing landscape. "Thanks, Harley. Seriously."

"Don't mention it."

Nothing would ever bring back his mom and dad, and it seemed unlikely that he'd find his way into the foster system again, but I hoped that he'd come to realize that we could be just as good. These were the cards that life had dealt him, and they sucked, but at least he wasn't alone anymore. The coven would have to be his family from now on, and I would do everything in my power to make sure that he felt loved. He deserved that much.

NINE

Harley

A day later, I paced the floor of my bedroom, giving myself a once-over in the mirror. I'd attempted to dress professionally, but I just felt plain uncomfortable. In a smart skirt, black pantyhose, and a white silky shirt, I looked like a little girl playing in her mom's closet. I eyed my jeans and T-shirt, which lay on the bed, and wondered if it mattered what I looked like. It was only an interview to see my parents' Grimoire; I wasn't running for state Senate or anything.

A knock at the door made me turn in surprise. Wade was supposed to come get me in half an hour. *I'm not ready...*

"Come in," I said loudly. My eyes flew wide as a figure entered, her dazzling smile and effortless chic making me feel about as glamorous as a sea cucumber. "Imogene? What are you doing here? Not that you're not welcome—I just... Sorry, I'm babbling. A bit of pre-show nerves."

She chuckled. "I was hoping to catch you before you left for New York. I heard about the interview and wanted to come and wish you good luck. Not that you'll need it."

"I'm not so sure about that."

"There's a great deal to be said for imagining people in their underwear. If nothing else, it will make you laugh. At least you'll be relaxed, then," she said, her eyes lighting up with playful mischief.

"I'll keep that in mind." The thought of seeing Salinger in nothing but his boxers made my stomach turn, although I wasn't sure who would actually be conducting my interview. Chances were, they'd be a bunch of people I'd never even met before.

"I also thought I'd bring you a good-luck gift," she went on, perching gracefully on the edge of my bed. The shame at seeing my dirty clothes scattered around the room made me want to open up a sinkhole and let it drag me down. Still, she didn't seem to notice. Either that, or she was pretending not to.

"A gift?"

She nodded. "I promised you one after your pledge, and I am a woman of my word, but with things being so hectic in the wake of this Katherine debacle, I haven't had the chance to come back here much. Besides, I had to make sure I selected the perfect gift—I am very particular about these things."

The warmth that always emanated from her surrounded me in a comforting blanket of calm, bringing my nerves down a notch. I hadn't known I needed her until she was here in the room with me. Glancing at the silver bracelet on her wrist, I wished I could delve into her true emotions again, the way I'd done at the pledge. I guessed her natural positive energy would have to do.

She opened the cream-leather clutch she'd tucked under her arm, and removed a box of varnished, black wood. Embedded in the surface was a yin-yang symbol, crafted from mother-of-pearl—one side white, the other black. Unbidden tears found their way into my eyes. *My mom and dad.*

"Thank you," I gasped, reaching for the beautiful box. "It's perfect."

She smiled. "The gift is *inside* the box, Harley."

"Oh... right." My cheeks reddened as I opened the silver clasp and lifted the lid. I'd have been happy with just the box, to be perfectly honest. However, as I set eyes on the gift inside, my heart leapt into my throat and those tears threatened to fall. Apparently, I was a crier now. Santana had opened some floodgates and I was having a hard time closing them again.

Set on a plump bed of black velvet lay a pendant that I'd seen before, in a distant dream. I lifted it out, the thin chain wrapping around my fingers as I let the pendant dangle. Colors danced against the wall as the sunlight glinted off the jewelry. It was made of sterling silver and shaped like a teardrop, with different, rough-cut gemstones mounted on the surface: red, white, blue, black, and pink. I didn't know what they were supposed to represent, but I knew this pendant as if it had always been in my possession. A memory came back to me of the night I'd first seen this. Even then, I'd sworn to remember the necklace if I ever saw it again. And here it was, in my hands.

"Where did you get this?" I murmured, practically speechless.

"I had it specially made for you, based on the design of an old Merlin heirloom. There's a picture of your Aunt Isadora wearing it in the New York Coven's alumni hall, so I had it copied. I imagine the original has been lost, but perhaps this is a suitable stand-in," she replied. "As I say, I always have to make sure my gifts are right. Presents should be special, and I hoped you might feel closer to your family if you had this. I know things haven't been easy for you, and I wanted to bring you some comfort. Especially as Alton tells me you're looking to clear your father's name—it is my fondest wish that you succeed, Harley. With this around your neck, you will feel Hiram's spirit close to your heart. Let that give you courage in the trials to come."

"Thank you so much," I choked, trying really hard not to bawl my eyes out in front of her.

"It is my pleasure, Harley."

"Does it have any magical ability, like an Esprit?" I wondered.

She shook her head. "It's simply a piece of jewelry, but there's magic in memory, Harley. This will give you strength and provide a tangible link to your past. It will remind you of your purpose, and that is an infinitely powerful thing to have."

"It's perfect."

"I did consider bringing something with power, but the pendant seemed more appropriate, given the circumstances of your interview today."

I nodded. "It's... yeah, it's totally perfect." I didn't know what else to say. The gift had left me tongue-tied and completely in awe. It might not have been the original that I'd seen in my dreams, but it would do exactly what Imogene had said it would—it would remind me of what I was fighting for, when things got tough.

"Speaking of Esprits, I did happen to hear that something had gone awry with yours," Imogene said, glancing at the broken jewelry on my hand. "My condolences. There's nothing more exasperating than suffering a breakage. We come to rely so heavily on these things, don't we?" She held up her hand, to show me the ring and bracelet of her own Esprit.

"Unless you're Nomura," I joked.

"Yes, but that man has the patience of a saint. I doubt the rest of us have the discipline. May I take a look at the broken part?"

I walked over to where she sat and held out my Esprit. Gingerly, she turned the interlinking chains and ran a finger over the empty sockets, eyeing them intently. A small frown furrowed her otherwise smooth brow.

"What's the verdict?"

"I believe it's fixable; you will simply need two replacement stones and a spell to embed them," she replied. "Yes, in fact, there's a spell in the New York Special Collections that might help you repair this. If memory serves, the book is called *Chanticleer's Art of the Réparateur*. It's a very rare tome from the fifteenth century, but if they'll allow you to look at it, then it may save you a great deal of expense and heartache. Esprit repair shops are notorious for conning young magicals. If you can, it's always better to do something yourself—a good motto to live by."

I gaped at her in girlish gratitude. "I don't know how to thank you for all of this, Imogene. Seriously, thank you. If I can repay you in any way, just say the word."

"There's no need for repayment, Harley. It's my honor to help you fulfill your potential, even if that is only by giving you a drop of courage and a useful suggestion to guide you on your way." She tucked her clutch back under her arm and turned toward the door. "Good luck with your interview. I mean it when I say you'll be fine. Don't let them intimidate you. Remember who you are, and what you stand for, and everything else will fall into place."

"I will."

"Now, I want to hear all about it the next time I see you, okay?" she said. "But, for now, I'll let you continue with your preparations. I hope everything works out for you today, and do look for that book if you can. Finding the right spell is half the battle. Once you have it, the rest shouldn't be too difficult."

With that, she walked out the door and left me to stare at the pendant some more. It was heartbreakingly beautiful, the sterling silver indented with tiny runic symbols that I couldn't read. I didn't know much about runes, but they looked pagan. A reminder of my heritage. Just holding it in my hand made me feel like I'd opened a gateway to my past—not just my recent history, but all the way back to Merlin himself. Our namesake, and arguably the most famous magical in all of time.

I went to the mirror and looped the long chain over my head, tucking the pendant beneath the silky lapels of my shirt. The cold metal on my skin shocked me for a moment, before the heat of my body warmed it up. Sensing the weight of it against my chest, I felt as though I could do anything and take on anyone. The original had seen my aunt and my dad through three years on the run from Katherine; it could get me through a little interview.

Maybe this thing is magic after all.

I met Wade in the Main Assembly Hall twenty minutes later, after telling him I'd meet him there instead of him picking me up. He was already waiting for me by the shimmering mirrors, tapping his foot impatiently. Nervous ripples flowed off him in a steady ebb, which added to my own anxiety.

"You look smart," he said. "That's good. They like smart."

"I feel ridiculous."

"You shouldn't. You look professional."

"Yeah, well, looking professional reminds me of my prep school days."

He smiled. "I can't even imagine you in a place like that."

"Yeah, it's best not to."

"New necklace?" He eyed the chain around my neck, a puzzled look on his face. "What happened to your St. Christopher medallion, or whatever it was?" I smiled at him shyly, surprised he'd even remembered me wearing it. It had been the first gift I'd ever received from a foster parent, and though I didn't wear it as often anymore, it still held a place in my heart. Even more so after seeing Mrs. Smith again. Man, I loved that woman.

"I still have it, but Imogene just gave this to me as a good-luck gift. It's based on a Merlin heirloom—she thought it'd make me feel closer to my family." I pulled the collar of my shirt up higher, covering the telltale chain. "Anyway, we should get going."

"Yeah, good thinking." He brushed a hand through his hair. "You ready for this?"

I nodded slowly. "How hard can it be, right?"

We approached the mirror that led to the New York Coven and stepped through without wasting another moment. A young woman met us on the other side, dressed in a dark blue pantsuit, her icy-blond hair plaited and draped over her shoulder. *Wow, Elsa's career really took a dive...* It was colder here than I'd remembered, the cavernous hallways echoing with busy footsteps.

"Harley Merlin?" the woman asked, her gaze fixed on me.

"Yes, that's me."

"Excellent. Then follow me. Please move as quickly as you can; the board doesn't like to be kept waiting and you're already a minute over schedule." Turning on her heel, she strode away down the corridor, leaving us to hurry after her.

We arrived outside an innocuous-looking door ten minutes later, the apex curved up in a church-like fashion. A black iron knocker hung in the center. The woman rapped it against the wood three times. Each thud echoed my heavy heartbeat, setting my nerves on edge. Without even thinking, I reached up to press the pendant, the solid weight of it bringing me comfort.

You've got this, Merlin.

"Are you coming in with me?" I asked Wade, who looked as nervous as I did.

"I'm not allowed."

"Right… of course not." The pendant was good, but I'd have felt even more comfortable if Wade was in the room with me.

"You'll do fine, Harley," he said, resting his hand on my shoulder. A rush of emotions coursed through me, filling me with his steady calm and reassurance. I thought back to the way he'd held me in the Luis Paoletti Room, the memory making my stomach flip-flop, and upsetting some of the calm he was pressing into my skin. *What would I have done if you'd kissed me?* I still didn't have the answer to that. Even so, it was a nice way of distracting my racing mind from what was about to happen.

"You may go in," the woman interrupted, holding the door open for me.

"Thanks." I flashed a worried look back at Wade, who lifted his hands in an awkward thumbs-up, and then I stepped into the room.

The room itself was nothing special, just an old hall with some medieval vibes, a single table at the far end. It almost felt like I was walking into a college interview or something. Not so long ago, I'd been dwelling on college aspirations, but all of that seemed to have disappeared with this Katherine stuff looming over me.

Four people sat behind the broad table, which had a solitary, poignantly empty chair in front of it. I didn't recognize any of them. There were two women—one, a middle-aged Korean woman with horn-rimmed spectacles and a severe black bob. The other had graying hair and a plump figure, and looked like she should be spending the year at the North Pole, helping Santa with his elves, rather than sitting here, scrutinizing me. Interspersed between the women were two men. One was much younger than I'd expected, with a mane of long, dark-blond hair and a blue-tinged tattoo that curved under his right eye. On the farthest side was an elderly gentleman. His face had sagged into long jowls that reminded me of a bloodhound, while his eyes were black and hollow behind silver spectacles, and what remained of his white hair had been slicked back.

All you've got to do is sell yourself. Easy-peasy. I'd spent years trying to convince people I was worthy of being fostered; I figured this should be a walk in the park.

Only Mrs. Claus smiled as I approached. "Harley Merlin, yes?"

"Yes."

"Please, take a seat." She gestured to the empty chair. Her accent was oddly whimsical, as though she had some Swedish heritage in her. I decided to focus on her as much as possible, since the others were less than friendly.

"Cain McLeod, Preceptor of Ancient Arts," the maned man said, in a faint Scottish accent. "Now, if you'd like to take us through your Reading, that would be great. Let's start with Light and Dark. Where does your affinity lie?"

Okay, so much for a "let's get to know each other" round.

"I don't know which side I lean more toward," I replied. "The Reading was inconclusive."

"Miriam Svalbard, Preceptor of Bestiary Studies," Mrs. Claus said. "It is exceptionally rare for someone to fall in neither category, or, rather, both categories. You understand that, don't you?"

I nodded.

"That blend of Light and Darkness has the potential to become imbalanced, depending on the type of spells you use throughout your magical life. If you favor the Dark spells, then it might prompt you to dwell more in the Darkness. The same goes for Light. Does that make sense to you?"

"I think so, Preceptor Svalbard. I need to make good choices, right?"

She smiled. "I suppose that is one way of looking at it. Essentially, you will have to be wary of how spells influence you."

"Gregoire Mountbatten, Preceptor of Hexes and Charms," the elderly gentleman chimed in, his accent flavored with French. "You fail to mention, Svalbard, zat if she is able to find a balance between Light and Dark, zen she would be able to perform feats zat have never been done before. It is *très* unique to have both within your grasp. So, you can see our concern? So much power and potential in one so young is a troubling thing."

"Blame my parents," I joked, lifting my shoulders in a shrug.

He chuckled. "Well, yes, you are quite correct. What I am trying to say is, we must be able to assure ourselves zat you pose no threat, before we allow you to visit your parents' Grimoire."

"Not to mention the way she might react to it," McLeod added. "Grimoires tend to have an effect on most people, but you might be more sensitive to their presence, given your remarkable blend of affinities. Don't think we are prejudiced against you, because of what you might be capable of; we simply ask that you understand our perspective. You are, as far as we know, like a proverbial bull in a china shop."

"Thanks," I muttered.

"It's a risky move for us," he replied. "We don't want you reacting strangely in the presence of the Grimoire."

My insides twisted up. I'd already found out that little chestnut the hard way. Although mentioning *that* to them was a complete and absolute no-no. If I breathed a word, it would almost definitely ruin any chance I had of getting to see the Grimoire again.

"So, if you wouldn't mind telling us *why* you want to see your parents' Grimoire, that might be a good place to start?" Svalbard prompted. I noticed that the Korean woman had yet to speak.

I took a breath. "Research."

"You'll have to be more specific zan zat," Mountbatten said.

"Both my mother and my father were linked in some way to Katherine Shipton. So, it stands to reason that there might be something valuable in there, that we can use against her," I explained. "Plus, that book belonged to my parents. I don't have anything left of theirs. I don't want to get all wallowy or anything, but I'd like to get close to something that they touched, that they wrote in, that they shared together. I'm guessing you've all lost someone you loved, at some point. Wouldn't you like to feel closer to them, through something of theirs, just once?"

"Sentiment is not a valid reason for visiting something like that," McLeod cut in. "The research aspect is more likely to persuade us."

I frowned at him, determined not to lose my cool. "I'm hoping there might be some information in there, or another spell, that we can use to fight Katherine—as I said."

The Korean woman snorted. "Not much use it would be to you. You know the Grimoire is unfinished, don't you?"

The other three chuckled at the idea. *Yeah, well you don't know what I can do.* It was a struggle to keep my mouth shut when I wanted to wipe the smirks off their faces so badly.

"That doesn't mean there won't be any intel in there," I protested.

"Kim Ha-na, Preceptor of Grimoire Studies," she replied, introducing herself at last. "I admire your tenacity, and I happen to think that sentiment is as valid a reason as any to want to visit an artifact like this. However, it will do you no good if you're looking for a spell. I realize you are relatively new to the magical world and do not understand how certain things work, but an unfinished Grimoire cannot be read from."

You'd think that, wouldn't you?

"I know that, Preceptor Kim. I'm just saying it might lead us in the right direction, if there's anything in there about Katherine. They can be like journals sometimes, can't they?"

Preceptor Kim nodded, a hint of respect on her face. "That is correct."

"Then, maybe my parents wrote something that wasn't a spell. Maybe they mentioned something about the Children of Chaos," I replied. "I don't know what's in there until I see it, but I have this feeling that there'll be something useful." *Because I already sneaked a peek, you stuffy red-tape lovers.*

"Even if you were to find any useful information in that Grimoire, I don't know what you think you'll do with it. You'll forgive us for saying it, but the SDC isn't exactly well-known for its efficacy. We've already heard of all these fluffs that Alton has been making in Katherine's investigation."

"I suppose it might keep them busy for a while, so the rest of us can get on with the real work," McLeod chipped in, smirking. "Do you think the National Council are just sitting on their laurels, Harley? You're probably better off waiting for them to make a breakthrough."

"Saying that, I don't suppose there's any harm in letting you have a go," Kim added, her tone bordering on condescension.

Their reaction irked me. It seemed laughable to them that the SDC could do anything to help with the Katherine Shipton case, and I was determined to prove them wrong. They would see what the SDC were capable of, if it was the last thing I did. *Let's just hope it's not though, okay?*

"So, is that a yes or a no?" I asked plainly. I was tired of their snobbery.

They mumbled amongst themselves for a while, leaving me to stare out the window at Central Park. The leaves were starting to change color on the trees, while birds wheeled and struggled against a breeze. I couldn't feel it, but I guessed it was cold out there. It made me long to be back in San Diego.

"We will grant you access to the Grimoire for one hour, on one condition," Svalbard announced, bringing my attention back.

"Yes?"

"That your boyfriend supervises you closely and reports to us if any adverse effects occur. The Crowleys have an excellent reputation. It's a shame he didn't choose to come here instead of the SDC. Pride can be a terrible thing."

I flushed with embarrassment. "Not my boyfriend, but I get the gist."

"Good—then you may go. Happy reading!"

"There's one other thing," I said, struggling not to snap against their condescension. "I've recently broken my Esprit, and was wondering if you had any spells that might help." *Namely, Chanticleer's book of fixy whatnot.*

"In your parents' Grimoire, you mean?" Mountbatten arched an eyebrow.

"No, not necessarily. I just mean any spell that can help."

"You may not find anything to fix your Esprit in the Grimoire, but there is a book in Special Collections that can help. Naturally, you'll have to submit another application to be granted temporary access to it, but we can facilitate that if you desire it," Svalbard chimed in, with that fixed smile that was starting to get a little eerie.

No way was I going to submit another application to them, although I knew I had to make it look like I was going to play by their rules. If Chanticleer's book was in Special Collections, I'd kill two birds with one stone; I'd get the fixing spell *and* look into my parents' Grimoire again. They wouldn't need to know about it, if I just wrote the Esprit spell down or took a photo. After all, it wasn't in a Grimoire—I didn't need to get all fancy in order to use it.

"I'll think about it," I said.

"Anything else?" Svalbard chirped.

"Nope... no, I'm good. Thanks."

"Then off you go, before we change our minds." She cackled as I turned to leave.

I could feel their mockery as I retraced my steps, their amusement tugging at my Empathy like a really annoying itch that I couldn't scratch. Resisting the urge to slam the door like a bratty teenager, I strode out into the hallway. At the end of all that, they hadn't seemed overly concerned about me visiting the Grimoire. Then again, why would they be? It was unfinished, and reading spells from an unfinished Grimoire was more or less unheard of.

Unfortunately for them, they had no idea what they were dealing with when it came to me.

Truth be told, I was the concerned one. After what had happened last time, terror and excitement mingled inside me. If I had Wade's calming hand to guide me, though, then maybe I'd be okay. Maybe I could stop the same thing from happening. Either way, I was glad I had Wade with me. Even if I had to come clean about my last visit, I was happy not to be alone. Somehow, his presence shouldered some of the weight.

TEN

Harley

"Wait here for a moment," the blond-haired woman instructed as I came out of my interview. Leaving us in the hallway, she went into the room and closed the door behind her. I figured they were about to have a nice little chat about me. Maybe they'd share a laugh about the "audacity" of the SDC thinking we could solve something that they hadn't managed to.

"How did it go?" Wade asked, breaking me out of my irritation.

I shrugged. "They said I could go and see it, as long as you came with me. It seems the Crowley name holds some weight here. Not so much the Merlins and the Shiptons, but I guess I can't blame them for that."

He smiled. "Well done. You must've impressed them."

"More like got myself laughed out of the room. They don't see us as a threat, which kind of works in our favor for this."

"Yeah, they're a little... prejudiced here."

"I'd have gone for 'up their own asses.'"

He laughed. "Still, we're getting what we came for. The rest doesn't matter. Let them have their prejudices—it'll make it even sweeter when we show them what we're made of."

"See, this is why I like... uh, this is why we're pals. On the same wavelength and whatever." I fumbled over my words, quickly dropping my gaze.

Little Miss Frozen saved my skin by exiting the interview room at that moment, a polite smile fixed on her face. "Here's your pass and the keys to Special Collections—the smaller one is for the Grimoire case. If anyone asks why you're here, or why you're going into the Special Collections room, just show them the ID card." She handed over an ordinary-looking lanyard with a card attached. "The big key will let you into the room."

"No password?" I asked, remembering the last time.

She frowned. "The password is only for New York Coven residents. This ensures that visitors can only enter once, and at our discretion."

"Makes perfect sense, my bad. Thanks," I said, taking it and looping it over my neck. Too eager to wait around, I started to move off down the corridor, only to be called back by the blond.

"Don't you need directions?" she asked pointedly.

Idiot... Don't give yourself away now!

I made a show of smacking my forehead. "Yes, of course. Directions."

She gave us a detailed map of the coven's layout, the Special Collections room helpfully circled. "Don't try and take the map out of the coven, though. It'll self-destruct as soon as you're out of the coven's perimeter." *Of course it will.*

With that, she sent us on our way. Wade glanced at me as we set off, a flicker of suspicion moving across his face. Had he noticed me trying to walk off without any directions? I hoped not.

Fifteen minutes later, after traipsing through the echoing hallways of the New York Coven, we arrived in the dingy wing that I recalled from last time. The air was even colder here, wind howling somewhere in the high arches above us, my body shivering beneath my leather jacket. *Does someone want to close the windows in this place? Geez!* I rubbed my arms to coax some warmth back into me, half-daydreaming about what it'd be like to snuggle up to Wade and steal some of his heat.

Once again, there was hardly anyone around. At every turn, I still expected a monster to come ambling out, moaning and reaching out clawed hands toward me. Heading past the Global Library that Salinger had guided our facsimiles around, I knew we were close to Special Collections, even without the map. Everything seemed familiar now.

"It's this one," Wade announced, stopping beside the right door. I tried to remember the password that had let me in the last time, but it was lost in the back of my mind.

"You sure?" I feigned ignorance.

"Well, this is the room she circled."

I stepped up to the curved doorway and fitted the ostentatiously large key into the lock, turning it until it clicked. A spark of green light flashed out of the keyhole, before the door swung open of its own accord. *Suitably creepy.* I half-expected Igor to be on the other side, hunched and beckoning us into his master's lair.

"Wow," Wade breathed as we entered.

"It's cool, right?" A wave of mixed energies rolled toward me, cascading from the Grimoires and books that lined the walls. There was so much power in this place, even without my parents' Grimoire secured in its glass case.

Without waiting for Wade, I set off across the room and mounted the wrought-iron steps to the second-floor platform, striding straight over to the glass case that had been tucked behind the bookcases. Even with the protective charms that surrounded the case, the Grimoire began to whisper. It knew me now, more intimately than before. It was almost like an addiction, my palms itching to touch the leather bindings and trace my fingertips across the embossed designs. *Mom, Dad, I'm here.*

Wade cleared his throat behind me, the sound making me jump. "Is this it?"

"Yeah, this is it." I couldn't take my eyes off the cover.

"How did you know it was here?"

"Uh… I could feel it." My mind was jangling all over the place, fixated on the Grimoire.

He put his hand on my shoulder and forced me to turn. "You've been here before, haven't you?"

"No…" I muttered sheepishly.

"You have! Don't lie to me, Harley. I knew something was up when you started wandering off before blondie had even said where to look."

I was faced with a choice: lie through my teeth and hope he believed me or come clean about everything. Right now, there didn't seem much point in lying to him. Judging by the expression on his face, he was already preparing to disbelieve anything I told him. True, I was scared of what he might say, and what he might tell Alton, but maybe he'd understand. Maybe, for me, he'd stay quiet about it.

"Promise me you won't get mad," I said.

"I can't promise that."

I rolled my eyes at him. "Fine… Yes, I snuck in here with Santana the last time we came through to New York. Salinger was otherwise occupied, and we saw an opportunity that we *had* to take. We got him a little tipsy and he told us where to find the Grimoire. Since we were in this part of the coven anyway, we figured we'd take a look—see what all the fuss was about." I didn't want to mention the summoning thing, but I figured I was going to have to, if only for safety reasons.

"You approached this thing without supervision?" Wade asked, before I could come clean.

I shrugged. "Yeah."

"Did anything happen?"

"Kind of. I sort of summoned something. Erebus, I think."

"Geez, Harley, you should've known better!" he barked. "You know what your affinities are like with this kind of stuff. Anything might have happened. And you had Santana with you, too—you could have put her in very real danger. We still don't know the extent of what you're capable of. You put both of your lives on the line by doing what you did. I hope you know that."

"Yes, I know that," I shot back. "I know I'm this terrifying bomb that everyone thinks might go off at any moment. I'm well aware of my responsibilities… but I couldn't walk past this place and *not* come in. I had to see it. I had to know what my parents had written. Don't you dare tell me that, in my position, you wouldn't have done the same."

"You could have been seriously hurt. Did you even think before you put yourself in that kind of danger?"

I balled my hands into fists. "Yes, I did. I weighed the risks and figured that discovering something in these pages was worth it." My insides twisted with guilt as I thought about what had almost happened. That definitely hadn't been worth it, considering the side effects Santana had experienced afterwards, but at least I now knew that I was capable of reading unfinished Grimoires.

"And did you?" His eyes narrowed.

"There are a couple of things about the Children of Chaos, yes. And that summoning spell that I performed—or at least that's what we guessed it was."

He shook his head in disbelief. "Why wouldn't you tell me about this?"

"Do you really want to know?" My voice held a challenge that took him by surprise.

"Of course I do. You should've told me."

"I didn't say anything, and I asked Santana not to, because I was terrified of what might happen to me," I replied.

"What do you mean? Nothing would've happened to you. You'd have gotten a slap on the wrist, and that'd be it."

I took a breath. *In for a dime, in for a dollar.* "No, if I'd told you the truth, all hell would've broken loose. Truth is… I can read from unfinished Grimoires. My parents' isn't complete. I go into a weird trance and the words come out. Garrett's seen me do it before, too. If I'd explained that to you, and you'd gone to Alton, and it had somehow got out—the Mage Council would've thrown me in a cell for the rest of my life. You really think they'd let someone with that ability just go free?"

He stared at me. "What? When did this thing happen with Garrett? He didn't say anything to me."

"We were in the Luis Paoletti Room. I did it by accident."

"Why the hell wouldn't you have told me that?"

"Same reason I didn't tell you about my last visit here."

He shook his head. "You can really do that—read unfinished Grimoires?"

"Yep. Lucky me, huh?" I ran a hand through my hair. "Santana thinks it has something to do with my heritage. I'm descended from the Primus Anglicus—the first magicals. Because of that, my roots are tied closer to the raw core of Chaos, and, with everything else I have going on inside me, it seems I got a few extra skills that haven't been seen in hundreds of years, such as unfinished-Grimoire reading. Apparently, mixing Shipton and Merlin blood is a *really* bad idea, if you don't want to end up with a potentially dangerous kid. Ticking timebomb, remember?"

"Why did you think I wouldn't keep your secret?" He sounded hurt.

I shrugged awkwardly, feeling flustered. "You love rules and authority, Wade. I knew you'd probably go to Alton about this, and I couldn't let that happen." I cast him a shy glance. "And, right now, I need to know that you won't go to him with this information. I don't want to sound dramatic, but my life might rely on it. My freedom, at the very least."

"I won't say anything to him," he promised, without missing a beat. "I won't put you in harm's way. I thought you'd have learned that by now. Rules and regulations are useful, but sometimes there are situations where they need to be bent a little."

"Do you mean it? You won't say anything?"

"I won't say anything." He smiled, though the feeling of disappointment lingered. "Just... don't go reading anything out loud while I'm here, okay?" The joke felt forced, but I was glad of the slight break in tension.

"You'll have to read it instead," I replied. "I don't *exactly* have control over it."

"You can stop that."

I arched an eyebrow. "What?"

"The self-deprecation. I know you do it to be funny, but you're good at what you do, Harley. I doubt anyone could have overcome the challenges of the Suppressor the way you have. You have more control than you think you do—take the fight with Katherine, for example. When it mattered, you stepped up to the plate. We'd probably all be dead if you hadn't."

"Was that a... compliment, Wade Crowley?"

He grinned. "Don't get used to it."

"So, you forgive me?"

"Give me a couple of hours, and I'll think about it."

That was good enough for me.

"Let's take a look, then," I said, using the smaller key to open the padlock. A shimmer of gold rippled across the case, loosening the charms so I could take the book out. It felt good to hold it in my hands again, the soft leather smooth against my skin.

"Wait—I'd like to try something first," he said, taking the book from my hands and setting it down at one of the nearby reading tables. A spike of jealousy shot through me at the Grimoire in Wade's grasp, but I forced the sensation down. *It's just the weird effect these things have on you, that's all.* Already, I was struggling against the pull of the pages. The words wanted to be read—I heard them begging for my voice.

"What?" I asked.

"You'll see." He disappeared down the stairs and returned a few minutes later with a book in his hands. By the looks of it, it was another Grimoire. As he brought it closer to me, the whispers grew louder.

"What's that for?"

He set it down on the table and gestured for me to sit. "If you can really do what you say you can, I want to test the limits of it. Might as well use the opportunity while we have it. I know there are some unfinished ones back at the SDC, but we're here now. This is another unfinished Grimoire—I want to know if it's only your parents' that you can read from, or if it's any unfinished one."

"I told you, I read from another one in the Luis Paoletti Room."

"Are you sure that one was unfinished?"

I frowned. "No, but—"

"Then we need to experiment." I'd never seen him so excited. The disappointment and surprise of discovering my new talent was par for the course, but this eagerness was a different aspect of Wade altogether. One I hadn't witnessed before.

I sat down at the table and flipped open the book. My impulses took over, filling me with a need to read what was on the pages. It felt like a physical tug, pulling me forward. Settling on a spell that seemed harmless enough, I let my eyes drift over the words. Suddenly, everything else fell away, leaving me in a strange bubble of darkness. I couldn't even see Wade anymore, only the book and the spell, brought to life in front of my eyes.

I heard myself saying something, but it sounded distant and echoey. *"Heart to heart and blood to blood, let you be me and I be you, and share and share alike,"* was all I could hear myself speak, though I knew words had come before it. A bright spark of white light shot out from the book, enveloping Wade and me. The darkness receded, bringing me back into the Special Collections room, the trance broken as the spell had come to an end.

Only, I was now standing where Wade had been, staring at myself in the seat a short distance away. Wondering if I'd performed some sort of teleportation spell, albeit it a small one, I frowned at my other self. I was still moving, my shoulders shaking as though I was laughing. *What the...*

"Well, this is weird," my seated self said, turning to look at me.

"What happened?" My voice came out way deeper than normal, startling me.

My other self smiled. "Look in the glass case over there."

Curious, I turned to check my reflection in the long pane of glass that held a series of ancient-looking books behind it. My mouth fell open as Wade's face stared back at me. I was in his body and he was in mine. *Oh, the possibilities...*

I smoothed my hands—or, rather, Wade's—over the taut abs of my stomach and admired how toned they were. I couldn't hear any of his thoughts or get into his head, but then I guessed that had transferred over to me.

"Don't even think about it, Merlin," he warned, as I glanced down.

"What—I wasn't going to do anything!"

He chuckled. "It's tempting, though, right? Haven't you ever wondered what it might be like to be the opposite sex for a day?"

"Maybe—but not you!" I was starting to freak out, hoping I could reverse this. I might've wanted to get closer to Wade, but this wasn't exactly what I'd had in mind. *Although it's a quick and painless way to get into his pants.* I flushed at the lewdness of my own brain.

"Well, now I know what it's like to be in Harley Merlin's shoes. It's weird. So much extra *stuff* buzzing about." I stared at him in horror. I didn't want him feeling too many of my hormones.

Determined not to let him embarrass me, I hurried over to the table and glanced down at the Grimoire, finding the reverse spell on the page beside it. Without waiting for Wade to say anything, I dipped back into the strange, trance-like state. Everything disappeared as my voice rang out, saying the words to undo what I'd done. *"Heart to heart, blood to blood, let me be me and you be you, and share no more of joined hearts."*

A blinding light burst outward, bringing me back into the room. Fortunately, this time, I was back in the seat at the reading table, with Wade looking over my shoulder. He looked far too pleased with himself.

"Let's never do that again," I mumbled in embarrassment.

"I don't know; I kind of liked it."

"Not a word of this to anyone!"

He laughed. "Okay, okay, I promise. Man, I never thought being a woman could be so—"

"What did I just say?"

He lifted his hands in surrender. "Sorry. My bad. Not a word." He drew his fingertips across his lips like a zipper, though mischief still twinkled in his deep-green eyes. "Well, at least we know it's not just your parents' Grimoire you can do this with."

"Yeah, thanks for that."

"It's got to be what Santana said—there's a power ingrained in you and your heritage that lets you do this with unfinished Grimoires, no matter who they belonged to."

"She told me that magicals used to be able to do it all the time, in the early days of magic. Since then, they've been sort of watered down.

Thanks to my combined bloodline, and the links it has to the first magicals, it must have triggered that ability in me."

"It's a neat trick. But, like you said, it'd put the Mage Council in panic mode."

I pulled a face. "I just wish we could take my parents' Grimoire out of here. I'm not sure if I can do a spell without having it in front of me. I think I need to be able to see it for it to work, if that makes sense?"

He nodded. "That tends to be the way with these things. We can test it, if you want."

"How?"

"Take a picture of this spell and go downstairs to try it out."

"Can we pick a different one?"

He grinned. "Sure."

I flipped the pages and picked a spell that seemed to turn objects into animals. Getting my phone out, I snapped a quick picture of it and headed back down the stairs. Wade followed me to the top of the staircase, peering over the platform's balcony as I took up my position and looked down at the image. This time, nothing happened. No whispers, no tug of power, no pleading for my voice.

"Anything?" he asked.

"Nope, nada."

"That's a shame. It'd have made things so much simpler if you could have used pictures."

I nodded. "Tell me about it."

Brushing the experiment off, finding that it'd left a sour taste in my mouth, I trudged back up the stairs and sat back down at the reading table. Pushing the test Grimoire away, I pulled the Merlin Grimoire toward me. My chest constricted as I smoothed my hands over the cover again, sensing the fierce power inside.

"Are you okay?" Wade asked, worried.

"Yeah, just keep an eye on me, okay? You should do the reading."

He sat down next to me and began to flip through the pages. I fought with the urge to reach out and touch it for myself, but I knew what might happen if I did. Still, every single leaf of thick vellum made my heart lurch and my senses light up with intense need. Each word wanted to drag me down, coaxing me into speaking the spell aloud. It took every ounce of strength I had not to give into it, a trickle of sweat meandering down the side of my face as I fought against the urges.

"There's a summoning spell here," he said, pointing to a familiar page. "It's used to summon Erebus—is this the one from last time?"

"Yeah, let's not use that one," I replied. "I'd like both of us to actually make it back to the SDC."

"Agreed. This stuff is terrifying. I don't even want to think about what you could have done, if you'd managed to read it all out. Stupidity doesn't even come close. It's giving me chills just mentioning it."

Wait... what? What might I have done? "What do you mean?"

"Erebus is always related to death," he explained. "He's known to be temperamental and can take lives as he pleases. He often takes a life in exchange for being summoned—at least, that's what the old books used to say."

I gulped. "Oh… yeah, let's not do that." I thought of Santana, and what Erebus might have done to her if I'd succeeded in summoning him. I doubted he'd have taken my life; otherwise, none of those ancient people would ever have bothered summoning him. No, it was more likely that he'd have taken the life of someone close to me. I shuddered at the thought. It was a good thing she'd stopped me when she had.

"There's this, too," Wade said, browsing a few more pages. "You can probably read this, since it's not a spell."

"Let me see…" I glanced down to find a section about the Children of Chaos. It referenced that the Children of Chaos could be found in their respective dimensions. To travel there, they suggested a number of transportation spells, though they weren't actually written in the Grimoire. The passage also mentioned a vague detail about drawing on raw energy first. Power seemed to be the main element in accomplishing this feat, but that wasn't something you could just pick up from the local store.

I reasoned that the National Council had probably seen this for themselves, but hadn't thought much of it. It wasn't like they'd be able to do this themselves, anyway. The process was too dark and terrible, crossing a whole bunch of moral lines. *Although I know one person who has no problem with that.*

It also made me think about Jacob's dad. He'd opened a portal to one of these places and had never come back. I wondered if he was still stuck there, trapped between the mortal world and these creepy other-worlds where the Children resided, or if something far worse had happened to him. I had a feeling that these deities didn't like to be accosted in their own homes, so to speak. Not without an invitation, anyway.

"What is it?" Wade pressed.

"It mentions that the Children of Chaos can be found in their respective dimensions. Nothing solid, just stories and suggestions. It's not easy to get to them on their own turf, though, by the looks of it." I showed him the page and felt his emotions sinking as he took in the lengthy process.

"We can bear that in mind, if we need to track them down," he said, though he didn't sound too convinced. "Is there anything else?"

I kept looking, but there was nothing else that related to the Children of Chaos. There were a couple of cool spells to do with improving strength, and one that seemed to allow a person to fly temporarily, but nothing that we could use against Katherine. The only one that seemed vaguely useful was a spell that mentioned being able to find things that were hidden, but if we couldn't take the Grimoire out of the Special Collections room, then it was as good as useless.

"There's a persuasion spell in here that we could use to get Emily Ryder to talk," I said. "Again, it's complicated, but it might help us locate the kids if we can squeeze the info out of her."

"Yeah—which we can't do if we have to leave the book here. There's no way the New York Coven will let us take it out of here," Wade replied grimly. "And even if we could, there'd be questions as to how you'd use it. Your secret would have to come out."

I slammed my hands down on the table in frustration. "This is ridiculous. My parents' Grimoire should belong to me. What right do they have to keep it here, locked away?"

"I'm sorry, Harley."

"Not as sorry as I am," I muttered. "We come *this* close and then we have to give up. I'm sick of it. We're getting nowhere! The longer Katherine has those kids in her grasp, the more chance she has to go through with her nasty little plan."

"We could explain to the covens what you can do, and see if they'll relent?"

I shook my head. "I'll never see the light of day again. They'll use me for what they want and then they'll throw me in Purgatory, or some-where just as bad. You know they will." Isadora's warning rang in my head—*Don't let the covens use you, or you'll never break free of the cycle.* I knew it was selfish to value my life over those of the kids, but I couldn't bear the thought of spending the rest of my days in a gloomy cell.

"Then what do you want to do?"

"Let's tell Alton about this 'respective dimension' angle, see if he can think of a way to expand it. If Katherine wants to become a Child of Chaos, chances are she'll have to come face-to-face with one. If we can somehow keep an eye on these places, wherever the heck they are, then we might be able to cut her off before she can do anything."

Wade nodded. "Sounds like a good idea."

"And, while we're here, I want to find a book by some guy named Chanticleer. Apparently, there's a spell in there that can help with my Esprit, but The New York Coven can go screw themselves if they think I'm bothering with another application." I got up and hurried down the stairs, realizing we were running out of time. Blondie would come and get us if we didn't leave within the given hour.

With me browsing the stacks on the right-hand side, while Wade took the left, we scoured the tomes. There didn't seem to be much of an order to them, at least not one that I understood. Wade seemed to be faring better, however, his face set in a determined expression. He was only focusing on one area of the books, scrutinizing each title closely.

"Here it is!" he shouted, pulling a book from the stack.

I raced over to him and took the book from his hands, placing it down on a nearby table with a puff of dust. Using the index, I quickly found the spell that I was looking for. The only trouble was, it was written in some form of archaic French. *Then why write the index in English? Ugh!* Undeterred, I snapped a picture of the spell and shoved my phone back in my pocket. From what I could make out, the spell required a lengthy list of ingredients. I just had to hope we had them in the SDC. That, and a French translator.

"Don't suppose you speak French, do you?" I asked, determined not to get downhearted.

"No, but I know a spell we can use." He flashed me an encouraging smile as he put his hand on my shoulder.

"See, *this* is why I like you, Wade Crowley." *If only you knew how much.*

"Why—because I go along with your crazy ideas?"

"Something like that."

After all of the last hour's disappointments, I wasn't going to give up on this. With my newfound determination to break the Suppressor, I needed my Esprit more than ever.

ELEVEN

Harley

After handing back the pass and the keys, we returned to the SDC and headed straight for the Luis Paoletti Room. The picture of the Esprit repair spell was pulled up on my phone. With the door closed behind us, I braced myself against the workbench. Memories of the other night came flooding back, but I tried hard not to think about them. My feelings for Wade could wait a while.

"So, what's this translation spell, then?" I asked.

"I'll find it while you write out the repairing spell," he replied.

"Wait—can't we just use the Internet?"

He laughed. "Apps are notoriously unreliable for this kind of thing. I doubt it'd even be able to read script like this—it's too close together and faded. Trust me, the old ways are the best ways for a reason."

"All right, Granddad," I said.

Setting to work, I grabbed a piece of paper and a pen from a nearby drawer and started to write out the words from my phone. The handwriting in the book was old and cursive, but I managed to do a decent job of getting it into clearer lettering. Meanwhile, Wade rummaged around in some of the Grimoire boxes on the top shelf. Finding the book he needed, he brought it to me and sat down at my side. His closeness made it hard to concentrate, but I was determined not to let my emotions get in the way of this. I'd ended up in Wade's room because Jacob had done just that; I wasn't about to make a similar mistake.

"Here it is," he said, turning to a page near the back. "Have you written everything out?"

I nodded.

"Good—then hand it over." I slid the paper along the workbench to him. He held out his hands and pressed them to the page, his ten rings lighting up with a soft, blue glow as he began to mutter the words from the Grimoire. My eyes were fixed on the paper, wondering what was going to happen. I found out soon enough, as the letters scrambled like a kaleidoscope, before settling into a pattern I could recognize. He had only translated the spell. The writing was still old-fashioned, with a lot of extraneous vowels on the ends of the words, but it was definitely English.

"I like that spell a lot," I said with a smile, as I browsed the list of necessary ingredients. It was long, but nothing stood out as being particularly hard to find. "Do we have all of this?"

Wade took a look at it and nodded slowly. "I think so: wolfsbane, devil's eye, three snowdrop bells, quicksilver, wild honey, red pringrape, maple sap, hartshorn, liquid gold, willow bark, spider's silk, and eye of newt."

I stared at him. "It doesn't say eye of newt."

"It does. See." He pointed to the words.

"What, like 'double, double, toil and trouble'? Should I get a cauldron and a stick? Should I be warning Macbeth about moving trees and stuff? Defy gravity, maybe?"

He chuckled. "No, but we will need a cast-iron pot."

"And we have one of those?"

"We should." He got up from his seat and wandered about the room, plucking things off shelves and placing them in the middle of the work-bench. I watched him work, feeling a bit useless. Making potions wasn't exactly my strong suit.

"Do we have it all?" I asked, as he came back and sat by my side.

"Not quite. We'll have to do some gathering."

"Where do we start?"

"Bellmore."

We spent the next hour running around the coven like headless chickens, gathering all the ingredients on the list. Some were in the Luis Paoletti Room, including a diamond and an emerald from a janky piece of jewelry that had been stuffed in the back of a drawer, but the majority weren't. Bellmore had a lot of what we needed, which she gave to us with a suspicious but willing air, both of us scrambling to explain that it was for a spell to fix my Esprit. It technically was, but she didn't need to know the details. However, the rest of the items had to come from the various storerooms that were located all over the place. We split up, searching for our given ingredients, before reconvening in the Luis Paoletti Room once we'd both gotten everything on our list. By the time I got back, I was sweating, wondering if I'd even have the energy to get the spell done. *Who am I kidding—I'd do this on my freaking deathbed.*

"Now, do you want to come back and do this later, or are you okay to start now?" Wade asked, catching his breath.

"Now."

"Okay, then take it away. I'll be here, if anything goes wrong."

I nodded and began to work through the list of steps. First, I added the three snowdrop bells, upside down, to the cast-iron pot. Three drops of the honey, the liquid gold, the quicksilver, the hartshorn, and the maple sap went into each bell, the curved flowers holding the fluid like little containers. Next came the pringrape, the tiny buds sprinkled into the mix, alongside the wolfsbane and the willow bark. I was careful to keep the measures exact. The devil's eye went in next. After that came the eye of newt, which I wasn't looking forward to. Reaching out for the small glass jar that held them, submerged in a viscous, amber liquid, I grimaced and took out three. Each one nestled in the basin of the snowdrop bells, sinking into the fluid that was already in each one. The last step, before putting the broken Esprit into the bowl, was the spider's silk. I took up the coil of it and wrapped it intricately around the three snowdrops, binding them together.

Reluctantly, I slipped off my Esprit and placed it in the bowl, the dead, empty sockets facing upward. *Please let this work.* Picking up the two new stones I'd pried out of the old relic in the drawer, I put them on top of the empty fixtures.

Turning back to the spell, I felt myself sink into a similarly trancelike state, though it wasn't as intense as with the Grimoires. I was still aware of Wade at my side, and nothing in the room disappeared—it simply went out of focus for a moment.

Taking a deep breath, I recited the words on the page: *"As Chaos binds you to me, let yourself be bound to Chaos. What is broken in you, may my spirit heal. What is damaged in me, may your Chaos nurture. We are one piece, let us be one piece once more."* I repeated it nine times, as instructed, my voice steady and even.

As soon as I was finished, I closed my eyes and hovered my hands over the top of the bowl. Drawing on my abilities, I struggled against my lack of control to pour small amounts of Air and Earth into the pot. The bowl shook as Air swirled, and the sides trembled as Earth rose up around it in a tangle of vines that gripped the table, creeping out of the floor like tentacles.

Come on, Harley... make it work. Remember, you're in control. You can do this.

The moment enough of my energy had been poured into the pot, I snatched my hands away, careful not to overdo it. I was breathing hard, cold sweat glistening on my skin.

Nothing happened.

"Did it work?" I whispered.

Wade shrugged. "I don't know. Look inside."

I reached for the bowl, only to draw my hands away as a surge of blinding silver light ripped out of the pot. It spiraled upward in a column of powerful energy, twisting like a tornado in a Kansas field. *Hold on to your stilettos, Dorothy.* In the very center of the spiral, I saw my Esprit, the new gemstones fitting back into place with the help of the spell's power. Gold energy mingled with the silver, a steady pulse emanating from within, like a heartbeat. The fine hairs on my forearms were standing up on end, the room crackling with electricity.

Wade lunged for me, knocking me off my chair and onto the floor. And not a moment too soon, since the minute we landed on the ground, an enormous explosion burst outward. A second blast erupted straight after, sending a pulse of raw energy over our heads and through the walls of the room. Déjà vu hit me as the interdimensional façade of the coven shook for a moment, the forcefield shivering and sparking. An expletive lingered on the tip of my tongue as I watched in horror, praying the Bestiary would restore it, the same way it had with Jacob's slip-up.

Two minutes later, the forcefield was still crackling sporadically.

Come on, come on, come on... Please, don't say I've broken the pocket. I watched it intently, willing it to come back to full force. If this place crumbled because of me, they'd lock me up even without knowing about my extra skills.

A wave of bronzed light surged across the walls; the Bestiary had done its job. Everything was settling back to normal. Although, with it being daytime, there was no way it would have gone unnoticed.

"Thank God," I murmured. Cursing under my breath at the near miss, I hastily scrambled to my feet and brushed the dust from my jeans. "What the heck was that?"

Wade stood. "I'm not sure. If the spell does what I think it does, then it requires the binding of Chaos to an object. When the new stones slotted into place in your Esprit, it might have caused a power surge of sorts. That would explain why there were two blasts, anyway."

"Why don't they write that kind of thing in the damn spell?" I snapped, my heart pounding. "All it'd take is a little footnote to say, 'Oh, and by the way, this may cause a huge explosion that might destroy things nearby.' Seriously, is that so hard to do?" I looked at the shelves around the room, to see if anything had been ruined or damaged. Fortunately, everything seemed to be intact. The power surge appeared to have affected the forcefield and nothing else.

"Hey, don't worry," Wade murmured. "The Bestiary took care of it and, even if it had failed, we've got the Aquarium as backup."

I shook my head. "I've really got to stop doing dangerous crap like this."

"You took the words right out of my mouth." He peered at the cast-iron pot. "Did it work?"

I put my hand into the bowl. The only thing that remained was my Esprit. No gunk, no eyes, no sticky stuff, just my Esprit. I turned my Esprit over in my hands. The gemstones that linked to Earth and Air glinted in the light, brimming with the same glow as the others.

At first, I wasn't sure if it was just a trick of the light, but the diamond and the emerald appeared darker than before. A heart of dark gray marred the previously perfect diamond, giving it a silvery sheen, while the emerald had deepened to an almost bottle-green shade. Slipping the Esprit back onto my hand, I couldn't help wondering if this was a bad omen. The gems had darkened; did that mean I was now leaning more toward the Dark side of things? Had I used the Dark side of me to perform the spell, giving that affinity the advantage? It worried me, though I didn't want to say anything to Wade.

I knew that being of Darkness didn't make me an inherently evil person or anything, but I felt uneasy about leaning that way. Darkness meant destruction, a lot of the time, and if I broke the Suppressor by force, using that sort of destruction, then what would it mean for me in the long run? Would I become a destructive force with unchecked power? *Katherine, eat your heart out.* I didn't like the prospect of that one bit. I needed the two to be in balance if I was going to have any control over my abilities.

To be honest, it planted a seed of doubt in my head about breaking the Suppressor, considering what it might mean for me. I had a tough enough time trying to control my suppressed powers—what the heck would I be like if they were allowed to run wild? They might take over, change me into something monstrous.

"Is everything back to normal?" Wade asked. He looked impatient.

"I think so."

He frowned. "Have they changed color?"

"I think it's just this light, making them look a bit weird. Or it might be that they're new stones—they looked a lot older than the previous ones."

"Are you sure?"

I hid my hand from him. "Uh… not entirely. They might've gotten a bit darker, too. Now, come on—we should find Alton and tell him what we found out about the Children of Chaos and their turf. I don't know if it'll help, since there wasn't much to go on, but it might. Plus, we should also explain why the forcefield almost disappeared—he's not going to be happy about that."

"You're sure you're okay? That was a lot of power you just used."

"I'm fine, honestly," I replied. As exasperated as I was, my heart fluttered at Wade's concern. "And thanks for diving on me again. If we keep doing this, I'll need to get head-to-toe padding."

He smiled. "Don't mention it."

With that, we headed out of the Luis Paoletti Room and made our way downstairs, walking toward Alton's office. The halls were weirdly quiet. If it had been nighttime, I'd have understood it, but this didn't make any sense. There should have been people everywhere.

"Does it seem a little quiet to you?" I whispered.

Wade nodded. "I was just about to say that."

I froze, grabbing Wade's arm and pulling him back as a shadow emerged up ahead. It loomed in the doorway that connected this hallway to the next. Hunched and snorting, it stood over seven feet, with bulging muscles and hooves that clipped on the marble floor. Two enormous horns bent out of its head, sharpened to a point. Its cow-like ears flicked back and forward angrily, as though listening for us, while two dark, beady eyes stared down the corridor in our direction.

"It's a minotaur," I hissed.

Wade shot me a look. "I can see that."

"Shouldn't it be in the Bestiary?"

"It must have escaped."

My heart sank as I realized what must have happened. My mishap with the power surge had likely damaged the integrity of the Bestiary, just for a couple of minutes. Clearly, that was long enough to let a minotaur out of its box. Alton was going to be *really* mad at me now.

"You take the left side; I'll take the right side," Wade said, bringing up his hands. I nodded and lifted my own palms, urging Fire into them.

The minotaur snorted and scraped its hooves across the floor. It had barely moved a yard when the first fireball struck it in the chest, stopping the creature in its tracks. Lifting its head, it let out a terrifying roar and pounded the injured spot with its fists. We hurtled a barrage of fireballs toward the beast and hit it again and again. With every impact, it roared louder, the sparks from the fireballs drifting up toward its face.

"Do you have a Mason jar on you?" I asked frantically, trying to keep up the artillery.

Wade shook his head. "I'm not Tobe; I don't have jars stuffed in my jacket twenty-four-seven. This jacket doesn't even have real pockets. Come on, we need to lead it back toward the Bestiary."

Switching to my Telekinesis, I sent out a lasso and wrapped it around the beast's neck. It struggled against me, but I held fast, pushing my power out. The creature was forced to stagger backward. Meanwhile, Wade continued in his fiery onslaught, the minotaur looking around in apparent panic as it tried to escape.

Two more figures appeared behind the beast. Astrid and Garrett had arrived, and they had the tools we needed to capture this thing. As they set to work with the green stones and the Mason jar, Wade and I kept up the distraction, keeping the minotaur's focus on us. If it spotted Astrid and Garrett, there was no telling what it might do. We'd riled it up pretty good.

Keeping the lasso around its neck, I used my left hand to shoot a bristling fireball at the beast. The sparking orb hit it straight in the forehead. It let out an almighty groan before tumbling to its knees, its head straining against the Telekinesis as I kept it on a tight leash. As it strained and roared, the bright green ropes shot up from the stones and crisscrossed over the beast's muscular back, pulling it down to the ground, where it finally lay still. Astrid skidded the Mason jar in front of the creature. The minotaur turned into black smoke as it was sucked into the glassware. She slammed the lid on.

"Nice job!" Astrid called to us.

"Yeah—nice of you to show up," Garrett added. "We could use some help in the Bestiary if you aren't too busy." Sarcasm dripped from his words.

I frowned. "Why—what's going on?"

"You'll see," Garrett replied.

The four of us hurried through the hallways toward the Bestiary, the Mason jar safely nestled in Astrid's arms. The corridors were empty of people—even the guards had disappeared. It made for a worrying sight. However, that was nothing compared to what awaited us in the Bestiary. My eyes flew wide as we threw open the huge double doors and witnessed the chaos beyond. Tobe was running around, whipping out jars as he tried to wrangle a mass of smaller creatures back into their cages. Most of the coven seemed to be here, too, helping get all the Purge beasts back behind charmed walls.

"What happened here?" I asked, fearing the answer.

"I cannot say for sure," Tobe replied, in the middle of hurling a small, toady-looking thing back into its box. "A large number of the creatures escaped at once."

My gaze settled on one box in particular, which was now empty. "Where's Quetzi?"

Tobe followed my line of sight. "No... That cannot be..."

"Where is he, Tobe?" My voice came out like a squeak. If Quetzi had escaped, then we were in a whole heap of trouble.

"I don't know," Tobe murmured in disbelief. "His box must have opened when the Bestiary faltered, and he used the ensuing mayhem to escape." He sank down on the edge of one of the glass boxes, a look of despair in his amber eyes.

Panic cut through me like a knife. This was all my fault. I'd fixed my Esprit, but at what cost? The Bestiary had failed because of me, and now the Purge beasts were everywhere. All the additional security personnel were running around, trying to capture the loose creatures from all across the globe. Big ones, small ones, calm ones, angry ones...

"The Ibong Adarna," Wade said, looking worried.

Tobe nodded. "You could be right, Wade. She hasn't come this way, but she may be loose in the halls at the back. I haven't seen anyone come out of there in a while."

"Right about what?" I asked.

"If the singing bird has found a way to free herself, then we are doomed," Tobe explained. "She will put us to sleep and kill us before we have the opportunity to restore her to her box."

"We'll take care of it," Wade said.

"Then you will need these." Tobe lifted his wing of endless wonders and took out a small box. He handed it to Wade, who removed four balls of dark red wax from inside.

Wade gave two to me and shot me a challenging smile. "Come on, Merlin—you're with me. Put those in your ears; you're going to need them."

"Why?"

"If you hear the song of the Ibong Adarna, you'll be asleep before you can so much as mutter the capture spell."

"You think she's managed to get free?"

"That's what we're about to find out." After grabbing a Mason jar from the side, he reached out and, unexpectedly, took my hand. With a sharp jolt that was anything but romantic, he yanked me down the central aisle of the Bestiary, leading me into the darker recesses I'd never visited before.

As we sprinted through the main chamber, I looked around for Jacob, wondering where he was. With so many creatures on the loose, I hoped he was safe. We pressed farther and farther back, moving down arched corridors where people were chasing Purge beasts. Eventually, we reached a part of the Bestiary where everything had fallen silent. The distant shouts of the others had become nothing more than a muffled echo. Stepping through into a cavernous hall, the walls gilded and carved with intricate designs that spoke of ancient beings and held statues of various creatures that I knew from old legends, my mouth fell open. People lay all across the floor, apparently asleep.

A beautiful bird perched on the chandelier in the middle of the room's domed ceiling, ruffling its exquisite feathers. It reminded me of a peacock blended with a phoenix, with a long tail of flowing feathers in every shade of the rainbow, ending in fluffy wisps tinged with white. A curled tuft swept back from its elegant face, its sharp beak menacing in the low light, as vast talons gripped the brass edges of the fixture, jangling the crystals.

It turned its head toward us, before opening out its majestic wings and soaring down to the floor. Evidently, it had no reason to fear humans, nor did it know we had balls of wax stuffed in our ears. Folding its wings back, it stalked toward us like a feathered dinosaur.

It paused a short distance away and opened its beak. Part of me desperately wanted to hear this beautiful, fabled song, but I knew that if I tried to listen, I'd end up asleep on the floor. Its long neck vibrated and trilled as the song poured out of its mouth, but neither Wade nor I could hear a note. Instead, we moved slowly toward it.

Once we were close enough, Wade passed me the green stones. He'd trained me on how to do this, so I hoped I could get it right. Tiptoeing closer, I slid the stones in a circle around the magnificent bird, who seemed so invested in her song that she had barely noticed us moving around her. I almost felt sorry for her. *A creature like this shouldn't have to live in a cage.* Then again, I didn't know the extent of what she'd done, out there in the world. One thing was for sure; she was more dangerous than she looked.

As I spoke the words of the capturing spell, drawing them out of my memory, the green ropes shot out and lashed themselves over the bird's sleek back. The creature's expression turned to one of confusion, her wings thrashing wildly against the ropes. For the first time, watching a capture like this broke my heart. I couldn't hear her, but I could sense her panic and distress. She didn't want to go back in the cage, but there was nothing else we could do. *I'm sorry...*

Wade placed the Mason jar in front of the bird, and her body swirled into black smoke as she was drawn into the glass center. As soon as the lid was closed, he removed the wax from his ears and cast me a smile. I took the plugs out of mine, too.

"Nice job, Merlin," he said.

"Yeah... thanks." My heart wasn't in it. I had a feeling that the Ibong Adarna's beautiful face, crushed under the strain of the ropes, would haunt me for a while. It was easy to capture the ugly or brutish-looking Purge beasts, but I'd forgotten that there were other creatures too— stunning, majestic beings—who suffered the same fate.

"Are you okay?"

I nodded. "It just seems like a shame."

"This bird could kill you in a heartbeat if it wanted to. I know it can be tough sometimes, but we have to do this in order to keep ourselves and the humans safe."

"I know, I'm just being silly."

He shook his head. "I don't think you're being silly. I think you're being compassionate. I used to feel the way you're feeling from time to time, but once you learn what these beasts can really do, it changes your mind."

Now, this is the reason I like you, Wade Crowley.

True, he could be a total jerk sometimes, and there were moments where I wanted to wring his neck. But when we shared a moment like this, all of that went away. I was reminded how intelligent and caring he could be... and that was sexier than anything.

Now, if only there was a singing bird who could make a certain man fall in love with me...

TWELVE

Astrid

"If the California Mage Council finds out about this, it'll be my head on the chopping block," Alton muttered as he grabbed three foxlike beings, avoiding the sparks of fire that shot up from their tails. They were Chinese Foxes, by my recollection—well-known polymorphs who tricked people into thinking they were old men or lost children. I'd read a few chapters about them a while ago.

The clean-up was going well, with only a few errant creatures to retrieve. The big ones had long been returned to their glass boxes, but the smaller ones were cunning and evasive, able to hide in all the available nooks and crannies. I myself was dealing with a particularly irate leprechaun. He kept trying to distract me, but if I looked away for even a second, he would be out of my hands and up to untold mischief. I shoved him in one of the boxes and slammed the door before he could evaporate into thin air.

"Which part of it?" I asked, tension still thick between us. His points had been valid in our former argument, but so had mine—a fact he would hopefully appreciate, or at least acknowledge, someday. Truthfully, had it not been the entire coven's safety at stake with all of these creatures darting around like maniacs, I would've made myself scarce.

Cowardly, perhaps, but I didn't have any taste for confrontation, especially not with my father.

As it happened, my services were called upon, as Smartie was exceptional at picking up the trace trails of these Purge beasts and tracking the remaining renegades throughout the building. Unfortunately, that ability didn't reach to the more ancient creatures, whose Purge trails had vanished thousands of years ago. Quetzi happened to be one such ancient beastie. I would rather have faced the minotaur again than have to fend off the mighty Quetzalcoatl and his rare prowess.

"I don't need your sass, Astrid," Alton replied sternly. "I mean all of it. Quetzi going missing is catastrophic, although I suppose this debacle with the Bestiary could have turned out a lot worse. Still, how he managed to cause so much damage and get out is beyond me."

"We're talking about the same creature, aren't we? Ancient being of enormous meteorological power, used to be worshiped as an Aztec god? He's had a long time to think about this."

"But why strike now?"

It was the very question I'd been pondering, and so had probably everyone else. From a practical perspective, there was a lot going on, and maybe Quetzi had used the furor to seize his moment. Although that still left the *why*. Unless he wanted to teach Katherine a lesson of his own and had decided that we weren't doing enough for the cause. But then, why would he act alone like this? Why wouldn't he have found a way to request our assistance, or offered his help in our fight against her—tapped it out in Morse code on the side of the box or something, or gotten Tobe to decipher for him? I knew beasts like him could be extraordinarily proud, but he wasn't foolish—he would know that there was strength in numbers, no matter how fearsome he was by himself.

"I don't know," was all I could say, which perplexed me. I usually had more answers than this.

Alton leaned against the box where he'd placed the Chinese Foxes and ran a hand through his hair. "It will take more than an AI to figure out that creature's thoughts."

I shrugged. "No matter what Quetzi has done, we need to find him before he gets us into even more trouble. We can't just let him slither free and cause this kind of chaos out in the human world."

"No... no, we can't." He looked to the rest of the Rag Team, who were all busy searching every corner for missing beasts. Raffe seemed to have a knack for it, his djinn giving him an affinity with these Purge beasts. The djinn wasn't exactly the same kind of monster, but they were both made of Chaos. At that very moment, he lifted two brownies up by their legs and hurled them into their glass box with a satisfied flourish.

"Everything okay, Alton?" Wade asked, his arm wedged behind a bookcase.

He nodded. "If you could all stop what you're doing for a moment, there's something I need to tell you. Leave the others to round up the rest of these Purge beasts—we can't get distracted by this."

"What do you mean, we can't get distracted by this?" Harley interjected. "If Quetzi is out, then we need to find him. We don't know what he's up to." She looked strange, as though burdened with guilt. I wondered what that was about.

"Why would Quetzi escape like this?" Santana asked.

"For Katherine, perhaps?" Tobe answered, dusting his hands on his feathers. "He may be able to sense her in a way that we can't. He may have escaped because he knows that she is coming and does not wish to be here when that happens."

I hadn't thought about that. Quetzi was fiercely powerful, and, from what I remembered, he knew Katherine from her days of visiting this Bestiary. His desire to avoid her was definitely the best explanation that I'd heard so far, not that anyone had been particularly forthcoming with their ruminations. Garrett had rather helpfully suggested that he "just wanted a break from being stuck in a glass box." He'd been so adorable when he'd said that, with such earnestness... Though Wade had laughed at him and set his mood on edge. He was still fuming away nearby, taking his anger out on a hobgoblin.

"Let's sweep the coven, see if we can track Quetzi down," Alton instructed.

Splitting into groups, the Rag Team headed out with some of the security personnel who weren't busy catching Purge beasts. We traipsed through the corridors for the better part of three hours, looking in every room, searching behind every door, turning over every possible hiding place. Wherever Quetzi had escaped to, he wasn't coming out. By the end of our search, it started to feel somewhat hopeless. The coven was enormous, and I couldn't find any sign of the serpent on the camera systems. A shadow here and there that might have been him, but we checked each location and still came up with nothing.

My phone pinged. A message from Alton flashed up: *Meet me in the Aquarium.* I wondered if he'd had any luck. My team of Raffe and Tatyana headed there with me right away.

Pushing through the fish-handled doors of the Aquarium, I glanced around at the enormous tanks to make sure that the integrity hadn't been compromised. It was attached to the Bestiary's central power, meaning it could well have been affected by the damage Quetzi's escape had caused, but everything seemed to be intact. A few beady eyes watched us from within the water, a selkie in her seal form swimming up to the glass before moving away again.

This place had always felt eerie to me. At least in the Bestiary you could see the black smoke of the beasts, if they didn't want to take their normal form, but the water creatures were harder to pick out. Then again, I hated water anyway, which didn't exactly help. Ever since I was a child and I'd almost drowned at the beach, I'd loathed the very idea of deep water, especially when I didn't know what was lurking beneath.

Alton turned as the Rag Team gathered in a semicircle around him. I found a way to be close to Garrett, my shoulder touching his. A frisson of excitement pulsed through my veins, my heart pounding. He glanced down at me with a warm smile, though the tightness in his jaw let me know that he'd yet to forgive Wade for his mockery.

"I know it seems as if we're in a perpetual state of doom and gloom, considering what has happened today, and it hasn't been helped by our inability to find Quetzi," Alton began stiffly. "However, there is some good news. I didn't want to announce it to the rest of the coven, as we have no way of knowing if it'll lead to success. Saying that, I'm hoping that it will be left in good hands if I tell you about some progress we've made."

"Progress?" Harley spoke up, her arms folded across her chest. Out of everyone, she continued to intrigue me. Power like hers didn't come along very often. In fact, I'd never read of anyone like her. It was hard not to sink into an unbidden state of heroine worship when I was around her, though I knew it couldn't be easy, living under a burden like that. At least, with being non-magical, there wasn't much of an expectation on my shoulders.

Alton nodded. "We spoke with the two guards we captured from the warehouse, and—"

"I thought we didn't get anywhere with them?" Wade interrupted, gaining a steely look from my father.

"Please listen without interjecting," he said curtly. "Yes, they proved tight-lipped during interrogation. Nevertheless, new information has come to light."

The room fell silent. Even the Aquarium creatures seemed to be holding their breath.

"Late last night, some unexpected files came through from the Reykjavik repository, by way of a certain Preceptor Salinger of the New York Coven," he went on, looking toward Harley for a fleeting moment. She dropped her gaze immediately, her face blanching, her manner becoming somewhat fidgety. Santana also seemed to be struggling to look at Alton, her expression sheepish.

What's going on with them? Why do they look like blushing schoolgirls facing the principal?

Nobody else in the Rag Team had noticed their sudden discomfort. Despite my curiosity, it wasn't the right time to ask about it. If they had something on their minds, then I wasn't about to expose them in front of everyone. I got the impression that my father was clued in, which was likely all that mattered.

"Wait… Reykjavik?" Tatyana asked, puzzled.

"Yes, Reykjavik, by way of New York," Alton replied.

"Did you order the files?" Wade chimed in, his eyes narrowed in confusion.

Alton smiled thinly. "In a way, yes." Harley and Santana looked like they were about to implode, their cheeks reddening. There was definitely something amiss here, but I held my tongue as my father spoke again. "Anyway, using those folders, and a copy of some of the information that Wade passed on to me from New York, I was able to find the name of one of Katherine's former associates. I left early this morning and visited him in Purgatory, to speak with him about Katherine. He was suitably silent on the matter, but the prison staff granted me access to go through a bag of his personal effects—the items he had arrived with—where I discovered an unusual medallion amongst his belongings."

"How does a medallion help us?" I asked, feeling slightly stunned by this revelation. He hadn't told me any of this, and I was normally his first port of call for advice. His residual anger had evidently taken me out of his inner circle, albeit temporarily. We'd argued before, and he always came around in the end. Although, if things continued with Garrett, I reasoned that my father and I might end up clashing more often in the near future. It didn't fill me with joy, but what else could I do? I wouldn't give up Garrett, but I couldn't give up my father, either. *Ah, to be lodged between a rock and a hard place.*

"There was a list of missing objects and spells from the Reykjavik repository," he answered, without any hint of snark. "One of those spells was a unification spell. Thieves and smugglers used them in the old days of magic, to speak in secret. It was placed in the repository as a means to prevent such secret conversations, in the hopes of bringing down the rates of magical crime. From what I can gather, it works like a transmitter of sorts, revealing coordinates to the whereabouts of anyone else who has one of the charmed objects enchanted with the same unification spell. These coordinates are only revealed for a short span of time, before disappearing. Complicated, I know, but bear with me."

"We're still with you," Dylan said.

Alton smiled. "Thank you. So, it appears that this medallion is precisely that—it's one of these charmed objects. The associate I spoke with—a grim individual named Cairo Pernice—allowed it to be taken from him, as it needs the spell in order to work. As the spell had been taken, I presume he thought he was off the hook. What he didn't realize was that the Reykjavik repository had made copies of all the spells they'd placed in the repository, in case anything like this happened and anyone was able to steal the originals. Reykjavik sent me this copy last night."

"Which means that Katherine doesn't know there's a copy, either?" I said, the thought popping into my head.

"Exactly," Alton replied with a thawing smile. "Reykjavik has also provided me with a powerful Suppressor, to hide the medallion's presence while allowing us to see the coordinates of Katherine's remaining associates. They appear to be more inclined to trust us than the American covens—so, all I can say is, thank God for the Icelanders and for Salinger's lack of thoroughness in checking what was in those folders."

Garrett frowned. "What—and you think these beacons will lead us to the kids? You think they'll still be operational?"

"I don't see why they wouldn't be," Alton answered. "Katherine doesn't know she's been potentially compromised, and the system is a useful one for her line of work. If she doesn't know it's broken, she has no reason to fix it."

"It will show us where Katherine's people are, right?" I asked.

Alton nodded.

"And we can be sure that the kids will be at one of the locations, at least. That should be our theory, going forward."

"Yes—that's my thought on it, anyway," Alton said.

I was still somewhat bothered about the fact that he hadn't spoken to me about this earlier, but then the course of familial love never did run smooth. It was petty of him, that was true, but he was a proud man. Telling me about this would have meant seeking me out and running the risk of starting our dispute afresh. His wanting to avoid that was something I could understand, as I would have done the same thing. Meanwhile, my mind was still racing with thoughts of Quetzi. We needed to get him back, pronto.

Harley barked out a weird laugh. "Wait—so does this mean we now have a way of finding the children? Are we finally getting somewhere?"

"If everything works out, then yes," Alton replied.

I raised a shy hand. "We should still pool our efforts into tracking down Quetzi, though, before he can get up to anything dangerous. Finding the kids is very important, but Quetzi is the biggest imminent threat to the coven and the surrounding areas."

Alton nodded. "Agreed. Let's continue in our search, though we must make his capture quick so we can get back to finding those children. Since our border alerts haven't been triggered, he's likely still in the coven somewhere, waiting for an opportunity to slip out unnoticed. Keep your eyes peeled, people, and get him back in his box before he can get out of the coven perimeter." He glanced around the room. "I trust I can leave it in your hands?"

A murmur of assent rippled around the Rag Team.

"Good—then I will expect an update on Quetzi first thing tomorrow morning. It's almost four, but we should continue to look for him through the evening. As for the coordinates, I will arrange for the unification spell to be undertaken this afternoon. I'll send word when the preparations are complete. You don't all need to be there, but I would appreciate a contingent of the Rag Team."

With that, he turned on his heel and walked out of the room, giving me no chance to speak with him about why he hadn't mentioned this to me earlier. *You can't avoid me forever, Father.*

"So, what's the plan of action?" Wade gathered us closer, a serious expression on his face. In all the time I'd known him, he was the one I still struggled to comprehend. He could never quite decide if he was superior or if he was one of us—that was my impression, anyway. We'd never been close, per se, and I got the feeling that my alliance to Garrett pushed me even further down his list of acquaintances. Still, what he lacked in warmth, I gained from Santana, Tatyana, and Harley. Although the latter was clearly besotted with him, and he with her. It was just a shame that his stern façade would probably always drive a wedge between them. Not that I claimed to know a whole lot about romance.

Still, for that reason, I was even more grateful for Garrett's bluntness—he'd come out and told me he liked me, plain and simple.

"I'll keep trying to scan the cameras for any sign of Quetzi. If he got out of the Bestiary, then there has to be footage of him somewhere."

"Good idea," Harley replied.

In theory, yes. Quetzi was a sly, intelligent serpent with a lot at stake —he'd have been careful in his escape, taking the appropriate precautions to avoid capture. But my technical wizardry could be clever enough to catch him.

THIRTEEN

Harley

A t noon, my phone pinged. The Rag Team and I were scouring the coven for Quetzi, using some footage that Astrid had found of a vague shadow moving down the hallway from the Bestiary. It wasn't much, but it was all we had. It could've been a hobgoblin or a Chinese Fox for all we knew, but Astrid was convinced she was on the right track. She'd never set us on the wrong path before.

Meet in my office in ten minutes, Alton's text said. I looked up to see if anyone else had gotten the same message, but nobody else's phone had gone off. Weird. Why was Alton asking to see me and none of the others? My stomach sank. I got the feeling we were about to have a little discussion about my casual use of the mirrors. After his sly dig earlier, that had to be it. He knew what I knew, and he knew I knew, so to speak.

"Guys, I'll meet you back here in a bit. Alton needs to see me about something," I said.

"About what?" Wade replied.

I shrugged. "He didn't give me details. I'll find out when I see him." I swallowed a spiky feeling of residual anger from what I'd read in Isadora's letter. I had to keep telling myself that he'd done it for a good reason, lying to me, but it was hard to rationalize.

"If it's the beacons, let us know how it goes," Astrid said, her voice slightly wounded. I wasn't sure what was going on between Astrid and Alton, but things had been odd between them this morning. Looked to me like the captain had had a bit of a dispute with the petty officer.

"Do you think that's what he wants you for?" Garrett asked, frowning.

"Like I said, he didn't exactly give me details."

"The golden girl gets the top spot again, huh?" Venom dripped from his words.

I shot him a cold look. "Don't call me that again, Garrett. I've got no idea why he wants to see me, but if it's to do with the beacons, I'll tell you everything when I get back. What do you want me to do—say no to him?"

"It'd be a first," Garrett muttered.

I knew he was pissed about the body cams, but that didn't give him the right to take it out on me. I wasn't the one who'd put them there. I thought about saying that to him, but there didn't seem to be much point. We'd only end up in a slinging match and I really wasn't in the mood. This whole Quetzi escape already had my nerves dancing on a knife-edge, and I didn't want to say something I might regret later. The truth was, I still had a feeling that I was responsible for him getting away. My Esprit's blasts had caused the Bestiary to fail for a moment, and Quetzi had used that to his advantage.

"I'll see you guys later," I said firmly, then headed off toward Alton's office. I could feel their eyes watching me as I left, and the vibes weren't happy ones. *What are you playing at, Alton?* Did he want them to start resenting me? If he did, he was going about it the right way. Then again, maybe he was trying to save my ass from their suspicions. Secrets weren't good things to have in a group as tight-knit as ours. If they found out about the mirrors and where I'd been going, Santana and Wade excluded, they might wonder why I hadn't told them.

I arrived at the vast black doors of Alton's office ten minutes later, rapping gently on the polished surface. My heart was pounding, my hands shaking as I knocked. *Stay cool, Harley. Stay cool.*

"Come in," Alton replied.

I peered around the doorway before stepping into the room. Books were piled high in every available space and papers scattered every surface until it was hard to see what kind of furniture sat underneath. *Sigmund Freud would have a field day with this.* It definitely didn't paint a good picture of Alton's mental state. Although I was having a hard time feeling sorry for him.

"Um, you look… busy. Do you want me to come back?" I glanced at the mess.

He shook his head. "There's method in this madness, I assure you. I know where everything is. If I move any of it, I may never find it again."

"I guess that makes sense. So, what did you want to see me about?" My tone was colder than I'd intended, getting a curious look from Alton.

He nodded toward a small table—the only one that wasn't covered in folders and files. A golden disc sat in the center, glowing steadily. I approached it with caution, not knowing if it might suddenly explode, given my track record with magical items. It reminded me of a computer's loading animation, the light swirling around and around the golden circle in a loop. I could've stared at it all day, it was so mesmerizing.

"Is this the medallion?" I asked.

"It is."

"Is it working?"

His expression darkened. "I've performed the required spell, but the result isn't as instantaneous as I might've liked. It could have something to do with the Suppressor, or the fact that this particular medallion has been offline for some time. Either way, it seems the medallion is scanning for the whereabouts of Katherine's associates, looking for their coordinates. When one is in the vicinity, if I'm right, it should light up and give us the location."

"How long will that take?"

"Your guess is as good as mine."

I frowned at him. "I don't know if I'm missing something here, but that doesn't explain why you called me to your office."

He chuckled. "I thought you and I might have a bit of a chat, away from the Rag Team. They'll no doubt presume I'm showing you the results of the unification spell, which gives us the perfect cover to discuss your last few trips through the mirrors. I thought you might prefer it this way, instead of me announcing it in front of them."

"I had a feeling that's what you wanted to talk to me about," I muttered, feeling sheepish. I was in the wrong here, too. "To be honest, I'm surprised we didn't have this discussion earlier. I knew you must've known about it—it's not as if people can just wander about this place without you knowing what they're up to, right? Since you didn't say anything, I figured you must've had your reasons for letting me get away with it."

"Like the Reykjavik information, you mean?"

I shrugged. "It helped, didn't it?" I was bordering on belligerent, but that was just my embarrassment talking. I'd been caught with my hands in the cookie jar, and there was no wriggling free of this one. Time to face the music and dance.

"You got lucky," he corrected.

"Pretty handy fluke, though, you've got to admit?"

"Like I said, you got lucky. If Salinger had thoroughly read the documents he sent through, chances are he would never have allowed us to have them," Alton said firmly. "The New York Coven doesn't want us to succeed in this. They've got their popcorn at the ready, eager to watch us fail in our mission. By going there and not informing me of it, you could have jeopardized this part of the investigation. We might never have managed to get our hands on this intel."

I sighed and sat down in one of the armchairs. "So, you're pissed at me—is that it? Do I get a slap on the wrist?" *I'm pissed at you too.*

"I'm not angry with you, Harley, but I *am* disappointed that you didn't come to me first. That is what I'm trying to get through to you. If you had spoken to me before you went through the mirrors, I would have given you my approval. I would've understood entirely. Heck, I might've even helped you," he replied. *Where have I heard this before?* Wade popped into my head, the words almost identical to what he'd said to me. "As for not broaching the subject earlier, I've been waiting in the hopes that you might come clean to me. I wanted you to, but you have forced my hand."

I stared at the swirling disc, unable to take my eyes off it. "I'm sorry about not coming to you before I went to New York and Purgatory, but I didn't think you'd understand why I wanted to go. I thought you'd try and talk me out of it, and then where'd we be? That information from Reykjavik only came through because of what I did, and Salinger probably didn't read the documents because he was too embarrassed about the state he was in when I met with him. I wouldn't be surprised if he just sent them on in case I told you about it. Plus, I was worried you might try to stop me from visiting my parents' Grimoire. Everyone gets a little weird about it, as though I might lose it completely."

"Are you talking about your first visit to the Grimoire or the second?" he asked, with a knowing look.

I grimaced. "I had to see it that first time, Alton. It was like a compulsion."

"That's what worries me."

"Why? Why does it keep worrying everyone? Isn't it perfectly natural to want to see something that belonged to your loved ones?"

He smiled. "Of course it is, but you aren't like normal people, Harley. You can't just do these reckless things without thinking properly about the consequences."

"What consequences?" I asked innocently, testing the waters of his knowledge. Clearly, he had guessed I'd snuck into Special Collections on that first visit and stolen a glance at my parents' Grimoire. He could read me like a book. He knew I'd spoken with Salinger and that information had been gathered about the Merlins and the Shiptons. Those folders had been passed on to him by Wade. But did he know what I'd done when I saw that Grimoire for the first time? I doubted it, though a spike of fear hit me regardless.

I'd thought about going the Erebus route to find out more about the

Children of Chaos, and how Katherine might use them for her own ends, but the prospect of actually summoning him was way too deadly. He'd take a life if I did, and I wasn't about to have that resting on my conscience.

"Fortunately for us, there were no consequences to your visits," he said. "However, what I'm trying to say is, there *might* have been. We still don't know the limits of your abilities. Anything might have happened while you were in there with your parents' Grimoire. It could have had a nasty effect on your affinities, or even on your general well-being. I have heard of people falling sick after just touching certain Grimoires."

So, he didn't know about the whole summoning thing, or my ability to read unfinished Grimoires. I heaved out a sigh of relief, knowing that was a good sign. Regardless, I wasn't about to talk to him about it now. There were some things I couldn't come clean about—not to him, anyway. After all, I was still scared that he might send for the men in white coats and have them lock me up for having too much power. It'd be "for my own good" no doubt, just to add the cherry on top of the crippling-terror cake.

"Well, you don't have to worry because both visits went just fine," I said coolly.

"Are you sure about that?"

I nodded. "Positive."

"You put Santana at risk, too. If you'd been caught, it would have been her reputation on the line as well."

"She insisted on coming along," I replied quietly. "It wasn't like I invited her. She wanted to keep me safe, that's all. She's nice like that."

"Nevertheless, if anything had happened, you could have risked her life as well as your own. I do think it a little suspect that she Purged so violently, so soon after returning from New York with you. You didn't have any part to play in that, did you?"

My mind jumped toward the first lie it could find. "I made her use her abilities to trick Salinger. She didn't want to, but I forced her into it. I'm not proud of it, but I was desperate to see that book, and I didn't think the New York Coven would let me if I applied. Anyway, it looked like a pretty draining spell—maybe that's what tipped her over the edge." *Wow, Harley, way to throw your pal under the bus.* I hoped that, by laying the blame on me and telling Alton that I made her do it, I might take some of the heat off Santana.

He tutted. "You can't do whatever you feel like, without thinking of the outcomes first. You understand that, don't you?"

"Please don't go all Spiderman on me."

He frowned. "I don't follow?"

"With great power comes great responsibility, right? I know that. I really do know that. It's just that, when it came to seeing that Grimoire, I couldn't help myself. I had to know what was in those pages. Nothing else seemed to matter." I took a shallow breath. "I know that sounds selfish and stupid, but I don't have anything of my parents. I wanted to be close to something that had belonged to them, you know? Does that make sense?" I wanted to confront him about his ruling on my father's death, but I swallowed the words. What good would it do now? It'd only make him more 'disappointed.'

The weight of the pendant around my neck gave me some fleeting comfort. Now, I had a replica of a Merlin heirloom, something close to my family. Still, it wasn't quite the same. I'd have exchanged it in a heartbeat for that Grimoire.

"It does make sense, Harley, though you have to assure me that you've learned your lesson. If you can't be trusted with the freedom of this place, including the mirrors, then certain restraints may have to be placed on you."

I nodded slowly. "I've learned my lesson, Alton."

"Is that why you stole a spell from Special Collections and used it to repair your Esprit?" he asked.

I gaped at him. "How do you—"

"Tobe traced a glitch in the Bestiary circuit back to the Luis Paoletti Room, where I found the remnants of a reparation spell. An old one, at that—ancient and powerful. There's only one place that has spells of that magnitude, and that is the New York Special Collections."

"Okay, so I've learned my lesson *now*." Guilt twisted in my stomach. I'd caused that glitch.

"Fortunately for you, that blast wasn't the cause of the disruption," he said.

"It wasn't?"

"No—that was caused by our reptilian escapee," he replied. "However, *this* is what I mean about consequences. You can't steal spells and hope for the best, not without speaking to someone first. I could've told you that the power surge of your Esprit stones reconnecting would have been immense, but you didn't think to ask."

"I spoke to Imogene," I murmured. "She told me to look for the spell, and she didn't mention anything like this could happen."

"Well, you ought to have double-checked with me first. Old spells can be very temperamental."

Relief and guilt sparked through my veins. I hadn't caused the blast, but I'd still gone against the rules, and I definitely hadn't checked in with Alton.

"It's not as if I had any other option, though," I said. "I'm sorry for stealing the spell, and I'm sorry for not coming to you about it first, but you didn't offer me any suggestions about fixing it. In fact, when I showed you the damage, you told me I'd have to train with Nomura until an Esprit repairer could be sourced for an Esprit like mine. No timescale, no cost; you just said I'd have to wait indefinitely. Do you have any idea what it's like to be told that, when you're already waiting to have a damn Suppressor taken out of you? It didn't exactly fill me with hope."

I thought he was going to yell at me but, instead, his expression softened. "That is my error, Harley. I should have realized how exasperating all of this must have been for you. You're right; when you came to me with your broken Esprit, I didn't give you much to go on. I should've done more. However, that doesn't—"

"It doesn't excuse my behavior. I know. I really am sorry for the trouble I've caused, but I needed to fix this Esprit, almost as much as I needed to see that Grimoire."

He glanced at the jewelry on my hand, his brows pinching together in a frown. "Has it changed color or do my eyes deceive me?"

"No, they've changed color," I admitted. After all, with him in a generous mood, I figured he might be able to help me. "They're new stones, but they're darker than they were before I started the spell. The Air and the Earth stones, anyway."

"Oh, dear…"

"You think I'm crossing over to the Dark side, Vader-style?"

He smiled tightly. "It would suggest that the way you conducted the reparation spell has tipped the balance slightly, though I don't suppose you'll feel it much with the Suppressor still working away inside you. Indeed, you probably drew more upon your Dark affinity to fix the stones into place, which has caused this… and likely those two huge blasts, also."

"Can I do anything to get the two sides back in balance?"

"This is near-untrodden territory, Harley," he said thoughtfully. "Although I recall reading about one spell, some years ago now. It was a Sanguine spell, if memory serves. A terrible business, but it had something to do with combining powerful Light and powerful Dark to restore equilibrium. Preceptor Nomura is the expert on this, rather than me. He is familiar with Suppressors and their various quirks, and I believe he's studied extensively in Sanguine spells."

My curiosity was piqued. "Equilibrium is exactly what I need…"

"I'm not saying that such spells should ever be attempted, mind you. The Sanguine spells are banned for a reason. In fact, I shouldn't have mentioned it at all. I don't even know where you'd find a spell like that these days. They've likely all been destroyed, which is a good thing if you ask me. Terrible, awful spells. Yes, good riddance."

He covered himself quickly, evidently realizing he'd said too much to the girl who broke rules for breakfast. So, Nomura was the one to speak to—he was the one who might be able to tell me how I could use Light and Dark to fix the division inside me, once the Suppressor was broken and all hell broke loose within me. This little tidbit was way more valuable than Alton understood. Now, all I had to do was get Nomura to spill a few beans.

It gave me a renewed sense of hope, though it also made me more afraid of what breaking the Suppressor might mean for me. If these Sanguine spells were banned, then what if I couldn't get my hands on one? What if I couldn't fix the divide? Even so, I was determined not to live within the artificial bounds I'd been given. In the fight against Katherine, we needed all the power we could get. With the Suppressor gone and my affinities living in harmony, I could become our not-so-secret weapon against her. I just had to decipher what Alton was leaving out.

Sanguine... that's to do with blood, right? So, what Alton was trying really hard not to let slip was that the blood of a Light magical and the blood of a Dark magical might somehow fix the mess that the Suppressor would leave behind. That was my guess, anyway. Like Alton had alluded, Nomura could clear up a few of these aspects for me. If I went in there all confident, with this information already under my belt, maybe he'd be more inclined to give me the rest of the information that I wanted to hear.

"Yeah, you're right," I said. "That sounds awful. Blood makes me squeamish."

He gawked at me. "Blood? Who said anything about blood?"

"Isn't that what Sanguine is about?"

"Ah… I see. Yes, very astute. Not that you should trouble yourself over it."

"Anyway, I really am sorry about using the mirrors without your permission. It was wrong of me to do that stuff without telling you. It won't happen again, I promise." Well, I half-promised. Me disobeying the rules was wholly circumstantial.

"I won't be so lenient on you again, if I discover that you've done something like this after today—is that clear?"

I nodded. "As crystal. Although you're not really one to lecture me on leniency." The words tumbled out before I could stop them, and I'd been doing so well, keeping my emotions back.

"Excuse me?"

Well, you've done it now. "What you told me about my dad's execution. That wasn't exactly true, was it?"

His face paled. "No... No, it wasn't."

"I just want to know why you lied, that's all."

He exhaled heavily. "I... I didn't want you to turn away from the coven, just because of a mistake I made so long ago. I was younger then, and more foolish. I listened to those around me, and made a judgment based on the opinions of others."

"He could've lived if you'd voted another way." I held on to my emotions, refusing to cry. My anger thrummed through my veins.

"I know, and I'll forever be sorry for that. I didn't know he was cursed. I did what I thought was best, so he couldn't hurt anyone else. Hardly anyone breaks out of Purgatory, but he had Katherine Shipton on his side. She was a snake, even then—slithering out of danger." He paused, his shoulders sagging. "If I apologize now, it would seem insincere, especially in light of what you discovered—the tattoo and punctures on his neck. However, I really am sorry for not telling you the truth. Would you believe me if I said I was ashamed?"

I stared at him in surprise. I hadn't expected that. I'd expected defensiveness and denial, not an apology like this. "I... uh, I think I would. It wouldn't change how I feel, though."

"I know that, but I would still ask that you believe my words. I am more ashamed than you know, and if I could change the past, I would. But none of us can do that, Harley. We must all live with the choices we have made." He looked genuinely upset, confusing my brain. "Still, I *am* sorry—for what I did, and for the lie that I told. I hope that you may find it in your heart to forgive me."

I swallowed hard. "Do you... Do you understand how painful it is, to know that he could've been saved if one vote had swung the other way —*your* vote?"

He nodded, pursing his lips.

I shook my head. "No, you can't. It's like having him snatched away, all over again. And it's even worse, now that we know he really was cursed. He could've lived, Alton. He could've lived if you'd just..."

He dipped his head. "I will apologize as often as I must, to get you to forgive me. I ask only one thing of you. Please don't leave the coven because of this. I lied, and that was wrong of me, but this place is your home now. That is what I wanted for you. If I had told you the truth... who knows where you might be."

"You deceived me," I said.

"I did it for your benefit, though my apology remains," he replied.

A mixture of emotions coursed through me. I couldn't forgive him, not yet—maybe not ever—but he was right about one thing. This place was my home, and his lie couldn't change that now. The SDC was embedded in my heart, and it would hurt like hell to break away now. My friends were here. Wade was here. *Very clever, Alton.* Maybe he knew I'd find out one day, but he wanted it to be a time when I was settled. A time when I couldn't leave.

"Just understand that things have changed," I said stiffly.

He nodded. "I understand. I can't blame you for your anger."

"You shouldn't have lied."

"No, I shouldn't."

"Do you accept responsibility for his death?" My eyes narrowed.

"I do. I bear it each day."

I cleared my throat. "Then maybe, one day, I'll find it in my heart to forgive you. Just not now. I can't do that now. It's still too fresh."

"I understand."

A tense silence stretched between us, neither of us knowing what to say. I scanned the room, desperate for a way to break it. He'd apologized, which didn't fix everything, but it was a good start. Yes, it'd warped my image of him, and knocked him off his pedestal, but did that make him a bad guy overall? No, probably not. He'd made a terrible mistake, but he wanted to repent for it.

I looked at the golden medallion, finding my icebreaker. I was still angry and bitter, but that wasn't going to help anyone right now, not with Quetzi on the loose.

"What about the beacons?" I muttered. "There really hasn't been anything at all?"

"There really hasn't. I'll send word to you as soon as they've found the whereabouts of Katherine's people," he answered. "It looks as though it may take some time to discover every coordinate, as they don't appear for long."

"Okay, I'll get back to finding Quetzi then." I was eager to get out of there.

"Any luck there?"

I shook my head. "Not yet."

"Keep me updated."

"I will, and thank you for not coming down hard on me about the Grimoire thing," I said, with a shy smile. "I mean it when I say I'm sorry. I've been on my own for so long that I sometimes forget what it's like to be part of a team."

"Just don't do it again, Harley. The mirrors aren't out of bounds, but don't abuse them—that's all I ask." He cast me a sorrowful look. "And, for what it's worth, I'm sorry too. I really would change it if I could."

"Thank you," I said quietly, pushing back tears. "I won't do it again."

"Then you can go." He nodded toward the door, before his eyes turned to fix on the swirling light of the gold medallion as I exited the room. Stepping back out into the hallway, it hit me how strange it was that he hadn't revoked my permission to use the mirrors. In fact, it made me wonder if he *wanted* me to follow my gut and do what instinct led me to do, since it had worked pretty well for us up to now. I'd have to test the waters at a later date. Either that, or I'd made him feel bad enough not to revoke my pass. Right now, there was a serpent on the loose and it had my name on it. *Now then, Quetzi, I've got a bone to pick with you.*

FOURTEEN

Harley

I pushed through the enormous doors of the Bestiary, having bypassed the security personnel who were still recovering from the madness of the earlier commotion. I'd texted the Rag Team to find out where they were and received one reply saying "Bestiary" from Santana, so I'd expected to find all of them there. But Santana sat alone on the edge of one of the glass boxes. She looked up as I entered, a nervous smile on her face. *Ah, the Thelma to my Louise.*

"How did it go?" she asked. "Was it the beacons?"

"Kind of. He did the spell, but we're still waiting on the results," I explained, joining her up on the side of the box. "He actually wanted to talk to me about the mirrors, and the way I've been using them with reckless abandon." I nudged her shoulder, trying to lighten the mood. She was anxious; I could feel it cascading off her in shivery waves that set my own nerves to jittering.

"Is he mad?"

I shook my head. "Nope, he's just disappointed. Typical father figure."

"Does he know that I was with you?"

"He does, but I told him you only came with me to make sure I was safe. Oh, and he also knows that you did a spell to trick Salinger. I told him I made you do it, but I only mentioned it to cover your intense Purge straight afterwards. He was asking too many questions about it, and I didn't want to mention the summoning thing in case he freaked out." I cast a sideways glance at her. "I'm sorry for bringing you into this, and I'm sorry I had to lie. I know that reading out of the Grimoire was my own fault, and I shouldn't make you suffer for it. I just panicked and didn't know what else to say to him about it."

She laughed. "That's some impressive quick thinking, Harley. I'd have buckled at the first sign of an interrogation with Alton. Flash a light in my face and ask where I was at two o'clock yesterday and I'd spill every secret I've ever heard."

"You sure you're not mad?"

"Why would I be? You didn't ask me to come to New York with you. I made you take me with you. I'm as much at fault for what happened that day as you are—we're in this together, *mi hermana*, whether you like it or not." This time, she nudged me. "I'm just happy it's all out in the open with Alton, aside from the whole summoning thing. Every time I see him, I've been having damned palpitations, thinking he's going to bring the whole Spanish Inquisition down on me. Now, I don't have to worry about it anymore. The air has been cleared, the demons have been exorcised, and this house is clean."

I chuckled. "I'm still sorry for dragging you into my secrets."

"As long as you're not going through them alone, I'm happy to be part of them."

"Thanks, Santana," I said, buoyed up on her positivity. "Anyway, where are the others? I thought you'd all be here to find out what Alton had to say."

She shook her head. "They got bored and went off to carry on the wild Quetzi hunt."

"Any leads?"

"None yet, though sitting in here waiting for you has given me a bit of an idea," she replied, looking from box to box. "What if we used my Purge beast as a lead? I mean, I'm no monster expert, but what if these two serpents were like snakes of a feather? They look the same, more or less. Mine is just on the small side. Then again, who's to say that Quetzi wasn't a tiny little snake when he was first Purged?"

I stared at her. "You're a genius, Santana Catemaco!"

"You think it'll work?"

"I think it's a better idea than following a vague outline of a shadow to nowhere in particular," I replied. "Smartie is an incredible piece of technology, but that shadow could've been anything. But this—*this* I can get on board with."

"Harley and Santana, the queens of *loco* ideas."

"Nothing else I'd rather be queen of," I said with a grin.

With that, we hopped down off the edge of the glass box and went in search of Tobe. We found him in one of the back halls, dealing with the sleeping figures that had fallen foul of the Ibong Adarna. It had been several hours since her song had knocked them out, and they were still snoozing. This wasn't her gilded hall, but it looked like her chaotic brand of birdsong had carried pretty far before Wade and I had managed to apprehend her. The poor Beast Master looked exhausted, though he scooped each sleeping human into his arms as if they weighed no more than a child. Part of me wondered what it might be like to be carried by Tobe, awakening a vague memory of someone carrying me out of a car in the dead of night, and tucking me up in my bed. I couldn't have been older than three, but the tactile memory was a new one. *Did my dad do that, when we were on the run?* It was the only explanation I could think of.

"Harley, Santana, how lovely to see you again so soon," Tobe said, unyielding in his politeness. "I thought you were joining the quest to capture Quetzi? I'd hate to think of the mischief he might cause if he manages to escape the coven altogether."

Santana and I exchanged a look. "Actually, that's why we're here," I replied. "Santana had an idea of how we might find Quetzi."

She nodded. "Yeah, I was hoping we could borrow my Purge beast for a little while, to see if my feathery serpent can't sniff out its big bro. I mean, gargoyles get friendly with other gargoyles, right? So, why wouldn't a serpent be able to find the location of another one of its kind?"

"It is much too dangerous," Tobe warned. "Your Purge beast might be small, but it's feisty."

"We can handle feisty," Santana replied, with a wink. "It's in my blood."

He tapped his chin in thought. "I suppose you might borrow it for a short time, if you listen to my instructions *very* carefully, and keep your eyes on the beast at all times. However, the last thing we need is another feathered serpent on the loose, especially as we do not know your beast's abilities as of yet. It's only a juvenile, though there is potential in what I have seen."

"Weather potential, like the weather magic Quetzi can do? Storms, rains, tornados—that kind of stuff?" I asked.

"That remains to be seen."

"So, how do we take little Fido out for a walk then?" Santana pressed, her eyes alight with excitement. I could tell how much she adored the beast that had come out of her. After the incident, it had taken her a couple of days to actually come down here and visit it, but once she had, she'd fallen in love. It really was like some kind of warped puppy to her, which was both cute and unsettling to watch. Then again, I supposed she liked the unusual things in life, Raffe being the main one.

The two of them practically smoldered whenever they were near each other, though thankfully they kept their PDAs to a minimum. I'd walked in on one of their smooch-fests while looking for a book in one of the reading rooms, but they'd been too busy to notice me and I hadn't breathed a word of it out of sheer embarrassment. Still, it was nice to see that they were progressing, even if it did give me a pang of envy. I wanted to be the one smooching in the reading room, without a care in the world, oblivious to anyone who walked in. I wanted to smolder next to Wade every time I stood beside him, instead of being a bumbling idiot who could barely get her words out. *You got a hug, Harley... baby steps are good, too.*

"I will show you," Tobe replied, leading us back through the Bestiary toward the glass box where Santana's Purge beast was kept. It was close to Quetzi's, making his absence all the stranger—why hadn't the little serpent gotten out, too?

The little feathered serpent, who had yet to be given a name, slithered up to the glass and flicked its forked tongue against the interior. Its eyes lit up as it saw Santana, its scales shivering in excitement. It definitely seemed as though the feeling was mutual—the beastie loved Santana as much as she loved it. She smiled down at it and ran her fingertips along the glass, the serpent chasing them happily, its body wriggling across the ground. I had to admit, it was cute.

"This is a Purge cord." Tobe pulled a length of flaxen rope out from under his left wing. "I will lasso this around the beast's neck. As soon as it has been pulled tight, it will remain in place until I remove it. It causes no harm to the creature, but make sure you keep hold of it at all times. This beast may appear sweet-natured, but there is cunning in all serpents."

Santana nodded. "Don't let go—got it."

"Very succinct." Tobe opened the door of the glass box and lunged inside. His strong arms wrangled with the serpent for a moment, before sliding the lassoed rope around its neck. He made it look improbably easy, as though he were merely snatching up a guinea pig for a bunch of kids to pet. Like a magnet pulling against metal, the cord fixed in place, unmoving as it attached itself to the serpent's scales.

Tobe led the beast out into the main aisle of the Bestiary, drawing the jealous stares of all the other creatures, still trapped inside their boxes. I wondered if Tobe ever walked any of them whenever the rest of the coven went to bed, giving them a bit of evening exercise. The image tickled me.

"Can I hold it?" Santana squeaked.

"You may—but, as I said, please do not let go of the rope," Tobe said.

"Thank you!" She reached out for the cord and took it in her hand, wrapping the excess around her wrist to make sure the serpent couldn't go slithering off without her say-so. I'd never seen her more excited, a broad grin fixed on her face. "Who needs a pug when you can have a feathered serpent?"

I laughed. "It suits you."

"Makes me look hella Mexican, right?"

"Your mom would be so proud."

"Ah, man, I'd totally take a selfie of this if I didn't think she'd cut me out of the family for dishonoring our ancestors. It might not be *the* Quetzalcoatl, but it'd be close enough to get a smack on the ass at the very least."

Before she could say another word, the Purge beast tugged hard against the leash. It wanted to head toward the main doors of the Bestiary. Seeing it strain against the rope, I leaned over and picked up a couple of Mason jars and a cluster of capturing stones that had been left out by the security personnel. Armed and ready, I smiled as Santana turned to me with a giddy shrug, the two of us hurrying behind the snake as we let it do its thing, like a serpent version of a water diviner. Only, we weren't looking for a spring; we were looking for a bigger serpent. That part of the process kind of worried me, but we'd have to cross that scary bridge when we came to it.

We sprinted through the coven corridors, turning endless lefts and rights along the labyrinthine layout, until my lungs began to burn, and my legs hurt. Santana did what she could to slow the serpent down, gripping the rope tighter in her hands and using her bodyweight to brace backward, but the serpent showed no signs of slowing. Its forked tongue flicked eagerly at the air, as though tasting something we couldn't.

On and on it pulled, leading us up to a strange panel in the side of the corridor wall. It headbutted the solid exterior with gentle thuds, determined to get to whatever lay beyond it. I couldn't see any hint of a lock or a secret button or anything, but Santana appeared to know how these things worked. Resting her palm flat on the side of the panel, she muttered a few words I couldn't understand, and the whole thing shifted to one side. Beyond it lay a concealed stairwell, a gust of ice-cold air spiraling up from the wrought-iron steps. The railings were covered in thick cobwebs and a blanket of fluffy gray dust that looked like it had been gathering for years.

My boots left crisp footprints on each rung as we made our way down into the underbelly of the coven, following the serpent on its unusual route. If this beast really was taking us to Quetzi, then at least now we knew how he'd managed to avoid the cameras. He'd used the secret passageways that no doubt littered this place, utilizing them to keep himself hidden from view.

"Stop!" I called out, as we pushed through an identical panel at the opposite end of the stairwell. I recognized this corridor, though it'd been a long time since I'd visited the subterranean world that lay beneath the coven. The dingy walls and clinical strip lighting were unmistakable, as were the metal-barred rooms on either side of the hallway. We were in the basement of the coven, where the prison cells were located.

"What's up?" Santana asked, fighting to keep her beast from slithering off.

"Why are we down here?" I looked around, expecting to see the usual contingent of security guards. Instead, the corridor was silent and empty. Not a mouse stirred. I guessed they'd all been called to help capture the escaped monsters, with it being DEFCON 1 and all.

"We might find Quetzi. I figured we should check everywhere."

I shook my head. "Why's it so quiet?"

"You're right... it is quiet," she murmured, switching to high alert. "Let's follow Slinky and see where he takes us."

I arched an eyebrow. "Slinky?"

"Cool name, don't you think? It just came to me."

"Very fitting."

Keeping our wits about us, we followed Slinky halfway down the hallway, until he stopped at the door to a cell that I recognized—one of the only occupied ones down here. The cell of Adley de la Barthe. While Santana battled with Slinky's fierce strength, I approached the cell door and peered inside. The lights were all off, casting a dense shadow across the room within. *Okay, something's definitely not right.* Tentatively, I pushed on the door. It swung wide without any force at all, creaking on its hinges as it gave way.

Lifting my hands, I forged a ball of bright fire and set it in the air above us, letting it hover there temporarily. The powerful glow cast its light across the cell, chasing away the shadows to reveal a terrifying sight. I clamped my free hand across my mouth to silence a scream as my gaze settled on a shape at the far side of the room, next to Adley's bed. A giant, freshly-shed snakeskin lay coiled on the floor, the gossamer material draped across the pale and staring face of Adley herself. It gave the impression of a horrifying mask, stretched across her features. Meanwhile, her body lay still, her chest no longer rising and falling with breath.

She was dead.

"*Dios mio*," Santana whispered, her eyes wide with shock. Neither of us needed to check her pulse. It was clear to both of us that she wasn't about to wake up. Ever. Her eyes were open and unblinking, all the color drained from her face.

"Oh, Adley," I murmured, sinking down to her side. I didn't dare touch her in case this place needed to be swept for clues. The giant snakeskin was a dead giveaway, but even that felt wrong somehow. I couldn't put my finger on what seemed amiss, but it gnawed away at the back of my mind like a determined woodpecker.

"What should we do?"

I stared down at Adley's dead body, feeling tears prick my eyes. No matter what she'd done, she didn't deserve this. Love had made her behave badly, but she wasn't a bad person. "You should take Slinky back up to the Bestiary. I'll call Alton and wait for him here."

"Are you sure? It can be uncomfortable to wait around the dead if you're not used to them. I don't mind staying here."

I shook my head. "I'll be okay. You get Slinky back to Tobe, and then come back here."

"Okay. I won't be long. If you start to feel cold or you see anything odd, don't panic—it's perfectly natural when a spirit is on its way out. I'll be back by your side before you can say 'what the freaking hell is going on in this place,' I promise," Santana insisted, before hurrying out of the room, dragging Slinky after her. The poor creature seemed much less eager to make the return trip.

With shaking hands, I lifted my phone out of my pocket and dialed Alton's number. He picked up on the second ring, his tone abrupt. "What is it? Have you found Quetzi?"

"No… not quite."

"What do you mean?"

"You need to get down to the prison cells right now," I explained, my voice trembling. "Adley is dead. She's been murdered."

A long pause followed. "I'll be down as quickly as I can," he said, at last. "Don't move her, okay?"

"Can you bring her back?" Tears trickled down my cheeks.

"I won't know until I get there," he replied calmly. "Now, hold on. I won't be long."

He hung up, leaving me alone in the cell with nothing but Adley's body and a giant snakeskin for company. I glanced over my shoulder, scared of every shadow, in case Quetzi was still hiding amongst them, blending into the background. Looking forward was just as unsettling. Adley's body was creepy and beautiful, all at the same time. She looked sad, her eyes glittering, her mouth turned down in sorrow.

Were you scared, Adley? Did you see what was coming for you before it took you?

My heart broke for her. All of this was Finch's fault. He'd led her to this, and I doubted he'd even care when he found out. He'd made his loyalties very clear, and Adley barely featured, even after all the sacrifices she'd made for him.

"I'm so sorry, Adley," I sobbed, wanting to reach out to take her cold, dead hand. She'd ended up like this because she fell in love with the wrong man. Love made her foolish, the same way it was making me stupid.

A glint caught my eye. A white object lay underneath the darkness of the bed, catching the glow of the fire orb above. Frowning, I carefully arched across Adley's body and picked up the item. As I turned it over in my hand, I realized it was a fang—long and pearly white, slightly curved with a sharp point. A snake's fang. Slipping it in my pocket, I made a mental note to give it to Astrid, to study further. She could find out almost anything using Smartie, and I wanted to know what the significance of this was. Did serpents leave their fangs as a sign of victory? Did they shed them along with their skins? I had to know why Quetzi had done this—and in forensics, teeth never lied.

Alton appeared at the doorway to the prison cell. He was breathing heavily, his hair messed up, his eyes carrying a haunted look. Without saying a word, he closed the gap between us and bent down, scooping Adley into his arms like Sleeping Beauty. Her body was limp in his grasp, her head lolling until he cradled it against his arm.

"Can you help her?" I asked, my voice catching in my throat.

He shook his head slowly. "It's too late. I got here too late." The words sent an eerie shiver up my spine.

"What do you mean?" I asked.

"Some spirits leave the body quicker than others. It varies from person to person. For some, it can take twenty-four hours; for others it can be a matter of a couple of hours. I've heard of some spirits leaving within ten minutes of death, before they're even cold. Adley is already gone."

My heart sank. "Then what will you do with her?"

"I'll take her to the infirmary and send security down."

"Isn't it too late for that?"

He sighed heavily, his shoulders sagging. "I can't help her, but I will see that she is treated with care as they perform a postmortem examination. She deserves that much. Indeed, she deserves so much more than this fate," he said, his voice strained. "I am sorry, Adley. I am so sorry."

"I found this," I said, lifting the fang. "Do you think it's important?"

He frowned, his voice choked. "We'll find out once the postmortem has taken place. If Quetzi did this, then that fang may be our murder weapon."

He turned and left with her in his arms before I could see a single tear fall from his eyes. Nevertheless, I could sense his heartbreaking guilt. This had happened under his watch and he hadn't been able to stop it. No matter what Adley had done, she'd been a fixture of this coven for a long time, before her crimes were discovered. She'd been a colleague of Alton's, if not a dear friend. True, she had kept secrets, but she hadn't known of Finch's true self. She'd been just as fooled as the rest of us.

Now, she was dead, and we had a killer snake on the loose.

FIFTEEN

Harley

———————

F eeling like I owed it to Adley, I loitered in the mortuary with Dr. Krieger while he performed the first stages of the post-mortem examination on her. A simple overview for now, though the grisly stuff would come later. She looked so still and almost peaceful on the slab, but the image haunted me. It was impossible to look at her and think she'd never do anything again. A few hours ago, her heart had been beating and there'd been breath in her lungs. Now, nothing so much as flinched.

Dr. Krieger moved around her, performing the procedure with dexterity and a gentle touch. I couldn't bring myself to watch him work, but I stayed close by, keeping my back turned. I didn't know how to explain it, but I wasn't ready to leave her alone. She'd died on her own—the least I could do was stay by her side at the very end.

"This is very puzzling," Krieger murmured to himself.

I glanced at him. "What is?"

"Well… you told me that you found a fang at the murder site, yes?"

I nodded.

"There are no puncture wounds from fangs on her body, and she doesn't seem to show any signs of constriction. I will run some tests to see if I can find poison in her veins or discover any damage to her internal organs that might suggest constriction, but this is a rather strange case if a serpent is supposed to have killed her."

My phone buzzed before I could ask any more questions. "Hold that thought; I'll be right back." With an apologetic glance to Krieger, I exited into the hallway outside the morgue. "Wade? What's up?"

"Where are you?"

"In the infirmary with Adley."

He was silent for a moment. "Are you okay?"

"I don't know. I guess."

"If you're busy, then that's fine, but we've had an arrival at the coven," he said.

"An arrival?"

"The security details that Alton sent out to visit the beacon sites are on their way back, and they're bringing the kids with them. They found them, Harley," he explained hurriedly.

Not long after we'd found Adley, the golden medallion had located the beacons of Katherine's associates. Several teams had been sent out as soon as the beacons started flashing. I was disappointed that we hadn't been allowed to go along, to rescue them, but Alton had insisted we stay inside the coven and recover from the Adley incident. I'd tried to argue, but he wasn't having any of it. Now, it seemed they'd found what they were looking for. *Taking the rough with the smooth, I guess.* Adley had supposedly been murdered by Quetzi, but the magical kids were on their way toward safety. Everything in warped balance. Still, I wished I could have been there to pick them up and bring them back, the way I'd promised myself I would.

"I'll join you," I said. Adley was in good hands with Dr. Krieger, and I didn't think I could be here when he started cracking her chest open. That was a step too far, even for my goodwill gesture. Plus, he'd know more when I got back.

"You sure? We can manage without you, if you want to stay there. I just thought you should know what was going on."

I shook my head, though he couldn't see me. "We've been waiting for this moment, and I need some good news. I'll be down in a few minutes. Where are they being dropped off?"

"The foyer of the Fleet Science Center," he replied.

"Have they been checked over, to make sure they're not bringing any vicious Shipton-style juju with them?"

"The security team aren't idiots, Harley. Yes, they've been checked. They got the all clear."

I smiled with excitement. "Hey, I was just checking. This is still Katherine we're talking about."

"They're fine, Harley. They're fine and they're on their way here."

"Okay, I'll see you in a bit," I said.

"See you then."

I hung up and poked my head through the mortuary door, flinching as a spatter of blood spurted from Krieger's first incision. "The Rag Team needs me downstairs. If you find anything, let us know."

"She'd be grateful for you staying by her side for this long," he replied kindly. "However, I was already going to suggest you make yourself scarce before the messy part begins. It won't be a pleasant sight."

"Take good care of her, Dr. Krieger."

He smiled. "I will, Harley."

I ducked back out of the mortuary and headed for the foyer of the Fleet Science Center. It was already late in the day, having just passed seven o'clock, meaning the Center would be closed to the public. Any outsiders would probably think a private school trip had arrived or something, though they'd be smuggled inside before anyone could look too closely. My heart leapt into my throat as I envisioned the missing magicals, finally coming home after weeks in Katherine's grasp. It was as exciting as it was frightening, considering Katherine's eventual reaction to us taking them back. She wasn't going to be happy about it, that was for sure. *Well, she can suck it, because she isn't snatching them again. No way.*

The rest of the Rag Team was gathered in the glass atrium of the Center's entrance hall, standing around anxiously, their eyes fixed on the revolving doors. Nobody else from the coven was here, meaning that Alton had decided to keep the children's arrival a secret. The fewer people who knew about this, the better. After all, we still had a spy on the loose. I joined the rest of my team, sensing the mixture of emotions that radiated off each person. Nerves, anticipation, fear, excitement, and an undercurrent of relief. I shared in the cocktail of feelings, fidgeting as we waited.

"How is everything up there?" Wade asked solemnly, as he came to stand at my side.

"Sad, grim, depressing, horrible," I replied.

"Does Dr. Krieger know how she died yet?"

I shook my head. "Inconclusive right now. He's puzzled because there aren't any bite marks or bruises, even though I found that fang, but he's still running tests. Bloodwork is next, I think, although he was about to start delving into her innards when I left."

"I don't know if I could watch that. It's weird when it's someone you knew, isn't it?"

"Really weird." I glanced over at Astrid, reminded of the fang in my pocket. "Can you give me a minute? I need to speak to Astrid."

He nodded. "Sure."

I hurried over to her, pulling her to one side. The kids would be here soon, and I didn't want to muddy the waters by asking her to look into the fang when they arrived. They'd be freaked out enough, being brought here by a bunch of burly security officers. I didn't want to make it worse by talking about killer serpents and murdered prisoners with them around.

"Astrid? Can I talk to you about something?" I asked.

She frowned. "What's up? Is it Adley? I heard what happened."

"You know that fang I found in her cell, under the bed?"

"Yes."

"I was wondering if you could look into this for me," I replied, pulling out the fang and handing it to her. "I don't know if it fell out of Quetzi's mouth or what, but I was hoping you could run some checks on it and see if we might be able to use it to track him. Plus, it might be useful to see if there's any reference to this kind of thing in the book of ancient serpents… if that exists?"

She turned the fang over in her hands, peering at it. "I'll have to connect Smartie to a mass spectrometer I customized for this kind of stuff, but yeah… I'll see what he can find out. It's definitely a serpent fang, isn't it? Do we still think he did it? I hate to admit it, but I can't help thinking it all seems a bit set-up."

It still amused me that she called Smartie "he," as though he were a real person and not a network of technical systems. There was a sweet innocence to it that made me want to wrap Astrid in cotton wool and shelter her from ever having that taken away. *If you hurt her, Garrett, you'll have all of us to answer to.*

"It's really weird," I agreed. "Krieger is stumped, but this might help us figure out what really happened down there. If you could check and see if it's got any connection to Adley, that'd be great. Some DNA or something, I don't know, so we can be sure it's Quetzi who did this. You're the whiz kid here. Alton knows about the fang, but some more info on it would be good. We can tell him what we find once you confirm if it has her DNA on it," I explained. I supposed that, deep down, I wanted to make amends for disappointing Alton, and I knew this might hold the key.

"Okay, I'll do some digging and get back to you. If I find anything useful, I'll let you know, and send any details over to Alton, too."

"Agreed."

We both turned to look at the revolving doors as three large SUVs pulled up on the curb outside. Men and women in dark suits and sunglasses stepped out, even though it was evening and the sun had set an hour ago. *Who do you think you are—Bono?* They moved toward the rear doors and opened them, urging the passengers out into the open. My heart soared as I saw the first of the missing children edge out of the cars, their eyes darting around in panic. They looked so small beside the officers.

"Where'd they even find them?" Raffe asked. I'd been wondering the same thing.

"An abandoned ferry port. Commander Beeton led the operation," Wade explained.

"Commander who?" I retorted. "Never heard of him."

"LA sent him. A bit of a bulldog by all accounts," Wade said.

I hated being out of the loop on something as important as this. I was even more miffed that Wade seemed to know more about it than the rest of us—why did he get the intel, and we didn't? This was personal to all of us. We should've been there. Even now, I was wondering if this whole thing was even real. Were we actually getting the kids back, after all this time?

"Okay, a few pointers to go over before they come in. There's no way we can hide the children in the coven," Wade declared, taking center stage. "So, our job is to get them down to the prison cells, using the concealed doorways and stairwells. Alton has gathered the rest of the coven into an urgent meeting, giving us a brief window to get them downstairs and out of harm's way. Hopefully, the spy won't know this is going on, which is why we have to keep this top secret. Understood?"

I stared at him. "The prison cells? You're kidding, right?"

"Sadly, no," he replied. "It's the only place safe enough to hide this number of people, without raising any suspicions. Micah and Marjorie will stay where they are, but these kids have to go downstairs."

"Wade, Adley died down there today," I said coolly.

Santana nodded. "We don't know if Quetzi is still hiding out nearby. Surely, this is putting the kids at even greater risk?"

"Security swept the area. It's clean of Quetzi," Wade replied.

"It's not wise to put young children so close to a fresh spirit," Tatyana added. "I can't feel her presence down there, but that doesn't mean she's crossed over. If she's feeling vengeful after her death, then it may affect the children. They have a greater affinity for these things than adults, as their minds have yet to be altered by their environment."

Wade sighed. "I hear you, and I agree that it sucks, but I'm following orders. I suggest you do the same. I imagine it'll be a temporary measure until we can find somewhere else to put them. Until that happens, that's where they're staying. End of discussion."

We had no chance to argue, as the children flowed in through the revolving doors, directed by the guiding hands of the security personnel. A few kids were pushing and shoving one another, while others cried quietly, and several looked around in abject fear.

"Hey, don't touch me!" one of the slightly older girls muttered, snatching her hand away from the littlest boy, who seemed desperate to find someone to cling to. *Samson Ledermeyer, age three, and Cassie Moore, age eleven.* I remembered their pictures from the folders. My heart broke for the little boy, who looked so lost and alone, tears brimming in his eyes.

It looked like the missing girls had formed a bit of a clique amongst themselves. Min-Ho Lee, the twelve-year-old Herculean with Earth abilities, stayed glued to the side of Cassie Moore, who was an Empath and a Morph, if memory served. I remembered the last ability because it had been such a strange one—the power to transfer consciousness into an animal. Sarah McCormick, the ten-year-old with unconfirmed Supersonic abilities, also stuck with the older group of girls. They glanced sourly at Samson, which irritated me. The little boy couldn't help being frightened. Then again, I knew what girls could be like, bullying because of their own insecurities.

I noticed Emilio Vasquez bringing up the rear, standing off to one side by himself. He was eight, with Fire and Herculean abilities. The little girl, Mina Travis, who was barely six, drifted away from the whispering gaggle of girls and clung to the hand of a shadowed figure at the very back of the group. They wore dark clothes with a hood over their head, masking their face from view. I couldn't tell if they belonged to the security team or not, but the two littlest ones—Samson and Mina—seemed to gravitate toward them, after being rebuffed by the mean girls.

I did a quick head count, realizing that two of our specified eleven children were missing—Andrew Prescott and Denzel Ford. Their abilities had been unconfirmed, but they'd been on our list of stolen kids. I looked through the glass front of the Fleet Science Center, waiting for more children to come out of the parked SUVs, but the doors were closed.

I walked over to the hooded figure, while the rest of the Rag Team edged forward to talk to the children and tell them about what was going to happen next. "Where are the other two?" I asked.

"We'll explain everything later, once the little ones are settled. They're our priority right now," a muffled, feminine voice replied, her chin dipped to her chest. The lip of the hood was so far forward that I couldn't make out a single feature of her face, as though she didn't want me to see. A sudden flash of fear shot through me.

Katherine... it's Katherine!

With panic searing through my veins, I lunged toward the figure and yanked down her hood. She shouted in alarm as she struggled to pull the hood back up, but I'd seen her face.

"Louella?" I gaped at her in disbelief. "How the—you're dead. We found two of your limbs. We had them on a slab in the mortuary."

She looked up angrily. "Well, I'm not, as you can see."

"How?" I wanted to pinch her, to make sure she was real. I'd seen the limbs myself, but she seemed to be intact—two arms, two legs, a body, and a head. All there, in one piece. Had Katherine patched her up? My nemesis was powerful, but I doubted even she could put limbs back where there weren't any.

"Stop causing a scene," Louella hissed, putting her hood back up and pulling me off to the side. She left Mina to hold Samson's hand, the two smallest children staring at their surroundings like startled puppies.

"Sorry, I'm just struggling to figure out how the heck you're alive?"

She sighed and glanced at the two little kids. "I'm a Regen. I didn't know what it was called before, but Katherine told me that's what I am," she explained quietly. "When the Ryder twins came after me, they trapped me in a magical snare. Only my leg and my arm were caught in the trap, so I shed them and made a run for it. I can regrow limbs at will and repair my body quickly. Not my head, though. If they took that, I'd be dead."

"Like a gecko?"

"Why does everyone say that?" she muttered. "Yes, like a gecko. I can shed limbs when I'm under threat."

"That's incredible," I replied, recalling how rare that ability was. In fact, if I remembered rightly, it had been on the list of obsolete abilities. *Looks like we've both got ourselves a few unusual powers in our veins, Louella.*

"Believe me, it's not as cool as it sounds. It can happen at the worst possible moments. An ex-boyfriend almost died of a heart attack when he reached for my hand while we were walking, and it just dropped off. He startled me, that's all. Try explaining that away as an April Fools' joke in the middle of July. Earned my weirdo badge then..."

I smiled at her. "Been there, done that, got several T-shirts."

"Really?" She looked surprised.

"Hey, I've been called every name under the sun. High school is a bitch, at the best of times. It's even worse when you're one of us, and I don't just mean a magical. Foster kids like you and me have it harder than most. Catnip for bullies."

A hint of a grin turned up the corners of her lips. "Tell me about it."

I gestured for her to start walking, the rest of the Rag Team leading the kids toward the prison corridor. "I mean, you'd think they'd give us a manual or something, to make it easier. Adding magical abilities to the foster mix is a damn nightmare. One time, I flung a crush across a class-room with my Telekinesis—he was out of school for a week with a concussion. As you can imagine, I didn't get invited to the junior prom that year."

She chuckled. "What's your name?"

"Harley Merlin—pleased to meet you." I stuck out my hand and shook hers, the two of us laughing at the formality of it. The break in tension was nice, though I knew I had to ruin it with more questions. "So, how did you end up getting caught, if you managed to get away from the Ryders?"

"Katherine had her minions everywhere." Her expression darkened. "I managed to stay hidden for a couple of days, but one of her team caught me on my way out to get food. It was late, like three in the morn-ing, and I was stupid enough to think that nighttime would give me some kind of cover. He'd been waiting for me to come out. He grabbed me before I could run, tying my whole body in this glowing rope thing so I couldn't shed and get away from him. He threw me in the trunk of his car and took me to this old ranch in the hills. That's where Katherine was keeping us, before we were taken to the old ferry port."

"Do you know who this guy was?"

She nodded. "Kenneth Willow. A freaking traitor. That scumbag has one hell of a superiority complex—struts about the place like a puffed-up peacock, thinking he's the big 'I am.' He wants to be Katherine's right-hand man, but he's just an idiot. He kept trying to make moves on me, but the Regen thing comes in handy when you don't want to be touched. In the end, I freaked him out enough to get him to stop. Plus, Katherine said she'd sear his balls off with a molten-hot spoon if he got too close to me again. Turns out she's not a big fan of guys in general, though that hasn't stopped him from trying."

I frowned. "Really?"

"Yeah, from what I could see, most of her associates are women. The ones in her inner circle, anyway."

"Hey, wait up!" one of the security guards called, making us stop at the doorway through to Kid City. "There's one more car coming."

Another SUV pulled up outside. I glanced over Louella's shoulder, my heart racing in anticipation. *Please let it be Andrew and Denzel... Come on, let them all be safe.* An officer got out of the passenger side and walked around to the rear door. Another came around the back of the car, holding what looked like a shock stick in his hands. Confused, I waited for them to open the door. Why did they need a shock stick for the kids?

My confusion increased as they dragged a figure from the backseat. Now, I understood—this was no kid, but Kenneth Willow himself. The two officers manhandled him toward the front doors of the Fleet Science Center, his face twisted up in a mask of rage as he thrashed against them. With a pair of Atomic Cuffs on his wrists, he couldn't do a thing about it.

How does it feel to be powerless, Kenneth? How does it feel to have your freedom taken away? He'd done the same to these kids, and I would never forgive him for that. His foster parents had almost died because of his actions, and many more hadn't made it. He wasn't wriggling free of this one, not if I had anything to do with it.

His scowl deepened as our eyes locked. "You!" he spat.

"Me," I replied.

"Katherine will see you all burn for this!"

What, no 'Katie'? You too inferior in her ranks for that?

"You're in no position to make threats," I said calmly.

"The Cult of Eris will come for all of you, and our almighty Goddess will raze you and every single place like this to the ground. She will make you beg for your lives, and she will take them anyway. She is the Goddess of Discord. She will bring a new world order, and not one of you will be worthy of a place in it."

I smiled at him. "The Cult of Eris? Sounds like a bad B-movie."

"We are almighty!" he howled, shaking his shoulder so his shirt slipped to the side. Bang in the center of his chest, nestled into his bare skin, was a golden tattoo. The flesh around it was scarred and livid, bringing a sudden, horrible realization: Katherine had poured molten gold onto his skin to form this mark. I peered closer, noting the intricate patterns that feathered and whorled into the shape of an apple, reminding me of aboriginal drawings—dots and lines and curves creating an overall picture. The metal and the flesh had combined to make this horribly beautiful image.

"An apple?" Was this some Garden of Eden, start-of-the-world stuff? It didn't fit with Katherine's Grecian aesthetic.

"The Apple of Discord," Astrid said, appearing at my side. "It's long been linked to the Goddess Eris. I read about it a while ago, when I was researching the Children of Chaos. It's been a long-held belief that, although we only know about Gaia and her four children, there are actually more Children than that. Eris has often been mentioned as one. The Greek gods especially used to take a lot of their influence from these Children. I didn't think it would have any relevance then, but now... I guess she's using it as her emblem."

"Has she done this to you, too?" I glanced at Louella.

She shook her head. "We hadn't been initiated yet."

"Thank God," I muttered, imagining these kids having to suffer through that.

"You would've *never* been initiated," Kenneth hissed. "You're scum! You deserve everything that's coming to you. Once our Goddess reaches the pinnacle of her power, you're all screwed. She will watch you all burn, and she'll laugh as the light goes out in your eyes!"

"Enough!" I roared, getting nose-to-nose with Kenneth. "You don't get to say another word unless we allow it! Do you understand?"

"Just try and silence me," he leered.

I smiled at him icily. "Oh, I'm the last person you want to try your luck with, Kenneth." I looked at the guards who held him. "Take him to Alton. Make sure he gets put in a secure room, away from the others. I don't want him to see daylight until he's ready to tell us everything he knows about Katherine and her cult," I said, then shifted my focus back on Kenneth. "Nobody is coming to save you. Katherine left her own son to rot in a prison cell—do you really think she'll lift a finger to help you?"

A look of confusion passed across his face. "Liar."

"Nope."

"Her son was a coward. A defector."

"Wrong again. He did everything she asked, obeyed her to the letter, and she left him with a life sentence in Purgatory. He's still there now, adamant that she's coming to break him out. It's like I told him—don't expect a wrecking ball to come crashing through the wall. Katherine will leave you to rot, same as him."

He fell silent, his brow furrowed.

Good—it's about time you understood what Katherine is really like.

As the guards led Kenneth away, his shoulders slumped, his arms no longer thrashing about, I returned my attention to Louella and the other kids. They were looking at me with a mixture of fear and awe, Samson's mouth wide open in shock. Even Wade seemed stunned by my outburst, a small smile playing on his lips.

"*Ay-ay*, Harley, I thought you were going to rip his head off!" Santana said with a stilted laugh. "I wouldn't be surprised if he leaves a puddle behind."

I shrugged. "He needed to understand what kind of mess he's gotten himself into."

"Nice job, Merlin," Dylan commended.

"You sure you don't have a secret Dark side in there?" Raffe added, with a knowing grin. But his words sent a cold shiver through my body. Was that why I lashed out like that? Was my Darkness seeping through already? I didn't have much of a temper, but Santana was right—I'd nearly ripped Kenneth's head off. I looked down at my altered Esprit and shuddered. This couldn't be happening now. I needed more time to get everything in balance.

"Come on, let's get these kids somewhere safe," I said, shoving the thought away. *That's right, everyone, looks like Miss Nice has left the building.* I just hoped I could find a way to bring her back.

SIXTEEN

Astrid

Alton had allowed the children time to settle in of their own accord, giving them chaperones in the form of a small squadron of security personnel. It unsettled me to think of them below ground, in the subterranean depths of the coven, but I supposed it was the safest place for them to be. Not that it would bring them much comfort. Prison cells were prison cells, no matter how they were gussied up with nice bedding and welcoming furniture, which the security staff had provided, courtesy of Director Waterhouse. I doubted they'd ever be able to "settle in" under these circumstances.

The following morning, Wade and Santana took over interrogational duties with Kenneth Willow. Harley had pleaded with Alton to be allowed to conduct the interview, but he'd forbidden it. Her impulsive reactions the previous night had been relayed to him by the guards, and he'd decided it'd be a bad idea to let her anywhere near Kenneth. I happened to agree with him, though it might've been useful to have a startling presence in there, to get him to talk. Harley had certainly proven that she had a streak of terror in her. I often wished I could come across as gutsy as she was, but my fiery persona needed a great deal of work, considering it was more or less nonexistent.

Quetzi was still at large, though Smartie hadn't picked up any sign of the evasive serpent. And so, with the fang in hand, I decided to visit my mom at Cabot's in Waterfront Park, to see if she could assist in the investigation. I'd told Harley I would run it through a Smartie-connected mass spectrometer, but I didn't get much out of it. I'd also run a tracking scenario on it via Smartie, to see if it might be possible for one of the others to put a spell on it, but it had come back as 'unviable.' It was definitely getting stranger, but I wasn't ready to give up. *If at first, and all that.* Smartie was an exceptional piece of technology, whom I adored heart and soul, but he couldn't replace a sharp mind like my mom's. She knew an awful lot about ancient beasts, from all her years in the industry, and I hoped her expertise might come in handy.

Something still felt wrong about Quetzi's involvement in Adley's murder. Everyone else seemed sure he was responsible, but I doubted that. Even in the good old days of his reign of godliness, flagrant murder had never been his modus operandi. He was much more devious and creative than that. Indeed, I was becoming more convinced that all of this was a setup, in order to remove the proverbial heat from someone else. I wasn't entirely certain, as thinking in absolutes tended to make a fool out of people, but my mom was wiser than me—in fact, despite her lack of Chaos abilities, she was far smarter than most magicals. Alton included.

"I'm very sorry to hear that," Mom said, as I relayed the previous day's tragedy to her. We were sitting in the corner, drinking tea. I didn't go into detail; I just told her that Adley had been found dead after a supposed encounter with Quetzi. It still pained me to talk about it so bluntly, but there was little time to waste with the feathered serpent still loose. Adley had always been kind to me and a constant feature of my reparative years at the coven. Sometimes, when my dad and I had one of our disputes, she used to let me sit in the infirmary until the dust settled. I always stole sweets from her candy jar, and she always pretended not to notice. My one rebellion.

"We're all still reeling," I replied. "She might've been a prisoner, but she was well-loved before she got mixed up with Finch. I know Alton is finding it hard to deal with. I think he blames himself. If he'd sent her on to Purgatory, or put her somewhere more secure, this might not have happened."

My mom smiled sadly. "He always took things harder than most folks. It's still weird to hear you call him 'Alton,' though. Have you two argued or something? Normally, you'll at least give him a 'father' or two."

I dropped my gaze. "He hates Garrett, that's all. We were on a date the other day and he stormed in and interrupted it. We argued a bit after that, about the usual stuff—the body cams, the Shapeshifters... you."

"Me?"

"Well, more his romantic history. I know I shouldn't use the past against him, Mom, but he'd riled me up so much, I couldn't help it. Before I knew what was happening, the words were spilling out of my mouth."

She rested her hand on mine. "I know our situation is hard for you sometimes, Astrid, but you can't let your anger take over. He made his mistakes, but he's also made amends for them. He could have abandoned me, pregnant and alone, but he didn't. And yes, he could be a bit... warmer at times, but he still loves you. There's no use in bearing grudges, not when it won't change anything." Her amber eyes sparkled with warmth, her voice like honey.

Everyone always commented on how closely we resembled one another, though her skin was a deeper shade of ebony than mine, her hair coiffed in a perfect afro that made her look like an African queen. There were hints of Spanish in her features too, which came from my grandmother. However, nobody ever saw any of Alton in my face, which was probably a fortuitous thing since we were keeping our familial ties a secret. Saying that, I knew it disappointed him sometimes, that he couldn't see any of himself in my features. It was evolutionary, that a father should see a hint of his DNA in the face of his offspring. A simple, human necessity, which I had failed to provide him with.

Plus, I knew he was disappointed that I hadn't ended up with any magical ability whatsoever. He'd likely been hoping for a magical child whom he could teach and train, the way he'd been taught by his parents. With children of half-magic, half-human origin, the genetic odds of becoming magical were the same as ending up with red hair—sometimes it happened and sometimes it didn't. I just hadn't gained the rare gene from my father that would've given me a bit of magical prowess. No red hair for me, metaphorically speaking.

"I know. I didn't mean to bring his past into it, and I didn't mean to bring up the fact that he hadn't been very dad-like, but he made me so mad," I said. "It's not as if he can give me advice on romance, not when he's left a trail of broken hearts behind him."

My mom chuckled. "I wouldn't call it a trail, Astrid. A few, maybe. My own, not really—sometimes, people just aren't meant to be. Anyway, what he lacks in romantic capability, he more than makes up for in loyalty to his coven, and to you. He was always resolute in that, even when it seemed like he'd disappeared. We both made the decision for you to live at the coven, because he realized he was messing up, and he didn't want to be an absentee father."

"I still can't understand how you can be so laid-back about him. You always put a positive spin on everything. Seriously, it's like a talent."

"I've learned to be very Zen," she replied, her tone amused. "Anyway, it's not as though I can get away from him, even if I wanted to. Which I don't, I should add. He's always calling me up and asking me for favors from the wonderful world of artifacts. Plus, he'll always be your dad. There's no reason not to be civil, when nobody has done anything wrong. It wasn't as easy to understand back then, and it wounded my pride a bit, but he fell in love with Isabel. Totally, totally in love. It was like a freight train that couldn't be stopped. Yes, in those early days when he first told me about her, I felt sad that he hadn't loved me that way, but I was mature enough to see that we would never have worked out. We'd have made each other miserable."

She took a slow breath, as though remembering that brief moment of pain. "See, there was a time, just after you were born, when I asked him to stay. I didn't love him, and he didn't love me, but I was so scared,

I didn't feel like I could do any of it on my own. We stayed together for a few more months, and I thought it'd get better over time. It didn't, and it was me who realized that it'd be easier for both of us if I let go, before anyone had the chance to get hurt. Now, like I said, it hurt my pride when he started dating Isabel, and I panicked that he'd up and leave us. Fortunately for him, it was true love, and Isabel became a part of who we are as a family—she made that happen, as much as he did. They have the kind of love that we'd never shared, not even at the beginning."

I stared at my mom in wonder. No matter what happened to her, she maintained a positive outlook on life. Even in her darkest moments of doubt, which she'd never admitted to me before, it seemed as though she'd always found a way to laugh and make everything better. I would never be able to fathom her endless grace. I just hoped that, one day, I'd have an iota of her patience and dignity. Even now, she refused to lay blame at anyone's door, or muddy anyone's name.

"He said he spoke to you last week about the tools for Harley's surgery," I said.

"Like I said, I can't get rid of the bastard." She flashed me a wink, her rich laughter filling Cabot's Esprit Emporium. The store was fairly empty for a weekday afternoon, for which I was glad. I liked to have my mom to myself whenever I could.

Cabot was her surname, while I'd chosen to take on my grandmother's surname of Hepler after arriving at the coven, to keep up the pretense of me being totally extraneous to my father. My mom had suggested it, as a nod of respect to my deceased grandparent, and I'd liked the idea. Thus, I'd become Astrid Hepler—an entity all my own.

"Did you know they were in love as soon as they met?" I asked quietly. "You don't have to answer if you don't want to. I'm just curious about it all. It's still hard for me to wrap my head around, even after you've said all of that."

She leaned against the table where we were sitting, propping her chin on her hand. "You know what... to be honest, and this may be a little too much information for your young ears, I always thought that he and Imogene Whitehall were going to get together. I called him out on it one year, after catching them smooching at the coven's Christmas party. We'd broken up recently, but we were on friendly terms, and he was so flustered about it, like I'd walked in on him with his hand in the cookie jar. I was convinced they were seeing each other for ages, but he'd never admit it to me. I never caught them in any more compromising positions, and he didn't mention her much, but that always stuck with me. The day he told me about Isabel, I was completely certain that he was going to tell me he was in a relationship with Imogene."

I gasped in shock. "*The* Imogene Whitehall?"

"You sound surprised?"

"I just… I didn't think any man would be good enough to tempt her, *especially* not him."

She paused, a ghost of a smile on her lips. "Well, turns out he wasn't. At least, I don't think they ever had a thing after that kiss. It didn't stop my suspicions though, considering I didn't even know who Isabel was when that happened. He hadn't said a word about Isabel. It was only when I saw them together, when they came to pick you up one Saturday morning, that I realized he was completely in love with her. That was when I decided to let go of any past feelings, and let bygones be bygones. I couldn't have given him a love like that, and life is worth nothing if you don't have true love in it. Fortunately, my angel, you're my true love—the only one I'll ever need. Men can suck it, quite frankly. I'm happier without one." She giggled, taking a sip of her cup of coffee.

I couldn't process this. "Still, though… Alton and *Imogene*? Are you sure we're talking about the same woman?"

"Willowy thing, great style, blond hair, looks like butter wouldn't melt in her mouth?"

"*Imogene?*"

"You really find that hard to believe, huh?"

"She always seems so nice! I couldn't imagine her doing anything like that. She's like innocence incarnate."

My mom shrugged with a laugh. "You can be nice and kiss guys, Astrid."

"You know what I mean. Drunken smooching at a Christmas party just doesn't seem like her style."

"It's always the quiet ones you've got to watch out for, especially beautiful ones like her. I'll be honest; I would've kissed her, too, at that Christmas party, with a few more Proseccos in me. She's not the sort of woman one could easily turn down."

"Mom!" I squeaked.

She laughed, clutching her stomach. "I'm just teasing. I was upset about that whole thing, back then, since we'd just broken up. In fact, I think that's the only time that Alton was glad I wasn't magical; otherwise, I'd have roasted his ass. Prime beef steak for dinner," she managed in between guffaws. "I'd have probably turned Imogene into a toad or something, for good measure. Anything to wreck that fine porcelain figure of hers. Not that I'm still bitter."

"I'll never get rid of that mental image of Dad's... ass. Ew," I lamented.

"Good. You let it serve you well, if this Garrett ever does anything like that to you," she replied, with a grin. "Mind you, you'll have a hard time stopping me from roasting his ass myself, magic or no magic, if I find out that he's hurt you."

I smiled. "Alton really hates him."

"Your dad is protective, that's all. It's his job to dislike your boyfriends. He wouldn't be a dad if he didn't. He drew the bad-cop straw when we split up, and I drew good cop."

"Do you think he's right, though? Do you think Garrett is bad news?"

"I take your question and raise you this—why does he dislike him?"

I shrugged. "Alton doesn't know him the way I do, but he's convinced that Garrett is going to end up hurting me. I don't know why, since Garrett hasn't done anything to suggest something like that. He was friends with Finch, yes, but he didn't know who Finch really was." I sat back and sighed. "The thing is, I know why he's worried about my safety, after everything that's happened with me, but I really wish he'd ease up on the Garrett aspect of things. Otherwise, we're going to keep arguing about it."

"Listen to me carefully, Astrid," my mom replied. "In matters of the heart, you have to trust your own judgment. Only you know how you feel, and only you know what Garrett is like with you. All I'd say is, make sure he's in it for the right reasons. Make sure he adores you the way you deserve and is respectful of you as your own person. If you start to doubt him, in any way, you need to listen to your gut instinct. It will never set you wrong. That little voice knows us better than we know ourselves. For a long time, I didn't listen to mine, and it ended with a lot of broken hearts."

I nodded slowly. "I trust him, Mom."

"Then trust him. And remember—roasted ass."

I smiled, though my mom's revelations had left me feeling a bit sad. She had been through so much and hadn't found her Prince Charming at the end of it. Then again, maybe that was admirable in and of itself. Life wasn't a fairytale. Life was tough and turbulent, and if you could come out of it all with a smile on your face and your heart beating as fierce as ever, then maybe that was the ultimate triumph over adversity. She certainly shone brighter than any woman I'd ever met.

"Actually, there was another reason I wanted to come and see you today," I said, remembering the fang in my pocket. "It's to do with Adley's death, and Quetzi's involvement in it. Harley found this at the crime scene and wanted me to see what I could find out about it that could prove or disprove that Quetzi is responsible. I figured you'd know better than anyone if this kind of thing is normal for such an ancient serpent and other similar monsters." I handed her the fang, giving her a moment to look it over.

Her brow furrowed. "This was found at the crime scene, you say? You're sure?"

I nodded.

"Do you know if there were any bite marks or bruising on Adley's body?"

"Krieger didn't report anything like that. He found venom in her veins, which he concluded to be the cause of her death, but no bite marks or bruises. Alton sent the report to me earlier."

My mom stared at me, an odd expression in her eyes. "Then Quetzi didn't do this."

"What do you mean?"

"Feathered serpents are venomous, yes, but the bite would be considerable. We're not talking tiddly little punctures here. Secondly, the fangs of beasts like him don't just fall out—they're not like shark teeth. Feathered serpents only get one set, to see them through the rest of their life. They're constrictors, ordinarily, if they don't possess any magical abilities. However, this Quetzi *does* have magical abilities, right?"

I nodded. "Right."

"And see this, here?" She pointed to a thin line of pinkish, organic matter that lined the edge of the tooth. "This isn't from a serpent's gum. If I were a betting woman, I'd say this fang was pried out of a different, though similar, creature, to make it look like Quetzi was responsible. If there was no bruising on Adley's body, from constriction, and Krieger is saying the venom killed her, then you may want to look for an injection puncture instead. Someone has done this to make it *seem* like a snake did it—I'd stake my life on it. Plus, Quetzi would probably have eaten Adley if it had been him, instead of leaving a body behind. Just give me a moment—I have something that may work." She took the fang and disappeared into the back room, bringing a small device back with her. She put the tooth in the center and pressed a button. Gold light swirled for a moment, before a red glow settled on the large orb-like object, and a spray of symbols shot upward.

"What *is* that?"

"It senses Chaos in objects."

"What does the red mean?"

My mom smiled. "It's made of resin. It's not a real tooth. It probably came off a necklace or something, like the ones you see surfers wear. A good copy, but it's fake."

I shook my head in disbelief. I'd had a feeling that Quetzi wasn't the one who'd killed Adley, but to hear it out loud surprised me. "Why would someone have set him up in such an elaborate way?"

"They might have wanted to cover up what they did, and pin the blame on the escaped serpent," she replied. "You mentioned there was a spy at large in the coven, yes?"

"Yes."

"Well, maybe they did this to stop the bigwigs getting called in. If everyone jumped to the conclusion that it was Quetzi, then there wouldn't need to be a bigger investigation. This spy, whoever they were, probably didn't want to draw too much attention to the murder of Adley. A better question would be *why* they wanted her dead."

I frowned. "Any ideas?"

"If they're working for Katherine, it might have been done on her order."

"You think they had a part in Quetzi's escape, too?"

"It's not implausible. He's a powerful creature, and very useful. Perhaps they stole Quetzi first, so they could cover the murder second," my mom said, tapping the corner of her mouth in thought.

"Well, if that's the case, they'll be long gone by now."

"Not necessarily. With so much heightened security about the place, it's unlikely they'll try to smuggle him out in broad daylight. My guess would be that they're waiting for the perfect moment to flee, so they can spirit him away without anyone seeing. Is there any event coming up, where the majority of the coven will be in one place?"

I racked my brains before settling on one such glaring opportunity. "Alton's monthly debrief, where he informs us of our points and our goals for the next month. It's happening next Sunday morning."

"That's probably when your spy will try and take Quetzi out of the coven. Until then, I'd imagine they're hiding the serpent, doing every-thing they can to keep a low profile until next week. I wouldn't be surprised if nothing bad happens in that time, as they're keeping them-selves on the down-low. One false step, and they'll risk blowing the whole thing wide open."

"Thank you so much." I kissed my mom on the cheek, before leaping down from the chair. "I'll call you tomorrow, okay?"

"I look forward to it. And, hey, don't give your dad too much of a hard time. He loves you more than anything in this world, you know. We might not have worked out, but you were the one glorious thing that shines through to this day. Neither one of us would know what to do if anything happened to you. And if he keeps hassling you about Garrett, just know that it comes from a place of love—he's scared of losing you, and he doesn't know how to show it properly. He never has."

I knew what she meant. Alton found it hard to show affection, though he'd displayed his love when he'd brought me back from the dead three times. Mom just didn't know about that, which was probably for the best. *Definitely no need for an ass-roasting.*

"I'll try not to. I love you, Mom."

"And I love you, angel. More than the universe and all its stars combined."

I hurried out of the shop and headed back to the coven in double-quick time. If my mom was right, then the Shapeshifter had Quetzi. Now, I just needed to find both of them. A daunting task, considering we'd spent weeks trying to discover the spy, and had yet to be success-ful. However, right now, I felt more determined than ever. With my mom's strength and wisdom guiding me, I would do the impossible.

SEVENTEEN

Astrid

I burst through the coven entrance and hurtled down the hallway toward the interrogation room that the Rag Team were using to interview Kenneth Willow. On the way, I almost collided with Harley. She had just come out of one of the reading rooms to the right. With lightning-quick reflexes, she grabbed my shoulders to stop me from tumbling over.

"Thank you," I panted.

"Is everything okay?"

I nodded, returning to a standing position. "I've just been to speak with... uh, someone who can detect Chaos in objects. She took a look at the fang you gave me. Quetzi isn't responsible for Adley's death. It was an elaborate ploy to throw us off the real culprit's scent."

She arched an eyebrow. "What do you mean? I saw the skin with my own eyes."

"No, that was part of it, too. Dr. Krieger said that Adley died from venom poisoning, right?"

"Yeah, he ended up finding two small puncture wounds in her side; they were just well hidden. I got the call literally ten minutes before you burst in here."

"Well, serpents like Quetzi have a huge bite, and they don't shed their fangs. If they lose a fang, it's permanent. They can't grow another. Anyway, my expert checked the fang and told me it was a fake—it's made of resin. Quetzi didn't do this, and I'd bet those puncture wounds were made by ordinary needles instead of fangs. The venom might have been injected by the real murderer, with the tooth and the skin being planted to make it look like Quetzi. "

"What?"

"What I'm saying is, *it couldn't* have been Quetzi. He's been set up by someone, and my guess is that our spy is the culprit. Whoever they are, they're still in the coven, and they're hiding Quetzi. In order to escape the coven without detection, they need to leave when everyone is otherwise distracted. Next Sunday is Alton's monthly debrief—the perfect time to make a break for freedom, with our reptilian friend in tow."

"Why would someone steal Quetzi, though?" Harley narrowed her eyes, the cogs visibly whirring in her mind.

"Maybe somebody asked them to snatch him. He is hugely powerful, after all. And who do we know to have a thirst for all things powerful?"

Her expression turned cold. "Katherine. This has her written all over it."

"My thoughts exactly."

"We should tell Alton," Harley said.

I nodded. "Good idea. Is he still watching the interrogation?"

"He should be. I still don't understand why he wouldn't let me take the lead on it."

"You gave us all a bit of a fright yesterday. He likely thinks you're too close to the case and may lash out if provoked."

"See, why couldn't he have just said that, instead of feeding me some bullcrap about O'Halloran being the muscle, and Wade and Santana being better negotiators?"

I smiled. "He doesn't really like confrontation."

"Yeah, I'm starting to see that."

We headed for the rooms that had been cordoned off for interrogation purposes. Several guards were on duty in the hallway preceding the interview room, their faces set in stern expressions. They reminded me of the fabled Queen's Guard at Buckingham Palace in London, who were required to remain stony-faced through any and all situations. It made me want to tickle them, or jump in front of them, in a vain effort to get them to laugh. They were used to us by now, knowing we were safe to let pass.

Harley knocked on the door and went in first. A two-way mirror lined the far wall, and Alton sat in front of it, his leg jiggling in agitation as he watched the proceedings unfold. Kenneth didn't appear to be cooperating, his arms folded across his chest, his eyes set in reptilian slits of pure rage. O'Halloran prowled around the small room with his eyes fixed on Kenneth, clearly trying to wig him out and get him to break. I jumped as he slammed his hands down on the desk, but Kenneth barely flinched. I had been gone for several hours, which meant the situation must have been dire. *Katherine certainly trains her minions well, especially in the art of silence.*

"Alton, we need to talk to you," Harley announced.

He glanced up at her. "Can it wait? I'm a bit busy at present."

"No, it can't wait. Astrid, tell him what you've found out."

I cleared my throat and relayed all of the information I'd gathered from my mother. "This expert friend of mine, Henrietta, is rarely wrong when it comes to matters of intuition, and I have reason to believe she's right. That device of hers doesn't lie, and it all makes sense. If we find the spy, then we'll find Quetzi," I concluded, knowing he'd understand exactly why I'd spoken to her. He might not have been a good partner to my mom, but he valued her as a specialist in her field.

He sat up straighter. "Good job, Astrid. Very good job."

"Thanks," I said, dropping my gaze.

"What are we going to do about this?" Harley asked, ever the pragmatist.

"I'm going to call small groups of the coven into a meeting. If we're going to find this traitor, then we need to redouble our efforts," he replied, his demeanor restless. "I want everyone interviewed, Shapeshifters included. I know they've got their body cams, but that doesn't exempt them from this. Astrid, can you conduct these inter-views and use that AI of yours?"

Harley nodded. "Yeah, do you have a way on that Smartie thing of yours to figure out who might be lying? A polygraph, maybe?"

"A polygraph wouldn't work. Those things are notoriously inaccu-rate and can be easily fooled if you have the know-how. However, I *can* configure a program that might work." I nodded, the ideas coming to me at a rapid pace. "I can use Smartie's internal database to match up the answers that the interviewees give me to the facts that are already stored on his hard drive—locations, times, whereabouts, alibis, etcetera, specifically for the timeframe that Quetzi went missing. If there are any contradictions, Smartie will be able to spot them. He works fast, so it's definitely manageable. The interviews will be the most time-consuming aspect."

Alton sat back, his shoulders relaxing slightly. "That sounds like an excellent plan, Astrid. While you figure out the minutiae, I'm going to make the announcement. Kenneth Willow isn't talking anyway, so we might as well use this room. He can wait his turn, as far as I'm concerned."

Harley frowned. "He's still not saying anything?"

"His lips might as well be sealed with that gold on his chest. Not a word about anything. He just keeps telling us that the Cult of Eris is going to make us pay, and we can't escape it, no matter where we run or how hard we fight. Stirring stuff, as you can imagine," he said wearily.

"You sure you won't let me have a go?"

He smiled wryly. "I want him alive, Harley. For now, I think it's best you stay away. Anyway, after tomorrow he's the Mage Council's prob-lem. They're not happy with our coven security, so they're coming to pick him up in the morning. They can interrogate him from there, since we're not getting anywhere. I'm afraid I have to admit defeat on this one."

"Are they letting the kids stay?"

"It seems so, yes."

She nodded. "Good… that's good. I'm making progress on that thing you asked about, so we might have some good news soon. At the very least, we'll have somewhere safer to put them."

"Yes, keep me updated on that," he replied, leaving me entirely out of the loop. Although I could guess what they were talking about—I was able to spot a Kaleido mask at ten paces. They were works of exquisite craftsmanship, but if you knew what to look for, you couldn't *not* see them. A slight prickle of energy when standing nearby, and a faint haze around the jawline. In fact, the moment Tarver had been introduced to us, I'd known he wasn't who he said he was. Harley and Alton's secrecy only confirmed my suspicions that he was actually Jacob, masquerading as this Tarver character. Not that I was going to tell them that—my knowing would only worry them, and I understood why Alton had given him such a mask. He wanted to protect Jacob, and I wanted the same thing. *You may keep your secrets for now.*

"I'll get the questions laid out," I said brightly. "Give me an hour and we can reconvene, if that works for you?"

Alton cast me a grateful look. "That's perfect, Astrid. Now, I have a call to make to Krieger."

Evening fell on the coven, silvery moonlight glancing in through the windows of the interview room. I tried hard not to look at the clock, but my gaze drifted there regardless. The hands read half past ten. I had been at this since noon, and I was beginning to tire. A yawn stretched my mouth open wide, making Harley imitate the same motions from the chair beside me. Nobody really knew why humans did that— yawning when other people did—but research had shown that it was an echo phenomenon, otherwise known as an automatic imitation of another person. Dogs and chimpanzees apparently suffered from the same impulse, though they'd yet to settle on a conclusion as to why. Another curious human attribute, like falling in love or crying at sad movies.

I'd managed to work my way through three-quarters of the populace, with no contradictions as of yet. The questions were simple, and the interviews were brief, though hours and hours of endless asking was not as easy as it appeared, and the detector program hadn't brought up any red flags. In fact, the only useful discovery we'd had was from Alton, telling us that the puncture wounds were indeed similar to those of hypodermic needles, which bolstered our theory. Harley had been helping me out, after Alton had agreed to let her sit in on the interviews. I supposed she wasn't a threat to these people, as she didn't want to punch them in the face for being generally unpleasant.

"Who's next on the list?" I asked.

"Garrett."

My heart almost stopped. Although, of course, that wasn't actually possible, not unless I was about to die again. It was more of an arrhythmia, brought on by thoughts of him. Dangerous, really, now that I'd actually contemplated the idea. All of this romance stuff couldn't be good for a person, not when it could cause increased adrenaline, heart palpitations, and an intense sensation of acute anxiety, with every neuron firing at once. Still, I had to admit it felt quite exciting.

The door opened, and Garrett was ushered inside by one of the officers. I knew the moment I saw him that this wasn't going to go well. He had that stubborn look on his face. Ordinarily, I found it adorable, but this wasn't the right setting for an expression like that. Here, I needed cooperation.

"This is ridiculous," he muttered, as he sat down on the opposite side of the table.

"It won't take long," I urged, forcing a smile onto my face.

He shook his head. "Ask me what you want—I'm not answering any of your stupid questions. This is totally ridiculous. Like, what is this? A dictatorship? What's next—Alton prancing around doing 'random' spot checks on people? I'm not standing for it, Astrid. I'm sorry, I'm just not."

"Come on, Garrett, everyone else is doing this," Harley interjected.

"I don't care—I'm not. Alton has already strapped these things to us —isn't that enough to prove I'm innocent?"

"Please, Garrett," I said quietly. Alton was watching us through the two-way mirror, and I could only imagine his current response. I admired Garrett's independent spirit, but I wished he would play along, just this once.

"No, Astrid. I'm not answering Alton's questions. Check the cameras if you want; I'm not doing this."

"They're my questions—does that make a difference?"

He smiled tightly. "Not this time."

"Please, Garrett. Let's just get this over with. They're easy questions, and I know you'll pass with flying colors."

"I'm not answering them. Nothing you can say will change my mind."

Panic made my heartbeat quicken. Alton would burst in here any moment, I knew it. He was probably already fuming in the next room, readying himself to rage at Garrett. Harley seemed to feel it too. Her entire body language had changed, stiffening with tension that didn't belong to her.

"Garrett, all you have to do is tell us where you were when Quetzi got taken," I encouraged softly. "That's all you have to do. Please, for me."

He leveled his gaze at me. "I've told you, I'm not answering these questions, not even for you. I'm sorry, I really am, but I'm not bowing to Alton's rules—not after the humiliation he's already put us Shapeshifters through."

"Are you hiding something?" Harley asked bluntly, saying what I couldn't.

"No," he replied, a beat too fast.

"Were you up to something the day that Quetzi went missing?"

"No."

"Then why won't you tell us what you were doing?"

"I'm not playing Alton's messed-up game."

I fidgeted in my seat, unable to suppress the thoughts that rushed into my mind. *Are you hiding something, Garrett?* It really felt as though he was. His manner, his words, his stubbornness. They all pointed toward deception. I might not have been an Empath, but I knew the signs of a liar—the tics that gave them away, like a poker player in the midst of an important game.

"Are you keeping secrets from me?" I asked, my voice barely louder than a whisper.

His eyes turned suddenly cold. "You're one to talk."

"What do you mean?" I recoiled, wounded by his frosty tone.

He shook his head. "Nothing. Forget about it."

"No, what did you mean?" I pressed, my heart pounding. What did he know? What had he been about to say?

"Nothing. I shouldn't have said anything. It's this room, it's winding me up," he muttered, visibly calming down. He ran a hand through his hair, turning his gaze toward the mirrored panel to the right of him. It definitely seemed like he'd wanted to say something. A revelation that I didn't want anyone finding out about, maybe? I didn't know what to be more concerned about—the fact that he might know about my familial ties to Alton, or the fact that he might use it against me, just to irritate my father.

Make sure he's in it for the right reasons. That's what my mom had said. Until that moment, I'd never questioned Garrett's motives. Now, however, my certainty about them had been thrown into turmoil.

"If you don't do the interview now, Alton will make you do it later," Harley said, defusing the prickly tension that had gathered like a storm between us.

"Fine, then he can make me do it later," Garrett replied. He scraped back his chair and stood up, leaving the room without another word. I watched him go, my heart sinking into my stomach. Again, not possible, but the sensation was rather poignant, and eminently convincing. I could almost feel it beating miserably in my abdomen.

"Are you okay?" Harley asked.

I nodded. "I think I need a brief recess, that's all."

"We can finish this in the morning. Go and do something else to take your mind off this stuff."

"Like what?"

She shrugged. "See what else you can find on the Cult of Eris, maybe?"

"Yes… yes, that sounds like a good idea."

"Want me to come with you?"

I shook my head. "No, I think I need a minute on my own."

"Okay, well, I'm a phone call away if you change your mind."

"Thanks, Harley."

She smiled. "Look, boys are a pain in the ass. Garrett's pissed at Alton, and he's taking it out on you. If it had been anyone else in the room, he'd have done the same thing. Don't worry about it too much, you hear me? He likes you. That's not going to change."

"I'll try not to worry."

"That's my girl. They're not worth it, most of the time."

Garrett is… At least, I thought he was.

Gathering my things, I ducked out into the hallway. Without bothering to stop and check in with Alton, I set off toward the library. Books always calmed my mind, and research was as good as a massage. Amongst the stacks and the shelves, I could make myself forget about Garrett entirely. If he *did* know about Alton being my father, did that mean he was going to hold it over me? If he did, I supposed I would learn what type of man he was.

Enough now. No more thoughts of Garrett Kyteler.

As my grandmother, the mighty Ariadne Hepler, had always said, "If you have time to think about boys, then you have too much time on your hands." Instead of worrying, I would find solace in discovering ways to uncover and destroy the Cult of Eris, along with bringing down Katherine Shipton. That could make me forget about almost anything else. Almost.

EIGHTEEN

Harley

The next morning, torn between helping Astrid out with the rest of the interviews and getting my chance to speak to Nomura, I joined the newcomers in a dawn training session at the preceptors' private facility. Jacob and I hadn't had much time to continue our work together, but he seemed happy enough to give it a rest for a couple of days. The blast had thrown his confidence, but he'd get back on the horse when the time came. Even if I had to force him back in the saddle.

Anyway, I figured Astrid wouldn't be starting until later, and Santana could always sit in the room with her if I wasn't finished in time. After what Alton had said to me about the Sanguine spell, and the potentially imminent threat of a pretty pissed-off Katherine, I needed to get Nomura's advice, sooner rather than later. As luck would have it, he was the one overseeing this dawn training session. Well, it wasn't so much luck as me checking with Alton that he'd be on duty, but still— this was my shot.

"No, not like that," Nomura instructed as Min-Ho Lee sent a shudder through the ground that almost split it in two. "You have to keep control of what you do at all times. You can't let your mind wander for even a second."

She flushed with embarrassment as her friends—Cassie and Sarah—laughed from the sidelines. "I don't understand what you mean."

"You can't just let it all pour out of you at once, then watch what happens, like you just did. It's about visualization and measured force," he explained. "Let it flow from your hands, but only as much as you need. Otherwise, we may end up having to evacuate the coven." He cast her an encouraging smile, but the girl was clearly mortified.

"I'm not sure I can do it, preceptor. It all comes out at once, whenever I try it," Min-Ho mumbled.

Nomura nodded. "You won't get it right away, but it's about persistence. Sarah, why don't you come and give it a try with your speed? You're a Supersonic, yes?"

She blanched. "I'd rather not, preceptor."

"Regardless, come and give it a go," he insisted.

Glancing back at Cassie, who shared in my Empath abilities, Sarah stepped toward Nomura. He positioned her in front of the white line that had been drawn on the floor and rested his hand on her shoulder for a second.

"What do you want me to do?"

He pointed to the far side of the room. "I want to see what you're capable of. Come on."

"Do you want me to clap like a seal, too?" she muttered. I could tell her nerves were making her lippy; she was hiding her insecurity behind rudeness.

"No, just the running will do, and if you speak to me like that again I'll make you run all day. On my count. Ready?"

"I guess so."

"One… two… three!"

The girl disappeared in the blink of an eye, a gust of wind sweeping back and hitting me in the face. A slight blur tore across the room, but you had to look closely for it. Everyone else turned to watch as Sarah McCormick appeared on the opposite side of the training room in less than two seconds flat. I gaped at her. I'd figured Supersonic had something to do with breaking glass, but this made sense, too. She darted back to the white line, disappearing and reappearing a second later at Nomura's side.

"How the heck did they catch you?" I blurted out.

She shot me a sour look. "They laid traps. Don't think I didn't try."

"Couldn't you have run away from Katherine?"

"And go where, exactly? Anyway, they put cuffs on me to stop me from using my abilities. Katherine's people only took them off when she wanted to see what I could do—inside a bubble thing, of course, so I couldn't make a break for it." Aside from the preteen attitude problem, Sarah was impressive. I'd never seen anything like it. She seemed tough. The foster system had hardened her, too.

"And what about you, Cassie?" I turned to the third member of the triad. "You're an Empath and a Morph, right?"

She shrugged. "I don't know what that means."

"You can put your consciousness in an animal, and sense what other people are feeling, right?"

"Then yeah, I guess that's me in a neat little box." I got the feeling that Cassie was nicer than she appeared, but fear had turned her wary and bitter, making her adapt to the attitude of the two girls who were always stuck to her side.

"Can we see the Morph ability?" I looked to Nomura for consent.

"I'm interested to see what else Sarah can do first, but Cassie, you'll be next," he replied.

Sarah sighed loudly. "Let me guess, you want to see me break something with my voice? Same as everyone else?"

"If you could."

She stepped up to a pitcher of water that had been set on a trestle table and braced her hands against the vinyl surface of the tabletop. Narrowing her eyes, she opened her mouth. A high-pitched shriek shivered out of her throat, my hands snapping to my ears to try and block out the sound. I half-expected an escaped Banshee from the Bestiary to appear, bringing an omen of death with it. Instead, the pitcher shuddered violently, before it exploded into a thousand tiny shards, sending water and glass in all directions. Fortunately, there wasn't anyone standing close enough to get hurt, and the shards bypassed Sarah completely, bending around the shrill scream of her voice.

Nomura whistled. "Impressive. Your control is very good indeed."

Sarah flashed a hint of a smile. "I've had my whole life to practice."

"It's not like she has to control a powerful Element. Her Fire is weak," Min-Ho muttered sourly, folding her arms across her chest. "Running and screaming is so much easier."

"No, it's not," Sarah protested.

"She doesn't even have an Esprit yet!" Min-Ho's was a jade hair barrette shaped like a seahorse, while Cassie's appeared to be a gold necklace with a green stone in the middle.

"All of you have abilities of equal difficulty, and having an Esprit isn't a sign of progression. It can take years to find one," Nomura interjected. "No matter how much of a natural you might be, every skill requires practice and dedication to master. There is no such thing as an 'easy' ability or a 'weak' ability. You would do well to learn that, if you don't take anything else away from these training sessions."

That silenced the girls, though they shot cold looks at each other. My guess was, by the time they headed to the Banquet Hall for breakfast, they'd be sitting apart. Girls were like that, as much as I wished they weren't. A shudder of déjà vu ran through me—this was a little too much like high school for my taste. Those years, and those tense relationships, were way behind me. *Good riddance.*

"Preceptor Nomura!" Mina Travis wailed from the bench on the right-hand side. "Micah is doing it again!"

My attention shot toward the two youngest kids, who were sitting off on their own. Micah cradled Fluffers in his arms, the cute scene not immediately worrying. However, the cat didn't seem to be moving. I hadn't seen what had happened, but there was a small pool of blood on the floor by Micah's feet. Neither of the kids seemed to be bleeding, which only left one victim. A moment later, Fluffers leapt up, nuzzling its furry forehead against Micah's smooth one. It mewled and pressed its claws into Micah's T-shirt, apparently fine after dying for the eighth time. *One left, pal. You might want to take things slower.*

"What happened?" I asked, walking over to the children.

"Fluffers pounced at me, and I used my Telekinesis," Mina sobbed. "I didn't mean to throw him so hard, but he scared me."

Nomura and I exchanged a look. It had come to light that Micah had secretly been Purging creatures after bringing his cat back to life. Just last night, after they'd headed down to the prison cells, Fluffers had eaten some of the rat poison that had been left out. He'd died in Micah's arms, only to be brought straight back. While it wasn't clear whether or not Micah Purged every time, he'd done so last night, resulting in a tiny imp that he'd tried to hide from the security personnel. Louella had been the one to find the creature and had reported it to one of the guards. Micah had been devastated when they took the imp away. According to him, they were his "pets," too, and he didn't like to be separated from them. I could only wonder what had happened to the previous ones. They were probably out there somewhere, causing havoc in the human world—the flashes people saw out of the corner of their eyes, or the reason behind things going missing in folks' houses.

It made me wonder how high that kid's pain threshold was, if he could Purge as if it was nothing. Was it another secret ability we didn't know about—Purging without effort? A weird one, but entirely possible. He was already freakishly powerful, and he was barely out of diapers.

"Do you feel okay?" Nomura asked Micah.

He nodded cheerfully. "Fluffers is awake."

"This is unbelievable," Nomura murmured.

I frowned. "What is?"

"Necromancers are notoriously powerful, by their very nature, but Micah must be extraordinarily gifted, if he can perform an act like that and not immediately Purge. Even Alton can't do that," he replied, in a low voice. "I wonder if something will turn up in his Reading."

"Do you think it might be the cat's size? Smaller creature, smaller consequence?"

He shrugged. "Maybe... but look at him. He's absolutely fine. It's like nothing happened. He's not even tired."

Of all the kids who had arrived back at the coven, Micah was the one I was most concerned about. If he was already this powerful, that power would only grow as he did. Once he reached adulthood, and even before then, he'd be a force to be reckoned with. It was a scary thought, considering how small and cute he looked now. Nomura seemed on edge about it, too. I could feel the anxiety emanating from him. The other kids were scared, as well—it poured off them in vibrant waves, blending with a childish sense of awe. To them, Micah was the equivalent of a classmate who could do a really neat trick, only they didn't want to be the ones on the receiving end of it.

"I'd say they really need to get their Readings done as soon as possible. They all wield at least one Element, but it's hard to tell with them like this," I said, turning my attention to Louella. She and Marjorie were locked in a fight in their own corner of the training room. Marjorie lunged forward to grab at Louella's arm, only for her to drop it to the floor. Marjorie screamed and backed off as a new limb pushed through Louella's hoodie sleeve. Her ability was creepy and cool in equal measure, though the arm lying on the floor did make me feel a bit sick.

"I did it!" Louella cried. "I did it without being scared!"

Nomura smiled. "Well done, Louella. Don't push it too hard, but very impressive work." He turned back to me. "The Readings have already been arranged for the end of the week. I'd be interested to see what comes out of Micah's. It may well be off the charts."

"He needs the right tutoring, otherwise he'll be screwed. You know what the Mage Council are like about super-powerful people," I said wryly. "I'm not having him put in some facility." The only reason I wasn't in one was because I was useful right now, and I had this Suppressor to stop me from getting out of hand. After I'd removed it, I wondered what their reaction would be. The fear of being locked up hit me like a punch to the gut, slamming renewed terror into me. If I ended up a Dark liability, I'd never see the light of day again.

"Yes, he'd certainly benefit from tutoring," Nomura said.

"Speaking of super-powerful people, I thought Regens and Morphs weren't around anymore?"

"Quite right—glad to see you've been learning. Morphs are rare, but there hasn't been a Regen for a hundred years," he replied. "There must have been a recent mutation, which has resulted in Cassie's ability. Supersonic is fairly unheard of, too."

"Must be something in the San Diego water, right?"

He chuckled. "It would seem that way. Although life has a way of working in cycles. This may simply be a revival of sorts, with those rare and dormant abilities coming back into the mainstream of magical society. It happens, just as the world moves through ice ages and returns to a time of warmth and prosperity."

"So, the magicals have been in an ice age?"

"Metaphorically speaking, it would appear so."

"Well, this is a hell of a way to thaw out."

"Indeed."

A thud distracted my attention away from Nomura, my eyes snapping back to the corner where Marjorie and Louella had been fighting. Marjorie lay on the floor, her knees tucked up to her chin, her eyes milky white. Her body shook violently, her mouth wide in a half-scream. Louella skidded to her side, trying to shake her out of her sudden trance, but Marjorie simply threw her head back, her neck arched at an inhuman angle.

I sprinted toward her, kneeling beside Louella. "Marjorie? Marjorie, can you hear me?"

Her eerie, milky eyes stared straight into my soul. "The traitor... is here. The traitor... is hiding. The traitor... has been here, in this room. I feel her... I feel him. He has stolen her face... he has stolen her body. They have been here... they have been in this room."

My mind frantically tried to piece together the little snippets Marjorie was giving. A bigger image danced just out of sight, the fractured fragments creating a confusing picture. *Who the heck can it be?* If they'd been in this room, did that mean they were here now? Was it one of the kids? That didn't seem likely. Jacob? Again, that didn't seem likely. *Does she mean the preceptors?* That was just as hard to validate in my head. Alton knew them all like the back of his hand, and he'd no doubt done some checks of his own when the spy first came to light. Then again, anyone could be the traitor. I thought about checking the camera footage for the room, even though it probably wouldn't be much help—lots of people used this room, and Marjorie's visions weren't always the most reliable. Plus, some cameras had been glitching like crazy after the Bestiary incident, like the ones in the prison corridor and the Bestiary itself. Still, I'd ask Astrid to look into it.

"What do you mean, Marjorie?" I urged, but the milky haze of her eyes was already receding, taking the vision with it.

"What happened?" she murmured as she came to.

"You had a vision. Can you remember any of it?"

She shook her head slowly. "I saw a face... it was so clear a moment ago. There was a man and a woman, but I don't know who was the traitor and who wasn't. I didn't recognize the guy, but the woman was familiar... maybe. Oh, I don't know. This is useless!"

"No, it isn't. You're doing great, you really are. Now, come on, what did they look like? Try to concentrate and see if you can make the image clearer."

"It was dark. I can't remember." She looked like she was about to burst into tears. "I'm sorry, Harley."

"Hey, you have no reason to be sorry. You can't control these things —it's not your fault. Honestly, every little tidbit you give us is worth so much."

"I should be better at this by now," she muttered.

I held her shoulders and looked her dead in the eyes. "You're doing incredible, Marjorie. Think about how far you've come since you first came here. And, hey, remember what Wade told you about my pledge? I nearly broke the place. When I got here, I didn't know my ass from my elbow when it came to magic stuff. It all shot out of me at once. I couldn't walk into a room without being deafened by people's emotions. I had no control, but I worked on it, and now I get to choose what I can and can't feel... most of the time. Crowds are still tricky, but I'm getting better with them, too. It's all progress."

Marjorie nodded slowly, and I smiled at her.

"You're making progress every day, I promise you," I continued. "Without you, we'd never have found Micah. I know you're struggling to believe it, but you're doing so well, and confidence will come in time. I need you to believe how good you are."

She glanced at me shyly. "I'll try."

"Why don't you go and see Astrid and get her to set you up with the camera footage for this room. It might take a while, but if you see anyone that jogs your memory, it might help us," I suggested.

"That'd be good. I'll do that."

"Cool. I'll make it happen."

"Yes, how about we all stop for the morning?" Nomura suggested. "You're all still exhausted from your ordeal with Katherine. Why don't you go with Marjorie to the Banquet Hall, before the rest of the coven starts coming down to breakfast? Gather up a bunch of food and take it all back to your rooms downstairs. Then, once you've eaten, I want you to rest and relax. Preceptor's orders."

A rumble of assent rippled around the room, and I helped Marjorie to her feet. She dusted herself off and stood tall, her features set in a determined expression that made me proud. With Louella at her side, the two older girls collected the others and headed out into the hallway, where a security team was waiting to escort them to breakfast. It still bugged me that we were missing two of the magical kids on our list, but Louella had been tight-lipped about their whereabouts. It wasn't a subject I wanted to press, considering what they'd all been through.

"Aren't you joining them, Harley?" Nomura asked, as the last of the kids filed out.

I shook my head. "Actually, I was hoping to talk to you about something."

"Oh?"

"It's kind of a delicate issue."

"Color me intrigued."

I took a breath. There was no going back now. "I don't know if you've heard anything about Krieger arranging for me to have surgery?"

"To get rid of your Suppressor? I heard about it. Congratulations."

"Yeah, I'm pretty grateful for all the hard work he's putting in. The thing is, I can't wait that long—he said it'd be months before everything was good to go, and it might be too late by then. Katherine is a threat *now*, and we need all the firepower we can get against her."

Nomura stared at me blankly. "You want to break it?"

"Uh… to put it simply, yeah."

"I thought you might," he said quietly, a note of hesitation in his voice. "In fact, I was wondering if you'd come to me for advice, given our current circumstances with Katherine and the spy."

"You were?"

He nodded, his brow furrowed. "I've seen your frustrations, Harley. You're not exactly the patient type, and I don't mean any offense when I say that," he replied. "I worked hard to master my abilities because I'm a Mediocre. You are anything but Mediocre but have been forced into a position that resembles it. Of course you're impatient."

"And you're an expert on Dempsey Suppressors, right?"

He eyed me curiously. "I have studied them a little, yes, though it would be naïve of me to call myself an expert. What did you want to ask about, specifically? I will see if I can help."

I smiled. "I'm just worried that, if I break the Suppressor by force, there's going to be this raw blast of energy. Even if that doesn't cause too much damage, I've got my affinities to worry about."

"You think you'll start leaning one way? Toward Darkness, judging by your expression?"

I nodded. *Damn, he's good. Not an expert, my ass.* "I want to be able to balance Light and Dark, once the Suppressor breaks. Otherwise, I'm going to struggle to control anything. I don't want to be destructive. I don't want to be a danger to anyone, but I also can't have this thing inside me much longer, without losing my mind."

"Have you spoken to Alton about this? I know it's not his field of expertise, but I would hate to be treading on his toes."

"He mentioned a Sanguine spell to me," I replied, bending the truth slightly. I was pretty sure Alton didn't want me following this particular trail, but he was the one who'd sowed the seed in my head. What else could he expect?

"He did?" Nomura sounded stunned.

"Yeah, he mentioned that I could balance my affinities using a spell like that—it had something to do with a powerful Dark magical and powerful Light magical."

"I'm a little surprised that he would talk to you about dangerous magic like that, but I suppose your situation is an unusual one. Sanguine spells are illegal to use in the United States without a license, although they're fairly commonplace in Europe and Asia. Your friend, Santana, is of a magical lineage who still use Sanguine spells, too."

"Is there anywhere in the States where you can use them on the down-low?" I flashed a conspiratorial wink.

He paused, as though weighing up his options. "Well... I suppose if you already know of the existence of Sanguine spells, maybe I can... yes, I suppose I must." He stayed silent a moment longer, making me wonder if he was going to tell me anything. "New Orleans still has practitioners," he replied evenly, at last. "You've heard of Voodoo, yes?"

I nodded. "Creepy dolls, pins in the eyes—that kind of stuff?"

He chuckled. "Not quite; that's a common misconception. Their magic is similar to that of the Santeria or the Kolduny, in that they serve spirits. However, they serve spirits known as the Loa—they make offerings to them and perform Sanguine spells to appeal for help, or ask for something, or gain strength, in the same way that Santana calls on her Orishas. The methodology is very similar."

"That's cool. I guess I'll learn more about it in International Cultures later down the line." Provided I survived Katherine, of course.

"Anyway, there are many powerful magicals in New Orleans who practice the art of Voodoo. A deal was struck with the New Orleans Coven, to ensure that Sanguine spells were isolated solely to the city. It requires a license to practice, as I've said, but it's still done there, with and without such permissions."

"What might *this* Sanguine spell be—the one Alton mentioned?"

"If it's the one I think it is, then you'd have to combine the blood of a very powerful Light magical and that of a very powerful Dark magical, in order to create the spell that would balance your internal equilibrium. It can be done, but it's very risky, and the spell itself is very rare and dangerous. Even getting blood like that would be hard. It can't just be any blood—it has to come from the type of magicals you'd probably only find in Purgatory. The Katherine Shipton types."

My heart sank. *Great... just what I wanted to hear.*

"Although it's funny you should mention this spell now... it's probably why it was on Alton's mind, now that I think about it."

My head snapped up. "What do you mean?"

"Well, that spell was one of the ones that came through from the Reykjavik repository. Katherine stole the original, but they had a copy."

It's in the coven! It's in the friggin' coven! I'd promised Alton I wasn't going to get myself into any more trouble, but this was different. This was a risk worth taking. In fact, this was worth everything. It could well be the bridge between us winning the fight against Katherine and losing it. He'd forgive me, eventually. And if he didn't... well, I could deal with that if it got there.

"Are you being serious?"

He smiled strangely. "There'd be no use in me lying to you now. If you didn't get the information out of me, you'd get it another way. It's an admirable quality in you, Harley—your determination. I just hope it doesn't get you caught up in something you can't get out of one of these days."

"I'll be careful," I said. Evidently, he was putting this big, dangerous, illegal ball in my court. I was grateful to him for that. He understood why I had to do this, in a way that Alton never could. Alton would have had me wait, even if it meant we failed.

"Please do. The only reason I've even mentioned this to you is because you might be the only person who has the power to overcome a spell like that and wrangle it to your purpose. If you were ordinary, it would swallow you whole, but you have the strength of will and of magic to control it. That is my hope, anyway."

"Thank you for this, Preceptor. You've got no idea what it means to me."

He sighed. "Don't make me regret it. If things look bad, come to me —promise me you'll do that."

"I promise."

With that, I left the training room, my mind racing with thoughts of the future. Quetzi was still on the loose, but things were looking up. If I could really break this Suppressor and get my affinities balanced, then we'd have the advantage we sorely needed against Katherine. Even so, one little gnawing concern nibbled away at the back of my brain. I hadn't been able to silence it since the kids arrived last night. We had nine of them back at the coven, but it had almost been too easy. The security teams had found them and brought them to us, seemingly without a fight.

Katherine Shipton, what are you up to?

NINETEEN

Harley

"Harley, there you are!" Astrid called, as I headed for the Banquet Hall. I needed some time to figure out how I was going to get my hands on that Sanguine spell. Even if I managed to find it, I'd have to get the blood that Nomura had mentioned.

The more I'd thought about it, the more a disappointing realization had started to dawn. Maybe Nomura hadn't given me that information to put the ball in my court. Maybe he'd told me all about it because he knew it was a near-impossible task. He'd spoken about magicals in Purgatory being the only ones who might be strong enough to fit the bill of what I needed. How the heck was I supposed to get in there and get some blood from a known criminal, without alerting anyone to what I was up to?

Cheers, Nomura... Way to build a girl up and let her down. Real sneaky.

"Sorry, I was just grabbing coffee and a bite to eat. I was on my way to the interrogation room, I swear," I replied. To be honest, I'd been coming up with excuses for the last half hour, trying to pick the best one. I had other things to be doing, instead of interviewing the entire coven. My time was better served elsewhere—I just didn't know how to break that to Astrid.

"Never mind that," she said urgently. "I wanted to tell you what I found out about the Cult of Eris. You were right—it really relaxed my brain last night. I haven't been able to stop reading since."

"Not really the point of relaxation, but whatever floats your boat."

She smiled. "I thought you'd be eager to hear what I discovered."

"Do you want to talk here?" I glanced around at the near-empty Banquet Hall. The newcomers had already taken their food downstairs, before the coven started to stir. Alton had orchestrated everything to perfection, forging a dance between the kids and the rest of the magicals so they passed each other like ships in the night. It was an impressive bit of logistics.

"I suppose so. I could do with one of those." She gestured to the huge mug of coffee in my hand.

"You *really* need to try a massage," I teased, taking up a seat at the top end of the far-left table, while she went to fetch herself a cup of coffee. She gulped it down as she set a fat folder on the tabletop.

"So, although I did a *lot* of reading, the information I managed to gather was weirdly sparse," Astrid began. "It's like chunks of history have been removed from all available repositories. That led me to delve deeper. I don't like censorship at the best of times, and I was certain there had to be *some* snippets of information somewhere."

"Hey, that folder looks pretty weighty to me."

She laughed. "It's mostly photos. I managed to get some prints of the Apple of Discord, just to be sure that it was the same as the horrible tattoo thing that Katherine mutilated Kenneth with. I already knew that the Apple was related to Eris, which ended up being my starting point for last night's research session. Do you know much about it?"

"Nada."

"Well, it's the apple that supposedly caused the Trojan War. In Greek mythology, the Goddess Eris decided to toss the apple into the mix during the feast of the gods, at the wedding of Peleus and Thetis. Inscribed on the golden exterior were the words 'to the most beautiful.' Naturally, this sparked something of a dispute amongst three of the other goddesses, each of them vying to be named the most beautiful—Aphrodite, Hera, and Athena. Are you following so far?"

"Yep. Although I'm also kind of thinking about a young Brad Pitt and Eric Bana in loincloths."

She grinned. "Well, while you drool, I'll tell you the rest of the story. So, our good friend Eris, the Goddess of Discord, wasn't invited to the wedding. Irked by the snub, she decided to cause a little ruckus to get her revenge and amuse herself, as a bonus. When she tossed the golden apple into the party, Aphrodite, Hera, and Athena claimed it as theirs, each of them thinking themselves the proverbial fairest of them all."

"Hang on a second… are we still talking about Troy here? That sounds an awful lot like *Snow White* to me."

"Walt Disney probably took some influence from it, same as *The Lion King* is just *Hamlet* with lions and a humorous warthog-meerkat duo. They're meant to be Rosencrantz and Guildenstern, in case you're interested," she replied.

"Whoa. Next, you'll tell me that *Beauty and the Beast* is supposed to be *Macbeth*." I chuckled.

"Anyway!" Astrid tried not to laugh. "The goddesses tried to get Zeus to judge who was the most beautiful. He didn't want to end up getting skewered during the night by an irritated goddess, so he decided that Paris, a Trojan mortal, should choose. There was some nudity involved I think, but we won't get into that, and each of the goddesses tried to bribe him. But, in the end, he settled on Aphrodite, because she offered him exactly what he wanted—Helen of Sparta."

I raised my hand. "You mean Helen of Troy?"

"Well, she was 'of Sparta' then. The 'of Troy' bit came later, when Paris snatched her and married her himself. See, she was already married to Menelaus, who was a Greek king. That's what caused the Trojan War, because Menelaus launched a campaign to get his wife back. And all because of a single golden apple, thrown into the mix by an unhappy Eris."

"I mean, personally, I hate weddings. I'd have been happy not to be invited."

Astrid snorted into her coffee. "Not exactly the point, Harley."

"No… I guess not."

"So, she's always intrinsically linked with this apple, as that story seems to be the only prominent one about her. Looks like Katherine is out to spread a little discord of her own, if this is anything to go by."

"Well, and all the crappy stuff she's been doing."

"Yes, that too."

"Right, now the apple makes sense. Anything else in that folder of yours?"

She pulled out a few sheets of paper and spread them evenly in front of her. "This is the majority of what I could find. A bit more Greek mythology, claiming her to be the Goddess of Strife and Discord, but we got most of that from the apple thing. However, she was also noted to be the equivalent of the Goddess of War, Enyo."

"Mrs. Smith liked to listen to her."

"Enyo, not Enya. Do you need another one of those?" She nodded at my coffee mug.

I laughed, taking another sip. "It'll kick in, in a minute. Bear with me until then."

"I'll try. Anyway, Enyo is a whole different kettle of fish. Discord and Strife aren't particularly heartwarming, but it's better than being the Goddess of War, Destruction, Conquest, and Bloodlust. Back then, from what we know, a lot of these gods and goddesses were interchangeable, and if Eris is the same as Enyo, then we're in a heap of trouble, if that's what Katherine is modeling her image on."

She took a nervous breath before continuing. "I managed to find out a lot more about this Enyo character. She's referred to as the 'Sister of War' and was a pretty bad egg, in most mythological accounts. She was responsible for the destruction of entire cities, loved all things warfare, and often rode into battle with Ares—the God of War himself. In fact, she even refused to take sides in a terrible battle between Zeus and the monster, Typhon. Here, there's a passage about it: *'Impartial Enyo held equal balance between the two sides, between Zeus and Typhon, while the thunderbolts with booming shots reveled like dancers in the sky.'*"

My heart stopped. "What did you just say?"

"'Impartial Enyo held equal balance between the two sides, between—'"

"No, that's cool—I got it." It was too similar to be coincidence. If Zeus had leaned toward the Light and Typhon toward the Dark, then Enyo had been the one to maintain the equilibrium between both.

Wait... does that mean I'm Enyo/Eris in this scenario?

"Everything okay? You disappeared for a moment there," Astrid said, her tone worried.

I nodded. "I'm fine, just a lot on my mind."

"Brad Pitt still?"

"If only," I replied, with a wry grin.

"Am I boring you?" She sounded hurt, her gaze dropping.

I touched her forearm. "Not at all. I love all this stuff. Like I said, I'm still waiting for the caffeine to hit, and when it does—man, it's going to hit me hard."

She smiled, clearly satisfied. "There were a few other quotes that I found, mostly about the split personality of these two amalgamated goddesses. Here, it mentions that 'After all, there was not one kind of Strife alone, but all over the earth there are two. As for the one, a man would praise her when he came to understand her; but the other is blameworthy: and they are wholly different in nature. For one fosters evil war and battle, being cruel: her, no man loves; but perforce, through the will of the deathless gods, men pay harsh Strife her honor due.' It has Katherine written all over it, if you ask me. I was quite startled by the parallels. This discord thing seems to be the concept she's creating for herself—a terrifying, ruthless, warlike goddess who has to be worshiped and feared by everyone."

What was with all this duality? It was starting to freak me out, not only because it sounded like Katherine's ball of twine, but because it resonated in my own head. Did this mean there was an opposite to Katherine, somewhere in the world? A person who could restore the balance of what she wanted to destroy? I wasn't arrogant enough to think it was me, but a gnawing suspicion remained. Maybe it was supposed to be Hester—Katherine's twin. With her gone, who else could step into that role?

What if Katherine has already killed the one thing that could stop her? I didn't want to dwell on it, in case it turned out to be true.

"Well, no man loved Katherine, that's for sure," I said bitterly. "Not without a nasty little curse, anyway."

"That's what I thought. As soon as I saw it, I got a picture of her in my head," Astrid agreed. "And the last bit: '...through the will of the deathless gods, men pay harsh Strife her honor due.' If she becomes a Child of Chaos, then *she* will be the deathless god."

I shuddered. "I don't want to find out what kind of honor we'll have to pay her, if that happens."

"There was another quote that I found quite interesting. This was apparently spoken by Eris herself: '*I am chaos. I am the substance from which your artists and scientists build rhythms. I am the spirit with which your children and clowns laugh in happy anarchy. I am chaos. I am alive, and I tell you that you are free.*' You know how I mentioned to you in the foyer that there's been a long-held belief that there are more than four children of Chaos?"

"Yeah."

"Well, this would suggest that Eris *is* Chaos itself, or at least another one of the Children."

"I'm not going to sleep well tonight," I muttered. None of this sounded good, though it was clear that Katherine was setting her sights high. If she could become Chaos itself, superseding the other Children, then there'd be no stopping her new world order—whatever that vision was. Kenneth still hadn't breathed a word about it.

My phone went off. Wade's name flashed up on the screen. I picked it up and gave Astrid an apologetic look, but she just smiled knowingly. I wanted to protest that it wasn't like that, but I'd already answered the call.

"Harley?"

"Yep, *you* called *me*, remember?"

"We don't have time for sarcasm," he shot back. "Imogene and

Remington arrived five minutes ago, on Levi's orders, and they want to take the kids away. Get down to the prison cells, now!"

"I'm on my way." I hung up and turned to Astrid. "Imogene and Remington are here. They want to take the kids."

Astrid frowned. "What? Does Alton know?"

"I guess so. Come on, we need to go—now."

She nodded, getting up from her seat and following me out of the Banquet Hall. We tore through the labyrinth of corridors, using one of the concealed stairwells to get down to the prison cells in double-quick time. As we burst through the door to the subterranean level, only Wade and Santana were there when we arrived, with Alton standing beside Remington, the two of them in the midst of a heated discussion. Their voices were low, but the hiss of anger was unmistakable, and I could feel it, too. Meanwhile, Imogene seemed to be looking over the children one by one, ticking them off on a sheet of paper she'd brought in an elegant leather binder. She was crouched low, speaking to them in soft tones.

"Where are the other two?" she asked gently. "Denzel Ford and Andrew Prescott—do you know where they are?"

I could sense fear rippling off the gathered children, though Imogene's soft voice seemed to calm them slightly. I remembered how in awe of her I'd been, the first time I'd met her. And, right now, she had the respect and attention of every single child, their eyes looking up at her as though she were their only hope.

To my surprise, Louella was the one to speak up. "Katherine killed them." Her voice cracked, her lower lip trembling.

I gasped, drawing Imogene's attention for a moment.

"Are you sure?" she asked.

Louella nodded. "I saw her do it. She decided their abilities weren't going to serve her, after all, and she killed them in front of us. She put her hands on their shoulders and muttered this weird spell—a fiery light shot through them, and they just disintegrated into golden specks. They screamed for her to stop, but she didn't care. She killed them anyway." She lifted her hand to her mouth as tears escaped down her cheeks.

Some of the smaller children began to cry, and even Sarah

McCormick had a glint of tears in her stony eyes. Looking at Wade, Santana, and Astrid, I saw my horror reflected in their faces. She'd killed children. That bitch had killed innocent little kids. Astrid looked the most shaken of us all, her gaze fixed on Imogene's face, a flurry of mixed emotions coming off her—sadness, shock, and something like anger. I understood exactly where she was coming from.

"I'm so sorry you had to endure such a terrible thing," Imogene said quietly, rubbing Louella's arm. "Really, I'm so sorry that you've had to suffer at her cruel hands, all this time. Please believe that we were doing all we could to help you, to save you. I'm so grateful you've been found at last. From now on, you will be safe, I promise. We'll make sure you get the best care and cannot be discovered by her again."

"Thank you, Miss Whitehall," Louella murmured, a sad smile on her face.

"Which is why we're taking you all with us," Imogene explained. "You cannot be properly protected here. The SDC has many excellent attributes, but with its past history, it isn't appropriate for you children to remain here. I can't force the two of you to come with us—Marjorie, Louella—as you are of an age where you may make the choice for yourselves, but I hope you will consider this offer of sanctuary."

Alton turned away from Remington and strode up to Imogene's side. "This is ludicrous, Imogene. Taking them away from here will only put them at greater risk. We're taking steps to find a better location for them to hide in, and we are close to a resolution. Please, let them stay here. They will be safe, I promise you."

She smiled apologetically. "You know I can't do that, Alton. It's beyond my jurisdiction. The National Council has ordered that we take them to a safer facility. They trust your ability to care for your own, but the choice has been taken from all of us. It will be better this way."

"And what about Micah? I can train him in the art of Necromancy. He'll learn more from me than he can elsewhere," Alton pleaded.

Hearing his name, Micah ran up to me and clung to my arm. His palms were sweaty and there were tears rolling down his rosy cheeks. All the while, Fluffers was perched on his shoulder, his hackles up.

Neither of them wanted to go, and I wasn't going to make them. Yes, the SDC wasn't perfect, but we could keep them safe. I knew we could.

"With the exception of the two older girls, should they choose to stay, the children are all coming with me. It really is for the best," Imogene insisted, her tone apologetic.

"Imogene, can't you see they're scared?" I interrupted. "Let them decide where they want to go—please."

"I know you want them to stay with you, but we have a secure place for them to live. It has all been prepared. They will be safe, at last. Really, truly safe."

"They're safe here!"

A flicker of frustration crossed her face, though it softened into a defeated sigh. "This is not negotiable, Harley. I'm sorry, but it's not. I have my orders from the National Council, and I can't defy them, as much as I might want to. We must all do what is best for these children, even if it seems difficult now."

At that, Remington stepped forward and wrenched Micah away from me. The cat leapt at his face in an attempt to defend his owner, but Remington cast the creature to one side with a sharp swipe of the hand, the animal dropping to the ground with a hiss. Micah let out a blood-curdling howl as he fought to reach his beloved pet, but Remington held him fast, bundling him into his arms. When it became clear that Micah wasn't going to stop, he tapped the boy on the head and whispered something. A second later, Micah went limp in his arms, sleeping like a baby.

"I didn't want it to be like this, Harley, I really didn't," Imogene said with a sigh. "I'm sorry for the unpleasantness. And to you, Alton." With a remorseful expression, she bent to pick up the irate cat and cradled it in her arms. It relaxed, purring as she scratched between its ears.

"You can still change your mind," I replied bitterly.

"It has been decided, Harley. Discussing it further won't change anything. These children will not be safe here, no matter what you may think. Would you have them stolen again, and used for Katherine's twisted purposes?"

"No," I mumbled.

"I didn't think so. None of us wants that. This is why you must let us take them." She turned to Louella and Marjorie. "Now, what is your decision? You are old enough, and wise enough, to make your own choices."

"I'm going to stay here," Louella said sheepishly. She couldn't meet Imogene's steady gaze.

Marjorie nodded. "I'll stay here too, for now. I need some time to think."

"Take all the time you need, girls. I am never far. If you decide you'd like to come with us, ask Alton to get in touch with me, and I'll come and collect you." She flashed her most charming smile at the other children. "Come, we have lovely rooms waiting for you. You will be safe, at last—somewhere that Katherine will never find you."

They didn't take much convincing. Slowly, they trailed after her, leaving the rest of us in the empty prison corridor.

TWENTY

Harley

A strid, Santana, and I stayed behind in the prison corridor for a
few hours and helped scour the area for anything the security
teams might have missed regarding Quetzi, while Alton and Wade went
off to make sure the kids were safely delivered through the mirrors.
Marjorie and Louella gave us a hand putting all the kids' stuff to one
side, though they didn't say much. The whole event had thrown us all
into silence. I couldn't come to grips with this stricter side of Imogene. I
mean, I knew she had to be some kind of bureaucrat to have worked her
way up to the Mage Council, but I'd never seen her have to get tough
with anyone.

I wiped my brow as we finished piling up the bedding, lights, and
toys. "Hey, I'm going to go upstairs to speak to O'Halloran, see if I can
look over the footage from the interview with Kenneth Willow. He
might have missed a detail about this spy."

Santana nodded. "Good idea. We'll be right behind you once we
finish up here."

"Yeah, we really should broaden our search field again," Astrid
added.

"Whoever this spy turns out to be, I'm going to wring their neck. I might wring Quetzi's neck, too, for letting himself get snatched like that," I muttered, flashing an apologetic look at Marjorie. She'd been beating herself up about the vision, and her inability to hold on to the image.

Santana laughed. "Get in line, *mi hermana*."

Leaving them to it, I headed upstairs in search of O'Halloran. Alton would've been easier to talk to, but I didn't want to disturb him while he was getting the kids to safety. Truthfully, I understood why Imogene and Remington had taken them; I just didn't like the way the National Council had given the order. If the National Council had spoken to Alton first, we could have arranged it and made it less of a shock to those poor children. Instead, they were being dragged from pillar to post again, left in a constant state of confusion and fear. That irked the foster kid in me.

All I could think about was Micah's hand, grabbing on to my arm in desperation. His terror had bled into me, and I was still struggling to get rid of it.

I set off toward the Security Office, hoping I could track O'Halloran down there. However, halfway down the corridor that led away from the living quarters, I skidded to a halt and ducked behind a bronzed dragon. My favorite hiding spot. A short distance away, I spotted Remington talking to Dylan, the children nowhere to be seen. *Have they been taken through already?* I supposed they'd had plenty of time, but I hadn't expected the Mage Council minions to stick around after the fact.

"So, you're still at college?" Remington asked. Bemusement whorled off Dylan as he scanned the corridor, clearly looking for a quick escape route.

"Yeah."

"And you play football?"

"Yeah."

Geez, what's with all the personal questions?

"How are your foster parents? Are they good to you?"

Dylan glanced at Remington suspiciously. "All good, thanks. They've got a nice place in the suburbs."

"Don't they worry about you being here?"

He shrugged. "Not really. They don't know much about it. They think it's a job."

"You were left at Children's Services, right?"

Seriously, what was his deal? I could sense a mixture of concern, nerves, and something close to affection flowing off him, though that didn't make anything clearer.

"A long time ago, yeah." Dylan spoke slowly, as if not sure how to react to Remington's barrage of questions.

"And you never found out who left you there."

"Nope."

"Didn't you want to?"

Dylan laughed bitterly. "Not much point. We call it the Dump for a reason. Nobody gets left there because someone's coming back for them."

A stab of sadness pierced my heart. Dylan and I knew how the fostering world worked. We'd both seen other foster kids waiting at the windows, and lingering by the doors, hoping their parents would turn up and take them back. Early on, I'd sit on the window ledge in my room and watch the road outside, convinced that a car would pull up with my parents inside it, and they'd walk back into my life.

"I'm sorry about that, Dylan," Remington said.

"Why would you be sorry?" A challenge flashed in his eyes.

"It must have been hard for you, that's all."

Dylan shrugged. "I'm over it. I've had good foster homes since then. I don't have much to complain about. So, my parents didn't want me—it doesn't bother me anymore."

"But you must have wondered?"

"I don't want to be rude or anything, but what's with all the questions? Do you know something I don't? Something you want to tell me?"

My ears pricked up in anticipation of Remington's answer.

Remington dropped his gaze. "Imogene chided me for being so rough with that child earlier. So, I want to better understand what it's like for those foster kids, given that we're taking so many under our wing. I thought you could provide some personal insight."

"I don't see you asking Harley all of this stuff," he retorted.

"No, she's a little too… how shall I say this—spiky. Besides, we know who her parents are now, and yours are still unaccounted for. That's why I was asking if you'd ever wondered who they were."

Dylan frowned, his eyes softening slightly. "When I was a kid, yeah, but I'm not a kid anymore. They must have had their reasons for leaving me there, and that's on them. Even if they walked through that door right now, I wouldn't care. It wouldn't change anything."

Remington fidgeted with his hands. "Even if the reasons were good ones?"

"Even if the reasons were good ones. You can be anywhere in the world and still write a letter."

"Yes… I suppose you're right." Remington glanced toward the adjoining corridor. "Well, I've taken up enough of your time. I should probably get back to the Assembly Hall and make sure all the paper-work is complete."

"Yeah, you do that," Dylan replied coolly. "Can I say one thing before you go?"

Remington nodded. "Anything."

"Make sure those kids know that they belong, okay? They've been moved around enough—make sure this is the last time. If you can find them homes after all of this is over, then do that, but only if you can guarantee they won't have to move again. Keep them in a coven if you have to—just don't drag them around anymore."

"I will see to it," Remington said, chastened.

"Good."

Dylan stood there a while longer as Remington walked away. Steeling myself, I stepped out from behind the dragon. He looked up in surprise as I approached, though I was glad he hadn't noticed me lurking in the shadows. Eavesdropping wasn't a good look on anyone.

"How's it going down there?" he asked. "Astrid called me a while ago. I was just on my way to join you. I think the rest of the Rag Team are coming to help search for Quetzi, too."

"It's slow," I admitted. "I was about to go and find O'Halloran when I saw you... and Remington."

A strange expression moved across his face, his emotions going on the defensive. "You heard that, huh?"

"Hey, I agree with everything you said. I hate to sound like an old woman, but those kids need stability. We've both been in their position, not knowing where we might be when we wake up. I'd like to see them taken care of, even if that means they can't stay here at the SDC."

He smiled. "Me, too."

"But why was he asking you all those questions? They seemed kind of personal."

He shrugged. "I'm not sure what his deal is. Could you feel his emotions?"

"Yeah, a big old jumble of stuff."

"Bad stuff?"

"No, not particularly."

"If he ever comes back here, I'll have to see if he continues being so nosy," Dylan said, in his casual way.

"You should probably keep tabs on that," I agreed. "So, did you move around a lot when you were a kid? Sounded like it, if you don't mind me saying."

"Yeah. I don't think I stayed in the same place for more than a year, maybe."

"The longest I managed was two years, and that was with the Smiths. You know, I wish I could've ended up with them earlier. They're the kind of foster family we all dream about, the ones who *just* might adopt us."

"That kind of family always come too late though, don't they?" He sounded sad. "My foster parents are like that, but it's the same for me—I wish I could've found them earlier so I didn't get hauled across the state as a kid."

I nodded. "School was the worst thing for me. I never settled anywhere."

"Nah, school was always my safe place. I think it's the football thing. If you're on the team, you fit in."

"See, everyone always said I should've been sportier," I said, with a wry laugh. "I was always the weirdo, even before my abilities started seeping out. I guess I give off that vibe—you know, the foster kid vibe."

"No way. Kids are just mean sometimes, I think," he replied. "It's like everyone's trying to find their place, and they imitate what they see so they can feel like they fit in. Take bullies for example—usually, they're the ones with the deepest issues. You go through their front door at home, and nine times out of ten, they're getting beaten by their dad or hounded by their brother or screamed at by their mom. So, they turn around and do the same to kids at school. Or their parents are working all hours of the day and they're latchkey kids who have to fend for themselves. I'm not saying it's an excuse, but one of my coaches used to have a saying, that 'hurt people hurt people.' I guess that kind of stuck with me."

"I didn't have you down as the poetic type," I said.

He grinned. "I can whip out a clever line when the moment's right. Tatyana makes me want to spew poetry all the time, but she'd probably just make fun of me. Man, I kind of like it when she does that, though. Is that weird?"

"No, I think that's the Tatyana Effect," I replied, chuckling. It brought Jacob to mind. "Although, if you're going to get poetic, I'd suggest using a word other than 'spew.' Word vomit isn't exactly sexy."

"I'll keep that in mind. Anyway, I should let you get to O'Halloran before the others start to think we're both shirking."

I smiled at him. "If you ever need to talk about this stuff, you know you can come to me, right?"

"I will. Thanks, Harley," he said. "I'm glad we talked."

"Cool, then I'll see you downstairs in a bit?"

"See you then." With a funny salute, he set off down the corridor, headed toward the prison hallway. Returning to my own task of finding

O'Halloran, I continued to wonder why Remington was taking such an interest in Dylan. He'd done the same thing the last time he was here, staring at Dylan as though he had a secret he couldn't mention. It seemed like a lot more than professional courtesy.

Are they related, maybe, and Dylan doesn't know? I pictured Remington's face, but the similarities weren't obvious enough for them to be tied together like that. *Then what's the secret, Remington?*

Shrugging it off, realizing it was none of my business, I hurried down the corridor.

I'd almost reached the Security Office when two familiar voices made me halt. Wade and Imogene were walking across the intersection up ahead, coming from the Assembly Hall. I ducked back behind the archway nearby and watched them head up the northern corridor. *What's he doing with her?* More to the point, why had both Remington and Imogene come back to the SDC, so soon after leaving with the kids? Paperwork and last checks seemed like the most logical solution, but I was eager to find out for sure. Plus, the jealous streak in me didn't like seeing them so close. Call me petty, but that was how I felt.

After watching Wade and Imogene walk further ahead, I ducked out of my hiding spot and followed them at a distance.

A few minutes later, they turned into a room on the right. From what I knew of the coven layout, it didn't lead to anywhere interesting, just one of the side offices that the staff used when they wanted some privacy from the coven. Wade followed Imogene inside, the door left ajar. I slowed to a creeping walk. Crouching down and peering through the gap, praying I didn't get caught, I glimpsed Wade's back.

"Stella and Channing spoke very highly of you, and they have recommended you for an apprenticeship position with us at the Mage Council," Imogene said. "I happen to agree that your future is in need of brightening, and I want to discuss that possibility with you."

"I know, but I don't understand why you picked me instead of one of the others," Wade replied. A green-tinged arrow of jealousy shot through me. *Yeah, Imogene, I'd like to know that, too.* From what I could sense, despite his obvious reluctance, Wade was crushing hard on Ms.

Whitehall. The feel of it flowing from him did nothing to ease my jealous streak. I mean, next to the glorious, Norse-goddess-esque stature of Imogene, I might as well have been a toad.

"You have untapped potential, Wade, and I worry that it's being wasted here," she explained silkily. "I know that Levi is eager to have you, and I share his enthusiasm. You're gifted, Wade, and you're of excellent lineage. You could be tremendous, if given the right guidance."

My heart stopped as she rose from her chair and moved around to Wade's side of the desk. Moving like a ballet dancer, she edged closer to him. She paused less than a yard from where he stood, leaning elegantly against the mahogany. I could hardly breathe, watching them together. Judging from Wade's body language, neither could he.

"You think I'm not getting the right guidance here?" he asked, his voice thick.

She smiled. "I think you're getting excellent guidance, but there are limits to what the SDC can offer you, and you're at an age where you need to make some difficult choices. A successful career awaits you, but you have to take the right opportunities."

"Like an apprenticeship?"

She shrugged. "That is one of the options, yes."

"Can we talk about this another time? I need to meet with my team soon."

"See, this is precisely what I mean. You have the makings of a superb leader."

He glanced away shyly. "Can I think about what you've said and get back to you?"

"Certainly. Maybe you'd care to join me for a drink, one day next week?"

His eyebrows shot up, and my eyes nearly fell out of my head. "A drink? I'm not sure if that's appropriate, Ms. Whitehall. I mean, I'm flattered by the offer, but… well, I kind of like someone else, and I don't want her to get the wrong impression by my going on a date with another woman."

Imogene laughed, placing her hand over her heart. "Goodness, Wade.

I didn't mean a drink in the *romantic* sense. I merely meant would you like to join me for a drink so that we can discuss business—as in, your future. Coffee or tea, not champagne and strawberries." Her smile lit up the room and sent Wade's cheeks a furious shade of beet. I clamped a hand to my mouth, stifling a giggle. *Man, that's embarrassing...* Although my own cheeks had flushed with heat after what he'd said about liking someone else. I really hoped he meant me.

"Oh, my God, I'm so sorry. I thought—"

"It's fine, Wade. I'm actually a little flattered to know I've still got it!" She laughed lightly. "As for this girl you like, I suggest you hurry along and tell her. Women don't enjoy the chase as much as you might think, and they certainly don't like to be kept waiting when it comes to matters of the heart." She smiled again, patting him on the arm as if he were a mischievous schoolboy. "If she could see you right now, I'm certain she'd be impressed by your loyalty."

I grinned like an idiot. Even faced with a misinterpreted offer of a date from Imogene freaking Whitehall, he'd turned her down for me. At least, I wanted that "someone else" to be me. Still, how the heck could I know, when he hadn't said a word about it? A near-kiss and a lingering hug didn't mean anything without the big guns of love to back it up.

My phone vibrated in my pocket, and I took it out. Astrid's name flashed on the screen, with a text underneath: *Are you coming back? Found something you wanna see.*

It was the perfect excuse to interrupt Wade and Imogene, without it looking like I'd been eavesdropping on their intimate little meeting. My jealousy had evaporated, leaving a fuzzy glow of hope from Wade, and a bit of guilt toward Imogene. She wasn't being a cougar, just a Council official with a job to do. I guessed I'd gotten a little too caught up in her attitude back in the prison corridor, which had shown me a different, less-patient side to her. We'd made things difficult for her and, by proxy, the frightened kids—of course she was going to get a little pissed at us. Plus, she had a point about their safety. We'd been compromised, after all. It had just hurt to see Micah taken away.

I knocked on the door. "Sorry to interrupt, Imogene, but we need

Wade downstairs. I just got a message from Astrid—she needs everyone on the Rag Team."

She nodded, smiling. "Harley, what a pleasant surprise. We were just talking about you."

Wade looked at her in horror, my insides fizzing with happiness and amusement. His expression said a thousand words, and so did his emotions. They were jumping all over themselves: panic, embarrassment, affection, surprise, the whole shebang.

"You know, about gifted members of the coven moving up in the world?" she prompted, nudging him in the arm.

His cheeks flushed. "Yeah, right... that. Of course."

"So, we'll continue this conversation later, yes?" Imogene said. "Harley, I was hoping to have a word with you at some point, too. It would appear that now is not the time, but I'll arrange a meeting with you when it's more appropriate. Would that be okay?"

"Absolutely," I replied.

"I also wanted to say I'm sorry for earlier. It's tough on all of us. I hate having to raise my voice, and I loathe confrontation even more. I hope you understand that I only did what I did for the children. They're my primary concern here."

"I see that now. Did they arrive safely?"

She nodded. "Yes, they're at the Mage Council headquarters, where they'll be sent on to a secure location. They'll benefit from round-the-clock security measures, though I have endeavored to make it as noninvasive as possible. They're only children, after all."

"Thank you, Imogene. I'm sorry, too, if I annoyed you back there. I know you were only doing your job."

"Nonsense. You were being protective, and that's one of your most admirable qualities. It will serve you well in all that you do—it was simply misplaced on this particular occasion," she replied. "Now, be gone with you, before I steal you both from under Alton's nose and put you on the Council training program!"

"The Council training program?" I asked innocently. I didn't want her to guess that I'd been eavesdropping.

She smiled. "A topic for another time. I should be getting back to headquarters, and there's still a large amount of paperwork. I will speak with you both soon, though, yes?"

I nodded. "One hundred percent."

"Yeah… for coffee or tea," Wade mumbled.

"Exactly." She chuckled, the sound warming my heart. Wade Crowley liked me. He'd picked me over a potential date with Imogene—he freaking liked me!

TWENTY-ONE

Astrid

"We came as soon as we could," Harley said breathlessly. Wade stood beside her, looking flushed. I didn't like to make assumptions, but he seemed somewhat awkward around her, unable to meet her gaze. *What's going on there?*

"What did you find?" Wade prompted.

"Ah, yes…" I snapped out of my thoughts, pulling Smartie out. "Since we didn't get to finish the interviews today, and we were sweeping for Quetzi evidence, I decided to review some of the camera footage from the night that Quetzi was taken. I found a glitch. Well, I thought it was a glitch, but it was actually another shadow that I missed before. I didn't think to re-check the footage down here till we were cleaning up, since the prison cameras were playing up after the Bestiary got hit." I replayed the frames, showing them the new images I'd dredged up from the depths of the coven's system. I'd had to look through them at a lower frame rate to make the picture clear.

"I don't see it," Harley said, frowning.

"Neither do I," Santana agreed, moving up to take a closer look. Tatyana, Raffe, and Dylan were also there, though I'd kept the news to myself until the entire Rag Team were in attendance. Only Garrett remained absent, which irked me somewhat. He should have been here with us.

"Here." I pointed to a smudge in the top right-hand corner of the footage. To the untrained eye, it appeared to be nothing but a fuzzy mark on the camera. However, I knew better. It was an unmistakable, moving shadow, edging up the prison corridor.

Harley gasped. "Holy hell, you're right. Are there more frames?"

"There are a few more, but they disappear at the far end of the hall-way. Now, there's only one place that this shadow could be heading, if it vanishes in the location that it does."

"Where?"

Tatyana answered before I could. "The Crypt."

"Yup," I replied. The fact had taken me by surprise, but now that I'd spoken it out loud, I was more convinced than ever. A locked doorway stood at the farthest end of the prison corridor, but only Alton knew the spell to gain entry. Well, him and I. He'd given me the privilege of learning its secret, in case I ever needed to go down there. Whoever this traitor was amongst us, they had somehow managed to bypass my father's fail-safe and broken into the Crypt—a restricted area, deep below the coven, that only Alton and the Mage Council had access to. My thought was that they'd stowed away Quetzi so they could wait out the rest of the week until Alton performed his usual monthly breakdown.

"Then what are we waiting for?" Dylan asked.

"Do you think the spy will be down there?" Raffe chimed in, his eyes flashing that worrying shade of red for a moment.

"Honestly, I don't know what we'll find down there," I replied. "You can keep your fiery friend on standby, though."

Raffe nodded. "No problem."

It felt odd to be the one leading the charge, but they followed me down the hallway regardless. Reaching the vast, black iron door at the end of the corridor, I paused. It was a beastly thing, forged from thick metal, with silver bolts indented in the exterior. It reminded me of the door to a bank vault, rather than a place for the dead to make their final slumber.

Pressing my hands against the central vein of the door, I recited the words Alton had taught me: "*Omnem dimittite spem, o vos intrantes.*" It had been my father's inside joke, to use the same words that were written above the gates of hell in Dante's *Inferno*—"Abandon all hope, ye who enter here"—though he'd translated the words into Latin to get the spell to work. I didn't see the funny side, even now. I supposed it was hilarious to a Necromancer, for whom death didn't have to be the end.

The locks whirred inside the door. With a soft click, the two sides swung open, revealing a long, dark tunnel beyond. The medieval architecture of the arched tunnel, complete with flickering torchlight in iron sconces, certainly screamed "Crypt" in every possible way. Now, I could understand why we were supposed to abandon all hope. Although Alton had given me the password to the door, he'd never allowed me in the Crypt. At least not while I'd been in a state of consciousness. He never liked to see me around death, and I supposed this brought back bad memories for him.

"Well, this is beyond creepy," Santana muttered, breaking the tension.

"Glad someone said it," Harley replied, with a nervous laugh.

As a group, we moved through the damp tunnel, which was slick with moss. The stone walls disappeared, revealing a wide platform. Flaming grates lit up as we neared, the fire roaring wildly, casting eerie shadows across the masonry. I lacked Tatyana's Kolduny abilities, but even I could sense the presence of spirits down here. They whispered in my ears and nipped at the back of my neck, setting my fine hairs on end. The others seemed to be equally perturbed, with the exception of our resident Ice Queen. She, as expected, was taking it in stride.

"Can you feel any spooks?" Dylan whispered, his arm around Tatyana's waist. I would never have called him out on it, but I sensed he was holding her due to his own fear, rather than hers.

"More than I can count," Tatyana replied calmly.

"Yeah, let's take that up a notch to *really* freaking creepy," Santana muttered.

A winding stone staircase met us at the end of the open plateau, curving down toward a cavernous space below. It looked like an ancient mine or a dilapidated temple, discovered by old-time explorers in pith helmets.

All along the far rock wall were the two-dimensional exteriors of mausoleums, running up five layers of strata. Stone stairwells and narrow ledges paved the way toward each one, my stomach plummeting at the thought of having to climb to the very top ones. Names had been carved into the lintels above some of them, but there were others that remained nameless. Either that, or the names had long been worn away by time and natural erosion.

"Let's get searching," Wade said firmly. "If we split up into groups, we'll cover more ground."

Tatyana stepped forward. "No need. If you give me a moment, I can ask the spirits if they've seen Quetzi here."

"Are you sure?" Dylan asked.

"Quite sure." Her tone held a warning.

We stood and watched her as her eyes lit up white, her body radiating with spiritual energy. Through her pale skin, her veins pulsated, each one brimming with that same white light. It was impressive, no matter how many times she did it. As she worked, I glanced over the edge at the mausoleums and wondered where Emmett Ryder was buried. Alton told me a lot of things, but he'd kept that secret to himself. Still, I worried that the dead Ryder twin might somehow take hold of Tatyana.

"The Angelov Tomb," Tatyana whispered breathily, her voice echoing with the cadence of another person. "A man came. He held a snake in glistening restraints. He brought the snake to the Tomb of Angelov and left it there with the door locked."

"When?" I prompted.

"On the day that the coven shivered," she replied.

Harley paled. "She means the day that Quetzi got taken. The force

field that holds this whole thing up glitched for a couple of minutes—
that has to be it."

Tatyana closed her eyes, the bright light fading. Her breath came in
short, sharp gasps as she came back into the real world, her hands trembling as the spirit left her. "He was strong," she murmured. "That spirit
—he was strong."

"Are you okay?" Dylan propped her up, his brow furrowed. *I wish
Garrett were here...*

She nodded. "I'll be fine. He didn't want to harm me. His strength
took me by surprise, that's all. It can happen from time to time, especially when I am out of practice." Ever since Oberon Marx had hijacked
her, she hadn't quite been as confident in her abilities, and hadn't used
them nearly as often. A natural reaction to almost being overwhelmed
by a ghost.

"Angelov... There, that's the one!" Raffe pointed to a mausoleum on
the third floor of the far wall.

We took off down the stone staircase and sprinted for the tomb.
Dylan was in front, running faster than the rest of us, given his
Herculean abilities. However, upon reaching the third level, and
standing in front of the given tomb, we found that the door was, indeed,
locked—just as the spirit had said. A huge, bronze padlock dangled
down, the rusted metal glinting in the dim light of the Crypt.

"I've got this one," Dylan said. He took a few steps back, his heel on
the ledge, then hurtled full speed at the door of the tomb. It shattered
into a hundred pieces of rubble as he careened through it. A fusty smell
seeped outward, while an impenetrable darkness faced us.

Harley and Wade conjured balls of fire to light up the shadows,
taking the first tentative steps into the gloom. The rest of the team
followed close behind them, using the glowing orbs as a point of guidance. I didn't know if it was because I'd been dead before, or almost
dead, but I felt invisible fingertips on my skin. They reached out for me
as if they knew I was one of them. I didn't want to be one of them, not
yet. It reminded me of Marjorie's vision—she had seen me, dead on the
ground. Now and again, since she'd revealed that to us, I'd awoken in a

cold sweat, my nightmares peppered with my own demise. Never had the possibility of her vision coming to pass seemed so tangible. All of us would die one day, but I heard that ticking clock louder than most.

"You took your time," a voice echoed from the darkness. "Silly, really, to think you were the intelligent ones. Even I'd guessed that someone might come for me before the spy snatched me from my box and threw me, like a sack of trash I might add, in here."

"Who's there?" Harley whispered.

"Idiots. I'm surrounded by idiots," it replied. "What did that hulking great mistake with the fancy wings like to call me? Quetzi, is it?"

Silence followed. Even I was shocked. I'd never heard any Purge beasts talk, aside from Tobe, and Quetzi had never done anything but hiss at most of us.

"Quetzi?" Harley gasped.

"I hate nicknames, but if you must call me that, then yes… here I am. You found me. Well done, you." The serpent's voice taunted us through the shadows. "Although I should warn you, if you think you're returning me to my former prison, you can think again. You have no idea how delicious freedom tastes."

Every sibilant letter carried a low hiss that sent a shiver through me. I imagined him lashing his tongue against the air, tasting out his surroundings. Could he sense our fear?

"You speak?" Harley asked.

A chuckle rippled toward us. "If I had hands, I would applaud your human obliviousness."

"Fair enough, that was probably a silly thing to say. It's just a little surprising to hear you, that's all," she retorted. "You haven't spoken before."

"Even if I had, you wouldn't have heard me through that charmed glass. Melodic, aren't I?"

"Uh… I guess so."

"Oh, and if you've come here to wreak revenge on me for that incident with the boyish woman, you can stop right there. I had nothing to do with it," he said firmly. "That cretin peeled the skin right off me, and

I wasn't even ready to shed. Not to mention the venom atrocity—stole it right from my fangs while I was out cold and thought I wouldn't notice. He might have killed her with it, but he took it against my will. I ought to wrap myself around him and squeeze the very life out of him for that. Had that nasty little Shapeshifter not had me bound, I'd have killed him where he stood. Nobody steals venom from me."

Harley cleared her throat. "We kind of did."

"No, I *let* you. There's a difference."

"Well, are you bound now?" I asked, emboldened. Back then, it hadn't seemed like he'd let us do anything. He'd put up a pretty good fight against Tobe for it to be a charade. I guessed he was trying to save face.

He laughed. "Ah, wouldn't you like to know, my little evader of death. I bet you're all quivering with anticipation, wanting to know if I'm safe to approach. Well, you'll only find out if you come a little closer. I won't bite, I swear."

"Do you know who the spy is?" I pressed.

"He kept changing his face—he wasn't someone I recognized, but I'd know him if I saw him again," Quetzi replied. "Although, you shouldn't bother asking me if I know his name. He wasn't generous enough to give one."

I frowned. "Why did the Shapeshifter make it look like you'd killed Adley?"

"Ah, so you're *not* here to punish me for crimes I did not commit? What a pleasant surprise," he mused. "I presume Adley is the boyish dead girl?"

"Yes, that's her," Santana chimed in. "Can I just say, it's an honor to hear you speak."

He dipped his head reverently. "It's always nice to see a Santeria. A *very* pleasant one at that."

"Why did the Shapeshifter set you up?" I repeated. Santana had stiffened at my side. Meeting a serpent like Quetzi had to be a big deal for her, although having one make flirtatious remarks was probably unexpected.

He hissed. "You probably know more than I do. I could understand him wanting to steal me, perhaps, but setting me up for murder seems like overkill. Honestly, your guess is as good as mine. Rude of the Shapeshifter to try and blame me. At least you weren't stupid enough to fall for *that*."

"If you come with us now, we'll make sure Alton finds somewhere better for you," Wade said.

Quetzi laughed again. "A glass box is a glass box, no matter the size or the finery you offer me. And I am fairly sure that Alton isn't about to let me roam free of my own accord, is he?"

"He might," I replied.

"Come now, you ought to know, better than anyone, that he never would. Why, he's almost like family to you, isn't he? You know him best of all."

My voice died on my lips. *He knows... How can he know?*

Before I could respond, a shadow surged forward and swept past the gathered group. Quetzi moved in a blur, slithering easily between our legs and out of the tomb door. Wade hurled his orb of fire at the serpent, but Quetzi dodged it deftly. One thing was for sure; he wasn't bound anymore.

We chased him out onto the ledge, but he'd already slid right over the lip. The serpent landed with a thump on the ground below. Harley threw her fireball at him, the sparking whorl almost glancing his tail, but he barely paid it any heed. Instead, he picked up speed, slithering toward the stone staircase that led out of the Crypt.

"Cut him off!" Wade roared, as he launched a barrage of fire at the beast.

Harley sent out a lasso of Telekinesis, but no matter where she sent it, Quetzi was always one slither ahead. Meanwhile, Dylan took off down the stairs at a Herculean sprint, as Tatyana lit up like the Fourth of July in an attempt to get the spirits to help her. Santana's Orishas were pouring out of her, and Raffe's skin turned a pale shade of scarlet. The latter took off after Dylan, black smoke billowing from his shoulders.

Not for the first time, I felt useless. There was nothing that Smartie and I could do to help stop Quetzi from getting away.

With the rest of the team, I ran back up the stone staircase and through the passageway, before the huge metal door blocked our path. I pressed my hands to the black iron and uttered the password, but it wouldn't budge.

"Get it open!" Wade shouted.

"I can't!"

He looked worried. "What do you mean?"

"I mean, it's not working. Quetzi has done something to keep it shut."

"Are you saying we're trapped down here?" Santana gasped, clutching her chest as she got her breath back.

I nodded. "I don't know if he whacked it with his tail, or did some weather spell on it, but until someone comes to rescue us, we're stuck here."

Wade slammed his fists into the door. "There's got to be a way out. Dylan, Harley, one of you use your Earth to break it."

"And cause a cave-in?" Harley shot back.

"Air then," Wade urged.

I shook my head. "That would do the same thing. If you tear this door out, it'll cause the rocks around it to crumble in. If we use Fire, we'll smoke ourselves out."

"Does this mean..." Dylan muttered, distracting me.

"Does this mean that Quetzi has escaped? Yeah, I think it does," Harley added bitterly. "He's managed to get into the coven and, if he gets his way, he's going to get out into the real world."

"No, someone will stop him before he can do that," Raffe said, though he lacked conviction.

"Who's going to do that?" Harley asked. "Nobody knows we're down here. Nobody knows we came to get Quetzi. Unless... Astrid, did you text Garrett the same thing you texted us?"

"I did, but he didn't come."

She sighed. "Right, then he might be our only way out of here. We've

244 • HARLEY MERLIN AND THE FIRST RITUAL

just got to hope he figures out something's up before that slimy little bastard gets out."

"Does anyone have a phone signal?" Tatyana asked.

"No," chorused the rest of the group. We were too deep beneath the coven for that.

"Great," Harley muttered. "So, Quetzi's going to get out into the human world, and we can be sure he's going to cause a little mayhem when he does. I mean, the guy's been locked up for so long that he must be in need of a bit of old-fashioned god-stuff. He'll be stretching his magical muscles before we even get out of here."

"Oh, yeah, there'll be some news reports tonight! Giant friggin' snake causes electrical storm over San Diego and demands all the gold in Fort Knox to make it stop," Santana agreed, sinking onto the floor.

Wade turned to me. "Why did he single you out like that, Astrid?"

My heart began to palpitate furiously. "I don't know."

"Come on, Wade, that was clearly just a distraction technique," Harley said. "And it worked. Man, how did we let that happen? We should have brought backup."

"What's done is done," Raffe replied. "We just have to fix it when we get out."

Tatyana shrugged as she sat down beside Santana. "At least we really know it wasn't Quetzi who killed Adley now. Maybe we can use her death to get Finch to talk. I know it may sound cold, but if he finds out that Katherine ordered Adley's death, he might be more willing to speak. Silver linings."

"I still can't figure out why she kept Finch alive, when she killed everyone else in the Shipton and Merlin clans. My aunt is the only other exception, and Katherine would have killed her if she could have. Unless she was already planning on using Isadora's powers for her own ends," Harley said, as she paced the floor. "Regardless, she just let Finch live. Do you think she couldn't do it, because he's her son? It's been bugging me for ages."

"That sounds like a logical reason," I replied. "Another question would be, why did she kill all the Shiptons in the first place? They weren't part of the Sál Vinna spell. Not that we know of, anyway. So, why would she have them all murdered?"

"My money's on vengeance," Raffe said.

Tatyana nodded. "Katherine evidently despised Hester, and if her family sided with Hester over Katherine in the Hiram triangle, then maybe she thought they deserved to die. It might have seemed like justice to her, albeit warped."

"Yeah, because she's a total crackpot who doesn't take kindly to rejection," Harley spat. "But she can't be doing all of this just because my dad wouldn't love her, and her sister stole her man. That'd be *complete* insanity."

"She's a psychopath, Harley. It might not be because of that, but that may have been the catalyst—the stressor that triggered the monster that was always lurking inside her," I suggested. "You hear of people who just snap one day and go on killing sprees, but that bad seed was growing inside her for a long time. I wouldn't be surprised if it was that break that led her toward what she's doing now; it opened up that new, dark world of psychopathy for her. It might have given her the... freedom isn't the right word, but you understand what I mean. Maybe, after that, she changed forever, and has no desire to ever change back. Now, she is who she was always meant to be, from the moment that first seed got planted."

"She might have felt trampled on," Dylan said. "Now, she's doing the trampling. Like, maybe it started off as a revenge thing, and it's just snowballed into this whole other thing."

Harley smacked her hand into the door. "What, like this Cult of Eris bullcrap—so she can feel all high and mighty and do some leveling of the playing field? So she can feel real good about herself, in her freaking astral, pure-Chaos form? Astrid, tell them what you found out about this Eris person. I think it's only right that we all hear just how insane Katherine is getting. You'll start shaking in your boots once you hear who she's modeling herself after."

I swallowed a nervous gulp and told them everything I'd told Harley, about the mythology of Eris and the worrying quotes I'd found out about her. They all listened in silence, their expressions morphing into identical masks of fear.

Santana raised her hand. "I just have one question."

"I'll do my best to answer it," I replied.

"If this is her game plan, to become this almighty, destructive force of war and discord, what part does Quetzi have to play in it?"

That, I couldn't answer. I had no idea.

TWENTY-TWO

Astrid

Over an hour later, a loud screeching distracted us from talk of Katherine and Quetzi, the iron doors pulling apart slowly. Through a gap in the center, Alton appeared with Garrett at his side. I wanted to be glad to see him, but concern lingered at the back of my mind. *Where were you?* Regardless of his absence, he'd evidently gotten my text. My message to him had been more specific than the one I sent to the others, and it was lucky I'd been more detailed. If I hadn't, I wondered how long it might have been until they found us down here.

"Thank goodness you're here," Alton said, letting us all out of the tunnel. "What happened?"

I explained everything to him, though I struggled to look him in the eyes in case it gave the others reason to put two and two together. Quetzi had almost exposed the truth about Alton being my father, and I didn't want to add fuel to any remaining fire.

Harley was the one to speak up. "We found Quetzi, but, uh… he got away from us."

"Quetzi is loose in the coven?" Alton's voice sounded strangled.

I nodded. "He broke the Crypt door on his way out."

"How long ago?"

"An hour, maybe."

"That's plenty of time for him to escape into the human world," Alton muttered. "I'll speak with security and see if anyone has noticed anything. Meanwhile, you should all get ready to go out in the field. If Quetzi has escaped the coven's perimeter, we'll need to go after him."

"No problem," Wade replied. "We're on it."

"Good, I'll call you when I know more." Alton turned and left, barely acknowledging me with a goodbye. I wasn't upset; he had other things on his mind. Besides, my attention was fixed on Garrett.

"Where were you?" I whispered.

He frowned. "What do you mean?"

"Before, when I texted you about Quetzi. Why didn't you come?"

"I was busy."

"With what?"

He shrugged. "Other stuff. I figured you didn't need me right away if you had the rest of the Rag Team with you. Good thing I didn't come down; otherwise, we'd all be screwed right now."

I couldn't let go of my nagging doubts. "But *where* were you? What were you doing?"

"I told you, I was busy."

Thanks to Quetzi, we now knew that the Shapeshifter was a man. Garrett hadn't been there initially when we'd all hurried to help with the collateral damage in the Bestiary. He'd turned up later—a good while later. And he hadn't been there when I told him to meet us in the prison corridor, sharing my suspicions about Quetzi's whereabouts. Had he been worried that Quetzi might give him away? I needed to tick him off the suspect list. It filled my focus entirely. Until I did that, I wouldn't be able to rest.

"You won't tell me what you were doing?" I pressed.

"It's not important. Just check the cameras if you're really bothered about it," he replied. I couldn't understand why he wouldn't just say what he'd been up to. Why the secrecy? We'd come so far, yet he was shutting me out.

"I don't want to do that," I said.

He shrugged. "Then trust me."

"I do trust you."

"Really?" He arched an eyebrow. "You really trust me?"

"Of course."

"Then promise me you won't look at the camera footage," he said.

"I… I promise."

"We'll see." His tone was cold, bringing me a wave of discomfort. "Anyway, now that you're all out of the Crypt, I've got some stuff to do. If you need me, call or something."

"Garrett…"

"What?"

I opened my mouth, but the words wouldn't come out. "Never mind."

He walked away, leaving me to wonder where this sudden change had come from. Maybe he was hiding something, after all. My fingers itched to bring out Smartie and check the cameras, precisely the way I'd promised not to.

I waited until he'd vanished from sight before I did it, hating myself for breaking his trust. *I'm sorry, Garrett. I have to know.* The others were heading up the hallway, too. Harley glanced back, her brow furrowed as she saw the tablet in my hands.

"You coming with us?" she asked.

I nodded. "I just want to check the security system for any sign of Quetzi," I lied. "I'll catch up with you in a bit."

"Okay. Do you want me to grab you something from the Banquet Hall? If we head out, we won't have any time to eat. I don't want you starving yourself because you're working too hard."

I smiled at her kindness. "A coffee would be great, and a sandwich if they're still out on the buffet table."

"No problem. Coffee and a sandwich. I'll text where we're at, okay?"

"Thanks."

Left alone in the corridor, I opened Smartie's interface and searched for the Shapeshifter body cam footage from the afternoon that Quetzi had been taken. I'd reviewed the footage a few times and never found anything, but perhaps I hadn't been looking close enough—namely at Garrett's individual frames.

The footage rolled smoothly enough, showing him asleep on his bed, the camera turned up toward his face. He looked sweet, breathing softly, his eyes closed. Nothing unusual immediately jumped out at me. *He was asleep when the Bestiary was attacked... I know that's why he didn't show up right away.*

I was about to turn it off, feeling satisfied that he wasn't involved in Quetzi being taken, when I noticed a flicker in the bottom-right corner of the screen. The shadow of an object, maybe a bird flying past the window, moved across his chest. However, a few seconds later, it did the same thing again, the pattern repeating over and over. I shifted to the footage from an hour or so ago, but the same thing seemed to be happening. He was lying on his bed, fast asleep, revealing a similar glitch. His right eye twitched subtly in his sleep, only to twitch again and again and again. I scrolled forward to find that the first repetitive clip lasted an hour, while the other one lasted closer to two hours.

There was no mistaking it: the footage had been doctored, playing on a loop to make it look as though he'd been sleeping the whole time.

No... this can't be true. Not Garrett.

All my fears and doubts crept in. I couldn't disagree with cold, hard facts, no matter how much I might have liked to. However, before I revealed this newfound information to Alton, I wanted to confront Garrett about it first. I wanted him to tell me his reasons before I threw him to the lions. Part of me hoped there was more to this than met the eye. Garrett couldn't be the traitor... could he?

I hurried down the corridor and clambered up to the main body of the coven, running through the hallway toward Garrett's room. I was so focused on what lay ahead that I almost didn't notice the slumped figure in one of the corridor's darkened recesses. Their chin rested on their chest, their neck bent, their legs sticking forward like a rag doll. A livid bruise wrapped around the exposed skin of their chest, where their shirt had come away slightly, spiraling all the way up to that unsettlingly bent neck.

Coming to a halt, I approached the figure. "Hello?"

Silence answered.

Tentatively, I ducked down and pressed my fingertips to the spot where a pulse should've been beating. There was no beat to be found. It was a man I didn't recognize, his lips blue, his bloodshot eyes looking down in a glassy stare. His skin was ice-cold to the touch. Whoever he was, he was dead.

My gaze flitted to the exposed line of his chest, where the buttons of his shirt had come undone, likely due to whatever had caused the bruising. A golden mark shone from the center of his sternum, surrounded by scarred flesh—the Apple of Discord, thrown amongst the SDC to cause chaos. The symbol of Eris.

With shaky hands, I dialed Harley's number. She answered on the second ring.

"Hey, I was just about to text and say we've got your coffee," she said brightly.

"Forget the coffee," I replied. "You need to come to the main hallway, just outside the Escher Reading Room. There's a body. I think... I think it's the spy."

A long pause followed. "We're on our way," she said, her tone dark. As soon as she hung up, I phoned Alton and told him the same thing.

Less than five minutes later, the Rag Team appeared around the corner, hurtling toward me at full pelt. I was surprised to see that Tarver was with them, or rather Jacob. I supposed Harley had gone to fill him in on what had been happening.

As soon as they saw the body, and the golden emblem on his chest, they stood around in awkward silence, none of them knowing what to do or what to say. This had been a *very* trying day for all of us, and there were still many hours to go. It was only when Alton arrived, a minute later, that some kind of sense started to be made of this event.

"Does anyone recognize him?" he asked firmly.

A "no" made its way around the group.

"No, me neither."

Jacob eyed the body. "I think he might be a Shapeshifter."

"How do you know?" Alton replied.

"Uh… well, I don't know for sure. It's just a guess." He eyed Alton curiously. "Should I say?"

Alton nodded. "It's okay. Since it's just the Rag Team here, they might as well know who you really are. Everyone, Jacob has been masquerading as Tarver, for means of protection." A ripple of surprise moved around the gathered group. Although not quite as much as I expected.

"Yeah, I kind of already knew," Santana said sheepishly.

"You knew?" Harley gasped.

Santana laughed. "Of course I knew; I can spot a mask like that a mile off. Plus, my Orishas sniffed it out and couldn't stop whispering about it."

"Me, too," Tatyana admitted. "I thought you must have had your reasons, given the current climate surrounding powerful magicals."

"Tatyana told me," Dylan added.

She nudged him in the arm. "Dylan!"

"What? It doesn't matter now."

Raffe nodded. "Yeah, Kadar spotted it, too."

"I didn't tell him, I swear!" Santana raised her hands in mock surrender.

"Well, then, you might as well take your mask off," Alton said to Jacob.

He peeled it away and threw it down. "Thank God. Do you have any idea how hot it gets in that thing, especially out here?"

"Well, aren't we all just *full* of secrets?" Garrett muttered, flashing a dark look my way that unsettled me.

"So, yeah… hi. Nice to meet you all for real this time. Anyway, subtle skills like Shapeshifting are harder to feel out, if that makes sense," Jacob explained. "But I can sense a similar thing in Garrett, so I'm guessing they have the same ability. I don't know for sure, though—I'm not exactly up to speed with the whole Sensate thing."

"Okay, well, the body seems like it's in good condition, and he couldn't have died too long ago. We might get lucky," Alton muttered, more to himself than anyone else. He scooped the dead man into his arms and kicked open the door to the Escher Reading Room, carrying him inside. Fortunately, there was nobody else within. "Clear a space on that table," he instructed.

Wade and Harley ran forward and swiped the books and papers off the long, wide reading table. Alton plonked the dead man down and tore open the rest of the guy's shirt. My father looked worried, scraping his bottom lip with his teeth in a tic of anxiety as he took off his own jacket.

"What are you doing?" Dylan asked.

"Bringing him back to life," Alton replied. "I'm not too late, which is good."

Jacob frowned. "What do you mean?"

"I have to reach people before a certain cutoff point, when the spirit leaves the body. Once it's gone, there's nothing I can do to bring them back."

I shuddered. I knew the basics of Necromancy—that was what he'd meant when he'd said he almost hadn't reached me in time, on one of my encounters with death. My spirit had almost abandoned my body, before my desperate father had snatched it right back.

Tatyana's eyes turned white for a moment. "The spirit hasn't left yet," she confirmed, the light dwindling as she came back from the place I liked to call the Phantom Zone. That usually made her laugh.

"Are you sure this is a good idea?" I asked, knowing how much it took out of Alton each time he did this. It drained him of everything, almost, and the recovery could be lengthy. Plus, he almost immediately went into a Purge state. This was a real person he was bringing back to life, not a cat.

"I don't have any choice," he said solemnly. "This guy might be able to give us valuable intel on both Katherine and Quetzi. I will be punished for this, if we can't get him back."

The group fell silent as Alton pressed his palms to the dead guy's chest. He closed his eyes, his breathing slowing to a steady rasp. I watched, enraptured. I hadn't actually seen him do this in person, as it had usually been me, cold on the proverbial slab. His eyes shot open, glowing a vibrant purple, mixed with black sparks that fizzed and crackled. The light ran through his entire body, and he pulsated with purple-tinged energy. Black fog rolled from within his chest, sweeping over his frame like dry ice. Everything in the room seemed to darken as the temperature dropped to below freezing. My teeth chattered, and I hugged myself to coax some warmth back into my skin.

While I was transfixed by my father, I felt arms wrap around me. I glanced up and saw Garrett standing behind me. His gaze was fixed forward, but the gesture showed he cared. My stomach turned over in a sickening feeling. I was torn between enjoying the warmth of his embrace and wondering how I was going to broach the subject of the body cam footage. I had to tell him what I'd found, but now definitely didn't seem like the right time. After all, given that the spy was on the table, it couldn't have been Garrett. So, why doctor the footage?

The black fog slithered toward the dead man, cascading down Alton's arms. Reaching his body, the mist percolated beneath the pale, dead skin and lifeless limbs. Alton was chanting now, reciting words that even I couldn't understand. Whatever he was saying, it wasn't of this world.

Alton's entire figure shivered and trembled as he poured more and more of the black fog into the dead man. His chants grew louder, the room turning to shadow, my breath visible in the air in front of me. A sheen of frost covered my father's bare skin, small icicles gathering in his hair. Turning to the others, I saw the same thing happening to them. Nobody else dared to move.

Without warning, everything whorled into a vortex and snapped into nothingness, the purple and black disappearing as quickly as it had appeared. Alton staggered back, Wade sprinting over to catch him before he could keel over. I wanted to do something to help, but I remained frozen to the spot, Garrett's arms still around me.

A few seconds later, the dead man sat up straight, clawing in a breath that startled everyone. He grabbed at his chest, his eyes wide in panic. Glancing around, his panic only increased. I doubted he'd expected to wake up, let alone wake up to a room full of the people he'd been working against.

"What the—?" he rasped, his eyes bloodshot. "That snake killed me. I felt him squeeze the life out of me. How can I be—what the hell is going on?"

Alton heaved out a breath and approached the table. "Who are you?"

A strange look flickered in the man's eyes. "Call me John Smith."

"Who are you *really*?" Alton pressed, pushing through his obvious exhaustion.

"Like I said... John Smith."

"Why did Quetzi kill you? Be *very* careful how you answer." Alton's tone held a warning.

"I know how this works," the man replied, his expression mocking. "You won't get anything from me."

Before anyone could stop her, Marjorie stepped forward and gripped the dead man's wrist. Her eyes turned milky white, John Smith's face blanching as he tried to wrestle free. She was surprisingly strong for a teenage girl, her Clairvoyance somehow feeding her mightiness. "I can see him," she said, in an odd, echoey voice. It reminded me of Tatyana's voice when a spirit took over. "I've seen him before. It's clouded, but he's... wait, I see him in a mirror. He looks like... no, it's gone again."

"Let me help you out," the spy said with a bitter laugh, his body morphing into someone else. All of us stared in shock as he turned into Preceptor Jacintha Parks. "All this time, I was pretending to be one of you, and you didn't even notice."

My heart dropped like a stone. We'd been needlessly watching the Shapeshifters, when *this* Shapeshifter had come from the outside. He wasn't from the coven, after all. He'd come in and posed as Jacintha Parks, and who knows how many others. Behind me, Garrett flinched, his grip on me tightening. I could feel his anger radiating out of him, even without turning to look at his face.

John Smith sneered. "You put cameras on the wrong people. I could wander around as free as I liked, and none of you batted an eyelid. As for your stupid interviews—you think someone can't lie their way through something like that? The systems you've got here are primitive. A monkey could hack them."

Did this guy set Garrett up? He might have heard about Garrett's defensive attitude surrounding the body cams and decided to use him as a scapegoat. I felt embarrassed and angry that I hadn't been able to tell the difference between the Jacintha I knew, and the Jacintha he'd pretended to be. I should have seen it in her quieter manner, or the way she'd been more distant than usual.

"Where is she?" Alton growled. "Where's the real one?"

John Smith smiled coldly. "No loose ends."

"What do you mean?" Alton looked about ready to pummel the man.

"She's dead, Director Waterhouse. I killed her. You should've seen the way the knife slipped in, buttery soft. Shame you couldn't have done this little trick with her, eh?" He gestured to himself, before morphing back into the body we'd found him in.

Alton lunged for him, grabbing him around the neck and dragging him off the table with a thud. "You'll pay for this, whoever you are. I'll see to it that you suffer, the same way you made Jacintha suffer. You can count on that. Nobody lays a hand on my people and gets away with it— do you understand me?" he spat in the man's ear. "Everybody out! There's a spell I need to do, to discover what this man knows. Dylan, help me strap him down!" he barked, lifting his weary head.

Dylan darted to John Smith's side, yanking his arms behind his back. Under Alton's instruction, the two of them tied the spy down using a set of entrapment stones. The spy writhed, laughing bitterly. One thing was for sure: the Mage Council would have to hear about this. Justice would have to be served for our fallen preceptor.

"Are you sure? Do you want us to stay?" Harley asked, tears running down her face.

"No—I don't want you around the spell I'm going to use," he replied firmly. "If it residually hits any of you, then it'll be bad news."

"What are you going to do to him, exactly?" Santana frowned.

"Use some old skills to interrogate him." A flurry of uncertainty moved around the room, but nobody felt like cutting the spy any slack. This was a job for the coven director.

Tears sprang to my eyes, as we exited the Reading Room and headed into the hallway beyond, with Dylan following behind. I'd known Jacintha well, and she'd always been kind to me. When I first arrived at the coven, to stay here for good, she'd been the one to make sure I had everything I needed. She'd always brought in cakes and treats, artisan coffee and sweets, and anything else to perk me up. Everyone thought highly of her, and her death would be a huge blow to all those who had known her—her students, her colleagues, her friends. I couldn't bear the thought of her, alone and most likely caught off guard, while that vicious cretin murdered her in cold blood. I hadn't seen her as much in the past few weeks. Now, I understood why.

I'm sorry, Jacintha. I should've known—I should have seen that it wasn't you.

"She's dead. I can't believe she's dead," Wade murmured.

"He must have trapped her soul, too," Tatyana said softly. "Otherwise, I would have sensed her near me. He must have put a spell on her, to keep her soul locked away. There is no fate worse than that, to be denied the ability to cross over."

I shook my head. "He killed her. How could we have been so blind?" A sob wracked my chest, prompting Garrett to put his arms back around me, holding me even tighter. He still didn't say a word, but having him close was a comfort.

"I think it's time for me to go," Marjorie whispered, her body shaking.

Harley glanced at her. "What do you mean? Go where?"

"To the LA Coven. I can't be here anymore. It's not what I signed up for."

"Hey, no one said it would be easy, but..." Harley replied, "...you're safer here than anywhere else. You're surrounded by people who care about you."

Marjorie scoffed. "Am I really safer here? After what we just found out—which, by the way, happened right under your noses? No, I'm sorry… I'm sorry to have to do this, but I can't be here anymore."

"You're ignoring the part about being surrounded by people who care," Jacob shot back. "You won't get that in LA."

"I'm willing to give it a try. Too much bad stuff happens here. I need to look out for myself, for once. I've had enough." Marjorie shook her head.

After everything that had happened since her arrival, I couldn't exactly blame her.

"Can you at least sleep on it before you talk to Imogene?" Harley asked, seemingly clinging on to the hope that she might be able to sway Marjorie in the end.

"I'd rather be with the other kids. Maybe, after this whole Katherine mess is over, I can come back, if the SDC will have me. Call me a coward if you want, but—"

"I wouldn't!" Harley cut her off, trying hard to keep her cool. "I just… I just don't want you to rush into something you might regret later."

Marjorie gave her a soft smile, though the sadness in her eyes didn't go away. "Harley, I care about you. I care about all of you. But I have to care about myself *more* right now."

Looking around the hallway, I sensed the colossal blow of her decision and the news of Jacintha's death. There wasn't a dry eye in the house. Even Tatyana's eyes were damp with tears. We'd failed Jacintha and Marjorie. We'd lost them both, with no chance of making it better.

TWENTY-THREE

Harley

Two days later, Alton stood at the altar, in the center of the Crypt, barely holding it together. His voice kept cracking as he committed Jacintha to her tomb, his gaze fixed on the paper in his hand. "From Chaos she was born, and to Chaos she will return, the essence of her being running free in the river of Gaia, where she will become one with the Earth once more. Ashes to ashes, dust to dust; may Chaos guide her back to where she belongs," he concluded, mopping his brow with the back of his jacket sleeve.

Sniffles and choked sobs peppered the stilted silence that followed. Only the Rag Team and the rest of the preceptors were here to witness Jacintha's burial, with the general memorial service having already taken place that morning. That had been even worse, my Empath senses going crazy as they picked up the sadness of an entire coven, joined in mourning for one of their own. The details of her death hadn't been released, but I knew the rest of the coven could guess what had happened, since the interviews had been called to a halt. The truth was, she'd been found dumped in another one of the tombs, hidden in a sarcophagus with a hundred-year-old skeleton.

Her body lay on a plinth in front of the altar, wrapped in silk of green, blue, white, and red, to signify the four Elements. She almost didn't look real. Alton and the security teams had been the ones to do a sweep of the coven and find her body. Anger pulsed in my veins at John Smith's disgusting disrespect. Killing her was bad enough, but to just dump her body like that… I wanted to wring his neck, but he was already dead. Alton had told us that he'd Purged violently while he was interrogating the spy, and the beast had killed John Smith on sight. It would have killed Alton, too, had Tobe not come to the rescue. A few scratches remained on Alton's face, where the creature had slashed at him.

"Ashes to ashes, dust to dust; may Chaos guide her back to where she belongs," the group repeated in an eerie chorus.

"Why didn't they do this for Adley?" I murmured to Wade, who stood beside me, his face stoic. He was doing his best to hold it together, too, though I could feel the overwhelming sadness inside him.

He cleared his throat. "She betrayed the coven. She isn't allowed to be buried here."

"So did Emmett Ryder, and he's here." The words came out colder than I'd intended.

"The top row is for criminals. Their souls are bound to them for fifty years after their death, so they can't escape to the other side. It's an insurance policy, in case they need to be questioned," he explained. "And anyway, the LA Coven claimed her as their own. She's buried there now."

"You think that's fair? Didn't she get a say in it, like a will or something?"

"No— no will. That's just the way it is."

I sighed and tried not to look at Jacintha's unmoving body. "Are we heading back out after this?"

He shook his head. "We need to keep looking for Quetzi, for sure, but all coven activity is suspended for the rest of the day. Magical mourning protocol."

We'd spent the past three days searching half of the San Diego area for Quetzi, with no luck as of yet, and I had too much frustration building up inside me to stay cooped up for the rest of the day, doing nothing but thinking about the woman we'd lost. Well, women. I needed justice, not only for Jacintha, but for everyone whom Katherine and her minions had targeted. Plus, I'd been dealing with my own guilt while scouring the city and its suburbs. Even though I hadn't known her well, I was ashamed I hadn't noticed that Preceptor Parks wasn't all she appeared to be. We all were. It showed on every single one of our faces.

"There'll be a feast in the Banquet Hall, in her honor," he went on.

I shook my head. "Do we all have to be there?"

"Mourn in your own way," he replied simply. "If you don't want to go, nobody's going to force you."

I needed to blow off steam. If I sat around, eating and being around people and their emotions, I'd snap. My own emotions were in total chaos, making it difficult to control my Empathy around others. I picked Nomura out of the congregation and decided to ask him if he'd spend a couple of hours training me. Even with my Esprit fixed, I was rusty and lacking confidence in my abilities. Somehow, these darker stones seemed to take more energy to use. It was like switching to a stick shift after having an automatic for years, and I couldn't afford to mess up.

As the group dispersed, I moved through the crowd toward him. He glanced at me as I approached, showing no surprise at all. I could've sworn this guy was psychic; he always seemed to be able to preempt people, figuring them out in a way that nobody else could. Myself included.

"Harley," he said, dipping his head in a polite nod.

"Preceptor Nomura, I was wondering if you were free to train for a while?"

"You don't want to attend the banquet?"

I shook my head. "I'm not good at being around people in situations like this."

"Me neither," he replied, with a solemn smile. "Shall we go to the training room?"

"That'd be good." I breathed a sigh of relief.

Following the rest of the group out of the Crypt, leaving Alton to make the final preparations with a couple of the coven staff, I made my excuses to the Rag Team and trailed Nomura to the preceptors' training room. Marjorie had hung around for the memorial service, but she was due to leave for LA that afternoon. I'd already said my goodbyes to her, but I couldn't face seeing her off. If I had to be there when she went, I'd spend the whole time trying to convince her to stay, which was pointless. She'd already made up her mind and, frankly, who could blame her? I wanted to believe that we could protect her. I was convinced we could have at least tried. She'd been spared until now, after all. But maybe this was for the best.

Entering the familiar space of the preceptors' private training room, I felt the rest of the world melt away for a moment. Here, I could pretend that nothing bad had happened outside these doors. Here, there was nothing but magic and focus—the perfect antidote for my scrambled brain.

"I thought we might start with Air and Earth, as they're your weakest," Nomura said, wasting no time. "Stand behind the white line and send a controlled burst of Air toward the wooden post." He moved to the far side of the room and grabbed a training post, bringing it into the center.

I did as he asked and stood behind the line. Lifting my hands, I took a deep breath and let Chaos flow through me. It raged in my veins, feeling hot and spiky in a way it never had before. Holding tight to my concentration, I gritted my teeth in determination and sent out a pulse of Air. It shot out of me wildly, sending me sprawling backward, a tornado appearing where I'd been standing. It tore toward the wooden post, twisting violently. It dragged the post straight up and slammed it into the ceiling. Rubble fell from the roof, and the stones hit the ground with a *tap-tap-tap*.

I jumped up and struggled to take control of the tornado. My nerves jangled, my mind racing with a million other thoughts, the glow of my Esprit flickering. Nomura stepped in, using his Telekinetic abilities to cut through it until the winds scattered and it fizzled away.

"You *must* concentrate," Nomura warned. "Let everything else disappear."

Easy for you to say, Captain Zen.

"I'll do better," I promised, taking up my position again. However, as I lifted my palms to try and hit the post that he'd replaced, the same thing happened. Only, this time, the swirling vortex took on a mind of its own. It rushed out of me with unexpected force, colliding with the far wall with a resounding boom that shook the floor. More rubble fell from the spot I'd hit in the ceiling, the face of a magical warrior now reduced to dust. *Ashes to ashes...*

"Your mind isn't in the right place for this," Nomura said softly.

"It is. It has to be," I replied. "Let me try again."

He sighed. "Try Fire instead. We'll work back up to Air. For the sake of the coven, I'd advise that we avoid Earth for the time being, until you're more settled in your thoughts."

"Fine... Fire it is," I muttered, my cheeks burning. I hated letting myself down like this. As an Empath, my role was to sense emotions. How could I do that, when I couldn't even control my own?

Taking up a power stance, my right foot forward, I lifted my hands and aimed at the wooden post. Without warning, my Esprit surged with red light, an enormous, crackling fireball hurtling out of my palms. It took out the post completely, reducing it to a smoldering matchstick, before it kept on going, smacking into the wall in an explosion of sparks. I stared at it in disbelief. *What the heck is going on?* Fire was usually the easy one, but my head and my Esprit were having none of it.

"It's your anger, Harley," Nomura said. "It's allowing the Darker, destructive side of your abilities to take control. Fire in balance, or Fire in Light tends to be calmer—you can tell from the texture of the fireballs you create. When they crackle like that and come out of you much larger and much more forceful, that's because Darkness is guiding them."

I shook my head. "It can't be taking over. I still have the Suppressor holding everything in balance."

He smiled. "The Suppressor does exactly that—it suppresses your abilities. It can't control which affinity channels your energies. By the looks of your Esprit, certain changes are already starting to occur inside you. The spell that fixed it wasn't done in balance or in Light. If it had been, the stones wouldn't look that way."

I fought against bitter tears. "This is ridiculous. It's like I don't even have control of my body anymore. These affinities and abilities, or whatever you want to call them, are doing whatever the hell they want. I'm sick of it. Don't I get a say?"

"You have the strength to control these things. It's all about focus and concentration. Everything is." He walked over to me. "Why don't we call it a day on the training and do something far more useful? We've both lost someone, and we're enduring grief in our own way. Meditation is often the best method to bring a warring mind back toward peace. I can teach you how, if you want?"

I glanced at him. "Can you show me how to sink into a state of Euphoria?" It'd been on my mind for a while now, ever since hearing about it. If I was going to break the Suppressor by myself, without causing a load of damage to the people and things around me, I figured that putting myself into that state might be the best way. Krieger had wanted me to learn for a reason. If I could apply it to my own, self-induced Suppressor break, maybe I could reduce the consequences, too.

He frowned. "I don't think that's appropriate for today, but if you'd like to learn, I can show you another time. It can be a helpful way to restore control over certain abilities, though it's not often done anymore. In your case, you may find it gives you greater clarity."

"Really?"

"Like I said, given your multitude of abilities, it may be a good option for you. Although I would advise that you don't come to rely on it, as it isn't always successful, and it's very time-consuming."

I smiled. "I'd still like to learn."

"Then we'll arrange it. But, for today, let us simply meditate awhile. It will calm you, without the need for Euphoria." He moved across the room toward the exit. "Follow me. All of my equipment is in my office."

"Equipment? What do you need equipment for? Isn't it all ohms and kumbayas?"

He laughed. "You'd be surprised at the objects necessary for meditation. Candles and incense, for starters. I call it equipment to make it sound more impressive."

I hurried after him, the two of us walking a short distance down the hallway. He opened a door to the right-hand side and let me go ahead of him. My mouth fell open at the sight beyond. It looked more like the interior of an ancient Samurai temple than an office. A low table sat in the center, with cushions around it, while golden statues of Buddha stood against the crisp white and black walls. Red and gold drapes hung down at even intervals. The ceiling had also been draped, softening the entire look of the place. Above the fireplace, two katanas in ebony sheathes were crossed in an "X."

"This place is so cool," I murmured.

"Thank you. I like to think of it as my sanctuary, when I need to detach my thoughts from the goings-on of the coven."

"I need to get me one of these."

He chuckled. "Take a seat, and we'll begin. Please, remove your shoes."

Taking off my boots, I picked my way across to one of the silky cushions and sat down, wiggling my socked feet as I watched Nomura. He moved over to a small table in the corner and prepared a ceramic pot of herbal tea. I could smell the spicy, bitter aroma from where I was sitting, the scent weirdly tantalizing. As he waited for the leaves to steep, he took a lighter and did a circle of the room, igniting the candles and stalks of incense that he had all over the place. Soon enough, the office glowed with warm, soothing light and smelled wonderfully smoky and sweet. Already, just being here, I felt calmer. *Yeah, I really have to get me one of these, and maybe one of those for Katherine.* I eyed the katanas.

A few minutes later, he brought over the pot of tea and two cups and set one in front of me. He did the pouring, a greenish liquid tumbling out. Heady steam rose from the cup.

"Drink," he urged, waiting for me to take a sip before he took a sip of his own.

"I'm not going to start tripping am I—seeing pink elephants on parade?"

He laughed. "No, this is just herbal tea, I assure you."

It tasted bitter on my tongue, my taste buds prickling at the new flavor. It was close to matcha but had a strong note of something earthy —like mushrooms, or sage. Still, it was hot and soothing, relaxing my tightly-wound muscles. I took another sip and set it down, Nomura instantly refilling it.

"I've just realized, I don't know much about you," I said. "Other than the fact that you are a preceptor, I don't know anything." After losing Jacintha, it somehow felt important to know more about people. I regretted not appreciating her more, seeing her as nothing but a teacher.

He smiled. "This isn't technically how you meditate. It's usually done without talking."

"Meditation can wait. I'd like to know more about you."

"What would you like to know?"

"How you came to be who you are, maybe? What keeps you going? What are your likes, your dislikes?"

He dipped his head. "Very well. At least close your eyes, so we can pretend we're meditating."

"Sounds fair." I closed my eyes and brought my cup to my lips.

"I always wanted to make myself a better person," he began. "As a teenager, I sensed I had potential, but my abilities let me down. Mediocrity was something of a curse back then. Even now, it carries a stigma, as you well know. However, I sought to become more than that label. I traveled the world and learned all I could, reading every book I came across. I learned from spiritual souls, from Native American shamans to Japanese monks, and Russian Kolduny. I spent some time with the Voodoo magicals that I told you about, and I've also studied with the Euphorics of Tromsø—the last people to practice the art in perpetuity. I have been all over, trying to bring myself out of Mediocrity, though it took me two decades to achieve."

"Sounds like a lot of hard work."

He chuckled. "It was, but it was worth every hour of study. As for what keeps me going—that would be my son, Shinsuke. He is also a Mediocre by label, but he's following in my footsteps. As we speak, he is in the Amazon, studying with the magical tribes there. I've not heard from him in several weeks, but I know he's succeeding in his task. He and I share talismans, which hold a piece of a loved one's soul. If anything should happen to him, the talisman would let me know. I'm very proud of him, for everything he's doing, and everything he has already achieved. One day, he will be more powerful than me, and I welcome it."

"No Mrs. Nomura?" I peeked under my lids as silence followed, wondering if he'd upped and left without me realizing. His face was clouded with sadness. "Sorry, that was rude. I've got a motormouth—it says stuff before my brain has the chance to stop it."

A hint of amusement broke through the clouds, before they drew together again, across his features. "It's a fair question. Unfortunately, my wife died several years ago. She was a gifted woman with a love for archaeology—that was her job, and she was forever exploring, aiding the Global Magical Department of Artifacts in their search for powerful objects. She went missing on a dig in Antarctica, looking for the remains of a cache that was buried by an ancient magical, and they recovered her body a month later, beneath the snow. An avalanche must have caught her off guard, and she didn't make it out."

"I'm so sorry." *See, this is why you don't ask personal questions!* I wished I'd kept my mouth shut.

"It was a troubling time. I have never known grief like that," he replied evenly. "It was around that time that I discovered meditation and spent a year with the Euphorics. My son came with me. That may have been the moment he decided to follow my path and pour his pain into something constructive. I don't need to tell you how hard it is to live without a parent."

I shook my head. "Yeah, it's a bitch all right."

"Have you ever considered literature? You have such a charming way with words," he teased.

"People keep telling me that," I replied, glad of the break in tension. I couldn't handle any more sadness, though the pain rolling off him was tangible, and not just because of my Empath abilities. He wore every memory of it on his open face, his closed eyes flickering.

"Even now, it seems strange that she won't walk through the door. That impossible absence is the hardest thing to get used to," he said. "I feel it for Jacintha now. She and I used to spend afternoons drinking tea and discussing global matters. It seems so absurd that she won't knock on that door and join me in my meditation ever again."

I sipped my tea. "Will you tell me about her?" I didn't know enough about her and it made me feel an overwhelming sense of guilt and grief. It was a bit late in the day, but I wanted to know more.

"I would be delighted to," he replied. "Do you know, in aboriginal culture, it's deemed inappropriate to mention the name of the deceased after they have passed?"

"I didn't."

"They believe it keeps the soul locked to the world of the living, preventing them from returning to the spirit world." He took a shallow breath. "Anyway, we may speak her name, so I will. Jacintha Parks was a bright woman with a wicked sense of humor. I remember on one occasion, she and I sat in here until the early hours, drinking sake and talking of our youth. I thought my ribs might break, I was laughing so hard. She was telling me a story about how she accidentally turned an ex-boyfriend into a lizard and had to hide him until she could figure out the reverse spell. Her father had come into her room, and she'd stuffed the lizard down her shirt. Every time he'd popped out, she'd had to shove him back down, while attempting to have a sensible conversation about college with her father. The way she acted it out… you likely had to be there, but I have never laughed so much in my entire life."

I chuckled at the image.

"She was kind, too—always helpful to the newcomers, though especially Astrid. Jacintha was the one to take her under her wing when she arrived, shy as a newborn foal. And, my word, Jacintha was an incredible cook. One time, she made this decadent stew for Astrid, who was sick with the flu. I tried to steal a bite—I couldn't help myself—and she slapped my hand away before I could even put the spoon in my mouth. The entire Staff Lounge erupted in laughter, naturally, with me standing there in front of the pot, spoonless and shocked."

"She sounds like quite the woman," I said, smiling. Nomura always seemed so poised and put-together; I couldn't imagine him standing there in such a funny manner, with an angry Jacintha swiping at him.

He nodded. "She was. Even when that monster killed her, I imagine she put up a fight."

"You think so?"

Nomura nodded. "Jacintha was always a fighter." I could hear the pain in his voice, making me realize just how human the preceptors were, beyond their formal, educational façades. It was like seeing a high school teacher in the mall, or at the movies. They loved, they lost, they hurt, they laughed, and they lived, just like the rest of us.

"I think we all wish we'd known her better," I replied.

"She thought highly of you."

"She did?"

He nodded. "Although she'd likely have broken my legs for telling you about the Sanguine spell."

"I haven't done anything about it, if you're worried."

"I'm not worried. It's up to you how you choose to use the information you are given. However, I think we can all understand your frustration surrounding the Suppressor, even Alton. I'm just able to admit it in a way that he's not. Given his role in this coven, he's not able to bend the rules as flexibly as others might."

"Hey, I'm in no position to go around blabbing about stuff," I assured him.

I hadn't dwelled on the Sanguine spell and the Suppressor break too much in the last few days, with everything else going on. Plus, with Jacintha's death and Quetzi's escape, now didn't feel like the right time to go around breaking rules or getting on Alton's bad side. His attitude toward me doing this wasn't ever going to change, but I needed to choose my moment more carefully, in case it got me kicked out or reported.

I couldn't lose this family, too.

TWENTY-FOUR

Harley

The following day, with a fresh determination in my mind, I set off for the Forbidden Section to find out more about Sanguine spells. Like, what was I supposed to do once I had the blood? Did I have to swallow it? The thought of that was almost enough to make me wait for Krieger to do the operation instead. If only we had the time for that. Sadly, we didn't.

I stopped on the threshold of the doorway to the library, startled by a figure sitting at the back of the room, hunched over a book, oblivious to my presence. *Louella...* What was she doing here? She shouldn't even have been able to gain entry. I thought back to her abilities, remembering the ones we'd yet to see her try out. As well as being a Regen, she had Telepathic and Audial abilities, though we had no idea how strong the last two were. We'd yet to see any sign of her Telepathy, though the ability, by its very nature, worried me. It made me understand how the others felt when I used my Empathy on them.

I cleared my throat. "Louella?"

She looked up in surprise. "Harley. Didn't see you there."

"You shouldn't be in here," I said.

"Oh, really? I thought this was just a library. I'll go. Sorry about that."

I smiled. "Not so fast there. How'd you get in? This place has a password, which I'm guessing you already know."

Her face paled.

"It's okay, I'm not Alton—I'm not going to snitch. I just want to know what you're doing in here… and *how* you got in here."

"I heard someone say it," she replied sheepishly. Relief washed over me as she made the admission. Her Audial ability I could handle, especially as it'd been the very thing that had helped her escape the Ryders the first time, at the Devereaux house, when she'd overheard what was happening and made a run for it. Meanwhile, the Regen powers had provided her escape the second time. I really didn't like the idea of Telepathy at all.

"I thought so," I said. "But your answer to my other question…?"

She eyed the door as if she wanted to dart past me. She must've thought better of it because, instead, she huffed out a breath and lifted the book in her hands. The spine read *Mysteries of the Otherworlds*. Glancing at her desk as I got closer, I noticed a few books on Greek mythology, too. A light bulb went off in my head as I put the pieces together. We'd looked through most of these books, aside from a few, trying to find information on the Children of Chaos and the five rituals that might make Katherine one of them.

"You're looking into the five rituals?" I asked.

She nodded. "I thought I'd make myself useful now that Marjorie's gone. Not much else to do."

"How do you even know about that?" I got the feeling I wasn't going to like the answer.

"I… uh, heard about it."

"Did you read someone's mind, Louella?" I sounded weirdly teacher-like, which was new for me.

Her gaze dropped. "I can't help when it happens. I don't have any control over it. Sometimes, I hear things loud and clear from people's heads; sometimes I can't hear anything at all. Plus, it gives me these killer migraines, so I try not to do it too often, if I can help it."

"Whose mind?"

"Astrid's," she replied stiffly. "I don't know if it's because she's a human or something, but she's easier to read than most people. With her, there aren't any walls or barriers to get through first. She's an open book."

"And these headaches—do you always have them when you use your Telepathy?"

Her mouth turned up in a grim smile. "No, it never used to be a problem. Kenneth poured some liquid thing down my throat while we were at that abandoned port, and I've had them ever since. I guess to stop me from reading their minds—not that I'm very good at it anyway."

"Have you spoken to Krieger about it?"

"He said the effects would wear off by themselves; he just couldn't tell me when, exactly. Could be days or weeks, depending on how much I swallowed."

I frowned. "Can you read my mind?"

"No. The others on your team have a *lot* of firewalls, but you—I can't get through your head at all. If I tried right now, migraines aside, I'd hit a wall. It literally feels like that, like I'm hitting a big, dark wall." I couldn't sense any deceit coming off her, only embarrassment and guilt. I realized that, in feeling out for her emotions, I was being a bit hypo-critical, but, hey, I had to know she wasn't lying to me.

"So, you've tried to read my mind, then?"

"Like I said, I can't control when it happens, and I don't like to do it with these headaches. It's different with Astrid—I can do it no problem —but with magicals I have to concentrate super hard. I thought I'd give it a go with you and your team, and risk a migraine, but your mind can shut me out completely. It's weird. You're doing it now and I bet you don't even know you're doing it."

I didn't know whether to feel proud or worried. In the end, I figured it was something to do with my Empath abilities, though I wasn't going to tell her that. If she was going around, secretly trying to use her abili-ties on people, then I needed to keep my cards a little closer to my chest.

"You know, you should leave that stuff to us—the intel stuff," I said, leaving the Telepathy for a bit.

She shrugged. "You didn't seem to be making much progress with that snake thing on the loose, so I thought I'd see what I could dig up. I've always been good at research."

"Even so… you shouldn't be worrying about this kind of thing."

Her eyes hardened. "How can I not, after what she did to us? You didn't have to watch those two boys get *murdered* in front of you, just because they weren't powerful enough for her. You didn't see her do what she did. You didn't have to wait each day, wondering if you were next on the chopping block, because you might've disappointed her or weren't 'rare' enough for her liking."

"Is that what this is, then? Is it—"

"Revenge." She finished my sentence before I could. "Yeah, it is. For my foster parents, and all those whom Katherine has hurt. And all the people she *wants* to hurt. I'm going to punish her, any way that I can, and I'm starting with these rituals. She has to be stopped, Harley. You have no idea what she'll become if she manages this." She shook the book at me.

"I do have some idea, believe me. However, there's not much in there," I said, my tone softening. "We've already looked."

"Well, you didn't look hard enough. You've got to read between the lines."

"You found something?"

She bit her lip nervously. "I'm not sure yet."

A thought popped into my mind. "Could you read any of Katherine's thoughts, when she was holding you hostage?"

"No, she's like you. I tried it before Kenneth poured that stuff down my throat."

My heart jumped in panic. "What do you mean?"

"That wall you've got in your head. She's got it, too. I couldn't even get close, and believe me, I tried," she replied. "If you're an Empath, maybe she's one, too."

My blood ran cold as a chilling realization dawned. Maybe Katherine *did* have some kind of Empath abilities, or some kind of power that allowed her to block out the feelers of other magicals. She'd blocked me when I'd tried to feel her out, back at the warehouse. Empathy seemed like an ironic ability for her, but there was definitely something about her skill set that suggested a blocking power. After all, she'd used something to stop us from finding the kids with a tracking spell. She'd blocked their magical signature. Maybe that was her skill, though I had no idea what it'd be called.

"Wait... how do you know I'm an Empath?" There went my closely-held cards.

She frowned. "Oh, is that what you are?"

"What did you think I was?"

"I thought you might've been like me. Still, Empathy isn't far off. See, even with that stuff in me, things slip through from time to time. That Wade guy was thinking, 'Please don't let Harley know I'm still thinking about her being in my bedroom,' all the way through breakfast this morning. I think I heard it because he was repeating it so much, but I kind of guessed what you were from that. I was wrong, but I'd say close enough."

What? A flood of girlish happiness swept through my veins. The timing wasn't great but, damn, it was good to hear that he was thinking about me. And in a kind of saucy way, too.

"I want her dead, Harley," Louella spat suddenly, her cheeks inflamed. "I want to kill her. I want to kill her, the way she killed my foster parents. Yeah, they were strict sometimes, but they were kind to me and I was happy there. They didn't deserve what she did to them. That evil bitch has ruined my entire life, and the lives of the other kids, and I'm not going to stop until she's dead."

I held up my hands. "Whoa, whoa, whoa! Slow down, there. We all feel the same, but you can't let your anger cloud your judgment. It'll only make you weaker—I learned that recently," I said. "I've got a thousand reasons I want to see her dead, too, but thinking only about vengeance isn't going to get any of us anywhere."

"I can't make it go away," she muttered, sitting back in her chair with a sigh.

"I'm not asking you to. I'm just saying, work *with* us, not away from us." I glanced at the rest of her book selection, a couple of them piquing my curiosity. "Where did you find these? I haven't seen them before." I pointed to a stack at the end of the table. From their spines, they didn't seem to have anything to do with the five rituals: *The Ancient Ways; Particles, and the Mythology of the Universe; The Fabric of Stars; Traversing the Cosmos.* I felt like Neil deGrasse Tyson was going to pop up and give me an impromptu lecture on Astrophysics for Dummies.

She smiled slyly. "Before Kenneth got the chance to pour that stuff down my throat, I heard him—he kept thinking about the five rituals. Like, it was *all* he could think about. The details were fuzzy, but I think Katherine might've given him a role to play in her plan, and he was so proud that he kept repeating things in his head. Things I shouldn't have heard. He didn't even realize it, the freaking dumbass, but it led me to these.

"See, they aren't specifically about the rituals, but that's the beauty— reading between the lines, like I said. The rituals are hidden inside, told through vague stories, scientific studies, and mythology. It's not about the Children of Chaos, not really. There are some essays about it, too, but they were all dumped in a box marked 'miscellaneous' up there." She gestured to the top shelf of a nearby bookcase.

"Geez, you're sharp," I blurted out. Frankly, I was astonished. I'd known she was bright, given the way she'd avoided the Ryders twice, but this was phenomenal, even with a little super-sensory help.

"Thanks. I guess *sharp* is better than *geek*." She flashed a wry smile, bordering on haughty.

I walked around to her side of the desk and sat down. "So, what did you find, since you're clearly a freaking genius?"

She pulled out the book called *The Ancient Ways*. "Well, see, each ritual has to do with one of the Children of Chaos, separately. It can't be done in one go—at least I don't think it can, not if I'm right. This book, for example, tells it in stories, of a warrior performing five tasks so that he can face one of the Children and gain untold power. It doesn't say what the tasks are precisely, but they seem to be linked to the attributes of the different Children. He succeeds in the tasks and the fight, and he has to decide whether to take the place of Nyx as a result. The warrior doesn't, but if he had, he would have *become* Nyx. Instead, he walks away with the power of Nyx, and is hailed as a kind of demigod. Anyway, what I can gather from the story is that a person can be transformed by sapping the energy from a Child of Chaos, most likely through that final fight, and taking on their abilities once they've done that."

"Holy crap," I mumbled. "What is this book?"

"Children's stories."

"Geez, that stuff would've given me nightmares as a kid. And you're sure it doesn't say what the tasks are?"

"Afraid not. It just says, "…each more dangerous than the last." There are pictures, but they've been worn away over time. I can't make anything out from them, other than a few bursts of light."

"Can I see?"

She showed me the book. I'd been hoping to find something she'd missed, but she was right—the yellowed pages had seen better days, the pictures fuzzed out beyond all recognition by age and water damage.

"That's a pain in the ass," I muttered.

She smiled. "There's more. One of the essays has a theory in it, that each ritual is very specific and has to be fueled by an enormous amount of power—the kind that no one is born with. If we reference this back to the myth, we can kind of tell that the only reason that the one warrior won was because they were already blessed by the gods. Hercules vibes, if you see what I mean?"

"So, already super powerful?"

"Exactly. That's why I think Katherine's collecting kids like us, because she wants to take our Chaos energy, to make herself even more powerful. That would be the only thing that would give her the ability to do these rituals-slash-tasks, whatever you want to call them. I mean, there were more kids in that ferry port than just us—she moved them before the security dudes came to get us. We were just the San Diego ones. She's got kids from all over."

I gaped at her. "Are you serious?"

"Do you think I'd lie?"

"No… no, I guess not. Have you told Alton?" He hadn't mentioned anything to us about extra kids.

"I told Alton about it, and he said he'd check with the other covens to see if they were missing anyone. Then again, they might be kids like us, who didn't belong to a coven."

I peered down at the book, swallowing my horror, letting it all sink in. Now, the lack of retribution for us taking back the kids made sense. She had backups. This way, by making it easy for us to get them back, she'd gotten us off her case. Why hadn't Alton mentioned anything to us about it? I guessed he might've wanted to run checks first. "Does it say what absorbing the energy of the Child of Chaos, in the final challenge, actually transforms a person into? I mean, do they become the exact same as the one they've defeated?"

Louella shook her head. "It's hard to tell. With the winning warrior, it simply mentions the word 'Ascension.' Here, it says, 'He had been marked for Ascension, whenever he chose to part with his mortal form.' Now, it doesn't say anything else about this warrior, so we don't know what happens next."

I shuddered at the thought of Katherine becoming some kind of avenging angel or Ascended being, or actually embodying the Goddess Eris whom she seemed to like so much. She was bad enough as a plain human.

"How do you even go about challenging a Child of Chaos?" I mused out loud. I knew, firsthand, that they could be summoned, but surely they'd know what was coming and just disappear before anything could happen. I doubted they were bound by duty to take challenges.

"The stories mention different places, where each Child of Chaos lives. Their home, kind of thing. They seem to be the locations where the five tasks have to happen. Tartarus is one of them, which seems to be Erebus's jam. Elysium is another, though it's not clear who that one belongs to. The Asphodel Meadows is number three. The Garden of Hesperides is four. And Lethe is the fifth, which seems to be some kind of pool. No clue where the final fight happens, though. I guess you have to pick, maybe?"

I frowned. "Tartarus?"

"Yeah."

"It's a real place?"

Louella shrugged. "No idea—those are just the places in these stories. Each one is linked to a different Child of Chaos, though indirectly. It's all in the mythology."

All this time, I'd thought that places like that were just stories, but now I was starting to think that they might be very real. Moreover, that they might have something to do with Katherine's pursuit of this Children of Chaos idea. Were these the locations where the five rituals had to take place, like Louella had guessed?

"Crazy, right?" Louella said.

"Yeah, you could say that." I had one more question that I wanted to ask her. "I don't suppose you found anything about a Librarian—capital 'L'—in any of these books, did you? They're meant to know everything there is to know about these rituals. More than a story can tell us, anyway."

Her face drained of color. "What did you just say?"

"*The* Librarian. Did you find anything in here about them?"

"Katherine had someone else captive," she said, after a tense pause. "Before the headaches came, I could hear a bunch of stuff going on in that woman's head. It was almost like she wanted me to listen. Not that it made much sense."

"What kind of stuff?"

She shrugged. "Words, Latin mostly. At least, I think they were Latin. I can't really remember. Even when I can use my Telepathy, the retention afterwards is pretty bad."

"How do you know that's her—the woman we're looking for?" I asked.

"Katherine called her the Librarian, just like you did. She never called her by her name."

My pulse quickened. "Is she alive? Does Katherine still have her?"

Louella nodded. "I think so. She took away the woman at the same time as the rest of the kids."

I was glad to hear that the Librarian was alive, but she was obviously in a heap of trouble. No doubt, that lady's knowledge was what Katherine needed to figure out the rituals. *How is she always one step ahead of us?* It was starting to piss me off.

"Did I say the wrong thing?" Louella asked.

"No, not at all. We need her, that's all—this woman. Without her, we'll have to guess how Katherine's going to do all of this. We need facts."

Determined, I flipped through the pile of essays Louella had gathered. Nothing really caught my attention, and I'd never heard any of the names before: *Alfonso Cotillo, Joel Pennington, Lisbeth Tawny, Foster McGinty, Finnoula O'Rourke, Aziriphale Gaiman, Remington Knightshade, Harriet Clarke, Marianna Gorge.* My eyes widened, my fingertips flipping back two pages. *Wait—what?!*

Remington Knightshade had written an essay on the Children of freaking Chaos. My eyes drank in his words, picking out the buzzwords I was looking for: energy, transformation, rituals—the whole shebang.

Katherine might have had the Librarian, but maybe all wasn't lost. I needed to give Remington a call.

TWENTY-FIVE

Astrid

Feeling drained after yesterday's memorial service, my eyes scratchy from so many spilled tears, I stretched out my arms and sat up in bed. Jacintha's loss continued to haunt me, and I hadn't slept well, thinking about her. Her body on the plinth, wrapped in the colorful silk, was an image that would take a long time to leave me. Attempting to put myself in a more positive mindset, as we had to head out into the field later to search for Quetzi, I pulled Smartie out from under my pillow and unlocked the screen. He chirped happily.

"Morning," I said, out of habit.

"Good morning," he replied. "Would you like a morning playlist?"

I shook my head. "No, thank you."

"No playlist. You have one note."

I frowned at the screen. "Open the note."

The screen flickered and shifted to one of the virtual post-its. I'd written it last night when I got in. *Check camera loop*, was all the note said. I must've fallen asleep before I could examine it further. I wanted to relieve the nagging feeling that had been plaguing me since the spy was captured. He'd mentioned how easy the system was to hack, which wasn't entirely false, but I wondered if there were more glitches like the one I'd found on Garrett's body cam footage. Had John Smith tried to set anyone else up to take the fall for his crimes?

With a yawn, I opened up the operating system that was in control of the cameras, and asked Smartie to find all the footage between the hours that Garrett's had been doctored. A flurry of windows opened. I spent the better half of an hour scanning through each one, but Garrett's seemed to be the only one that had been tampered with. Determined to find out what had actually gone on in that window of time, I went back to the most important cameras—the ones I'd initially checked when the Bestiary had been thrown into mayhem. The cameras in the Bestiary itself had malfunctioned during the energy overflow, but there was one still working in the hallway outside.

Squinting over the top of my glasses, I watched the footage. Four security guards stood in the hallway, barely moving. For five minutes, they continued to do nothing. And then, very subtly, the screen flickered. It was barely noticeable, but I was looking out for the tiniest of glitches. The security guards continued to stand there, but it was clear the footage was on a loop. The tap of one of their feet on the floor gave it away.

A few minutes after that, another flicker shivered through the image. The moment it glitched, the image changed to one of the security guards running toward the Bestiary. I hadn't noticed it before, when I'd first looked over the cameras after the incident, but the security guards were very clearly running much faster than I'd have expected, with it being such a short distance between the hallway and the Bestiary. It almost looked as if they'd come from farther away, like they hadn't been standing in the hallway when the blast went off. Someone had doctored this footage and pieced it back together to make the timeline fit.

"Smartie, can you retrieve deleted video files from before the explosion in the Bestiary?" I said.

"I can, though it may take a moment. Would you like to proceed?" he answered, in his soothing, clipped voice.

"Yes, please."

"Very good." The screen turned black, showing a whirling circle that chased its tail. I couldn't tear my fatigued eyes away from it, the movement hypnotic. "Deleted files recovered," Smartie chirped. The screen shifted back to the camera footage, showing the same four guards standing languidly in the hallway. Once again, the closest man to the camera tapped his foot in apparent boredom. However, as the clock ticked past the five-minute mark, where the doctored footage had shifted to the loop, this one didn't. A figure stepped up to the security guards with their hood up. I couldn't hear anything, but the figure was clearly speaking to them about something. They looked at him like they knew him, exchanging glances before wandering off down the hallway, out of shot.

The shrouded figure turned up toward the camera for a second, revealing a face I didn't want to see. Alton snapped his head back around and hurried up to the doors of the Bestiary, placing a small, silvery object on the ground. I gasped and almost dropped Smartic on my face, my clammy palms gripping the sides of the tablet. My heart rate spiked, my eyes widening in horror. *No, no, no, no, no... This can't be right.*

My father whirled back around and hurried back the way he'd come. A few minutes later, a second figure strode up to the door and picked up the abandoned object. I knew it had to be the Shapeshifter spy, but they weren't wearing a familiar guise—not John Smith, not Alton, not Preceptor Parks, but someone else entirely. *Very cunning.*

With no guards around to stop him, the Shapeshifter opened the door and skimmed the silvery object inside. The blast went off ten seconds later, the figure darting in through the fog that rolled out. He sprinted back out soon after, with Quetzi slung over his shoulder, the serpent's tail dragging behind him. He was clearly struggling with the feathered serpent, the weight slowing him down, but Quetzi didn't move or fight back, a shimmering golden rope wrapped around him. Running as fast as he could with the added weight, the spy disappeared out of the camera's sight, no doubt using the nearby concealed stairwell to get down to the Crypt.

I realized I'd been holding my breath, and I let it all out in one shaky exhale. Alton had facilitated Quetzi's release. He'd made it possible for John Smith to get in and get out, with Quetzi in his arms. Alton had, by proxy, caused the chaos in the Bestiary. And, presumably, he'd been the one to cover these tracks.

But why? Why would you do this?

I threw on clothes, grabbed Smartie off the desk, and sprinted toward my father's office to confront him. Furious tears meandered down my cheeks, my broken heart too overwhelmed to stop them. None of this made any logical sense to me. Why would Alton have done all of that for the spy? A sickening feeling wrenched inside me. *Please tell me you aren't working for her.*

I burst through the hefty doors of his office, to find him sitting behind his expansive desk. He looked up in alarm, shoving something into the top drawer before I could catch sight of it. A memory came pinging back into my mind—his suspicious behavior the last time I'd been in here, when he'd pushed documents and something shiny into his desk.

"Why did you do it?" I barked, my voice cracking with emotion.

He frowned. "Do what, Astrid?"

"Why did you do it? Why did you set things up so Quetzi could be stolen? Why are you working with Katherine? Tell me *now!*" My body shook violently, my heart racing so hard I thought I might suffer a cardiac arrest at any moment.

"This is preposterous. Astrid, you need to calm down. Who has been feeding you these lies?"

"You're the only one who's been feeding me lies, Father!" I snapped, breathless. "I saw you. I found a glitch in the camera footage, and I recovered the deleted files. It showed me the real footage. You left an object for the spy so he could get into the Bestiary and take Quetzi. All that mess, all those escaped beasts, it happened because of *you*. I want to know why, and *now*." Anger spiked through my veins. "You blamed

Garrett, when all this time *you* were the one doing the betraying. How could you?"

His face turned as white as a sheet. "You did what?"

"I found the original footage, Father. You can't wipe anything permanently from the coven's system—even you should know that. The doctoring was well done, I'll grant you that, but I have a keener eye for detail than most. I saw you. I saw what you did."

"Nonsense. You don't know what you're talking about."

"Are you really going to lie to my face?" I turned Smartie around and played the footage to him, his eyes getting wider and wider as the images danced across the screen, revealing the truth—the unmistakable facts, in vivid Technicolor.

He sank back down into his chair, holding his head in his hands. From the purple circles under his eyes, and the drawn, sunken look of his skin, it was clear he was still exhausted from his Necromancy and the Purge that had ended John Smith. Still, I could muster no shred of sympathy, not after what he'd done. He had brought all of this on himself.

"I'm sorry. I won't lie to you again," he whispered, tears brimming in his eyes. I'd never seen my father cry before, and the sight was deeply unsettling. Part of me wanted to hug him, while the other part wanted to smack him hard in the face. "I made a deal with Katherine—Quetzi, in exchange for the missing children. I didn't find that medallion at Purgatory. The spy brought it to me, from her, though he was impersonating someone else at the time. I didn't know who he really was, I swear. I didn't know he was pretending to be Jacintha, and I definitely didn't know what he'd done to her. If I had, I would never have gone ahead with it."

He paused, taking a shallow breath, his face contorted in pain. "Katherine threatened to kill you and destroy your body before I'd get the chance to resurrect you. Out of devotion for the coven and the magical world, it wasn't an easy choice to make—I thought about it for a while before I gave her anything, weighing up my options. I wondered if I would put the lives of others above yours... Katherine was so eager to get Quetzi, she even offered the San Diego kids, to 'sweeten the deal,' in her own words. I said yes, but not with an easy heart. I figured Quetzi would be powerful and smart enough to get away from whoever she sent here to collect him. It was a huge risk, I know, but… you're my daughter, Astrid. I couldn't let anything happen to you. I had to keep you safe."

I stared at him, not knowing what to say. There were some reasons in there that I could understand, but my life wasn't worth all of this mayhem. I wasn't more important, just because I was his daughter. If Katherine fulfilled the ritual because of this, then what was the point? There wasn't one. And what if Katherine had been bluffing? She wasn't known for doing that, but what if she'd known she could bend Alton to her will by saying something like that?

"Katherine might succeed because of you," I said coldly.

"You think I don't know that? You don't think I feel the weight of that?" His eyes burned with grief, his bottom lip trembling.

I frowned. "What if Quetzi hadn't escaped?"

"I planned to help the serpent out, when the spy tried to take him during my monthly debrief. I had a fail-safe in place, but then you went looking for Quetzi, and now he's gone. Katherine is out to get him now, and she won't stop until she gets what she wants. Which is why I sent you all after Quetzi. I wanted you to find him before Katherine does."

"Why did you even bring that evil man back to life?"

Alton sighed. "I wanted to know who he really was, and if Quetzi had told him anything prior to his death."

Realization hit me like a stab in the chest. "Did you… kill John Smith? That story about you Purging and the beast killing him—was that true, or was that another lie?"

"That is how it happened. That wasn't a lie. I'd intended to wipe his memory of me and hand him over to the Mage Council, but everything hit me at once. I was so tired and angry, and I Purged before I could get him to safety. The Purge beast *did* kill him, but that wasn't my intention."

"You expect me to believe that?"

"It's the truth, at least with that aspect of it," he replied solemnly.

"Pretty handy, though, right? That took the spy out of the picture, in case he let anything slip."

Alton's eyes hardened. "Either way, I couldn't have anyone finding out about what I'd done, not when I'd planned to make things right. But I did *not* mean for him to die like that. There's been enough death in this coven."

Everything they'd said during their exchange in the Escher Reading Room made sense now. Alton had told John Smith to be very careful how he answered, presumably warning him not to reveal his involvement. John Smith had replied by saying he knew how this worked, and that he wouldn't say anything. It had been a silent agreement between the two of them, and we'd all been duped.

"Why did you try to set Garrett up, when it was you all along?" I hissed, tears falling.

"I didn't know that it wasn't Garrett. When I checked the footage myself, I saw that his body cam had been set on a loop. It made me suspect him even more, though I realize now that I was wrong. The spy must have hacked the system to make it look like Garrett was responsible, just as I'd done to cover the images of me in the hallway outside the Bestiary."

"You can't just be forgiven for this," I murmured.

He nodded. "I know... but I beg of you, please don't tell a soul about what you've seen. We have to find Quetzi before Katherine does, and you will need me for that. I can make this right, but I can't do that if everyone finds out what I did. No one will trust me, no matter how good my intentions might have been."

"You could have told me. I would have understood. I could have helped you." My voice came out as little more than a squeak, my eyes blurry with weeping. Alton had always been loyal to the coven, almost to a fault. This betrayal did not compute with my brain—it was a crime against the very thing he adored, and surely would have ended up with him in Purgatory, or the coven prison at the very least. I couldn't get the pieces to fit properly. It was as though I were still in my bed, half-waking from a terrible nightmare.

"You would have talked me out of it," he replied bluntly. "I was terrified of losing you. I couldn't let her do anything to you."

"So, you've actually spoken with her?" I gaped at him. I'd presumed that all communications had been made via the spy, with Alton using the medallion solely as a means of locating the children.

He nodded. "Yes."

"You're making deals with the devil now?"

"You would never have seen it from any other perspective. I *had* to do this—she would have stopped at nothing to make me accept the deal!"

I shook my head. "Do you truly believe this deal will keep any of us safe from her? And what did it accomplish? She's got to have an alternative in place—more kids to use. It was all too easy, Father—even you have to be able to see that. She wouldn't just give them up unless she also had a fail-safe in mind."

He sank deeper into his chair. "She does have more children. Louella told me about it. I'd already realized that when the security teams picked them up without so much as a fight, but Louella confirmed it. The report explained that there were more cages in that abandoned ferry port—empty ones."

"I know that saving some of the kids is better than saving none, but my life isn't worth all of this, not when she'll come for me anyway, next time she needs you to do her bidding."

"Your life is worth it, to me. I couldn't take the chance. I couldn't live in fear of wondering when she would come to take you away. You can't understand that, I know you can't, but my intentions were good. You're my only child—I wasn't about to let you die, when I could stop it from happening." He looked up in desperation, his voice oddly boyish and vulnerable. "Besides, we still have time to fix this, if we find Quetzi. Although, in order to do that, I'm going to need your silence a while longer."

"Fine." I stalked out of the room, my head brimming with a thousand emotions, all in turmoil. I heard his chair scrape back as I exited, and the sound of footsteps hurrying behind me. I kept my gaze fixed on the end of the hallway, walking quickly.

He didn't follow me, nor did he call out, but I could feel his eyes on my retreating back. I kept right on, wondering what on earth I was going to do now.

TWENTY-SIX

Astrid

"A re you busy?" I asked Garrett over the phone. I'd more or less stopped the endless tears from falling, angry and hot down my cheeks. My phone had been ringing ceaselessly, with Alton's name flashing up. In the end, I'd forwarded all of his calls to voicemail, unable to bear the sound of him or even acknowledge him. I had yet to fully process everything, and until I'd done that, I didn't trust myself to talk to him again.

"Not really. Why, what's up?" Garrett said.

"Can we meet?" I asked.

He paused. "I guess so."

"Dragon garden in ten?"

"Can we pick somewhere else?" His words wounded me a little. Why didn't he want to meet me there, in the place we'd had our date? More to the point, why did he sound so standoffish? Things had been normal between us during the memorial service, and even before then, when he'd held me during Alton's Necromancy. What had changed since then? I wasn't sure, but there was a newfound strangeness to his tone that brought back memories of the other day, when he'd said that I was one to talk about secrets.

"Uh… the library?"

"Sure. I'll see you there." He hung up without saying goodbye. Ordinarily, I might have thought very little of his behavior, but I was already on the brink of losing my mind. I couldn't add Garrett's coldness to the list of things that were bothering me, not when I needed his comfort more than ever. *Whatever it is, I can fix it when I see him.*

Feeling somewhat better, I walked in the direction of the main library. I arrived long before he did, taking up a seat in one of the corner desks, close to the window. It was out of the way of the main space, sheltered from prying eyes. Although, there weren't many other people around. After Jacintha's memorial service, the coven had been more subdued, with most of its residents choosing to spend time away from its walls. Even the preceptors' students had been given the week off, to cope with the loss, and they certainly weren't using the free days to study.

Garrett appeared fifteen minutes late, waltzing in with a casual air. He wore dark jeans and a gray T-shirt, his short, dark hair freshly cut. His piercing blue eyes scoured the room for me. I raised my hand, waving him over. Not even then could he muster a smile for me, his brow furrowed as he crossed the gap between us and sat down with a thump.

"What's up?" he asked brusquely. "Were none of your other buddies free?"

I stared at him, struggling to hide my sudden hurt. "I wanted to speak to you."

"Oh, so now you trust me?"

"What do you mean?"

He sighed, running a hand through his hair. "You basically accused me of being the traitor, because I wouldn't do that stupid interview. Have I heard a single word of apology from you since the real one was found? No, I haven't. What—did you think I'd just gloss over it and everything would be peachy?"

Tears brimmed in my eyes again. "I… I thought we were good?"

"Why, because I held you during all of that scary Necromancy crap?"

I nodded slowly.

"I held you because it was crazy cold. I haven't stopped caring about you, Astrid, but you treated me like dirt. You can't expect me to just get over that. You're supposed to be the one person in this place who trusts me, but you just bought into the same old trash as the others."

"No, I *do* trust you," I insisted, my voice thick. It calmed me to know he still cared, but the rest worried me. Did this mean we weren't good anymore? It certainly felt that way, much to my horror. I didn't want to lose him.

"No, you didn't. You looked into my eyes and asked me where I was, and when I didn't give you the answer you wanted, you judged me, same as everyone else. I asked you to trust me, the way any couple should be able to, and you didn't. You don't, Astrid. You jumped on the Shapeshifters-are-bad bandwagon and you doubted me. I let you have your secrets and I don't say a word, but you won't let me have mine? Seems a little hypocritical, doesn't it?"

"I know it wasn't you!" I blurted out, warring with my fractious emotions.

"You do now, but only after the spy got caught." He smiled sadly. "Did you look at the camera footage?"

My heart plummeted. I was a terrible liar at the best of times, with the exception of about who my father was. Somehow, I knew that if I lied, he would see right through me.

"You don't need to tell me," he said. "I know you did, because you didn't trust me. That's who you are. You always need to get to the bottom of everything, and I admire you for that, but not when I'm the one in the line of fire. I wish I could say I hoped you wouldn't, or that I knew you'd trust in me enough not to, but then you wouldn't be you. As soon as I said it, I figured you'd check the footage."

My cheeks were fiery hot. "I wanted to check you off the list, that's all."

"All you had to do was believe me," he replied evenly. "But you couldn't, could you? Alton put the seed of doubt in your head, and you had to know for yourself. My words didn't matter. See, regardless of what you think, or feel, about me, you'll always side with Alton and do as he tells you. He's your dad—what else are you going to do?"

My eyes felt as though they were bulging out of my head. "What did you say?"

"I know, Astrid. I wasn't going to say anything because, hey, families are hard enough as they are without other people getting involved. Plus, I thought I'd bide my time, see if you came clean about it on your own. But then you had the nerve to question my honesty, after the lies you've been telling everyone?"

I shook my head effusively. "How can you even know that?"

"See, even with this, he's your first thought. You don't care about my feelings, or how this might have affected me; you're only bothered about your secret with dear old Dad." He huffed out a breath. "I followed you, after he took you away from our date. I overheard your argument."

"You—"

"Yeah, I probably shouldn't have eavesdropped, but I wanted to make sure you were okay. He seemed mad, and I didn't want him upsetting you. Little did I know I'd get *that* gem—that he's your dad. I suppose I should've guessed, considering how close the two of you are. He wouldn't bring just *anyone* back to life three times."

"I'm sorry," I wheezed. "I'm sorry I didn't tell you. I'm sorry I doubted you. I'm sorry I… I'm sorry I looked at the footage. But you have to know why I did it, right? I kept asking where you were, and you wouldn't answer me."

"This is what I mean about trust. You don't need to know my every movement—that's not right, or healthy."

"Then why was the footage doctored?" I couldn't help myself. "It was doctored during the Bestiary explosion and when we were stuck in the Crypt."

He shook his head. "That first time, during the blast, I'd gone to try and visit Finch. I got to the reception of Purgatory before I turned back and changed my mind. I guess the spy must have found the change I made to the system and used it to frame me." He looked me dead in the eyes. "The second time, when you were all stuck in the Crypt, I tried to visit Finch again. I didn't turn back that time. When we spoke about him—you and I—it made me realize I had to swallow my fears and talk to him, to find closure or something. At the time, that was something I needed to keep from Alton, for obvious reasons, but it had nothing to do with Katherine or Quetzi, not directly."

"You… you went to see Finch?" If that was the case, then I could understand his reason for not wanting to let on about it, on either occasion. My father would have had a field day with that information, using it to smear Garrett's character even more, to cover his own tracks. *That explains why one loop was longer than the other, at least.*

"Yeah, I did."

"Why?"

He frowned. "You going to accuse me of siding with him?"

"No, I'm just interested," I said. "I want to know."

"I just wanted to speak with him, that's all. See if he knew anything about these rituals."

"Did he?"

"No, I didn't get anything out of him, otherwise I'd have *had* to say something," he replied bluntly. "Anyway, since I didn't find anything out, I didn't want Alton to know in case it gave him more reason to suspect me. Now the spy's been caught, I guess it doesn't matter anymore. Either way, it doesn't change what you did," he muttered. "I thought you were different. I know people say that all the time to folks they care about, but I really thought you were something special. You've got no idea how much it kills me, to know you're just the same."

I bit my lip. "That's not fair. I care about you. I did trust you; I just needed to know where you were during the time Quetzi was taken and the time we were stuck. If you'd said you were with Finch, I'd have understood, given Alton's track record with you. All you needed to do was explain. I needed to rule you out, that was all."

"Well, you can."

"What?"

"Rule me out," he said coldly. "I'm done with this."

"Done with what?" I could barely utter the sentence.

"With whatever this might have been." He gestured to me.

"Please, don't be like this. You have to understand my reasoning. It's common sense, surely?" I felt foolish. What few people were around had started to stare.

He laughed bitterly. "You should have thought about that before you lied to me, and called me a traitor to my face. Even if you'd apologized, I might've forgiven you, but you're so caught up in this place and Alton that it's not worth it for me anymore."

"Please, please don't do this. Just see it from my perspective." Panic spread through me like ice.

"I'm sorry, Astrid."

"You have to understand… if people knew I was his daughter, they'd treat me differently."

"Then you'd know what it feels like to be a Shapeshifter."

Tears trickled down my cheeks. His expression shifted for the briefest of moments, the edges softening slightly, before they hardened right back up again. His eyes were steely and blank, his mouth set in a line.

I scraped back my chair and stood, unable to look at him. Wiping the tears away, I turned around and exited the library. My first foray into romance had ended in a tragedy of my own creation, but what did people always say about more fish? I didn't want to hook one, but it was easier to tell myself that there were more.

Mom will know what to do, I told myself, as I walked quicker, tears blurring my vision again. Waterfront Park beckoned—my only sanctuary, away from this place and everything bad inside it.

———

I burst into Cabot's, trying not to appear like a teary waif who'd strayed in from outside, and sought my mom out. She was busy helping a customer, but she noticed me as I frantically waved and hurried through to the back of the store. My hands shook as I fixed a cup of tea and sat down at the small table beside a window that looked out on the park. Children were playing on the jungle-gym, but I could find no joy in watching them. Instead, I envied them. Being an adult was filled with pitfalls and humiliations I couldn't have compre-hended back then, when everything was simple and the worst injury was a grazed knee. I'd have taken a thousand of those over a bruised heart.

My mom came in a few minutes later, looking suitably worried. I'd never been an emotional kind of girl, and tears were a clear warning sign.

"Astrid? Is everything okay?" She sat down and took my hand.

I shook my head. "It's Garrett." Alton's betrayal weighed heavily on my mind too, but I didn't want to tell my mom that. Not right now.

"Do I need to roast some ass?" She tried to coax a smile out of me, but I couldn't muster one.

"No, I think we were both at fault," I replied solemnly. "We had an argument. I didn't trust him when he told me he wasn't the spy, and I didn't apologize when I found out he wasn't. I checked up on him, Mom. I shouldn't have done it, I know I shouldn't have, but I couldn't help myself. And then, he told me he knew about me and Dad, and he was upset that I hadn't trusted him enough to tell him about it."

Fresh tears fell, which was strange, considering I'd thought I'd squeezed them all out. I realized I'd called Alton "Dad" for the first time in a long time, which only made matters worse. Maybe Garrett was right. Maybe I *would* always side with Alton, because I felt I owed him my loyalty. Even after he'd made that deal with Katherine, I still couldn't bring myself to hate him.

"Oh, my sweet, sweet girl."

"I really liked him, and now he wants nothing to do with me," I sobbed. My mom wrapped her arms around me and pulled me close. She rocked me like a child, smoothing down my springy curls. "I should've trusted him. I should've known better than to meddle." *I should have seen what my dad was up to. I should've stopped him.* Both men had broken my heart today.

"Why didn't you trust him?" she asked softly, into my hair.

"I asked him where he was when Quetzi got taken, and he wouldn't tell me."

"Okay, so it sounds like you had reason to doubt him. Did he tell you where he was, after the spy was discovered?"

"He did just before, when we argued."

"So, he had secrets too. He has every right to feel hurt, but he can't play innocent if he wasn't clear with you earlier, either," she said. "You might have been at fault, but so was he. I'm sure he's just angry right now. Once that subsides, you may find you can have a more mature conversation about things. We often let our emotions get the better of us, and I imagine his wounded feelings have played a part in this. Give him time, and give yourself time, and see what happens."

"He won't speak to me ever again," I muttered.

"He will, if the boy has any sense."

"I should've trusted him! I'm so mad at myself."

She held my cheeks and pulled away, looking straight into my eyes. "Astrid, trust is a very fragile thing and, once it's broken, it can be very hard to repair. However, if you care enough about each other to try, then it's not impossible. Plus, trust goes both ways. He lied to you; you lied to him. That makes the reparation all the easier, if you choose to do it, because neither of you is the innocent party. In that way, you can fix it together, instead of one of you doing all the picking up of the pieces."

"What if it can't be fixed?" I blinked away the last of my tears. I was thinking of Alton, too. A big part of me wanted to tell her about what he'd done, but I didn't know what to say. Where did I even start?

"Then it wasn't worth putting back together again." She smiled, and brushed the streaks from my cheeks. "If it's something that can be saved, you'll find a way to resolve your issues."

I was about to ask her how, when my phone pinged in my pocket. Terrified it was the Rag Team, ready to go out into the field and wondering where I'd gone, I plucked it out and looked at the screen. Instead, I found a series of message alerts from Smartie, which had been rerouted to my phone. They'd come from the technological setups I had implemented across San Diego, which notified me of any unusual social media or newsfeeds. Each alert showed a number of weather anomalies, popping up all over the place.

"It's him," I whispered.

My mom frowned. "Who?"

"Quetzi."

TWENTY-SEVEN

Harley

At two o'clock, I met the rest of the Rag Team in the Banquet Hall to get ready to head out. Astrid wasn't here yet, but I figured she'd be on her way. Garrett, on the other hand, was standing around with a grim expression on his face. There was clearly a lot on his mind. I wondered if something had happened between them, after the dispute in the interview room. Then again, they'd seemed fine in the Escher Room, when he'd put his arms around her.

Couples, huh? Who'd be in one? I cast a shy glance at Wade, who was busy circling places on the map where we still had to look for Quetzi.

"So, turns out Louella's quite the historical sleuth," I announced to the distracted group.

"The Devereaux girl?" Tatyana asked.

I nodded. "Yeah, I caught her in the Forbidden Section. She's found quite a lot of stuff that we missed in the old books."

"Like what?" Raffe said, leaning forward over the table.

I gave them a quick debrief of what Louella had told me, from the texts she'd gathered and the essay Remington had written. They watched me in silent awe as I regaled them with her findings. There were a few confused looks, too, but I got that—I'd looked at Louella the same way, through most of what she'd told me. As I finished up my tale, Dylan let out a low whistle.

"So, this Librarian chick is still alive?"

"Looks like it," I replied.

"Might as well be dead, for all the good she'll do us. If she's with Katherine Shipton, she's out of our reach," Garrett muttered.

"Loving that uplifting attitude, Kyteler," I shot back. "Wanna flash some pom-poms while you're at it?"

He scowled. "I'm just telling it like it is. No point going after the Librarian if Katherine's got her. We tried that already with the kids, and it took rummaging through a criminal's belongings to get them back. What do we have to do to get the Librarian, huh? Send a fruit basket and a harem to Purgatory to get one of those scumbags to talk?"

"Who pissed on your cornflakes?" Santana asked, arching an eyebrow.

He sighed. "Forget it. Long day."

"Listen, we need to view this as a positive," Wade chimed in. "If the Librarian is still alive, then there's a slim chance we can rescue her. Slim, yes, but not impossible. If we can do that, we could find out how these rituals work, thanks to all the information she's gathered over the years, through her souped-up Clairvoyance abilities. Louella's information is good too, but it's all from books and old texts—we can't be sure what's real and what's fiction. Facts would be better, and the Librarian knows those facts. At least, that's the theory."

"You don't think it could be reality masked as fiction?" I replied.

He shrugged. "We need something clearer than a myth. Either that, or we need proof that she's on the right track."

"Well, thanks for taking the wind out of my sails." I cast him a teasing smile. He was right, of course he was, but I wasn't about to give up on Louella's theories. If I could add some facts from Remington, then maybe it'd be enough to bolster the evidence that she was onto something.

"It's not that; I just think we should focus on one thing at a time. First order of business: Quetzi."

"Then myths?"

He smiled. "Then myths."

"Harley, can I speak to you over here for a moment?" Tatyana asked unexpectedly. She was standing close to the table, perfectly poised as ever.

"Sure." I followed her a few steps away from the group. "What's up?"

"What we were talking about just then—all these myths and legends —it reminded me that I needed to talk to you. I've been preoccupied lately, with everything that's been going on. Anyway, I spoke to my parents about your family, as I said I would," she explained, her voice low. "I was waiting until I'd compiled all the information before I said anything to you, but I think I have everything now."

My eyes widened. "What did you find out?"

"There have been some new developments regarding your more-ancient past," she went on. "According to my parents, it is believed that your family—both sides—were thought to be some of the first magicals born on this Earth."

"The Primus Anglicus, right?"

She seemed surprised. "Yes, exactly. You already knew that?"

"Spoilers." I gave her an apologetic smile.

"Well, then, you must know that they were responsible for many good and bad things over the course of time. There doesn't seem to be an in-between—either they were exemplary magicals, or they were into some dark and unsettling endeavors. Leaders and criminals, in an almost even split."

I grimaced. "The Dark and the Light?"

"In most cases. You must know that not all Light magicals are good, though, yes? Same as not all Dark magicals are bad. I mean, I lean towards Darkness and I'm nice most of the time." She cast me a smile.

"Yeah, it's just hard to wrap my head around."

"I mean, there was a case a couple of years ago about an extraordinarily powerful Light magical called Giverny le Fay, who launched an attack on the annual meeting of the European covens, in an attempt to overthrow the regime and take over," she said. "She succeeded in killing several leaders, but was stopped by the Angels before she could murder them all. She's rotting in Purgatory now, for her crimes."

"Angels?"

"The secret security services in charge of protecting the European covens."

"Like the CIA?"

She nodded. "But with added magic."

"Do we have a group like that?" We could really have done with some Angels right about now.

"Sadly not. The United Covens of America decided against having a secret service, preferring to keep things in-house."

I frowned. "Wait… did you say le Fay? As in Morgan le Fay?"

"She is descended from her, yes."

"And she's a Light magical?"

"Yes. Are you listening to anything I'm saying?"

I laughed nervously. "Just making sure I've got my facts straight." If this Light magical was as powerful as Tatyana made out, then she might be *exactly* the kind of person I needed for the Light side of the Sanguine spell. Getting to her would be the hard part, but I'd navigated Purgatory before. Maybe I'd get lucky, like I had with my visit to Finch.

"Anyway, what I'm saying is, Light can mean destruction, too," she continued. "Some of the Light side of your family have been involved in terrible things, while some of the Dark have done a great deal of good."

"Nice to know."

"As for your mother and father, and Katherine's involvement," she said, "my mom said that the real troubles began when your mother invited Hiram for Christmas at the Shipton household. Now, it's not exactly clear, but it appears that Katherine was asked not to attend if she was going to cause a fuss. Apparently, she showed up and tried to rekindle her previous relationship with your father at the Christmas party, and he exposed her seduction efforts to the entire family."

"Sounds about the right shade of messed-up."

"Naturally, Hester was furious and told her to leave. Katherine had expected the support of her family, but the rest of the Shiptons agreed it would be better for everyone if Katherine spent the festive season else-where. The coven obviously heard what had happened when Hester and Hiram returned. With Hiram and Hester considered the golden couple back then, Katherine lost her potential position on the board, she lost the man she wanted, and she lost the respect of her family, all at once."

Anger burned in my veins. "So, she killed them?"

"She killed them all at the Christmas party she'd been cast out from the previous year—everyone but Hester. As you know, she left her to... well, we don't need to go over that."

"Yeah, that psychopath wanted my dad to kill my mom—she wanted to force him to do it, so she could have that sick, twisted satisfaction. I know that bit," I said through gritted teeth. "Was there anything else?"

"Well, apparently Katherine was a favorite of their grandfather—Drake Shipton—who was always suspected of being evilly inclined. He died shortly before the wedding of your mother and father, and she was banned from attending the funeral. It appears that he was the one who first gave Katherine the idea of how to defeat or use your parents to her benefit."

I frowned. "How do your parents know all of this?"

"Various sources. Most of it is firsthand knowledge, or information passed to them through mutual friends. They also read her files, prior to her entry into the New York Coven, and when they had to reassess her after the incident with Hiram," she explained. "They thought she was a little unstable, but they admired her power, and her intelligence was more than impressive. I guess they took the power over the possible instability. Either that, or New York thought they could tame her."

"Well, they thought wrong."

"Oh, undoubtedly."

There was plenty of overlap between what Tatyana had told me and what I'd read in Isadora's letter. If my mom knew about Katherine's obsession, which she likely did, then maybe she'd been trying to come up with spells that could combat her. It certainly explained why there was a large chunk about summoning a Child of Chaos in my parents' Grimoire.

Is Erebus the key? I didn't feel comfortable with the idea of summoning him in order to find out, not after what I'd been told about him. If I summoned him, I had to give a life in return. *Nope... not doing that.*

Katherine had really gone through some tough times. It couldn't have been easy for anyone to get rebuffed and ousted by their own family. But being sent away for causing trouble wasn't a good enough reason to kill your entire family and put an evil curse on the man you loved. There were countless serial killers out there who might've disagreed with me, but I wasn't unhinged enough to see things from that kind of perspective. *Although, if I break this Suppressor, who knows?* I shuddered at the thought.

One thing was for sure—Katherine Shipton was ruled by her emotions. More so than most people. It worried me, given my Empath abilities, and the way my emotions seemed to affect my powers. I'd already experienced what could happen when my emotions got the better of me: sinkholes, training posts reduced to matchsticks, almost killing a room full of people with a chandelier. I didn't mean to do it, but that didn't remove the responsibility on my shoulders, or the conse-quences of those actions. Then again, that already set me apart from Katherine, because she *definitely* meant to do the things she'd done.

"Are you okay?" Tatyana asked, with unexpected warmth. "If I said too much, please tell me."

"No, you didn't say too much. I needed to hear it. It's just... well, it's a lot to take in at once."

"You should see the notes I made, trying to remember everything they said at the Family Gathering. There are pages and pages. Russian is much faster than English, but I think I caught everything they had to say," she said, smiling.

"Thank you for doing that. I mean it."

She dipped her head. "It was my pleasure. It's vital to know one's history, no matter how bad it may be. That way, we can ensure it does not repeat itself."

"How'd you get so wise, huh?" I teased.

"It's the Vasilis way."

A beep in my pocket took my attention away from Tatyana. A series of similar beeps went off around the room, the rest of the Rag Team looking to their phones. I did the same, seeing Astrid's name pop up. There was a message attached, with links to a series of news reports of local weather anomalies. It simply read: *Think we've found Quetzi. Alton knows. He wants us to go to each location—we need to leave now. Meet me in the foyer in five.*

"It's always Alton this, Alton that, Alton said we have to go here," Garrett muttered.

"Yeah, because he's our Director, dumbass. What's your problem?" I barked.

"It's not my problem, it's Astrid's," he said coldly.

"What are you talking about?"

He pulled a sour face. "All of you, following him like sheep. And she's just as bad."

"You got something you want to say?" Wade stepped in.

"You're all blind, every single one of you."

"Spit it out, Garrett," Santana pressed. "You've clearly got something on your mind."

"Look at you all, ganging up on me because I dare to speak a bad word about Alton friggin' Waterhouse. You all think the sun shines out his ass, when he has no problem keeping secrets from you."

"What secrets?" I asked.

"Both of them, they're liars."

"Who?" Tatyana asked.

"Astrid and Alton. Aw, how cute, they've even got the same first letter."

"Garrett, what the hell are you harping on about? We've got places to be, so either say what you clearly want to say, or shut your trap so we can leave," Santana cut in, clearly irritated that he was getting in the way of us going after Quetzi. I shared her annoyance.

His eyes flashed with anger. "She's his daughter, you idiots. They've been lying to you this whole time. She's probably been spying on us all for him, feeding back to him all of our private conversations and having a good laugh about it. You ever wonder how he already knows everything, before we've even told him? It's not because she's his right-hand woman, it's because she's his *kid*."

I could see the exasperated fury in his stiff shoulders and twisted, half-hurt expression. To be honest, I had no idea what to do with this sudden burst of information. I already had enough swimming around in my head. Still, it was a hell of a shock. The rest of the group were staring at him as though he'd just sprouted another head.

He shrugged. "What? You all deserve to know who you're dealing with. She isn't this little innocent, vulnerable thing you all think she is." *Yep, he's definitely dealing with some issues here.* What had they argued about? Whatever it was, it had left its mark on him. His tone was borderline spiteful.

"Look, we don't have time to talk about this now," Wade said, breaking the tense silence. "We need to get after Quetzi before he disappears again. I suggest you rein in whatever this anger is about, and try and get your head in the game. If you can't do that, you should probably stay here."

Garrett glared at Wade. "I'll be fine. I'm coming with you."

"Right, then, let's go."

As we ran for the exit of the coven, I wondered if it was true. Could Astrid really be Alton's daughter? Now that I thought about it in a different light, it did make a lot of sense. Alton's unwavering reliance on her, for one.

TWENTY-EIGHT

Harley

D aisy skidded to a halt beside one of the locations from Astrid, the engine falling silent as I turned the keys. Wade's Jeep pulled up a moment later, with an almighty screech of tires. I had Astrid, Tatyana, Raffe, and Jacob—our honorary Rag Team member—in Daisy with me, while Santana, Garrett, Dylan, and Wade were in the Jeep. We all spilled out and sprinted for an expanse of barren wasteland up ahead, on the outskirts of La Jolla.

It didn't look like much, at first glance. An abandoned parking lot. But the charred bodies that lay sprawled on the dried-out earth made it clear that something awful had happened here. Their limbs were bent at awkward angles, dead eyes looking up or facing the dirt. We edged forward to take a closer look. I glanced at the body of the closest one, shuddering at the sight of the golden emblem embedded in the carbonized flesh. The Apple of Discord—a sure sign this person was part of the Cult of Eris.

"Look for the symbol," I said to the others. They nodded and picked through the ten figures who'd lost their lives. Yeah, they were evil and deserved punishment for their unpardonable affiliations, but the only person I wanted to see dead on the ground like this was Katherine herself. Everyone else could just rot in Purgatory.

"There's one here," Raffe shouted, from the opposite side of the wasteland.

"Another here," Astrid added.

"Yep, this one too," Dylan said.

Wade lifted his head. "And this one."

It took a few more minutes of checking to conclude that they were all part of the Cult of Eris. "They must've come looking for Quetzi," I mused aloud. The others nodded.

"Looks like he fought back, and then some," Santana replied. "There's no mention of a Fire ability in the old stories about him."

I glanced at her. "What about lightning?"

"Right! Quetzalcoatl is known to manipulate the weather—lightning included. Makes sense, judging by these bodies." They were charred and smoking, but their veins were doing strange things beneath the clear stretches of skin that could still be seen. Weird patterns had bloomed, fanning out like the branches and leaves of a tree. I'd seen pictures of victims who'd been struck by lightning, and a lot of them had these same, odd patterns all over, where the current had blitzed through them.

"Do you think he's still here?" Raffe whispered.

As if summoned by the mere mention, the ground around us quivered. It started small, a vague vibration, before gathering strength. A howling wind tore across the dry landscape, the Rag Team bowing against the powerful gale. The vortex dragged in debris, and I shielded my eyes against the dirt and dust. It twisted into a terrifying tornado that powered up from the earth in a swift rush, growing bigger and bigger until it threatened to swallow us whole.

We backed off as best we could, but the winds kept trying to knock us off our feet, buffeting us this way and that until it was impossible to know which direction would lead us to safety. It all happened so suddenly that we had no chance to run back to the cars. I couldn't even see them through the dusty haze that settled over the wasteland. The miasma was too dense.

Quetzi, what are you doing? We're not here to hurt you!

I racked my brain for a way out of this as a gust made me stagger back. Astrid and Jacob had already hit the deck, both of them scrabbling around to try and get back on their feet. Tatyana's eyes were glowing white, her spiritual energy holding her to the earth. Santana seemed to be doing a similar thing with her Orishas, while Dylan and Raffe were leaning so far forward I thought they might tip over. Still, it appeared to be working, their muscle power giving them some leverage against the winds. Wade, meanwhile, had his arm wrapped around his eyes to block out the dust. I was struggling, too; my mouth, nostrils, eyes, ears all filled with scratchy particles that itched like crazy.

An idea sparked in my head, though it was a risky one. *Fight fire with fire. How about air with air?*

Lifting my palms as best I could, though the gales pummeled against them, I drew on my Chaos energy and let it flow through my veins. It ran, hot and cold, and syrup-thick to the edges of my fingertips. I closed my eyes and forced my thoughts to drift away, leaving nothing but the idea of Air, and what I wanted to use it for. Nomura had told me I had to concentrate, so that's what I was damn well going to do.

Air spiraled out of my hands, erupting in a burst of powerful wind. My eyes flew open, my nerves on edge at the thought that it might backfire horribly, the way it had done before.

Come on... here goes nothing.

Tensing my muscles, I sent the gust of Air toward the tornado, using it to combat the vortex and divert it away from us. It thundered upward in a shimmering blockade of pure Elemental force, pushing against the tornado and edging it back to a safer distance.

For a split second, I saw something in the center of the vortex—a familiar, reptilian shape. Sweat poured down my face, trickling all the way down my spine. Despite the titanic effort, I was in awe of my own control. My Esprit glowed vibrantly, the darkened diamond practically spitting with energy.

Yes, Merlin! This is the stuff!

The tornado swept forward again, my entire body feeling the push of it against my Air wall. I sent out more and heaved it into the tornado. It jolted backward in a drunken tilt, the top part wobbling violently, like an ice skater about to tumble to the rink. Quetzi was doing this, I had no doubt about that, and the history books were right—he was crazy strong. It was all I could do just to keep the tornado at a safe distance. If I was going to get to Quetzi and stop him, I needed to get into the eye of the storm.

Leaving the others behind, I trudged through the powerful gusts, the dust and sand whipping against my face as I reached the edge of the tornado. Each particle dragged across my skin, a trickle of liquid finding its way into my mouth. From the familiar, metallic taste, I knew it was blood. My blood. Undeterred, I pressed on, sending out another flow of Air to form a bubble around me as I forced my way inside. It wavered and swayed but, miraculously, it held, letting less of the violent tornado get its gusty tentacles on me.

Without warning, the wind died. The roar of the tornado echoed around me as it twisted up and up, but it didn't touch me. Even without my bubble, everything was weirdly still inside the eye of the storm, my boots firmly on the ground. At the center, Quetzi slithered toward me and rose up to his full height, balancing on the back end of his thick tail. His feathers ruffled as he eyed me closely. He was a serpent, but I could've sworn he smiled at me.

"Very impressive," he said. "But you should know I'm still not going back."

"You can't stay out here, Quetzi," I replied. "You're already making headlines."

"Am I? That's exciting. I haven't been in the spotlight for years."

"I mean it. You need to come back with us now. Maybe we can speak to Alton, see if he'll give you a better place to live."

"No."

"That's it? No?"

"Why waste time on fancy words, when a simple 'no' works very well by itself?"

I rolled my eyes. "If you stay out here, Katherine is going to catch up with you. I don't even want to know what she's going to do to you when she gets her hands on your scaly ass."

Quetzi tutted. "I'm one of the most powerful creatures of raw Chaos. Please, show the appropriate level of respect. Besides, as far as I can tell, we serpents don't have asses."

"Sorry, it's just that we're kind of running out of time here. Judging by the bodies on the ground, she's got a hell of a lot of people after you."

"You saw what I did to them, yes?"

"Yes."

"So, why worry? She'll keep sending her people, and I'll keep frying them. Eventually, she'll get the picture, and I can find myself a nice little part of the world to live out the rest of my days. Everyone wins."

"And if *she* comes for you?"

He lashed out his tongue. "Oh, I'm counting on it."

"You are? Is that what this showy display is for—to entice her here?"

"I don't whip up these kinds of frenzies for just *anyone*, although it's nice to stretch my muscles a bit. Hundreds of years in a box is terrible for the physical body. I already have aches in places I didn't know existed. Just this morning, I had the awful feeling I'd grown limbs—honestly, I could feel this terrible ache in a leg I don't even have."

I couldn't help but smirk. "What's your beef with Katherine, anyway? I know why I hate her. Why do you?"

"She's a vile specimen," he said simply.

"Come on, there's got to be more to it than that."

His scales rattled. "I don't believe in mortals becoming gods, and that's what she wants. You think this is a recent occurrence, but it's not. Even before she did away with your dear old *Papi*, she had this plan. Katherine has been at it for years."

"What? How do you know this?"

"She used to come into the Bestiary and talk to her gargoyles about it

—about how she planned to become this almighty being and make everyone else pay. She talked of judgment, and a new world order, all ruled over by her and created in the image she'd envisioned. Had she a mirror, she would have asked it if she was the fairest in the land. You, Ms. Merlin, would've ended up with a poison apple shoved in your mouth."

"So, you want to kill her before that can happen."

He chuckled. "Before she kills *me*, yes. Even if I were to go back to the coven with you, which is by no means going to happen, she'd find her way to me eventually. Whether it's today or tomorrow, or a month from now, one of her maggots would weasel in and take me. Here, at least, I'm on even footing. Here, I can fight. The Bestiary box renders me limp and useless."

"Is that what she wants you for—to kill you?"

"You're quick." Sarcasm dripped from his fangs, both of them where they ought to be.

"If that's the case, *why* does she want you dead? Seems like a lot of work if she's just going to end you."

"A much better question. Smart witch," he replied. "Katherine requires the sacrifice of an ancient god for the first ritual. Ancient god meaning me. I was worshiped as one, so, technically speaking, I qualify. Not to mention the purest Chaos at my heart—gifted to me as I was Purged from the Princess of Culhuacan, Atotoztli. A woman of exceptional prowess, her power more formidable than any before her. She was said to have birthed the entire Aztec Empire from her womb. So, you see, there aren't many creatures like me left, with godlike powers. What do you think of that? I'm precious, aren't I?"

Wow, someone thinks a little too highly of themselves. Then again, he was, like we already knew, worshiped as a god, once upon a time. That clearly made him legit. How the mighty had fallen. Now, more than ever, I could understand how frustrating it must have been, being cooped up in a glass box all these years. Still, that didn't mean I wouldn't drag him back there by his tail, if I had to.

"What about the other rituals? Do you know anything about them?"

He flicked his tongue. "Sadly not, or else I'd tell you."

"Well, shouldn't you be hiding, too, if Katherine is after you?"

"There's no point. I thought I explained that already. She will come after me regardless. Hmm, just when I thought you were making progress, you go back to dim-human mode." He fluffed out his feathers. "Anyway, most of those weather signs that you picked up on were an attempt to throw these pestilent agents off my tail. That failed, and they keep chasing me, in annoying swarms, so I've decided to switch to all-out warfare. She can come for me, and I will be ready for her."

"We can protect you, Quetzi."

He snorted. "You can't even protect yourselves. That Shapeshifter was running about for weeks before you bothered to notice something was amiss. Sorry that you had to clean up after me, but I had to kill him. I'm not usually a creature of impulse, but he'd disrespected me."

"Alton brought him back to life," I said.

His eyes glinted. "He didn't!"

"He did. And then he died again. Purge beast got him."

Quetzi chuckled. "Well, at least *I* got to enjoy watching the light go out in him once, thanks to my coils. Most delicious. Reminded me of my less benevolent days as a god."

"We're running out of time, Quetzi. You have to come with us."

"You know, you're so focused on protecting *me* from Katherine, that you're forgetting about yourself. You're important in all of this some-how, or so I heard the Shapeshifter say. I have no idea why, as you seem as inferior as any other magical. Maybe you've got a bit more oomph in you, but I don't imagine it's enough to entice Katherine's sensibilities. Not yet, anyway. Maybe that's it—maybe she's waiting. Who can say? All I know is that you have your part in this, Ms. Merlin. You're the flavor of the month."

"I'm not the one she's after right now," I shot back. "We need to get you out of here."

"Never again," he said slowly. At least, it sounded slow. I blinked rapidly, trying to get my eyes to focus, but everything looked blurry and odd. A strange, silvery mist seemed to rise from the serpent's scales, seeping out from under them and rolling toward me. The smell was musty and metallic, stinging my nostrils as it crept in. It tickled the back of my throat, my tongue fuzzy and numb.

"What did you do?" I slurred.

"Like I said, I won't go back in a box. I have to face her. But this isn't your time… not yet."

Before I knew what was happening, he nudged me back into the tornado with a gentle push. That was all it took—my legs were like jelly, unable to hold me up as I staggered into the swirling vortex. My body shot straight up to the top of the towering cyclone, limp against the rushing current. I couldn't even fight it; my brain disconnected from the rest of me. With great effort, I twisted my neck to look down into the eye of the storm, noticing the dense fog that had settled down there. A figure stepped through, and my heart stopped.

Katherine had arrived, right behind Quetzi.

I wanted to scream, to warn him, but I couldn't. Dread clutched my jaws tight, my tongue twisted and paralyzed.

Quetzi didn't get a chance to react. By the time he sensed her presence and turned around, she lunged forward, wielding a shimmering gold rope in her hands. It left her hands and wrapped around the serpent. It crackled with energy as he thrashed against it. Katherine hurled Quetzi's long body in a tangled mess over her shoulder and dragged him away. She disappeared through the haze as quickly as she'd come, leaving the eye of the storm empty.

Quetzi had been protecting me when he'd tossed me up into the vortex, and wasted valuable time in doing so. *That doesn't seem like him.* Maybe a snake could change its scales, if it wanted to. Maybe I'd misjudged him.

Either way, determination took the place of crippling terror and filled me to the brim. I wasn't going to let Quetzi die by Katherine's hand. There was just one teeny, tiny problem—*how am I supposed to get down from here without breaking every bone in my body?*

TWENTY-NINE

Harley

I got my answer quickly. The tornado collapsed without warning, the dust spiraling up and disappearing into the atmosphere. A scream burst from my throat as empty air opened up below me, and I crashed toward the ground.

I fought to forge a cushion of Air, but I was falling too fast, my limbs thrashing as if that could somehow slow me down. Beneath, I caught sight of Wade darting forward, his eyes fixed on me as he held out his arms to break my fall. I'd expected to land all dainty and graceful into his grasp, but it didn't quite work like that. Instead, I slammed into him with the full force of my weight, the two of us splayed out painfully on the baked earth.

I lay across his stomach, the wind knocked out of me. Staying still for a moment, I wiggled my hands and feet, checking for any breaks or any shooting pains that might reveal one. Fortunately, everything seemed to be intact, though my ribcage had taken a beating. Underneath me, Wade rasped in sharp breaths, his hand on his chest as it rose and fell. I got the feeling he regretted his act of heroism, but I was grateful for the Wade-shaped cushion that had stopped me barreling headfirst into the ground.

With a gruff groan, he sat up slowly. "Remind me never to do that again."

"Are you okay? Anything broken?" I twisted around in his lap and checked his face for any cuts or bruises, very aware that I was balanced on his thighs. His arms snaked around me for a moment, and my heart pounded like a racehorse on steroids.

"No, but you're crushing my… um." He grimaced. I shimmied off his legs and hauled myself to my feet, glancing back toward where the tornado had just been.

"Katherine took him," I murmured, freaking out slightly as the realization caught up to me.

He frowned. "We didn't see her."

"She came through the tornado and snatched him, before he even had the chance to fight back. If you didn't see her, she must still be using Isadora to portal her from place to place."

The dust was still settling, a reddish haze obscuring the nearby landscape, but there were shadows stalking toward us through the miasma. Vague, and still at a fair distance, but they were on their way, whoever they were.

Jacob sprinted through the haze behind me. "Harley! Are you okay? What happened?"

"Katherine took Quetzi! He wouldn't come with me, and Katherine took him. I think she disappeared using Isadora. They're gone!"

Jacob nodded. "Yeah, I can smell that burnt-toast thing. They were definitely here."

I gasped at him, my heart racing. "You can? Can you open a portal to wherever they've gone?"

His face paled. "Uh… I can try?"

"Okay, you get started on that while we deal with these punks." I nodded to the approaching figures—more of Katherine's goons, come to distract us. Only, this time, we didn't have Quetzi to strike them down with a handy bolt of lightning. Fear pulsed through my veins. Right now, we had no idea what we were up against.

I turned to call for the rest of the Rag Team, peering through the fading dust. My heart lurched as I noticed Astrid on the ground, her hands gripping her knee. Blood trickled out between her fingers. I hadn't forgotten Marjorie's vision of her, dead on the ground with nobody there to resurrect her, but this didn't seem to be the moment. She was alive and kicking, if a little on the broken side. Tatyana also seemed to be dealing with an injury, dabbing a torn strip of fabric to the side of her head, where a rock or something had collided with her temple. She was muttering a healing spell, too, to quicken the repair. Evidently, when the tornado got swept away, it had decided to cause a bit more mayhem before it exited for good.

Dylan was at Tatyana's side, pressing the fabric deeper into the wound to keep pressure on it, while Tatyana moved to focus on Astrid, helping her out with her cut. Meanwhile, Garrett was standing off like a spare part, glancing anxiously at Astrid. I wondered why he wasn't running to her side. After his attitude in the Banquet Hall before we'd left, I'd guessed that he and Astrid had had an argument or something, but this was ridiculous.

"What are you just standing there for? We've got goons inbound!" I snapped, drawing Garrett's attention. He looked like a little boy who'd forgotten what was right and what was wrong. Now wasn't the time for personal grudges, whatever they were. They'd break through the haze at any moment, and we had to be ready for anything that faced us.

"Everybody in position!" I roared.

Wade stood beside me and lifted his palms, his ten rings glowing. Santana took up her position on the other side of me, her guitar keychain glowing bright as she geared up her Esprit. Astrid retreated to the Jeep, while Tatyana and Dylan moved beside Santana, Dylan dipping low to the ground and pressing his hands on the parched earth. His graduation ring burned fiercely, the first rumbles of his Earth ability shivering through the dirt. Meanwhile, Tatyana's silver bracelet, embellished with a perfect sapphire, burst into a fierce blue radiance, and her eyes turned white.

Raffe bounded up to Santana's side a few seconds later. His skin was already halfway to scarlet, his eyes shining like rubies, the black smoke beginning to rise from his body. I'd never seen his Esprit, but I didn't know how it worked if you had a djinn inside you. Maybe the djinn *was* his Esprit. Garrett shot him a cold look that only I saw, as he moved to stand by Wade, his palms raising up as his watch took on a steady, golden glimmer.

"Jacob, get back!" I shouted. "Protect Astrid and focus on following the portal trail. Understand?"

He nodded and darted to the Jeep, as bronzed threads of Chaos began to twirl between his fingers like vines. His eyes were glued to a speck in the distance, his mouth moving silently.

"I can help! I've got bombs!" Astrid yelled, holding up a satchel. She winced in pain.

"Save them—we might need them later! Stay where you are," I ordered, knowing how vulnerable she was, even with a satchel full of explosives. With a disappointed look, she stayed where she was.

My head snapped back, just in time to see six creatures emerge through the haze. Two were hulking golems that looked as though they'd been carved from rock, cracked boulders replacing biceps. They provided the bookends to this nasty squad, with a black bear that stood over eight feet on its hind legs, a lizard-looking beast with tiny wings, a tall dude with a fish head and long fangs protruding from its mandible, and a blue-and-white-feathered cockatrice—wyvern-like with a cocker-el's head—making up the central quartet. These weren't magicals… these were Purge monsters. They must've come from the wild, though. The Bestiary was secured.

"Everybody ready!" Wade's voice bellowed across the wasteland.

"Do we capture them?" Dylan asked.

"No Mason jars. We kill them," Tatyana replied bluntly.

I nodded. "No choice this time."

"We kill them before they kill us," Garrett growled.

"And get our asses to wherever Katherine has zipped off to," Santana added.

Raffe grinned eerily, making me realize that our friend was no longer in control of the ship, so to speak. The djinn was. Since he'd manifested during my face-to-face battle with Katherine, I could tell the difference. Plus, Wade had let slip the nature of Raffe's inner Hyde after that fight. Raffe knew that I knew, and I knew that he knew—we'd never needed to get into the nitty-gritty of it.

Raffe tore off toward the golem on the left and pounced onto the monstrous beast's shoulders. He slammed his fists down into the golem's shoulder blades, rock splintering off at all angles. The lizard creature tried to leap up to stop him, but Raffe blasted the reptile in the face with a savage kick and kept pummeling the golem in the shoulders. Its clumsy hands tried to reach up to pull Raffe down, but he was far stronger.

Taking Raffe's lead, the rest of us charged toward the monsters. Tatyana and Santana were the only ones who stayed back, mustering their spirits and Orishas. Santana gathered Fire to her palms and sent her Orishas to distract the beasts, the darting streaks of each one sinking beneath the skin of the vast bear. It swiped at the wisps with its paws, but there was nothing it could do against Santeria power.

"Fish or lizard?" Wade shouted to me as we sprinted for the central two beasts. Dylan and Garrett were busy with one of the golems, pummeling it into the ground.

"Fish," I replied. Behind me, icicles shot forward and knocked the cockatrice back. Tatyana had drawn water from the tower at the end of the road, pulling it from a hatch, the freezing-cold temperature of her surrounding spirits turning it to ice before it hit its mark.

He nodded. "Lizard for me, then." His ten rings glowed as he hurled a fireball at the lizard, and the crackling orb hit it head-on. It hissed and lashed out its tongue, scrabbling at its eyes with its clawed hands. Wade leapt through the air and grasped it by the neck, wrestling it to the ground like a prize linebacker.

I left them to it, lizard and man rolling around in the dust, while I turned to face the fish man. He held two electrical scythes in his hands, crossing them over his chest. I skidded to a halt a few yards away and sent out the first barrage of fireballs, then ducked down and sent a shiver of a quake under his webbed feet. With this being a fish man, there wasn't much use in me drawing on Water, and I didn't want to hurt anyone else with my Air.

The fish man's knees buckled, his silvery scales flashing as he crumpled to the ground. He jumped back up to his feet a moment later and threw one of the scythes. It whizzed past my face like a boomerang, then sliced back through the air and into the fish man's hand.

An idea came to me, though I didn't like what the outcome might be. Thinking fast, as the second scythe barreled toward me, I bent back out of its way and sent out a lasso of Telekinesis. It gripped the fish man tight, trapping his arms at his sides as the lasso drew about his middle. I focused all my energy on keeping him fixed to the spot, so that he was unable to move out of the way of the returning scythe. His bulging eyes opened even wider as the scythe flew back toward him with a *whub-whub-whub-whub*. Keeping him fixed to the spot, I squeezed my eyes shut as the scythe's sharp edge sliced straight through him. There were some things I couldn't watch.

"Delicious!" Raffe shrieked, as he stood triumphantly on top of the motionless golem. A moment later, the scarlet faded from his skin, his eyes turning from red to midnight blue. *Back down you go, Mr. Hyde.*

Garrett and Dylan had been similarly successful with their golem, who had gone up in a puff of black smoke. The same with Wade's lizard creature. Meanwhile, Tatyana had suitably skewered the cockatrice with her icicles of doom, while Santana had done a mean job of taking the bear out of action with Fire. For some reason, that was the one that made me saddest, seeing the bear splayed out on the ground, unmoving. I knew we'd had to, but still…

Their bodies disintegrated, each particle peeling away and turning into a wispy trail of black smoke. Up and up the smoke spiraled, until there was nothing left on the ground below. A gust blew across the wasteland, carrying the remains of the Purge beasts with it.

"We need to go after Katherine," I replied, breathing hard. "Jacob, how're you getting on with the tracking?"

"I think I can manage it, if I can combine the 'scent' with my Sensate ability, which should boost the signature that Isadora left behind," he replied.

"Isadora had that spell on her, right?" Dylan asked.

"Yeah, which should mean she's close to Katherine at all times," I replied.

"Well, are we going or not?" Garrett grumbled. "We're wasting time, standing around chatting about it."

Tatyana crossed her arms over her chest. "I hate to say it, but Garrett's right. We need to make a decision, and quickly. We don't know how long this 'scent' may last, and if there will be more to follow on the other side of this initial portal."

"Jacob, are you sure you're good to try this?" I asked, feeling my doubts surface. I couldn't shake my fear of his powers, after what I'd seen him do in the training room. Plus, he still hadn't entirely mastered getting portals to go to the right place.

"I need to," he replied defiantly. "Quetzi needs our help."

He stepped past me and walked toward a seemingly innocuous patch of ground nearby. He paused there and closed his eyes, feeling out for something we couldn't see. At a certain spot, he stopped and held out his hands. Bronzed tendrils seeped out of his fingertips, the thin strands almost tasting the air. Faint particles glittered, though they weren't coming from Jacob. They were feeding down from the atmosphere, drawn to the magnetism of Jacob's abilities and dancing to his call. *The Pied Piper of Portals, eh?*

His body went rigid and glowed with bright, bronze light, his veins pulsating with radiance beneath his skin. As he drew on more and more Chaos, a burst of power surged out of him and flowed into the break in time and space that Katherine and Isadora had left behind. It tore it open again with a thundering roar, like a healing wound being ripped afresh.

"You did it!" I whooped, punching the air.

He looked at me, straining not to show his exhaustion. I could feel it coming off him. "Then we'd better get going. I don't know how long I can keep it open."

"Everybody, go!" I shouted, feeling worried about Jacob. Doing this had clearly taken a lot out of him, but what other choice did we have?

We all ran for the portal and jumped through, with Jacob bringing up the rear. I stayed close to him in case he faltered. After all, we'd need him to create another portal to get back. Only as my foot crossed the threshold of the fabric of time and space did I realize that nobody would know where we were. Trepidation shot through me. Considering I had no idea where we were going, it looked like we were flying blind on this one. We'd have to take on Katherine by ourselves, at least for long enough to rescue Quetzi and get the hell out of Dodge.

Right, then... Potential death, here we come.

THIRTY

Harley

We tumbled from the portal into a world of eternal night, with starlight gleaming in a blanket of black velvet overhead. There was no moon here, which struck me as odd, but the glow of the stars seemed to cast enough radiance on the world below. Dark fields stretched into the distance, the glint of a faraway lake reflecting the stars. Torchlight flickered on the horizon, too, although I couldn't make out any people wandering about. Everything was eerily silent, with not even a hint of a breeze. The trees stayed perfectly still, the grass unmoving, the air strange and stilted in my lungs.

Ahead of us stood a set of ruins, with pillars and arches that had once belonged to a greater, more elaborate building. By the looks of it, the roof and most of the walls had caved in a long time ago, leaving nothing but chunks of rubble. Statues with missing limbs flanked the entrance, their sad eyes turned up to the clear night sky. Clearly, we weren't in Kansas anymore. We weren't in California, either. Had it not been for the lack of moon, I might've guessed that we'd crossed the globe and ended up somewhere in a different time zone. Instead, it looked like we'd entered a completely different world. An otherworld.

It brought back a vision of my parents' Grimoire, and the mention of respective dimensions. Whose had we landed in? Judging by the land-scape, I wondered if it could be Nyx, given the ethereal nighttime vibes. I stared around in a state of abject awe.

"Good freaking job, Jacob! Any idea where we are?" I whispered, my voice carrying on the windless air.

"No idea," Jacob replied. The others stared at him in wonder, with Raffe even clapping him on the back. He'd done this. He'd made it work! I'd never been prouder, or more afraid. We were in strange territory now. Strange, dangerous, awe-inspiring territory.

"This place reminds me of the Asphodel Meadows in Greek mythol-ogy," Astrid replied. "It was the realm of the underworld where those who hadn't done much with their lives went. It was for the ordinary folk—the ones who were neither good nor bad and hadn't done anything remarkable. It's described like this, and it would explain the lack of moon."

I nodded slowly. "Well... it's weird."

"Why's it so quiet?" Santana asked, glancing around anxiously.

"Wait... do you hear that?" Dylan cut in, his eyes darting toward the interior of the ruins. A deep, rumbling percussion pulsed beneath the ground, sounding all the more powerful as it roared through the silence around us. The torchlight in the distance went out.

"What is it?" Raffe asked. No sooner had he spoken than a pillar of light shot up from the inside of the ruins, behind a wall in the center. Streaked with blue and gold, the spiral of magical energy continued to rise upward, until it sliced through the night itself. It crackled and sparked, twisting like one of Quetzi's tornados, sending gusts of violent air through the atmosphere.

"I don't know *what* it is, but I've got a good guess *who* it is," I hissed.

"Katherine," Wade said, before I could. "Everyone, come closer."

The Rag Team did as he asked, forming a huddle. Fear was written on all of our faces, and I felt the collective bristle of it with my Empathy. I couldn't blame anyone for feeling completely terrified. I did, too. Here we were, in a strange world, in a different dimension altogether, with nobody coming to rescue us. This was us against Katherine, in the purest form.

"We need to approach from all sides and do everything we can to stop her from doing... well, whatever it is she's doing," Wade said, glancing at every single one of us. "If we all fan out once we reach the ruins, we should be able to sneak up on her. Hopefully, she'll be too distracted to notice us."

"Let's go," I urged, my stomach twisting in knots. I wanted to know what she was doing with Quetzi. Judging by the spiraling tornado of raw energy, it didn't look good for him. Plus, we were evidently in this weird otherworld for a reason. She wouldn't have come here for the fun of it—there was method in every scrap of her madness.

We crept toward the ruins, the roar of the energy vortex drowning out our movements. We edged around either side of the ruins, with Wade, Santana, Dylan, Jacob, and I taking the right-hand side, while Raffe, Garrett, Tatyana, and Astrid took the left. The light grew more blinding as we neared the epicenter, swathes of liquid-like glow pooling out of the gaps in the walls. It was all I could do not to burn out my retinas as I peered around the edge of the crumbling exterior. Nerves spiked through every vein as I took in the sight before me, my heart thundering like a stampede of wild horses.

Katherine stood at the center of the ruins, her arms outstretched in front of a golden altar. Quetzi had been strapped down to a marble slab at the top of the golden altar, his body thrashing as he fought to escape her clutches. Whatever spell she had put on him, it had rendered him helpless.

Nevertheless, the sparking tornado appeared to be coming from within him, tearing him apart, atom by atom. It was like when the portal had almost disintegrated Jacob, back in the training room, but this was on another level entirely. Each time the vortex ripped deeper into the serpent, it released a flurry of bronze particles, the thunderous energy burrowing into every layer of his being. The particles sank into Katherine's skin. Her eyes glowed with each addition, her body pulsating with a bronze-tinged light. I could practically see her veins throbbing from where I stood.

"We have to help him!" I whispered, anger replacing my fear. Who the hell did she think she was, snatching an ancient Aztec creature and defiling him like this? Her disrespect for the lives of others was sickening, and it only got worse with each person she killed.

"Wait... she's not alone," Santana murmured, pointing to a figure lurking in the corner.

I'd almost missed the creature steeped in shadow. Tall and elegant, with white wings tucked down her back, a Purge beast stood with her muscled arms crossed over a furred chest. Talons tapped at her feet, while her entire body was covered in white fur, her figure and face the unmistakable shape of a tigress. She reminded me of Tobe, only far fiercer. There was anger and pride in the way she carried herself, her muscles twitching as though on constant alert. Bright-yellow eyes peered into the gloom, scanning the surrounding area. We ducked back; I hoped she hadn't seen us.

"Who is she?" I whispered.

Jacob stared at the figure, terror spiking in him. "Could be the Recruiter that Louella told me about."

"Recruiter? What Recruiter? I haven't heard anything about that," I replied.

"While we were training the other day, Louella said that Katherine had a right-hand woman, and she was the one who planned out all the magical-kid grabs, and where to look for fresh meat. Although, she said that this woman was always covered head-to-toe in a black cloak, but walked in a weird way. Maybe the talons are the reason she walks funny. I figured Louella would have told you all about her."

"This is the first I'm hearing about any Recruiter, though I suppose it makes sense that Katherine has a lieutenant of sorts." I shuddered. "All I know is she's going to be a pain to take down."

"I agree," Wade replied. "We need to cause a distraction, so the other team can strike at this Tobe lookalike from behind. Jacob, you should stay out of this one—we'll need you later. You're the only one who can get us back. Understood?" His voice carried a warning not to argue, which I was glad of. It sounded silly, with so much danger in front of us, but I didn't want Jacob getting in harm's way. He was my responsibility now, and I wouldn't shirk that.

"Astrid, you should stay back, too," I said, turning to her. This was going to get nasty—it wasn't a fight for a human to get caught up in.

"Let's go full force," Dylan said.

Wade nodded. "Esprits up and ready."

I crouched low and lifted my palms, the pearl of my Telekinesis ability lighting up. I glanced at the lioness beast, preparing to take out her legs so the others could pile in. Katherine was my main focus, but we needed to take out this Recruiter of hers first, if we were to stand any chance of stopping her from completing the spell. Wade's rings shone red as he readied his Fire, while Dylan pressed his palms to the ground. Behind me, I could hear the whoosh and whisper of Santana's Orishas. Looking through the gloom, I tried to make out the others on the opposite side, but they were well hidden.

"Now!" Wade yelled. The four of us lunged forward. Jacob kept behind the wall, a sullen expression on his face. I understood his desire to get involved, but now wasn't the time. There was already too much at stake.

I charged across the ground and lashed my lasso at the lioness's legs, whipping the invisible rope back and knocking her to the dirt. Before she could get up, Dylan leapt onto her and wrestled her into submission, his hands wrenching her arms up behind her back. She roared in fury, her biceps bulging as she fought back. I wasn't sure how long he'd be able to hold her. Already, she was thrashing and snapping wildly, Dylan's expression slightly more panicked than it had been a moment ago.

Garrett and Raffe joined in against the lioness, while Tatyana made for Katherine. Astrid darted behind the wall, keeping out of the way. I saw the green glint of capture stones as the boys tried to wrestle the Recruiter, but she seemed to be fighting them fang and talon. Wade, Santana, and I made toward Katherine too, using every ounce of our combined strength to try and make a break in the protective wall she'd built around herself. It shimmered and fizzed, but none of our abilities could pierce the outer shell. She'd made herself nice and cozy in there, with Quetzi at the center of it all, losing himself, particle by particle. I could only imagine the pain of it.

"Here, take one of these!" Astrid shouted, ducking out of her hiding place. She grabbed orb-shaped objects from the bagful of explosive goodies she'd brought from the coven. She hurled one at each of us. "Press the button in the middle and throw them at that force field. Then, run and duck for cover. We'll have five seconds, maybe."

"Maybe?" I glanced at her.

"They're prototypes. I didn't have time to get them fully functioning."

I caught mine and looked to the others. "On three! One, two, three!"

We pressed the central buttons and lobbed them at the force field. Turning on our heels, we sprinted for the nearest piles of rubble and army-rolled behind them. Four seconds later, everything fell deathly silent. The orbs had somehow latched on to Katherine's protective bubble, each one absorbing sound and light and energy of every kind.

With a silent explosion, the force field came tumbling down. It evaporated into thin air, leaving only the impact of the tornado as a means of protecting Katherine. She lowered her palms and drew on every scrap of energy that came drifting off Quetzi.

"From Chaos you were made, and to Chaos you must return. Feed my soul with your ashes," she cried, the words cold and terrifying.

We darted out from behind our hiding places, but nothing we did seemed to even touch Katherine, even with the force field gone. My fireballs physically refracted away from the sparking vortex, like magnets bending water. Wade's fireballs were bending away, too, while Santana's Orishas were cowering from the magic. Whatever she was using, it was Dark magic. Dylan had tried to send up a quake, but it had dissipated just shy of the altar. The same went for Tatyana's Water ability, and Garrett's Fire.

"Can't the spirits help us?" I asked Tatyana, as I sent my millionth barrage of fireballs toward Katherine. Not a single one even grazed her.

"There aren't any here. There's nothing but silence," she explained rapidly.

"What is she doing?" Garrett muttered.

"Absorbing Chaos into herself," Tatyana replied. "I think she might be powering herself up through the first ritual."

"Well, we are in one of their dimensions. Louella said these rituals took place on their home turf, with each ritual related to one of the Children," I replied. "I wonder if step one is the Nyx-related ritual?" I didn't quite know how, or why, an ancient Purge beast would be related to Nyx, but the location definitely fit.

Tatyana nodded. "I think you're right."

We continued our onslaught against Katherine, but she was unstoppable. The ritual process was slow, and the peeling away of Quetzi's atoms was time-consuming, but it didn't matter. Nothing we did had any effect. However, it looked like we *had* managed to wrangle the lioness, after a lengthy battle between her, Dylan, Raffe, and Garrett. She was bound in the green ropes of entrapment stones, though struggling to break free.

"You won't get through." Katherine chuckled. "The stage is mine now, and you my rapt audience. You will see me rise before your very eyes. Aren't you the lucky ones?"

"Go to hell, you old witch!" I spat back, firing a ball of flames at her.

An idea popped into my head. If we were going to stop this ritual, we needed to think outside of the box. Ordinary magical abilities weren't working, which meant it was time for the big guns. Catching sight of Jacob, I tore across the ruins toward him. His eyes were fixed on something at the far edge of the ruins, behind the altar, but I couldn't quite make out what he was looking at.

"Jacob, we need you," I gasped.

"Isadora…"

I frowned. "What do you mean?"

"She's right there. Don't you see her?"

I peered at the spot where Jacob was looking and saw a crouched figure behind a fallen block of pillar. Her hands were bound, and her mouth was gagged, but it was definitely Isadora. I'd have known her profile anywhere. She wasn't looking at us, her head lolling to one side. It was a worrying sight, but we'd have to deal with it once we'd figured out a way to stop this Quetzi ritual. Those particles were sinking into Katherine's skin with increasing speed, and I didn't want to see what happened once she was done with it.

"We'll get her out of here, Jake," I assured him. "But right now, I need you to do something for me, okay?"

He turned to me nervously. "What is it?"

"I need you to open a short-range portal to that altar. I'm going to snatch Quetzi. It's the magic that's strapping him down, not the rope itself. If I use my Telekinesis, I should be able to swipe him in one go. I've seen you do short-range before. You've got this, I know you do." I patted him on the back, my faith unwavering.

He shook his head. "I don't know if I can, with all that energy next to the altar."

I took him by the shoulders and looked him dead in the eye. "You *have* to do this, Jacob. Quetzi will die if you don't, and Katherine will finish this ritual. All you need to do is concentrate and let the Chaos flow through your Esprit. Think of your dad, and of your heritage, and let that guide you."

"Do you think my dad ended up here?"

"I don't know, but we can always try searching these otherworlds for him, if we survive this. Maybe he's trapped in one of these places. But you won't ever find out, unless we put a stop to this right now."

"And what about Isadora?"

"We'll come back for her, Jake. Even if we can't get to her now, we'll find a way."

He nodded slowly. "I'll open it for you."

"I knew you would." I took a step back. "Whenever you're ready."

He lifted his hands, the black stone of his Esprit lighting up. An electrical crackle filled the air around him, bringing with it the scent of a storm as he opened up a portal in front of him. The tear was smaller than his usual creations, the edges vibrating as he stepped into the fabric of time and space. I was about to step toward it when he pushed me backward, diving into it himself. My heart lurched as I watched him go, the portal snapping shut behind him.

"Jacob, NO!" I roared, but it was too late.

Another portal opened a short distance away from the altar. Panic shot through my veins. *Why, Jacob? Why?* A second later, he jumped out and grasped Isadora in his arms, before jumping straight back through the portal he'd just made. I had no idea where they might reappear, but without Jacob we were completely screwed. We'd be stuck here, with no way out.

"JACOB!" I screamed, unable to believe my eyes. I loved my aunt with all my heart, but she was under Katherine's spell. Katherine could kill her at any moment. Taking her from this place was futile, without a way of breaking that spell. Plus, we needed to stop Katherine. That was the most important thing. I wanted to throttle Jacob for doing it. I wanted to scream at him until I was blue in the face. Exasperation didn't even cover it.

He'd taken Isadora instead, and now we had no way of getting to Quetzi. He'd not only snatched my aunt, but he'd snatched away our only hope.

"You sneaky little—" Katherine swore loudly, pausing for a moment before returning to the spell. Jacob had taken her only mode of transport, and ours too.

More to the point, something weird was happening with the interdimensional tear. The vortex was being dragged into the portal itself, attracted to the raw energy that had forged it. Not even Katherine could do anything to stop the blue and gold spiral from seeping into the portal, though I could see her trying to regain control. Suddenly, the portal snapped shut, severing the link to this otherworld, and the raw energy that had been dragged inside.

In a terrifying nightmare of déjà vu, a thin line of light remained after the portal was shut. It thrummed violently, mixing with some of the vortex, until the jangling, overexcited particles had nothing else to do but explode. A huge blast erupted across the ruins, knocking everyone flat on the ground, while several walls crumbled to dust around us. Raffe barreled into Santana, plucking her out of the way of a falling façade of solid stone. Dylan braced his body over Tatyana's, taking the pummeling of the tumbling debris. Fortunately, I was nowhere near the falling walls, and Wade was otherwise occupied with being slammed into the ground by the explosion.

I hit the deck with a painful thud, catching a glimpse of the blast knocking Katherine sideways. A shiver ran up the central column of twisting energy, making it burn red. *What the hell does that mean?* It couldn't be good. We'd done something to interrupt an intricate and very powerful spell, and that could only end in destruction when there was a Shipton at the helm.

With the blast subsiding, I dragged myself to my feet and looked toward the altar. The explosion had done something weird to Quetzi. The serpent's body was ablaze with blue and gold light, the particles twisting out of him in vine-like wisps instead of handfuls of tiny sparks. Somehow, whatever Jacob had done with the portal had sped up the ritual process. Quetzi was writhing, his mouth snapping silently as the magic disintegrated him, piece by piece. Katherine leaned over Quetzi, absorbing the wisps as they were released, drawing each one into her body much faster, gulping down every drop until there was nothing left.

"No," I whispered, as Quetzi disappeared before my eyes. The enchanted ropes that had held him sagged, lying flat on the altar where he'd just been. I couldn't move, my heart sinking like a stone in my chest.

Jacob had made the choice to save Isadora—and now Quetzi was dead. Not only that, but that spell was still on her, the one that could sputter out her life in an instant if she tried to run. Although I knew his heart would've been in the right place, it looked as though Jacob had signed her death warrant, too.

"Now, you will see Eris rise! I have taken the first step toward true greatness!" Katherine bellowed, her arms shooting up.

With a deafening crack like a thunderbolt, the vortex switched direction, all of it powering into her body. I just couldn't look away, even as her scream filled the air. Light poured out of her eyes and her mouth. Only as the last stream disappeared into her did the glow begin to fade, though not by much. Her eyes had turned golden, and her entire being seemed to light up from the inside. She looked like an avenging angel—the stuff of nightmares, rather than biblical prose.

"There's no way we can beat her like this," Santana whispered, her eyes wide. "My Orishas are freaking out. They're telling us to run."

"Run? Run where?" I muttered.

"We need to get out of here," Wade agreed.

Garrett glowered. "How far do you think we'll get, huh? Jacob's left us high and dry and now we're screwed. The best thing to do would be to beg for her forgiveness, and hope she'll show mercy."

"Are you kidding?" Astrid snapped, hurrying out of her hiding place. "She'd kill us for being cowardly."

"She wouldn't kill Harley. Harley can make a deal for our lives," Garrett replied.

I glanced at him in disbelief. "Oh, yeah, why not make me the sacrificial lamb?"

"I can hear every word you're saying." Katherine's voice drifted across the ruins, echoey and otherworldly. "I'd rather enjoy listening to you all beg for your lives. Then again, desperation is such an unsavory look on you."

"You should let us go," Garrett said, raising his voice.

"With what? Your little space-hopper has taken *my* space-hopper, and so it looks like we'll all have to stay here awhile, and get to know one another better," she purred. "Maybe I'll play a little game, and let you choose who dies first. I can be merciful when I want to, though, and, considering I feel like a shiny goddess right now, I'm open to suggestions. Who do I spare?"

"Not a chance!" I shot back.

"Now, how did I know you were going to say that?" Katherine said. "Always so predictable in your feistiness. I could raise you up to greatness, Harley, if you'd only let me. However, rest assured, you're not dying tonight. You're still useful."

"You won't be getting any surrenders from us," I said, Fire burning in my palms.

"We'll see," she replied flatly. "First point of business: I'd ask that you release my associate, Naima. How would you like it if you had two young men strapping you to the ground in such a rough manner? I mean, I'm not one to judge different tastes, but it's really very degrading."

"Spare us, and we'll spare her," Wade growled.

Katherine laughed. "It doesn't work like that. Not anymore." With a flick of her wrist, two thick darts of gold shot out of her palms and sent Raffe and Dylan hurtling into the back wall of the ruins. They sank down, dazed. "I did ask politely. It isn't my fault if you want to play silly beggars. People will get hurt that way," she tutted, smirking.

If we couldn't defeat her with traditional means, and she could knock us back with a simple flick of her wrist, then I needed to use something she wasn't going to expect. What I was about to do was incredibly dangerous, with huge risks, but what else could I do? We needed something extreme. Still, that didn't make it any easier. I was quaking in my boots just thinking about it. *I'm going to give you something to cry about, Katherine Shipton.*

I thought of the summoning spell from my parents' Grimoire. The words suddenly came back to me, taking me by surprise, and the spell tumbled out of my mouth. My blood ran cold. My heart rate slowed. Everything fell away, as it had before, leaving nothing but darkness around me. I couldn't see Katherine, or the Rag Team, or the Asphodel Meadows with its moonless sky. I couldn't see anything.

Power coursed through my body, building with each sentence I recited. I could feel the black fog gathering around me. Terror gripped my chest, my heart thundering, my limbs shaking. *This is too much... It's too much for me to hold on to.* Panic came at me in a flood, bombarding my senses. I should never have done this, but it was too late to back out now.

A jolt of pain ricocheted through my nerves, hot and agonizing. Deep inside, I felt something crack—not break, but splinter. *No... Is it the Suppressor?* I had no way of knowing, but the overwhelming pain that followed seemed to suggest it was.

Something pulsed out of me, and my body shook from the violence of it. I didn't know what I'd sent out, but it felt powerful. In that dark world of my trance, I could see a beast emerging from the sky overhead, starting as wispy, black fog and growing clearer by the second.

"Harley, STOP!" Wade yelled. A harsh impact collided with me, knocking me to the ground before Erebus could fully manifest. The dark world receded, bringing me back to the eternal night of the Nyx's dimension. I lay on the dirt with Wade over me, his hands shaking my shoulders. Beside me, Santana was working her magic to get the summoned beast to disappear, back into the sky from whence it came.

"Oh, my God!" Tatyana's eyes were wide, her hand clamped to her mouth. I sat up, ignoring the pain in my muscles, following her line of sight. Two figures lay on the ground, one poking out from behind the altar, and one in front of it. Whatever I'd done, I'd knocked Katherine out, her body enveloped in a hazy shield that sparked dangerously. Whatever she'd sucked out of Quetzi was defending her, albeit a little too late. I couldn't feel any joy in knocking her flat, not as my gaze rested on a small figure who lay crumpled at the foot of the altar. She held one of those bomb balls in her hand.

Astrid... No...

The blast that had surged out of me had knocked her into the stone as she'd tried to edge back toward the walls of the ruin. Blood trickled down her temple and out of her ear, pooling on the dust beside her.

"Is she—?" I choked out.

"Her spirit is about to leave her body," Tatyana gasped, her breath coming in short, sharp drags. "We have to get her to Alton—now! She can't hold on much longer."

I jumped up, despite the weakness in my limbs, and sprinted for Astrid with the rest of the Rag Team. Santana had managed to dispense with the shadow beast and followed close behind us. Garrett was the one who scooped Astrid into his arms, cradling her limp head, though none of us knew what we were going to do next. There was no way out of this place, and Astrid was fading fast. If we didn't get her to Alton soon… I couldn't even think about it.

"How do we get out of here?" Garrett asked through gritted teeth.

"And what do we do about her?" Santana pointed to Katherine. She started to stir at that very moment, dragging herself up from the ground. Her body still glowed with the energy she'd absorbed, though the shield was fading, and we'd soon be on the receiving end. Meanwhile, Naima was still bound by the entrapment stones, but the blast seemed to have weakened them.

No sooner had Katherine started to get to her feet than a loud snap burst through the air. A portal gaped open close by. Jacob stepped out of it.

He scanned the ruins until he found us. "Come on!" he yelled. Isadora was nowhere to be seen. My eyes narrowed at him, a pulsing rage bursting inside me. This had all gone to crap because he'd made the wrong choice. With anger still bubbling within me, we ran for the tear, and leapt through it, leaving Katherine and this weird underworld to each other.

THIRTY-ONE

Harley

"We're running out of time!" Tatyana cried as we raced down the corridor toward the infirmary. "She's almost gone!" Jacob had deposited us in the Aquarium, on the opposite side of the coven, giving us a lengthy run.

"Alton, you need to get to us *now*!" Wade shouted down the phone. "We're heading for the infirmary. Astrid needs you. Tatyana keeps saying she doesn't have long, that she's almost gone." His face said everything I needed to know. We were losing Astrid. Necromancy was still a pretty mysterious thing, but I guessed there had to be a limit on when you could and couldn't perform a resurrection. Maybe, if a spirit was too far gone, there was nothing to be done.

Come on, Astrid, just hold on! I looked at her, limp in Garrett's arms. Her lips were pale, her eyes closed, her body lolling like a rag doll. Garrett was doing his best to cradle her head, but speed was of the essence, and that speed wasn't particularly graceful. Tears rolled down his cheeks as he clutched her to him. It was painful to watch, not only because I shared in his grief, but because they'd argued. If she died now, he'd never be able to make peace with her. She'd be gone, and there'd be nothing we could do about it.

"She isn't going to make it," Garrett rasped. "By the time we get her to the infirmary, she'll be dead. Tatyana, is there anything you can do for her? There has to be something. There *has* to be."

Tatyana had tears in her eyes. "I wish I could, but I can only speak with spirits. I can't stop them from leaving this world. Her ties to the land of the living are looser than most of ours, because of her previous deaths. She's finding it very hard to hold on this time."

"You can see her?"

Tatyana's face crumpled. "Yes. She's standing beside you. She's holding on to your arm, because she thinks it might ground her enough to buy another few minutes. She is doing everything she can, but the light is pulling her."

"Please don't go," Garrett begged, staring down at her closed eyes.

"Stay with us," Tatyana urged. "Alton will be here soon."

Jacob had made himself scarce, slinking off to wherever he'd taken Isadora. Part of me had wanted to go after him and confront him, but right now Astrid's life was on the line. If I abandoned her now, I would never forgive myself. My wrath toward Jacob's selfish actions would come later, though I couldn't make any promises that I'd be calmer about it. There was one silver lining in all of this—Isadora was safe for now. I knew Katherine well enough; she would dangle that killing spell over us, until she was certain she couldn't get Isadora back. Isadora was valuable to her, after all.

Alton appeared a few minutes later as we turned the corner onto the main stretch of hallway. His face was deathly white, his eyes wide in panic. He hurtled toward us at breakneck speed. Garrett skidded to a halt and laid Astrid down on the marble floor—we didn't have time to waste on getting her all the way to the infirmary, not when Alton could work his magic here.

Breathless from the sprint, Alton sank to his knees and pulled Astrid into his arms. Now that we all knew the real relationship between them, it broke my heart all the more. He'd done this three times for her. He'd lost his daughter three times, and had been forced to bring her back from the grips of death. I couldn't even begin to imagine the weight of that, being carried around every day of his life.

"Oh, Astrid," he whispered, pulling her face close to his as he rocked her gently. "Stay with me."

He closed his eyes and held her in one arm, his hand positioned on her ribcage while his other palm flattened against her chest. His fingertips lit up with purple energy, flecked with black, the rippling vines sinking deep beneath Astrid's skin. This wasn't the same process we'd seen on the table in the Escher Reading Room, but I could sense that the magic was the same. The freezing temperatures were already creeping across the ground toward us, my breath coming out in hot plumes. Alton's veins pulsated with that dark, purple power. His eyes stayed closed, and his face twisted up in a mask of agony as the purple threads found their way into Astrid.

After resurrecting the Shapeshifter, I knew he had to be exhausted already. Astrid had told us that it took a lot out of him every time he performed Necromancy like this, and the recovery was lengthy. Not enough time had passed for him to be fully himself again, his abilities weakened. I could see the strain on his face as he struggled to control the energy.

His emotions were all over the place, flooding my senses with grief, and sorrow, and anger, and pain, and desperation, and love... above all, love. That kept him going. His love for Astrid stopped him from giving in, though I could feel his fatigue. It would have been easy for me to shut his emotions out, but I couldn't bring myself to block them. Instead, I concentrated my mind and tried to reverse the feelings he was sending me, offering encouragement and strength back to him in an invisible wave of hazy energy. His body seemed to straighten up as that expression hit him. Somehow, it had worked. I'd sent good emotions back to him, feeding them into his soul, so he might find the last scraps of resilience to see him through this.

That crack I'd felt earlier, during my summoning of Erebus—it hit me like a punch to the gut that I might've actually cracked my Suppressor, allowing my abilities to expand to the point where I could do this...

where I could transfer emotions into someone, instead of just feeling them.

"Stay with me," Alton murmured against her blood-soaked hair, as he forced wave after wave after wave of purple energy into her system. Wherever Astrid was, she was clearly in a deeper state of crossing over than the Shapeshifter had been. Tatyana was right about that. Alton was fighting to keep her in this world. It was clear from the sweat pouring off him.

"Is she still in the spirit world?" I whispered to Tatyana, whose eyes were still lit up with white.

She nodded. "It's taking a lot for her to come back this time. I'm with her. I'm helping her, but it is hard."

"Don't leave," Alton pleaded. "You can't go yet."

We all stood and watched as Alton waged war against death. I thought of a surgeon hand-pumping a heart long after the patient has already passed the point of no return. Alton refused to give up, though his own strength was waning with every minute that passed. The color had all but gone from his face, his body vibrating with Necromantic energy.

Slowly, Alton stopped conjuring the purple-tinged magic, his body sagging into an exhausted heap. He wrapped his arms around his daughter, but I doubted he could expend more energy without killing himself, too. Judging by the emotions coming off him, I got the feeling he would have welcomed death over a lifetime without Astrid, but he was too tired to keep going. Self-loathing and despair found their way into the mix of his feelings, my senses reacting to every bombardment of it. Here lay a broken man, holding his dead daughter in his arms.

I sank down to my knees. My blast had caused this. I'd knocked her into the altar. Tears poured down my face, a choked sob rasping from my throat. She was dead because of me, and all the cracked Suppressors in the world couldn't change that.

"Is she here?" Santana asked Tatyana.

"I can't tell anymore."

Alton shook his head miserably. "I can't feel her presence."

"Is that good or bad?" I murmured, my voice catching in my throat.

"Bad," Wade replied, his face stoic. Nevertheless, his eyes held a glimmer of tears.

"I think… I think she's gone," Alton wept. "I was too late. Her spirit was already too far gone."

"She was struggling this time," Tatyana replied sadly.

Dylan folded his arms across his chest. "She can't be gone. No way."

"Are you sure she isn't here still?" Raffe added.

Only Garrett remained silent, his eyes fixed on Astrid's face. His eyes held a haunted expression, his mouth agape. Tears rolled down his cheeks unchecked, his hands trembling. With him being a Shapeshifter, I couldn't feel his emotions, but I didn't need to. They were etched onto his features. Loss… devastating loss.

I leant back in fright as Astrid sat up suddenly, her lungs clawing for air with a terrifying rasp. She dragged the oxygen down in heaving gulps, the whites of her eyes showing as she glanced around in confusion. Alton grasped her, rocking her in his arms, smoothing down her hair. She was clearly in a state of shock, her body reacting violently to being brought back to life.

"Hush, my little one, you're safe now. You're okay," Alton murmured. "Everything is going to be okay. You're in the coven, you're surrounded by friends, and you're doing just fine. You've had a nasty shock, that's all, but you'll be okay again soon. I promise."

"Astrid!" My voice came out as a tight squeak. She was alive. Thank God, she was alive!

She continued to look about her, a weird look in her eyes. My joy turned to confusion as a weird sensation hit me. I couldn't put my finger on it, but something wasn't quite right about her. I mean, I knew she'd just come back from the dead, but the Shapeshifter hadn't been like this when he'd been resurrected. Her limbs were shaking and her teeth were chattering, while her eyes simply stared at things, as though hardly recognizing what she saw. It was like she was overwhelmed by life somehow.

I reached toward her with Empathy. Immediately, I withdrew my feelers, like a snake recoiling in fear. Where there ought to have been clear emotions, I felt nothing but a gaping void—an absence of feeling. It was cold and odd and unsettling. She wouldn't meet my eye as I tried to catch her gaze, her whole demeanor panicked and confused.

"Are you okay?" Alton asked softly.

Astrid turned to him. "I'm fine," she said, her voice flat.

"Are you sure?"

"I feel fine. A bit tired, maybe." That same dead tone exited her lips.

Alton pulled her closer, relief washing over all of us. "I thought I'd lost you, my little one. I thought I got to you too late. Every time I reached for you, you got further and further away, and I felt you slipping… oh, I felt you slipping out of my hands. I didn't think I could hold on to you. I'm so sorry, Astrid. I should never have let this happen. I should never have let you out of my sight."

"You can't stop me from living," she replied. "My team needed me. I felt you reaching for me, but I didn't think I would make it, either. For a moment, I thought I hadn't." The others were smiling and crying. I couldn't stop focusing on the void inside her. It was in every hollow word, and I couldn't understand why nobody else was hearing it. There was no smile in her eyes or on her lips, only a blank expression that didn't fit with the words she was saying.

"We should get you to Krieger so he can run a full checkup on you," Alton suggested.

Astrid nodded slowly. "I agree."

Is nobody hearing this? Seriously? Something was wrong with her. Her whole manner was off. It was like she'd turned into a changeling—an echo of the person she used to be. I realized, with a sinking feeling, that we hadn't got her back quick enough. Alton had fought with everything he had, but he hadn't been able to bring every part of her back to the land of the living. It broke my heart, to think of what Astrid must be going through. She must have been so lost and baffled, having been a spirit one moment, and then being dragged back into the human world a moment later. I hoped that it might only be temporary, a brief side effect of being resurrected after being dead too long.

Alton helped Astrid to her feet and lifted her into his arms. They set off down the corridor together. It was a sweet sight, marred only by the knowledge of what was going on inside her. The infirmary wasn't much further, but none of us felt as though we should follow. They needed some father-daughter time, after what they had just endured. Plus, Alton was probably going to have to disappear to Purge as soon as he'd taken her to Krieger.

"So, what now?" Dylan asked, wiping his eyes.

"We debrief Alton once he's done in the infirmary and done with the Purge that is probably going to hit him soon, and we try and send a team back through to the Asphodel Meadows. Katherine may still be there and, if she is, we will need stronger firepower," Wade replied. "After that, we set to work on figuring out the rest of these rituals, to try and stay ahead of her."

I shook my head. "We can't send a team back there. Isadora is too weak, and Jacob will be exhausted by now. If he can even reopen a portal there, we've got no assurances that he'll be able to get back. Not now, at any rate."

"So... what? We just let her go?"

"She already completed the ritual, Wade. Sending a team back there would be a suicide mission," I explained. "It's going to take her a while to get out of that place, with no Portal Opener to use. That gives *us* some time to look into the next rituals and try and get the jump on her. We need to use this window wisely, instead of risking more lives."

"I agree," Santana said. "While she's stuck there, she's not causing trouble for us. I say we use the time to get ahead of the game, before she and her pet lioness find a way out."

"Weird, wasn't it, seeing another Purge beast like Tobe walking about?" Dylan said. It was a welcome break in tension.

"Very weird," I agreed. "It was like Tobe in drag."

"She was kind of pretty for a Purge beast," Raffe mused, getting a punch in the arm from Santana.

Garrett still hadn't spoken.

"You okay?" I asked.

"I can't stand around here talking like nothing has happened," he replied wearily. "Sorry, but I need to go to the infirmary. I need to know she's okay. I'll come back and find you later for the debriefing, but I have to be with her right now."

I put my hand on his arm. "We understand, Garrett. We'll be along soon; I think it'd just be better if we didn't crowd her at the minute. You go, be with her. She'll want you there." Before I told anyone about the weirdness that I'd felt from her, I wanted to find out what was wrong with her myself. Maybe it would go away in its own time. Maybe it was just the residual effect of being brought back so many times.

Garrett nodded and hurried away toward the infirmary. The rest of us stood around uncertainly, though a plan of action was steadily forming in my head. Jacob had put us in a dangerous position back there, and some words needed to be had. Although I had to admit I was eager to see Isadora again, despite my anger.

"I can't believe Quetzi is dead," Santana said quietly.

"What was she even doing to him?" Dylan replied.

I sighed heavily. "Absorbing his energy to make herself stronger. I think she might have sapped some energy from Nyx's dimension too, using Quetzi as the conduit. It's the first step in this plan of hers, and it worked. That woman is crazy powerful now, and there's nothing we can do about it."

"Says you, with your weird, foggy beast," Raffe teased. Part of me wondered if the djinn was in there, having a laugh at my expense. The djinns were closely related to Erebus, and I'd almost brought him down from whichever dimension he existed in.

"Yeah, you and I need to have a little chat about that summoning stuff," Wade said suddenly, shattering my reverie.

"Not now," I shot back.

"You could've hurt yourself back there, not to mention the rest of us."

That stung, after what had happened to Astrid. "I had to stop Katherine, and I didn't see any other option. I know it could've ended badly, but Katherine was about to slaughter us. You saw the way she flicked

Dylan and Raffe, like they were annoying little bugs. Imagine what else she could have done." I turned to Santana. "I'm sorry you had to deal with the aftermath, though. I just wanted a way to stop Katherine. I figured that, if I managed to call Erebus, I could offer Katherine's life as payment. That way, we wouldn't have to worry about her anymore."

Santana put her arm around my shoulders. "You're forgiven. Although," she lowered her voice, "I still don't know how you did that without the book. You think it's your parents' mojo, giving you some extra juice?"

"That's what I was thinking. I couldn't read any of the unfinished ones in New York without the book in front of me, but I didn't try it with my mom and dad's."

"Could be the blood tie you have to it, then. Man, it was scary impressive though."

"I'm still sorry. I know you could've gotten hurt, cleaning up after me."

She smiled. "Apology accepted. I get what you were trying to do, and if it had worked, I'd have been grateful. Just don't go making a habit out of this summoning stuff, you hear me?"

"I promise."

Wade frowned. "Do I get the same promise?"

"I promise—no more summoning all-powerful entities."

"Glad to hear it." He eyed me cautiously. "What's your plan for now, until Alton comes out of the infirmary?"

"I'm going to find Jacob and deliver a couple of harsh truths."

"You want company?"

I shook my head. "Not for this one."

"Call me if you need backup. They're hiding out in one of the rooms at the back of the Aquarium, by the way. I saw Jacob sneak off while we were running with Astrid."

"Thanks, Wade." I looked up at him, wanting to say so much more but not knowing where to begin. My stomach had tied itself in knots.

I set off toward the Aquarium, ready to launch a tirade at Jacob. Not all of my anger was directed at him, but he had messed up big-time, and that couldn't go unpunished. Plus, I wasn't exactly dealing with Quetzi's death well. I had wanted to save him, and I'd failed. After all, the serpent had saved me from Katherine, and she'd literally torn him apart.

Anger and grief were mixing in a great big ball inside my stomach, twisting and turning, and tearing me up. If Jacob had done as I'd asked, would things have turned out differently? It was like missing a train by a couple of minutes. All of the could-haves and might-have-beens came swarming into my brain.

Right now, I was on the warpath.

THIRTY-TWO

Harley

I stormed through the double doors of the Aquarium with anger pulsing in my veins. Not the best way to go about speaking to someone, but I couldn't get my feelings to simmer down.

Before I could open my mouth to call out for Jacob and Isadora, though, a searing pain shot through me. It was white-hot, like a million blades being pushed through my veins. I sank to my knees, clamping a hand to my chest. A cry escaped my lips, and my eyes squeezed shut as I fought against the sudden pain. What the hell was going on? I hadn't been hurt in the blast, aside from a couple of scrapes and bruises.

Oh, no...

My overwhelming anger and the intense pain were linked, I'd have staked my life on it. I'd cracked the Suppressor by calling on Erebus, and this was the result. Deep inside me, some of the pent-up energy was leaking out, tipping the balance toward Darkness. Everything I'd striven to avoid had happened. Now, I felt as though I was in a worse position than the one I'd started in. At least, before, there'd been no crack in the Suppressor, meaning everything was sort of in balance. But what now— would it keep on leaking, and pushing me toward the Dark?

"Harley?" a sheepish voice called from the shadows.

"Jacob, get out of here now," I shot back, sweat dripping down the back of my neck. With enormous effort, I hauled myself back into a standing position. I wasn't going to speak to Jacob on my knees, looking like I was on the edge of an aneurysm.

Two figures emerged, though one was limping. Jacob and Isadora, reunited. For a moment, I lost all sense of my anger. It was good to see her in a safe place again, away from Katherine's clutches. Then again, with the hex looming over her, there was no telling how long she'd actually be safe for. That notion spurred on my fury at what Jacob had done. I could see on his face that he was expecting a lecture, and I wasn't about to disappoint.

"What the hell were you thinking?" I hissed, my body pulsating. The light was dim in the Aquarium, but I was convinced that there were black veins throbbing beneath my skin. I blinked, and they disappeared, but the paranoia remained. *What's happening to me?*

"I had to save her," Jacob replied firmly.

"At the expense of everything we'd been working toward? We could've stopped Katherine, right there and then, if you'd just done as I'd asked. We could've prevented her from completing the first ritual!"

Isadora stepped in front of Jacob. "You know that isn't true, Harley. Katherine would have found a way out of the situation, as she does every time. I'm not saying that what he did was right, but don't lay that sort of blame at his feet. She had already absorbed a great deal of Quetzi's energy before Jacob jumped through that portal—she would've been too strong to defeat, regardless."

"He messed up, Isadora," I said, my eyes narrowing.

"He knows what he did, and he's sorry for it," she replied evenly. "He was doing what he thought was best. And besides, we will have the chance to stop her from completing the next rituals. Yes, it's troubling, but all is not lost."

"No, if we'd stopped her killing Quetzi, then we'd have stopped her completing the first ritual and becoming even more powerful. She managed it, and that's on Jacob." I needed to calm down, but the fury was pouring out of me like molten metal. "I asked him to help me take

Quetzi. We wouldn't have left you behind, Isadora. We'd have found a way to rescue you."

She put her hand on my shoulder. "I know you would have, Harley. As I said, Jacob knows he made an error in judgment back there."

"I've yet to hear *him* say a word about it. Is that what you've been doing here, huh? Having a chat about how to spin this in a better light?" I wiped the sweat from my brow with the back of my hand, the pain subsiding.

"I'm sorry," Jacob muttered. "I saw her, and I couldn't help it. I had to save her. It felt like the right thing to do, at the time."

Don't tell me, your intentions were good? I knew the dangers of doing things with good intentions. I'd convinced the coven to leave Micah and the other magical kids with their foster parents, under magical supervision, even though the Ryders were circling. And look how well that had turned out.

"Yeah, and some of the most catastrophic things that have happened on this planet were done with the best intentions. Atomic bomb, anyone? That research was supposed to be used for good, not to build a great big nuke that could decimate cities and affect generations afterwards." My words were tumbling out at a rapid pace, my breath coming in stilted gasps.

"Are you okay?" Isadora asked, her brows pinched in worry.

"No… I don't think I am." I staggered forward, losing my balance. Jacob caught me and held me up as I forced my legs to stop shaking.

"Maybe we should sit down," Isadora suggested. Rather than risk sinking to my knees again, I agreed, plonking myself down in the center of the Aquarium's marble floor. Some of the sea creatures were edging nearer to the glass, to take a closer look at us. Either that, or they were drawn by the energy that was leaking out of my Suppressor, the same way Katherine drew gargoyles to her.

"What happened to you?" Jacob said quietly, seeming afraid to meet my gaze.

I tilted my head from side to side, trying to get my vision to clear. "What happened to me? I'll tell you what happened to me—because of your little stunt, I had to think of something big to distract Katherine. I summoned Erebus—or partially summoned him, anyway. I wanted to sacrifice Katherine's life, in return for summoning him, but I didn't get that far. Somewhere along the line, while I was doing my magical best, the spell's power cracked my Suppressor. It's not fully broken, because I can still feel the limitations, but there's definitely something not right. Hence the falling and sweating and overwhelming anger."

Isadora sighed. "I warned you about this."

"Hey, I didn't do it on purpose. Not exactly. I mean, yeah, I did the spell, but only because we needed a way to get out of there. We had no idea if Jacob was even coming back!"

"I'd never have left you there," Jacob murmured.

"I know you wouldn't, but it was terrifying to be abandoned in some otherworld," I shot back.

"I'm not blaming you for performing the spell, Harley," Isadora said. "I'm angry with myself, that I didn't predict this in some way. I should have tried to put a fail-safe in place or done more to bolster the defenses around the Suppressor—at least for a little while."

I turned to her. "I don't need more defenses; I need a quicker, safer way of breaking this thing. If you'd given me that, then we could've avoided all of this. Hell, if you and dad hadn't put this stupid thing in me in the first place, that'd have been swell." I knew it was the leaking energy talking, but I couldn't get my mouth to stop yapping.

She shook her head. "We installed the Suppressor to keep you safe from detection. You know that."

"It doesn't make it easier to swallow," I muttered.

"I know it doesn't, and I know you're frustrated by it, but all of that means nothing now anyway." Isadora dropped her gaze, her foot tapping on the marble floor. Sadness drifted off her, peppered with regret.

I arched an eyebrow. "What do you mean?"

"If the Suppressor is cracked, then you need to break it properly as soon as you can. The leaking energy can become poisonous to you, as it's being fed through your system in waves, almost like adrenaline. If you inject too much adrenaline in one go, then your heart can't cope. It's the same with the Chaos energy inside you. At least, with one release—though that comes at great risk—it's able to dissipate as soon as it's been sent outward. With these smaller batches, it almost has nowhere to go, and builds up in a dangerous way."

I lifted my hands in confusion. "Wait… so now you *want* me to break it?"

"It's not a case of wanting, it's a case of needing."

"How long do I have?"

Isadora shrugged. "It's hard to say. Days, maybe, or weeks. It depends on how badly the Suppressor has cracked."

"Can you help me?" My voice was tinged with desperation.

"I don't know enough about these things, Harley. I'm so sorry," she replied, tears flashing in her eyes. "Aside from the spell that cracked the Suppressor in the first place, I can't think of another one that would be strong enough. Plus, I wouldn't advise you using that spell again, if it caused that much damage. Anything to do with Erebus is an accident waiting to happen."

"Would a Sanguine spell work?"

Her eyes shot up. "How do you know about those?"

"I've been doing some research of my own," I replied.

"A Sanguine spell might work, if you had the right one. You'd need something powerful enough to break the Suppressor, which also balanced out the Light and Dark within you. If you can't get your affinities in equilibrium, then there's no telling what might start happening to you."

"And if I knew of a spell like that?" The Sanguine spell that Alton had mentioned popped into my head—the one that had been sent over from the Reykjavik repository. I hadn't managed to get my hands on it, but from what Alton had said, it seemed like the jackpot. Breaking and balancing, rolled into one. All I'd need was the blood of a powerful Light magical and a powerful Dark magical. No easy task, but not impossible.

She frowned. "I'd start to worry what kind of coven you'd ended up in."

"But say I *did* have a spell like that? Is there anything else I could do to make the break safer? I mean, I've already caused enough mayhem with Erebus. I don't want to put anyone else in danger, if I can help it." My heart was in my throat, the anticipation killing me.

"Have you ever heard of something called Euphoria?" she replied. I could hear the reluctance in her voice, but what choice did we have now? I'd put a crack in this thing, and I needed it gone if I was going to survive. I'd put her in a bit of a dilemma, the concerned aunt warring with the careful guider.

I nodded. "Alton and Krieger wanted me to learn how to do it, before my surgery."

"Surgery?" Isadora's voice went up an octave.

"Long story. I was supposed to get this Suppressor carved out of me in a couple of months' time, but it looks like I've messed up everyone's plans. Anyway, there's a preceptor here who said he'd teach me how to enter a state of Euphoria, if I needed it."

She shook her head. "You can't learn how to fall into a state of Euphoria that quickly, Harley. It takes practice and focus."

"You said I have days, maybe weeks before this leak starts to properly hurt me. Can I learn how to get into a state of Euphoria in that timeframe—yes, or no?"

"It's not that simple, Harley," she replied, her lip trembling. She looked genuinely scared.

"Yes, or no?"

"Theoretically, yes, but it will take a lot out of you. You may find that you don't have enough energy to break the actual Suppressor, once you're done. And, with all of this pent-up Chaos leaking out, you'll have to endure the side effects of that, too. It'll be too much for you to bear." She looked up at me with utter despair.

"What else can I do, Isadora?" I asked plainly. "Let this thing kill me?"

"No, but maybe this Krieger can perform the surgery he promised to, instead?"

I smiled sadly. "The tools haven't arrived yet; that's why it's taking so long. And, right now, I don't have the luxury of time. Not that we ever did, but it looks like things just got a kick in the ass."

Jacob nodded. "He wanted to do it sooner, but there's all this paperwork that needs to be filled out before you can get the tools and stuff. I was there when he explained it all to Harley."

Isadora's face crumpled. "Well... who is this preceptor, anyway? Does he know what he's doing with Euphoric practices? I'm not foisting you off to any Tom, Dick, or Harry who thinks he can do ancient meditation because he read it in a book once."

A wry chuckle slipped from the back of my throat. "He studied with the Euphorics of Tromsø, if that makes his credentials any better?"

"They let an ordinary magical into their inner circle?" she gasped. "No, I don't believe it. This charlatan is clearly bluffing. There's no way the Euphorics would allow an outsider into their group. For starters, very few people even know of their whereabouts."

"Nomura does," I replied. "He's got no reason to lie to me."

She frowned. "Wait... Hiro Nomura?"

"The very same."

"Oh."

I smiled. "Does that change anything?"

"A little bit, though I still don't like it. Hiro Nomura is very well respected in most circles and has an aptitude for Dempsey Suppressors. It's not a common subject, but judging from what you've said about him and the Euphorics, common subjects aren't really his thing. I'm guessing you already know all of this, but I'm trying to talk myself into letting this happen." She cast me a lopsided grin, though the humor didn't reach her mournful eyes.

"This will work," I promised. "The only reason I didn't do something like this in the first place was to reduce the risks of hurting people around me. That's still my main focus. If I can master Euphoria, then I know I can keep to that."

"I still don't like it, Harley," she murmured.

"You're not supposed to. You're my aunt—you think you have to protect me, because it's what Dad would've wanted. And while I'm very grateful to have a guardian angel watching over me, I know that I can do this." I cast her a sad look. "Plus, it's not like I have other options, unless I want to end up with magical radiation poisoning."

She sighed. "If there was another way, you know I would tell you."

"I know."

"If you need help with any of these madcap endeavors, you know where to find me."

I frowned. "You're staying at the coven, right? You're not thinking about disappearing again?"

She shook her head. "I will need to speak with this Krieger, to see if he has a means of removing the spell that Katherine put on me. I'd try to do it myself, but it's drained me of much of my strength. I suppose that was the point. Anyway, if I'm to speak with him and get this hex removed, I need to be here… temporarily, at least."

Jacob cleared his throat. "Or, you could speak to Preceptor Bellmore."

We turned to him in surprise.

"She's the expert on Charms and Hexes, right?" he said. "Plus, I did a bit of digging after Katherine took Isadora. There's definitely a reversal; it'll just take someone like Bellmore to do it. She took a crazy strong hex off Krieger—she can do it with Isadora, too."

I smiled. "Were you thinking of that when you snatched Isadora?"

He nodded sheepishly. "Does that make it any better?"

"Very, *very* marginally."

"Plus, it means you'll be near both of us, Isadora," Jacob continued, though he still couldn't meet my gaze. I found that my anger toward him had settled slightly, with the fading of the white-hot pain in my body. Isadora had been the first parental figure, aside from the Smiths, who'd treated him like he was wanted. In the moment, he'd acted on impulse, and saved the person who meant the most to him. Quetzi likely hadn't even compared. I could understand that, in a way. Besides, my aunt was probably right about us not doing much to dampen Katherine's determination. Even if we'd managed to get Quetzi out of there, she'd have been too strong to defeat, with all of that energy inside her.

The trouble was, even though I tried to rationalize it all, Quetzi was still dead. He wasn't coming back. I couldn't help but feel crushed by that fact.

"It's a temporary measure, that's all," Isadora reiterated. "You know my feelings about covens in general. I don't like to stay long in any one place, especially as Katherine will likely come after me. I've proven very useful to her, and I doubt she'd want to give up instantaneous travel. However, Jacob and I might get a better fighting chance if we stay here with you, at least for a little while."

I nodded. "I get why you can't stay here for good, I really do," I replied, thinking of her letter. "Stay as long as you need to. I can't promise that nobody will try and stop you from leaving when you decide it's time, but I won't stand in your way. And we'll carry on taking care of Jacob when you leave so we can keep him away from Katherine. Just make sure you say goodbye first, okay?"

"I will, I swear it. No more midnight flits."

"Good to hear. Now, I've got a lot to do, so I should probably let you rest up," I said, glancing around at the watching sea creatures. They were sniffing out the raw energy in me; I could sense it. "Don't stay here, though. Go up to the infirmary where they can see to that hex."

Isadora helped me to my feet, though she was pretty shaky on hers. "Jacob might have made a mistake in saving me, and it might sound selfish, but I'm glad to be here." She folded me into a hug. I let her hold me, my own arms encircling her as we stopped for a moment and let ourselves be family. A minute later, I turned my face to Jacob. "You might as well get in here, though you're not off the hook. Wade and the others might have a couple of things to say to you, but I'll try and make them go easy."

He paled. "Thank you, Harley. I really am sorry for what I did... and also not sorry, because she's here, and she's safe for a while."

I gathered him into our huddle, the three of us hugging it out—getting rid of all the anger and upset and pain. There was no use crying over spilt milk, and the milk was everywhere right now. I needed to calm down, or risk letting the Darkness take over. Already, I could feel a tingling in my body, as if something cold was making its way through my veins. The Suppressor had been cracked, and I had to deal with the consequences of that. I had to calm down, slow down, and get the bastard fully broken before it ended up killing me.

To do that, I needed to pay a visit to Nomura and then Alton. I needed to know if this was possible, not just in theory but also in practice. That Sanguine spell was in the coven somewhere, and I was going to get my hands on it before time ran out. I had some idea of where to get the blood from a powerful Light magical—that le Fay woman was rotting in Purgatory at that very moment, her blood brimming with the right kind of ferocity. Actually, getting the blood might be a little trickier, but maybe I could persuade her that I was on her side—that I intended to use the blood for nefarious means only. As a Shipton and a Merlin, I doubted it would be too hard to convince her. My lineage spoke for itself.

The Dark blood was a different story. I'd have to look into that a bit more, as I didn't know of anyone that powerful who leaned toward the Dark. Katherine could be a potential "donor," but that came with two issues—one, I didn't know for sure that she *did* lean toward Darkness, and, two, I had no way of getting close enough to snatch some blood from her without getting myself trapped in the process. However, there was one place that called my name, louder than any other, a place that seemed to hold all the secrets I needed to explore. Once I'd managed to find the Sanguine spell located within these walls, and had a better grasp of Euphoria, there was only one city I wanted to visit.

New Orleans.

THIRTY-THREE

Astrid

I lay in the infirmary bed and looked up blankly at the ceiling. Ever since waking up in my dad's arms, the life forced back into me, I'd been feeling strange and disoriented. My body was cold, but I couldn't shiver—the cold was much deeper than that, sitting like a rock in the pit of my stomach and spreading outward slowly. It gripped my lungs and my heart, and crept all the way up to my brain, where this odd emptiness reigned supreme. I could still think and function and get my mouth to speak and my limbs to move, but there was a sluggishness to everything I did, like wading through molasses. I wanted to cry each time I thought about it, but the tears wouldn't come—truthfully, I felt like a part of me was missing. The real world seemed too bright and too loud; the lights burned my eyes and even a whisper grated on my senses.

I came back wrong. Some of me stayed behind.

Worst of all was the memory of almost crossing over. On the last three occasions that this had happened to me, I'd had no memory of the event at all, but this time… this time, it lingered in my mind like a black fog. I remembered the warmth and the silence, reaching out toward me across a great divide. I remembered a voice, telling me it was all okay, and that I wouldn't be in pain anymore. It had been like falling asleep and sinking into the sweetest dream, where nothing ached, and my body felt light, and my mind was free.

And then... I'd been ripped out of there, torn from the warmth and the sweetness, wrenched out of the dream. I could remember the violent tug of it, of my father wrestling with the underworld to get me back. Everything had gone black, and those voices had drifted further away, taking paradise with them.

The terrifying truth was, when everything had seemed still and calm and peaceful, I hadn't wanted to come back. I thought of those I was leaving behind, but I knew they'd be okay without me. Selfish, maybe, but it had been so serene... until it wasn't. Until reality barreled into me, my spirit being dragged kicking and screaming back into the real world. Evidently, my reluctance had caused this missing piece—that fragment still somewhere in the underworld, no doubt.

"Are you awake?" Alton asked, distracting my attention. He sat at my bedside, where he'd been for the past hour after disappearing for a while to Purge. He hadn't said anything since he'd come back; he'd just sat there looking sad and exhausted.

Garrett had followed us when my father had brought me here, but he hadn't hung around for long. I didn't remember him leaving, but I presumed he must have gone while Krieger was running his preliminary checks. He hadn't said anything either, just loitered in the doorway and disappeared soon after.

"I'm awake." I shuddered at the tone of my voice. Everything felt flat and empty, as though someone had put soundproofing on everything I did and said.

"How do you feel?"

"Like I've just been brought back from the dead."

He smiled stiffly, fidgeting with his hands. "I mean, is everything okay? Do you feel normal? It was much harder this time. The others— they brought you back almost too late, and I had to struggle to find you, let alone bring you back. I was worried that something might have happened, that you might not be quite—"

"Myself?"

He nodded. "It can happen sometimes. I'm good at what I do, but even the best Necromancers in the world can't always get it right. I was still recovering from the last one, too, so I suppose I'm more worried about it than I usually would be."

"You got it right. I'm fine," I lied. I didn't have the heart to tell him that I felt as if I'd come back half-formed, even if it was an undeniable truth. He was my dad; he didn't need that kind of weight on his already-burdened shoulders. He'd only blame himself, and I didn't want that. However, the more I lay there, willing the void to go away, the more intense it became. My insides felt empty, my mind blank. There was no restless chatter in there, like there usually was, which was more unsettling than anything else. I relied on my mind chatter, and it was horribly silent without it.

"Are you sure?"

I nodded. "I'm a-okay. A little tired, but that's to be expected."

"It just feels like something went wrong."

I touched his hand. "It didn't. I'm fine, honestly."

"You would tell me if something was the matter, wouldn't you?"

"I would."

"Where did you go, anyway?" he asked, holding my hand gingerly.

I frowned. "When I died?"

"No, no, no… I mean, where did you and the Rag Team go? We tried to get in contact, but there was no answer. Another security team arrived at the site where you'd gone, but you weren't there anymore. The cars were there, and the place was trashed, but you were nowhere to be found."

"We went to the Asphodel Meadows. Katherine was there, performing one of the rituals with Quetzi," I explained. "He's dead, but Isadora should be in the building somewhere. Jacob brought her here."

Alton gasped, visibly shocked. "You went to the dimension of a Child of Chaos? That's supposed to be just a myth."

"Apparently not."

He shook his head in disbelief. "And Quetzi is dead?"

"Yeah, looks like he wasn't so good at escaping after all." The words came out unfeeling, my mind shocked by the lack of sentiment. I hadn't known Quetzi very well, but he had been a fixture of this place ever since we'd been granted the Bestiary. Why couldn't I muster any emotion at all? I hated it. It made my skin crawl.

"Did Katherine get away?"

"No idea. From what I've read of these Children, they don't like people overstaying their welcome. There's a good chance that Nyx kicked her out, once she'd finished absorbing Quetzi's power. She'll be long gone."

"You think so?"

I nodded. "She's like an octopus—she can get out of any tight spot, even if it's a Child of Chaos kicking her out."

"You may be right about that. No matter where she is, or what she's up to, she's impossible to trace. I tried to locate the source of her transmission, when she sent it through the medallion, but all I found were dead ends." He sighed wearily. "Did Jacob come back safely? I didn't see him with the rest of you, although I was..." His voice caught in his throat. "Well, I was somewhat busy at the time."

"Jacob made it back, and he has Isadora with him," I said weakly.

He nodded, evidently skirting around a difficult question. It took him a couple of moments to spit it out. "I'm guessing from the way the rest of the Rag Team reacted to me that you didn't tell them about the Quetzi-Katherine-kids deal? I was expecting a tirade when you all got back." He dropped his chin to his chest, shamefaced.

"I haven't told them about it, but you should," I said simply. "Sooner rather than later. You can't play into enemy hands and then cover it all up, not with them."

"And when I lose my place here?"

I shrugged. "Then you lose your place."

"And if someone worse *takes* my place?"

"We'll deal with that if it comes to it. I'm not saying you have to tell everyone, but you absolutely have to tell the Rag Team. They deserve to know."

Alton seemed torn, his brow furrowed in thought. "Can I have some time to decide on a course of action? I'm not asking you to lie for me—just don't say anything until I've figured out what I'm going to do. I'm sorry for even asking, but it's necessary right now. With the coven in turmoil, there's a lot I need to think about."

How are you going to get yourself out of this one? My father would never give up his place in the coven, not for anything. He'd thought he was doing the right thing, in protecting me and getting the children back. I wondered how that felt to him now, as I'd almost died anyway. I guessed he was finally realizing that it might not have been the greatest idea. Still, that didn't mean he wouldn't fight to keep hold of his position as director. I could see it in his face—the weighing of options. I had expected it, to be honest. He was a proud man, who enjoyed the respect that came with being director. It would not be easy for him to relinquish, nor did I think he would. On any other day, that would have made me feel nothing but disappointment.

"I won't tell them for a while," I agreed. "I'll give you some time to come up with your own way of breaking it to them, but that's not an indefinite silence. You can't just sweep it under the rug."

He nodded. "I know."

"I'm feeling quite tired, actually. I'm not kicking you out or anything; I'm just going to go to sleep now, see if that makes me feel any chirpier."

He smiled and leaned over, kissing me on the forehead. "Goodnight, little one."

"You haven't called me that in years," I said, surprised.

"I miss it," he replied. "Now, get some rest. I'll come back in a few hours and check on you."

I stared at him as he went, trying to muster some kind of nostalgic happiness at being called that name again. It reminded me of long car journeys when I was very little, when he'd take me out of my car seat and carry me to my bed. It reminded me of him reading me stories at night, and of baking on a Sunday afternoon. He was terrible at it, but he did it because I wanted to. It reminded me of happy times, but I couldn't feel anything. I could recall the memories, but they held no emotion whatsoever. I couldn't cry, couldn't smile, couldn't laugh. My heart went on beating, but it might as well have been dead.

Turning over in the bed, I closed my eyes and pulled the covers up to my chin. As soon as darkness slid beneath my eyelids, a thousand screaming nightmares burst into my head. I tried to open my eyes again, but they were fixed shut. I was trapped in the gloom, lost amongst the souls surrounding me. I heard voices in the black oblivion, begging me to let them cross over to paradise. I heard the lapping of water, somewhere in the distance, and the cries of the desperate, asking for my dad's mercy—asking him to bring them back, the way he'd done with me. Somehow, a crack had opened between the underworld and the real world, and I was the gateway.

I came back wrong, I came back wrong, I came back wrong...

It took a long time for sleep to come, and when it did, I wasn't even sure I was sleeping. The nightmares stayed, and no matter what I tried, I couldn't get my eyes to blink awake.

Had I been able to, I would've cried at the sight of the sun streaming in through the infirmary windows, waking me up. The nightmares had been chased away, and the voices had disappeared, though I still couldn't get rid of the weird, empty feeling inside. It looked as though sleep hadn't exactly healed me, nor had it brought back the missing part of me. That was still lost out there, somewhere I couldn't find it.

Feeling achy and sore, I swung my legs over the edge of the bed and hauled myself out. Physically, I wasn't too bad: a bit unsteady, but nothing was peeling off and I wasn't visibly decaying. I had a tendency to dwell on the zombie aspect of the resurrected, considering I sort of was one. A sentient, more or less fully functioning one, but a zombie nonetheless. I padded over to the chair in the corner of the room, where fresh clothes had been laid out. Throwing them on, I wandered to the door of my hospital room and peered out. The place was empty, except for one solitary, pacing figure.

Garrett...

"Oh… you're up," he said as he saw me. "I didn't think you would be for a while."

"Yeah, I'm feeling much better."

"What'd the doc say?"

I shrugged. "My tests all came back negative. I am, as they say, in perfect health, aside from the fatigue and near-death flashbacks." I leveled my gaze at him. "What are you doing here, Garrett?"

"Alton came to visit you a while ago. He said that, if you woke up before ten, I should bring you down to his office—but only if you're feeling up to it. I need to be there, too, but I thought I'd wait a little longer before I checked in on you. Didn't want to bother you if you were sleeping." He looked flustered, running a hand through his hair.

I nodded. "No problem. Let's get down there now."

"You don't have to, if you're still feeling sick."

"It's fine, Garrett. I'll be just fine."

He eyed me suspiciously. "You sure? You look dazed."

"Honestly, I just need to take a walk and clear my head. If I feel poorly again, I'll come right back." I made to walk past him, but he grabbed my arm, pulling me back.

"Can we talk for a minute?"

"What about?" I asked, exhausted.

He took a deep breath. "You. Me. All of this mess."

"You made your perspective on that very clear. We don't have to talk about it again."

"Astrid… I carried your dead body in my arms yesterday. I held you, and I was praying to any god that would listen to keep you in the land of the living. I was begging for you to hold on," he said, his face contorted with pain. "It showed me something. It showed me that none of the other stuff matters. We argued, we had some big issues, but I care about you so much. I don't want to lose you. If we can fix this… well, I want to. I think this is worth fixing."

My mom's words came back to me, echoey and strange. *If something is worth fixing...*

"I don't know if now is the time," I replied stiffly. I couldn't feel anything.

"It's just that…" He trailed off, clearly struggling to put the right words together. "You remember I told you that I'd been to visit Finch in Purgatory?"

"Yes." *What does that have to do with us?*

"Well, I didn't just go there to get some kind of closure. I actually went to tell him that Adley was dead. I figured he ought to know," he explained. "It was pretty bad, as you can imagine. The guy was totally torn up about it. Back then, I didn't think I could ever imagine what that might feel like, but then yesterday happened. I understood, then. I felt it —that unbearable grief. It made everything else seem insignificant. And then you came back, and I realized that I had a chance that Finch won't ever get—I've got the chance to make this work."

I looked at him, willing the emotions to come… but they didn't. "I'm sorry, Garrett. I can't talk about this now. It's not that I don't care, it's just that I need to sort my head out first."

"If you don't feel the same, I'll understand."

I shook my head. "It's not that. The thing is… I don't feel anything."

"What?"

My chest gripped, as though a weight was sitting on my ribcage. "I'm hollow inside."

"I don't understand." He looked worried, as if this was entirely because of him—as if he'd been the one to hollow me out and leave me empty. I wanted to reassure him that it wasn't the case, but the words evaded me.

"Forget it, I shouldn't have mentioned it," I said. "Can we talk about this some other time? I'm finding everything a bit… uh, overwhelming right now."

He nodded. "Sure, of course. I should have waited until you felt better."

"I do care though, Garrett." *At least, I think I do, somewhere deep down.*

A wave of relief washed over his face. "You do?"

"I never stopped."

"So… another time?"

I forced a smile onto my face, the action strange and almost unnatural. "Another time."

"Are you sure you're okay?"

"I will be," I lied. I had no idea if I would be.

"You don't have to come to this meeting if you want to stay in bed."

"I want to. I'll be fine." With that, I walked through the infirmary and headed to Alton's office, with Garrett in tow. After what my father and I had discussed last night, I wondered if this might be on the same subject. It was just as likely to be a debrief over what had happened yesterday.

I walked in to find the rest of the Rag Team already gathered, all of them swiveling around to look at me as I entered. Expressions of concern greeted me, changing to surprise as they saw Garrett behind me. He moved swiftly over to the far side of the room, by the desk, a worried look on his face. I made myself smile at him, and he smiled back.

"Astrid! How're you feeling?" Harley asked.

"Sleepy but okay," I replied. "I'm a little hungry, too."

"For brains?" Raffe joked, getting a swift smack in the back of the head from Santana.

"That's not funny, Raffe," she chided.

I smiled stiffly. "I don't know, I thought it was pretty funny."

"It's good to see you on your feet again," Tatyana interjected.

"Yeah, you had us worried for a minute there," Dylan added.

Garrett held my gaze. "Really worried."

"Can I get you anything?" Wade chimed in. "Coffee, water, something to eat?"

I shook my head. "I'll get all that later. I just came to hear what all the fuss was about."

"Well, I was about to begin, so your timing could not be more perfect," Alton said, his voice tight and strained. "Please, take a seat."

I did so, Raffe making his chair available for me, the invalid. I thanked him and sank into the soft cushion, letting it take my weight for a while. I hadn't been lying about the tiredness—everything felt heavy and uncomfortable, my bones creaking.

"I haven't been entirely honest with you all," Alton began, keeping his head up. "You see, the reason we managed to get the children back had nothing to do with the discovery of a magical medallion that could lead us to Katherine's associates. In fact, it only led to one place, and that location was given to me by Katherine herself. I made a deal with her, to get the children back, as I believed it was the only way to stop her from killing them, and taking their Chaos for herself, or using them as weapons in her war."

I glanced at the others, trying to gauge their reactions. Harley looked stunned, Wade looked horrified, Santana looked about ready to explode, Raffe looked blank, Dylan looked confused, Tatyana looked furious, and Garrett looked downright murderous. I couldn't blame Garrett for being the angriest amongst them—my father had accused him of being a traitor for so long, when it was actually Alton who was the traitor. Hypocrisy at its finest. I wouldn't have been shocked if Garrett had socked him in the face, right then and there, though I hoped he wouldn't. Alton was still my father, regardless of what he had done. The group stood in silence, waiting for Alton to continue.

"I agreed to exchange Quetzi for the children, with the hope that Quetzi would be strong enough to escape and evade Katherine," Alton said. "The spy wouldn't have left the coven with Quetzi; I had a fail-safe in place to ensure that, but… I didn't expect Quetzi to want to fight her, face-to-face." He paused, taking a shaky breath. "Am I sorry for doing it? Yes, in many ways. Do I think it was worth it? I'm not sure. It has come to my attention that there were more children being held at the facility. In which case, my actions have been fairly futile. Although the children we rescued are alive and well, which is always a victory, however small." His voice trembled, his hands riffling through papers as a means of distraction from the emotion in his words. In a way, it was hard to watch.

"This is a joke, right?" Harley choked out.

Alton shook his head. "I'm afraid not."

"You sold out to *her*? What the actual hell, Alton?" Harley looked about ready to implode.

"There is one more aspect to it," he replied quietly. "Katherine threatened to kill Astrid if I didn't comply, and I could not have that happen. You all know this by now, after yesterday, but she's my daughter. I could not let Katherine murder her and take away any chance I might have of resurrecting her."

"There must have been another way," Santana interjected. "Couldn't you have tried to entrap her, while you were making the exchange? Couldn't you have bluffed?"

"That was part of my initial plan, but she used her spy wisely. I wasn't allowed to know of their identity, and we never met face-to-face. It was all done through transmissions and orders," he explained.

"The Bestiary... was that you?" Raffe gaped in horror.

To me, that was definitely the worst part of it. Anything could've happened if the spy had sabotaged the place. My father had put his trust in a foolish place, and I could only partially understand why. My life wasn't worth that risk.

"In order to cover Quetzi's escape, some mayhem needed to be created. I didn't expect it to cause quite so much chaos, but everything was swiftly resolved thanks to yourselves and Tobe, and the security teams who helped in getting the beasts back in their boxes," he said.

"You realize you could have lost your job then and there, if the Mage Council had found out about it? You understand that, yes?" Tatyana cut in coldly. "You would be in Purgatory right now, no matter what your reasons were."

He dipped his head. "I know. I didn't mean for any of this to happen —well, not quite like this, anyway. I didn't mean for Quetzi to die, and for Katherine to sap his energy. I was supposed to stop it all before it got that far."

"So, you messed up?" Garrett muttered. "Believe me, I can understand not wanting to put Astrid in harm's way, but you can't know that Katherine will keep her promise. Now that she's all super-powerful and stuff, what's she going to do? Ritual number two will be the first thing on her mind, and none of us know what that entails."

"We'll have to figure it out," Harley shot back. "We can't give up because of this. The Librarian knows all of the spells that have ever been written, and she's in Katherine's grasp. Our next action should be to launch a rescue for her. If we want to stop Katherine, we need this Librarian."

"There is one more thing," Alton announced. "I wish it weren't so, but it may make your next steps more difficult. However, I can see no other option. I must make amends for this deal."

The Rag Team stared at him expectantly.

"I have decided to step down as director of this coven," he said, surveying the room with concerned eyes. "I will announce the news of my resignation to the rest of the coven this afternoon. In the meantime, the Mage Council have already been informed and will send an appropriate substitute for me, until a permanent director can be found. I don't know who that substitute will be, but they will be suitably qualified for the role."

"Tell me this is another joke?" Harley yelled. "You're upping and leaving us now?"

"I have to."

Tatyana shook her head. "You have made a grave mistake, but what if this new director prevents us from taking measures against Katherine? You know how everyone feels about the SDC. They'll take it out of our hands."

"Can't you save it for a while?" Dylan said. "Put it off until this is over?"

Alton sighed. "That would be dishonest. I've lost your trust, and this can't work without that. You'll always be wondering if I'm still making deals with her."

"We'll forget about it," Raffe promised. "Temporarily."

"You can't do this to us," Santana added, her expression cold.

"It has already been done," Alton said.

I looked at him. "Wait, did you tell the Mage Council what you did?"

He cleared his throat. "I didn't. I simply handed in my resignation, and said I no longer had confidence in my abilities to run the SDC. I was trying to protect you, Astrid. I know I did wrong, but I don't want to go to Purgatory for it."

"So, you want us to cover for you?" Harley asked.

"It's a big request, and I will understand if you don't want to. However, I can continue to be your eyes if I am allowed my freedom. I can still help, just not in an official capacity."

"You don't have to do this, Alton," Santana urged.

He smiled. "I do. It is my duty."

Garrett folded his arms across his chest. "I think it's a good idea. He's right; we can't trust him. It might be a pain in the ass, but at least we'll know we're not being lied to," he said. "Then again, it doesn't affect *me* much... I guess this is as good a time as any to tell you all, since Alton has just announced his resignation. I've been given my own assignments by the LA Coven, now that Stella and Channing aren't here anymore. So, I'll be leaving the Rag Team, and working independently with the LA Coven and some of the security teams here."

I sat up straighter, surprised he hadn't mentioned this earlier in the infirmary. "What's your assignment?"

He flashed me an apologetic look. "I can't tell you. It's top secret from the LA Coven."

"There's no such thing as top secret when you're in my coven," Alton said firmly.

"Well, it isn't *your* coven anymore, is it?" Garrett fired back, his eyes burning with anger. My father had the common sense not to retaliate, no doubt realizing just how furious Garrett was, after all the accusations and the body cams. "Oh, and we'll all be taking these things off now. I don't want to hear a word of disagreement. There's no need for us to wear them anymore, so you can shove them where the sun doesn't shine." He tore off his body cam and threw it in the trash, an icy smile of victory turning up the corners of his lips. Even then, Alton didn't move a muscle. He had no leg to stand on.

With the two most important men in my life leaving the group and the coven, respectively, I started to wonder what might be on the horizon. There were going to be a whole bunch of drastic changes and, given my current state, it was going to be even harder to deal with. Without Alton as director, even the day-to-day running of things—the tiniest idiosyncrasies—would get an overhaul. This place had been a huge part of his life for so long, and now he was stepping away from it, because I'd urged him to. I worried about his future. Plus, without him here, it would feel strange—he'd been my solid link to the coven. I'd always felt apart from the others in this place, but now I felt completely alone. A human in a crowd of magicals wasn't a comfortable place to be.

Then again, this was the *only* place I belonged. This was the only place where someone like me fit in. Besides, if I was going to have any hope of recovering from whatever was going on inside me, being here was where I needed to be.

THIRTY-FOUR

Harley

R eeling from the news we'd just received, I half-staggered out of Alton's office. It didn't feel real. How could he have betrayed us like that? I understood the motives, I really did, but there had to have been another way he could've gone about it. Yeah, we'd saved the children and he'd made the deal to protect Astrid, and I was so happy that we had, but what did that mean now? Katherine had managed to wrap Alton around her little finger and gotten everything she wanted out of it. Hell, she'd probably been one step ahead of him the whole time. If he'd even tried to stop the spy from leaving, I had no doubts in my mind that Katherine would already have had a contingency plan in place. She didn't do things halfway.

More to the point, who's the replacement going to be? Alton had clearly done a bad thing, but what if we were burdened with someone who wasn't as forgiving as Alton was? I had a spell to steal and an undercover trip to New Orleans to take, to speak with some Voodoo practitioners about Sanguine spells, not to mention the sly visit to Purgatory I'd need to undertake. For that, I needed a director with a bit of leniency, who wouldn't kick me out the minute they found out why I'd done these things.

With talk of Katherine's rituals still barging about in my head, I pushed the idea of New Orleans, Purgatory, and Nomura to one side for now. I'd come right back to it, given the urgency of magic pooling into me, but there was another person I needed to speak with first. *Remington Knightshade.* If he knew about the rituals, then he was our man. Now, more than ever, we needed to cut Katherine off before she could get to ritual number two… whatever that was.

"Astrid, wait up!" I called. She was walking slowly down the side of the hallway, her head dipped.

She turned sluggishly. "Oh, hey, Harley."

"Can you believe that?" I gasped, running a hand through my hair. "Alton making deals with Katherine. I can't even wrap my head around it. What was he thinking?"

"He wanted to save me. I think he wanted to be heroic, even though Katherine does what she wants regardless."

"Yeah, well, it hasn't ended well," I murmured.

"No, it hasn't."

"Did you try and talk him out of leaving?"

"No."

"So, you're cool with it?"

She smiled. "I feel the same as all of you. Although, a small part of me is sort of proud. I didn't think he'd give up the directorship for anything, but it looks like he's attempting to do the right thing, to make up for his mistakes."

"I hadn't thought of it like that," I said. "I guess he could have kept it a secret from us, and none of us would have known."

"That doesn't mean I'm not angry with him, by the way," she said.

"No, me neither." I glanced sideways at her, taking in her fatigued features. I could still feel that odd, gaping void, where emotions should have been. "How are you, anyway?"

"Fine."

I frowned. "I mean, how are you *really*? I didn't want to say anything, but I know something's up. I can… uh, feel it, sort of."

Astrid's eyes widened. "You can?"

"Yeah, I didn't mean to reach out for your emotions, and I wasn't prying, but I just felt this weird… I don't know how to explain it. It's like there's a—"

"Missing piece inside me?"

"I guess you could describe it like that."

She nodded, with a half-smile. "I've been pretending to everyone that I'm okay, but I feel anything but," she said softly. "I think I came back wrong, with something missing. I was wrenched out of wherever I was, and when Alton pulled me back into the real world, a bit got left behind. Judging by how I feel, it was an important bit. Most of the time, I just feel empty and heavy, but when I close my eyes, I see a black void and there are voices in it, calling to me."

"I'm so sorry." My heart broke for her. As if dying wasn't bad enough, she was now having to deal with all this creepy stuff. As per usual, she was trying to put a brave face on it, but I could tell she was broken by this.

"I don't really know how I'm going to get through all of this," she admitted.

I stopped mid-step and whirled her around, holding her by the shoulders. "We'll be here for you, no matter what. When it gets bad, you can count on us to do everything we can to cheer you up, and keep things feeling normal. And if we can't cheer you up, we'll just be there for you. I know it'll be weird without your dad here, but you've still got the rest of us hanging around like bad smells. We aren't going anywhere. Even Garrett will be around—he just won't be hanging with us so often. All these changes are bound to make you feel strange and have bad thoughts, but we'll be here to help you through it. I promise. And if this new director tries to get too high-and-mighty, changing everything up, they'll have the whole Rag Team to deal with."

"Without Garrett, though, like you said," she murmured.

"He'll come back around, I know he will. And anyway, him leaving the team doesn't change his feelings about you. He's totally smitten," I said. "You should have seen him yesterday, when he thought you were gone. I thought he might have smashed the barrier between heaven and earth with his bare hands, if it would have brought you back. He adores you."

"Maybe." Her tone was oddly flat. "What do you think they're talking about in there?"

I glanced back at Alton's office. "I think they're having one last tête-à-tête before the Mage Council sends Alton's replacement. I guess they've got a lot to discuss after the whole body cam fiasco." An idea came to me. "Hey, while they're hashing out their issues, why don't you come with me to visit Remington? He's got the goods about the rituals, and we need information more than ever."

She paused for a moment, before nodding. "Okay… I guess that would be a good distraction."

I flashed her an overenthusiastic smile. "Excellent. Then let's get our mirror on and go and pay old Remy a visit. Speaking of which—do you know where we can find him?"

A genuine laugh rippled from her throat, startling me. "I do."

In a companionable, if slightly eerie, silence, we made our way to the Assembly Hall and stepped through the mirror to the farthest left. I hadn't been through this one before, though I wasn't sure if the mirrors *only* went to one place, or if the locations could be changed. A moment later, we arrived in a strange underground hallway that looked like it had been carved out of rock, reminding me of a fairy glen or a grotto. Glowing lights flickered in their rocky recesses. A small desk sat to one side, with a bored-looking male receptionist staring at us in surprise. *I guess you don't get many visitors, huh?*

"And who might you be?" he asked.

"We've come from the San Diego Coven to speak with Remington Knightshade." I flashed Astrid a look. "Apparently, he's here?"

"Does he know you're coming?"

I shrugged. "Sort of. Tell him it's to do with Dylan Blight."

"But it isn't," Astrid whispered.

"Two birds, one stone. I've been meaning to talk to him about Dylan, too."

Astrid frowned. "About them being related?"

"You think so too?"

"No idea, but I've seen the way he looks at Dylan, like he's a lost puppy or something."

The receptionist cleared his throat. "When you've stopped chattering amongst yourselves, might I ask your names? We rarely get visitors here at the SFC, so this is most unorthodox." *So, what do you do all day if you've got no one to greet?* I imagined him with his phone out, playing endless games of Candy Crush.

"SFC?" I whispered to Astrid.

"San Francisco Coven. Right now, we're under Alcatraz."

"Under it?" I gasped.

She nodded. "The architects liked the isolation."

"Names?" the receptionist barked in exasperation.

"Oh, yeah, sorry. Harley Merlin and Astrid Hepler," I replied, putting on my most saccharine smile.

"Thank you," he huffed, before picking up the phone and dialing a number. He turned his face away, casting us furtive looks as he spoke to someone on the other end. Remington, presumably. I didn't understand all the cloak-and-dagger routine, but maybe spending days on end in this dank, dark room under Alcatraz could do that to a person.

"We good to go?" I asked, as he put the phone down.

"Mr. Knightshade will come and collect you shortly." He spun his chair around and faced the wall, paying us no attention whatsoever. Had it not been for the glowing lights, all I'd have been able to see of him would've been the blue screen of his phone glaring up at his face.

Five minutes later, footsteps approached from the far end of the rock-hewn hallway. Remington appeared beneath the strip lights like a villain in a Bond movie, all long coat and gruff demeanor. The tattoos that curved up the side of his neck added to his bad-guy image, though I kind of liked them. I'd always wanted a tattoo but had never known what to get. He frowned at us as he approached, shoving his hands into his pockets.

"You wanted to speak to me?" he asked.

I nodded. "Yeah, if you're not busy."

"I'm not the substitute director, if that's what you're here to find out."

"No, no, we wanted to talk to you about something a little more sensitive than that," I replied, keeping my answer vague and intriguing. "It's to do with Dylan... and some of your research."

He eyed us curiously. "Well, I guess I can spare twenty minutes. Follow me."

We trailed him down a network of equally ethereal corridors, with quaint wooden doors branching off from each one, until we reached a doorway at the end of a short hallway. His name was written on a plaque to the side. After touching the door handle and speaking a quiet couple of words, the door opened, with him ushering us inside before he stepped into the room. The space beyond was beautiful and cozy, with bookcases nestled into the bare rock walls, flickering sconces, and a fire roaring on the left-hand side, while a porthole window looked out on San Francisco Bay. *Nice digs.*

"So, what did you want to talk to me about? You mentioned Dylan?" he asked, as he took a seat behind a varnished black desk. Astrid and I sat on the other side, positioning ourselves awkwardly in the high-backed leather chairs. These kinds of seats seemed to be all the rage for the high-and-mighty of the magical order. Alton had a pair, and I was sure Imogene would have a cream pair.

"Yeah, we were kind of wondering what your deal with him was," I said. "Are you related or something? He can't see it, but I can sense the way you feel about him, as if you have some connection to him."

Remington sighed and sat back in his chair. "I'm not ready to tell him yet. I want him to come to his own conclusions."

"How is he supposed to do that? You'll keep asking him questions, and he'll keep answering them, and neither of you will make any progress," Astrid cut in.

"It's a sensitive subject," Remington said defensively.

"Are you his dad?" I guessed.

"No."

"Then what?" I pressed.

Remington looked torn. "If I tell you, you must promise not to say a word to Dylan. Let me break the news to him—I don't want him to hear it from you."

"I promise," Astrid and I choused.

"Well… I'm his uncle. His father was my brother. I've been looking for him for a long time, but children's services changed his name, and wouldn't tell me where they were putting him. I was in with a bad crowd for a while, when I was much, much younger, and the authorities didn't trust my lengthy rap sheet. I wanted to take him out of there, but they wouldn't let me," he explained. "And now, I don't know how to tell him. He must be so angry, at being left there."

My heart swelled. It wasn't often that us foster kids actually ended up being wanted. "Why did he get left there in the first place?"

"Dylan's mom died from complications, after a routine surgery," he went on. "My brother never recovered, and… well, he delivered Dylan to the orphanage and killed himself afterwards. He jumped off the Golden Gate Bridge."

My swollen heart broke in an instant. "Oh, my God…"

"That's awful," Astrid said, in her odd, flat voice. "Poor Dylan."

"Anyway, I'd appreciate it if you didn't say anything to Dylan. As you can see, it's a delicate topic, and I want to be able to broach it in the right way. I need to figure out how I'm going to tell him, and when. I'll do it—I just need more time."

I nodded. "We can do that. But you've got to tell him, okay? There's nothing worse for a foster kid than thinking they have nobody in the world. Sure, he'll be angry at his dad for that, but it's better that he knows."

"I will tell him, I promise," Remington said quietly. "Now, you said you had another point of business?"

"Yes, we came across an old thesis of yours in the SDC's library," I began, covering my Empathy toward Dylan with proactivity. "And we wanted to know if you could help us gather some information on the Children of Chaos. More specifically, *how* one might go about becoming one, if they wanted to. Not me, but someone very powerful —Katherine Shipton. You might've heard of her." I cast him a sarcastic look, which made him smile. However, it quickly turned to a frown.

"I was wondering where that thesis went. I have no idea how it ended up in the SDC, but at least someone has found it," he replied thoughtfully. "You came to the right man. I've been working on theorems for many years now. In truth, I did not think it within Katherine's realm of possibility to even attempt it, but it's a subject that has interested me for a long time. I thought it best to study the practicalities, in case anyone ever tried to become a Child of Chaos. It's pretty exciting stuff, to be honest. I always wondered, personally, what it might be like to be one. I'd never try it, of course, but it's always a curious topic to think about." He turned his face toward the firelight, his eyes fixed.

"Where did you get all of this information, if you don't mind me asking?" I asked tentatively. "We've searched a bunch of places and couldn't find anything."

He smiled. "I studied for a long time with a woman called Odette. She was a remarkable woman, with the most powerful Clairvoyance abilities I have ever seen. Her memory was beyond anything I've ever witnessed, too—it was like a library in that head of hers."

My eyes widened. "Wait, are you talking about the Librarian?"

"There were some who called her by that nickname, though I'd forgotten that. Yes, the Librarian. She hated it. Anyway, she has fallen into legend, somewhat, but she knew more about everything in the magical world than anyone I've ever come across, the Children of Chaos included. I haven't spoken to her in a long while, but that's where much of my intel came from. She knows everything there is to know about every spell in the world... including rituals that might help a person become a Child of Chaos. I'm sure of it. She never showed me any of those, but, if Katherine's got her sights on the task, then Odette must know a way to accomplish it."

"And if Katherine *had* your friend, Odette?" I said bluntly.

He looked up in alarm. "Does she?"

"We have reason to believe so, which is why we need your help on this," I replied.

Astrid nodded. "For starters, do you know of a way we might stop Katherine?"

He was silent for a while, letting our words sink in. "You really think Katherine might have Odette?"

"Like I said, we have reason to believe that's probably the case, unless Odette's found a way to escape her," I said firmly. This might be just the nugget of information we needed to get him to spill every single bean in the jar.

He tapped his chin anxiously, his eyes showing a glimpse of inner turmoil. He evidently knew he shouldn't really be telling us this kind of stuff, but his friend was in danger and we were right there, willing to help. "Well... you could always inform one of the Children of Chaos, face-to-face, and ask them to stop her. It's not an easy task, by any means."

"How would we go about doing that?" I asked.

"Well, you'd have to summon one," he replied.

I nodded, feigning ignorance. "And if we could do that?"

"Well, you'd either be incredibly brave or incredibly stupid," he replied. "Summoning isn't done anymore, because it carries enormous risks. A Child of Chaos will often ask for a trade, in return for being summoned, and they can pretty much ask for anything they want. With that in mind, the level of difficulty also depends on who it is you're summoning."

"Uh... let's use Erebus as an example," Astrid prompted, flashing me a conspiratorial look.

He laughed tightly. "Forget about it. You couldn't pick a worse one."

"Well, are there spells to summon the other Children of Chaos?" I asked, determined.

"There are, but I don't have them. The only person who would know about them would be Odette, but if she's with Katherine, then there's no telling where she might be right now or what state she's in." He cast us a warning look. "Then again, I wouldn't advise those spells anyway, even if you had Odette's help. Summoning isn't something that should be taken lightly. It's extremely dangerous at best, deadly at worst."

"Would they listen to what we had to say if they were summoned?" Astrid jumped in. We already knew how deadly summoning could be; we didn't need Remington to tell us that.

"The Children, I hate to say it, have grown lazy in their decades in this universe. They stopped listening to mortals a long time ago."

"Even when these mortals have warnings to give?" Astrid said.

He nodded. "Even then. They don't think they're at any risk of being challenged or overcome, because nobody has tried in millennia. They'll make promises and say whatever the summoner wants to hear, just to get them to go away. You'd have to make the argument very persuasive, and they might still choose to ignore you."

"How would someone go about persuading them like that, to really make 'em listen—theoretically speaking?" I pressed.

He tapped his chin. "Astral projection would work, I suppose. It forms a link through the summoning gateway, connecting the summoner's mind to whoever has been called. That way, they'd have less chance of ignoring what was being said. It'd be seared into their mind."

Astrid gasped. "A person can do that?"

"Again, it's a very difficult, rarely performed practice that hasn't been seen in a long time. According to the history books, the knowledge of it died with a powerful magical named Marie Laveau. All of that information is buried with her, quite literally—all of her writings and her Grimoire are down there in her tomb. At least, that's the myth. Nobody knows for sure, since nobody would dare to break into her grave to steal it, not unless they wanted to be cursed."

"Marie Laveau? Why do I know that name?" I tapped my chin.

"The Voodoo Queen of New Orleans, right?" Astrid chimed in. "Most powerful Dark witch who ever lived, according to the history books."

I almost choked. "Did you say New Orleans?"

Astrid nodded. "Yeah, she's famous down there—a bit of a colorful history. Apparently, if you go to her grave and make an offering, she'll grant you a wish. I'm not one for superstitions and things like that, but hers I believe. She was a fiercely powerful magical when she was alive, like I said, and she's no less powerful in death. A true Voodoo Queen."

Now, more than ever, my path was clear. Marie Laveau was the woman, or spirit, who could have the answers I needed. If I wanted to break this Suppressor properly, and stop Katherine from performing the next ritual, then I'd have to head to New Orleans. If Marie Laveau was a Voodoo Queen, then there was a good chance that she—or rather, her spirit—knew where I could find the Dark blood I needed for the Sanguine spell. After all, according to the history books, she was the greatest Dark witch of her time. As a Voodoo Queen, Sanguine spells were literally her life-and-death's work, meaning she might be able to teach me how to do it right, to stop anyone else from getting hurt. Plus, it'd be useful to have that spell on astral projection, in case we ever decided to risk a summoning again. Although, to speak with this Marie Laveau, I was going to need Tatyana's help.

I just hoped the thorns of this leaking Suppressor wouldn't drag me back before I could manage it. *Give me the strength to do this... one last push.* If we could get these tasks done, then Katherine was on borrowed time.

THIRTY-FIVE

Harley

Astrid was called in to join Alton in a meeting with the Mage Council, as soon as we got back from the San Francisco Coven, leaving me to wander the hallways with my thoughts. My mind was racing and my heart was, too. There was a lot to take in, and I didn't have much time to dwell on everything. This Suppressor would poison me soon enough. My life was on the line.

First off, I need that Sanguine spell.

Since Alton was leaving anyway, I figured I might have a window of opportunity to ask him for it. I had my doubts that he'd just hand it to me after what he'd said about this type of magic. The only trouble was, I had to wait for him to come out of that Mage Council meeting. Or grilling, depending on Levi's mood.

Determined to meet with Alton once the meeting was over, I was about to head to the library to dig up some research on Marie Laveau when a familiar figure appeared at the far end of the corridor. It felt like a lifetime since I'd seen him, when in reality it hadn't been that long at all. A few hours, maybe. Was this the Suppressor's doing, turning me into this melodramatic mess? Was I about to run into his arms in slow motion? Maybe a field would appear, with him in some medieval get-up and me in a flowy dress. I smirked at the image. Wade wasn't exactly the knight-in-shining-armor type.

"There you are," he said stiffly. "I've been calling you for the past hour. Something up with your phone?"

I pulled it out of my pocket and saw the missed calls. "Sorry about that. I had it on silent. Astrid and I went to see Remington in San Francisco. Cool place. Anyway, what did you want to see me about?"

"You want to tell me about San Francisco first?"

"Oh… right." Keeping it as brief as possible, I relayed everything we'd learned from Remington about the Children of Chaos.

He frowned. "You think summoning them is a good idea? That was a terrifying thing you did back there, in the Asphodel Meadows. And that blast… I thought we were all done for. I'm glad you're all right now, though."

A warm feeling flowed off him. My emotions rose like a tidal wave inside me, mingling with the affection and fear coming from him. It was like they had a mind of their own, feeding their way toward him and sinking beneath his skin. I could almost see them. *What the—?*

"Do you feel that?" Wade asked, glancing around as if he'd just felt a chill on the back of his neck.

"Uh… no. Feel what?"

"I don't know. It was like static electricity."

I shook my head. "I didn't feel anything." My body was ablaze with sudden and all-consuming passion, my eyes wider, my heart pounding, my blood rushing in my ears. My cheeks felt hot, my stomach flip-flopping violently. *Not now, not now, not now.*

He turned back toward me with a strange look in his eyes. "You're something else, Merlin. Not because of your abilities, or your lineage, but because of who you are as a person."

I gaped at him. "Are you feeling okay?"

"Never better," he said, stepping toward me.

I gulped, overcome with emotions. His and mine, intertwining in the most intense way. Without warning, he grabbed my hand and pulled me close. I knew this was my Empathy working in reverse, my power amplified by the crack in the Suppressor, heightening both our emotions. It was pushing my desires and feelings into him, while bolstering my own. This could only end badly. This wasn't all him, and yet... the way he was looking at me was magnetic. I couldn't have pulled away from the longing expression on his face, not when it was reflected on my own.

"I've tried so hard to keep this from you," he murmured. He lifted his hand and toyed with a strand of my red hair, twirling it around his finger before pushing it behind my ear. "You know already though, don't you?" A smile turned up the corners of his delicious lips. I knew I should've been thinking about New Orleans, and the Sanguine spell, and the state of Euphoria, but my Suppressor's leaking energy had taken over. My feelings for Wade were well and truly in control now.

"I don't know what you're talking about."

"Man, I don't know how to say this." He laughed awkwardly, his eyes darting away from my face. "I just... I like you, Harley. I really like you."

I fought to rein in the Suppressor, but there was nothing I could do. I was being dragged down with him, in the best possible way. The emotions were ours, but the leaking energy was bringing them to the forefront, making them impossible to ignore.

"I like you, too," I said. It felt so damn good to say it out loud.

He rubbed a hand over his face. "I've lost my mind. I was coming to talk to you because I was worried about the risk you'd taken, doing that summoning spell again, but now I'm... It's weird. I can't help it. Uh... tell me, Harley. Why'd you try that summoning spell again? You did it to distract Katherine, right? You did it to buy us time?"

I nodded. "That was the idea."

"See, you're always on the front line, even when things get dangerous." His eyes glittered with admiration, though the sight was bittersweet. *This is the energy talking... This isn't him.* If he hadn't been affected by my accidental push of Chaos, he'd have been telling me off right now, telling me not to be so reckless.

I opened my mouth to explain what was really going on, when he suddenly moved closer, his hands cupping my face. With him so close, I couldn't speak. The words wouldn't come out. *Oh God... He's going to...* His lips grazed mine tenderly, his thumb brushing my cheek. My heart stopped. I should have pulled away, but instead my palms pressed against his muscled chest, his heartbeat thudding against my hand. Closing my eyes, I kissed him back fiercely, like a woman possessed. He was all I could think about. Nothing else mattered in that moment. His mouth moved against mine with sensual passion, before he traced delicate kisses along my jaw and down my neck, pulling me close with his arm wrapping around my waist.

A jolt of pain shot through me—the same kind I'd experienced in the Aquarium. It started deep in my core and spread out like a ripple, jabbing at my chest and heart, pushing through every nerve ending. It felt as though I'd fallen down on a bed of nails, with every sharp spike stabbing into my skin. Wade caught me as I crumpled to my knees, a scream of agony tearing out of my throat.

Whatever spell had been cast on the two of us, it broke in that instant. His eyes turned from amorous to frightened in a split second, his brow furrowed in concern. He scooped me up into his arms and set me down on a nearby bench, kneeling at my feet.

"Harley, what's the matter? Tell me what hurts."

I grimaced, clutching at my stomach. "Everything."

"What's going on?"

"The Suppressor... it cracked... when I summoned... Erebus," I wheezed, my lungs on fire.

He gasped. "It broke?"

"No... it just cracked. There's... energy leaking... out. It's going to... kill me if I don't... break it properly. It's poisoning... me."

"What?" He stared at me in shock.

"It's leaking... into my system in... small pulses. Isadora told me... it'll kill me within weeks, if not sooner." The pain began to subside, allowing me a second to catch my breath.

"But the tools for the surgery won't arrive for months," he said, panicked. "We could tell the Council and have it expedited, maybe? But then... no. They'd never agree to it if they found out the Suppressor was already cracked. The conditions would be too volatile for a surgery that precise."

"I know. That's why... I have to find another way. In fact, I've already... found one."

He frowned. "You have? Please don't tell me it's something dangerous."

"I assume that was a rhetorical question... When was anything Suppressor-related easy?"

"Harley..."

I groaned. "Do you want to know or not?"

He paused for a moment, before sighing. "I want to know."

"There's a Sanguine spell that arrived from the Reykjavik repository. Alton has it and I need it. I could ask him for it, but I need to do it before he leaves. Whoever this new director is, there's no way they'll give it to me. They'd have no reason to."

"A Sanguine spell? You're kidding me, right?"

"Nope, I'm perfectly serious. It can break this thing and balance my affinities."

He pulled a face. "You know you need blood for that kind of stuff, though."

"I know."

"And that might be just as dangerous as performing a massively powerful spell. You're putting yourself at risk here, Harley." He held my hand, his thumb brushing circles across my skin. I looked into his eyes, my lips tingling from his kiss. Part of me couldn't even believe that we'd done that, after wanting to for so long.

"And I'll die if I don't. Besides, I'm going to ask Nomura to teach me how to fall into a state of Euphoria. If it was supposed to work during the surgery, then chances are it might work for me when I break this myself," I replied, sounding more confident than I felt. I had a lot to do and not a lot of time to do it in.

He shook his head. "You can't die, Harley." His voice was so sad that I wanted to put my arms around him, but the Suppressor had given the reins back and my boldness had faded with it.

"I don't want to. That's why I'm going to do this."

He looked up into my eyes. "Then, I'll help you. Whatever you need, I'll be there."

"Is this the Suppressor talking?"

"What do you mean?"

I eyed him suspiciously. "You remember what just happened, right?"

He cleared his throat, glancing down, all bashful. "We kissed."

"I think I might've made it happen, by accident. The crack is making my abilities and emotions go a bit crazy, and I *may* have fed some of my Empathy into you. At least, I think that's what happened. It's really hard to say."

He frowned. "Did you mean what you said?"

"Did *you*?"

"Yeah, I meant it."

I took a breath, trying to process what he was saying. Before I could speak, Wade cut in.

"But let's focus on getting the Suppressor out of you, one way or another. We can talk about this... whatever *this* is, later. When you're out of danger. I'm not letting you do this alone, and I'm sure as hell not going to let you die. Not a chance. You got that, Merlin?" His mouth was set in a grim, determined line. The mouth I'd just kissed and wanted to kiss again.

I wrestled with my feelings, praying he was right. Truthfully, I'd been acting a little too casual about the whole this-Suppressor-might-kill-me thing. It was my defense mechanism, to put on a brave face, but I couldn't hide my fear from Wade. I didn't want to. I was scared of dying —terrified, even. I'd cracked the Suppressor in trying to kill Katherine, and now it was poisoning me. *How's that for a slice of divine irony.* And though I had ideas in place, there were no assurances that I'd survive. Krieger had spoken of side effects, and that was in a secure, surgical environment. Isadora had spoken of side effects, and that was in a less secure, more volatile environment. What I planned to do was somewhere in between, but definitely riddled with potential problems. Not just in the logistics but in the outcome, too.

"I don't want to die," I whispered, my resolve crumbling in front of him. Tears trickled from my eyes, and his hands reached up to wipe them away. Before I knew it, I was in his arms again. He pulled me from the bench and cradled me gently in his lap, the two of us sitting on the floor. I buried my face in his neck as he stroked my hair, kissing my forehead softly.

"We'll make this work, Harley," he promised.

"The Sanguine spell or us?" I teased.

He smiled. "The spell first."

I held him tighter. "It'll be too hard if this doesn't have the outcome I want."

I felt him smile against my forehead. "The Sanguine spell or us?"

"The spell, of course."

"None of this is going to be easy, but I'll be by your side throughout it all. I promise you that," he said firmly. "After all, someone has to keep you from doing anything reckless."

"How do you feel about New Orleans?" I asked.

"Love the place. I might not give off the vibe, but I'm something of a jazz aficionado."

I mustered a small chuckle. "Is that right?"

"Absolutely. So, is that where we're headed?"

I nodded. "Once we have that Sanguine spell, that's the next place on my list."

"Then we'd better get to Alton before he packs his bags."

I might've been scared of actually dying, but I wasn't giving up without a fight. I was a Merlin, and Merlins didn't back down from a challenge. My Suppressor needed breaking, and nothing in this world—or the next, or even the otherworlds, for that matter—would stop me.

Ready for the next part of Harley's story?

Dear Reader,

Thank you for reading *Harley Merlin and the First Ritual*. I hope you enjoyed it!

I'm excited to announce Book 5 - ***Harley Merlin and the Broken Spell*** - which releases **January 21st, 2019**.

Whose head, aside from Harley's, will we get a peek into next? ;)

Visit: www.bellaforrest.net for details.

I'll see you in the New Year! I hope you have a great holiday season.

Love,

Bella x

P.S. Sign up to my VIP email list and you'll be the first to know when my next book releases: **www.morebellaforrest.com**

(Your email will be kept 100% private and you can unsubscribe at any time.)

P.P.S. I'd also love to hear from you. Come say hi on Facebook: Facebook.com/BellaForrestAuthor. Or Twitter: @ashadeofvampire. Or Instagram: @ashadeofvampire.

Read more by Bella Forrest

HARLEY MERLIN

Harley Merlin and the Secret Coven (Book 1)

Harley Merlin and the Mystery Twins (Book 2)

Harley Merlin and the Stolen Magicals (Book 3)

Harley Merlin and the First Ritual (Book 4)

Harley Merlin and the Broken Spell (Book 5)

THE GENDER GAME

(Action-adventure/romance. Completed series.)

The Gender Game (Book 1)

The Gender Secret (Book 2)

The Gender Lie (Book 3)

The Gender War (Book 4)

The Gender Fall (Book 5)

The Gender Plan (Book 6)

The Gender End (Book 7)

THE GIRL WHO DARED TO THINK

(Action-adventure/romance. Completed series.)

The Girl Who Dared to Think (Book 1)

The Girl Who Dared to Stand (Book 2)

The Girl Who Dared to Descend (Book 3)

The Girl Who Dared to Rise (Book 4)

The Girl Who Dared to Lead (Book 5)

The Girl Who Dared to Endure (Book 6)

The Girl Who Dared to Fight (Book 7)

THE CHILD THIEF

(Action-adventure/romance.)

The Child Thief (Book 1)

Deep Shadows (Book 2)

Thin Lines (Book 3)

Little Lies (Book 4)

Ghost Towns (Book 5)

HOTBLOODS

(Supernatural romance. Completed series.)

Hotbloods (Book 1)

Coldbloods (Book 2)

Renegades (Book 3)

Venturers (Book 4)

Traitors (Book 5)

Allies (Book 6)

Invaders (Book 7)

Stargazers (Book 8)

A SHADE OF VAMPIRE SERIES

(Supernatural romance)

Series 1: Derek & Sofia's story

A Shade of Vampire (Book 1)

A Shade of Blood (Book 2)

A Castle of Sand (Book 3)

A Shadow of Light (Book 4)

A Blaze of Sun (Book 5)

A Gate of Night (Book 6)

A Break of Day (Book 7)

Series 2: Rose & Caleb's story

A Shade of Novak (Book 8)

A Bond of Blood (Book 9)

A Spell of Time (Book 10)

A Chase of Prey (Book 11)

A Shade of Doubt (Book 12)

A Turn of Tides (Book 13)

A Dawn of Strength (Book 14)

A Fall of Secrets (Book 15)

An End of Night (Book 16)

Series 3: The Shade continues with a new hero...

A Wind of Change (Book 17)

A Trail of Echoes (Book 18)

A Soldier of Shadows (Book 19)

A Hero of Realms (Book 20)

A Vial of Life (Book 21)

A Fork of Paths (Book 22)

A Flight of Souls (Book 23)

A Bridge of Stars (Book 24)

Series 4: A Clan of Novaks

A Clan of Novaks (Book 25)

A World of New (Book 26)

A Web of Lies (Book 27)

A Touch of Truth (Book 28)

An Hour of Need (Book 29)

A Game of Risk (Book 30)

A Twist of Fates (Book 31)

A Day of Glory (Book 32)

Series 5: A Dawn of Guardians

A Dawn of Guardians (Book 33)

A Sword of Chance (Book 34)

A Race of Trials (Book 35)

A King of Shadow (Book 36)

An Empire of Stones (Book 37)

A Power of Old (Book 38)

A Rip of Realms (Book 39)

A Throne of Fire (Book 40)

A Tide of War (Book 41)

Series 6: A Gift of Three

A Gift of Three (Book 42)

A House of Mysteries (Book 43)

A Tangle of Hearts (Book 44)

A Meet of Tribes (Book 45)

A Ride of Peril (Book 46)

A Passage of Threats (Book 47)

A Tip of Balance (Book 48)

A Shield of Glass (Book 49)

A Clash of Storms (Book 50)

Series 7: A Call of Vampires

A Call of Vampires (Book 51)

A Valley of Darkness (Book 52)

A Hunt of Fiends (Book 53)

A Den of Tricks (Book 54)

A City of Lies (Book 55)

A League of Exiles (Book 56)

A Charge of Allies (Book 57)

A Snare of Vengeance (Book 58)

A Battle of Souls (Book 59)

Series 8: A Voyage of Founders

A Voyage of Founders (Book 60)

A Land of Perfects (Book 61)

A Citadel of Captives (Book 62)

A Jungle of Rogues (Book 63)

A Camp of Savages (Book 64)

A Plague of Deceit (Book 65)

An Edge of Malice (Book 66)

A Dome of Blood (Book 67)

A Purge of Nature (Book 68)

A SHADE OF DRAGON TRILOGY

A Shade of Dragon 1

A Shade of Dragon 2

A Shade of Dragon 3

A SHADE OF KIEV TRILOGY

A Shade of Kiev 1

A Shade of Kiev 2

A Shade of Kiev 3

THE SECRET OF SPELLSHADOW MANOR

(Supernatural/Magic YA. Completed series)

The Secret of Spellshadow Manor (Book 1)

The Breaker (Book 2)

The Chain (Book 3)

The Keep (Book 4)

The Test (Book 5)

The Spell (Book 6)

BEAUTIFUL MONSTER DUOLOGY

(Supernatural romance)

Beautiful Monster 1

Beautiful Monster 2

DETECTIVE ERIN BOND

(Adult thriller/mystery)

Lights, Camera, GONE

Write, Edit, KILL

For an updated list of Bella's books, please visit her website:
www.bellaforrest.net

Join Bella's VIP email list and she'll send you an email reminder as soon as her next book is out. Visit: www.morebellaforrest.com

Made in the USA
Coppell, TX
25 August 2020

34801068R00236